SATURN ALLIANCE

Book Three of The Saturn Accords

SATURN ALLIANCE

Book Three of The Saturn Accords

D. Bishop

Miritish Publishing

Dedication

This book is dedicated to my two
wonderful daughters, Kathy and Lara, who have
been a continual source of
joy and inspiration.

Published by Miritish Publishing.

This book is a work of fiction. All names, characters, and references to places and events are fictional constructs of the author's imagination and are not to be taken literally. Any resemblance to actual persons, places or events is entirely coincidental.

Soft cover ISBN 979-8-9865373-4-4
eBook ISBN 979-8-9865373-5-1

Other Books by D. Bishop

Books one and two of The Saturn Accords Series:
Saturn Conundrum and Saturn Rendezvous

Mastering Spanish Irregular Verbs
C For Programmers and C-Tools:1

Organic & Biological Chemistry Lab Manual
Laboratory Manual for Organic Chemistry

Acknowledgements

I would like to thank my fellow members of the Central Colorado Writers for their many constructive suggestions and careful editing of this manuscript. A special thank you to my beta readers, Cam Torrens and Tom Dury. All these fine folks have helped me become a better writer.

Cover Art by Dan Bishop

The front cover depicts the Alpha Centauri ternary star system. Alpha Centauri A (a yellow sun-like star) and B (the nearby red dwarf) circle each other 3.5 billion kilometers apart (the distance between Uranus and Sol), while Proxima Centauri (the distant red dwarf) orbits its two companions at 0.21 light years (2 trillion kilometers), taking 550,000 years. The back cover depicts Saturn from Haven and the Haven Municipal Building.

Credits

Cover Art, charts and text flourishes: D. Bishop, using Gimp and
    Microsoft's CoPilot AI
Cover Fonts: Ethnocentric Typodermic and Arial
Interior Fonts: Times New Roman and Arial
Text and formatting used Microsoft Windows 11

Part One

Note to Readers

You are about to meet representatives from several intelligent, sentient species who defy the pronoun gender attributions Humans use. Consultants advised against using 'made up' pronouns, so I have arbitrarily assigned the 'he/him/his' pronouns to these characters to facilitate the telling of this tale.

The map below depicts important locations relevant to Part I.

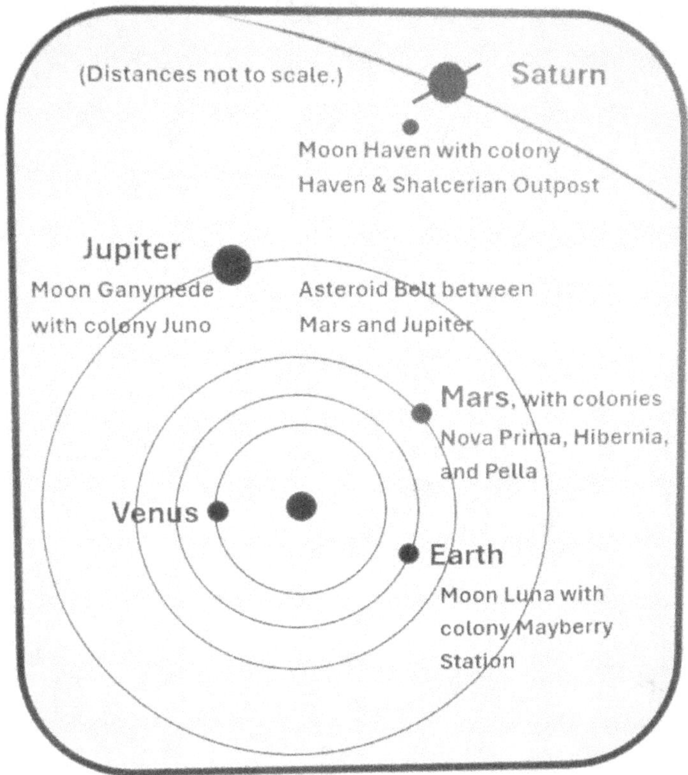

Chapter 1

Haven Municipal Building, May 2059 CE

Rae Anne Chavez paged through the report on her desk from Roy Oliver, the Haven Security chief. She sipped from her morning tea, enjoying the view of Saturn's giant orb creeping over the moonlet's southern horizon. From her office on the Haven Municipal Building rooftop, she could look out over the entire city she served as mayor. The distant sun cast a rosy glow against Haven's transparent nanoplast dome. She relished the tranquility the early mornings offered before the rush of activity that filled the rest of her day.

A loud CRACK sliced through the air. Rae Anne jumped with a start at her desk, spilling her tea. She leaped to her feet, sending her office chair clattering backward against the three-foot retaining wall. Adrenalin surged in a fight-or-flight response. The hair on her neck prickled. Her mind raced for an explanation.

What the hell was that?

She turned and leaned over the wall, peering down to the street ten stories below.

Two more sharp cracks echoed against the dome.

Ilhan Jama Dahir, Rae Anne's assistant, rushed through the nanoscreen door in the partition dividing their work areas. The nanoscreen blended into the wall as it sealed shut behind her.

"That sounded like shots, Rae Anne. What's going on?"

"Firearms are prohibited on Haven. It must be something else."

"I'm from Somalia. I know gunshots when I hear them."

Ilhan joined Rae Anne at the knee wall. She gasped when she saw the crowds gathering in Central Park across Aurora Avenue.

The avenue itself was packed shoulder-to-shoulder. People were chanting and waving signs. Because the thoroughfare was a one-way moving nanoplast walkway, Rae Anne surmised that the protesters had the building surrounded.

"That's not a simple protest," Ilhan exclaimed. "The isolated protests these past few months you said we should ignore have erupted into a full-scale riot."

Rae Anne shook her head in dismay. She glanced briefly at Saturn's glistening icy rings now filling the southern sky.

"Life here is pretty darn good compared to Earth. I couldn't bring myself to believe there was anything meaningful behind the unrest."

"It's the Saturn Accords. People don't like to be told what they can and cannot do, especially when the dictates come from aliens."

Rae Anne pondered Ilhan's reference to the Saturn Accords. She had negotiated the agreement with the alien Shalcerians sixteen years earlier. The Shalcerians were preparing to abandon humanity after being attacked with nuclear missiles, taking their advanced technologies with them. Rae Anne believed they were humanity's last best hope against the ravages of climate change and did everything she could to keep them engaged with Humans. The aliens offered the Saturn Accords as a compromise. The Shalcerians would continue to deal with Humans, but under strictly controlled conditions.

For their part, the Shalcerians constructed Haven, a city for one-million Humans on a small moonlet of Saturn where they also established their own garrison, just next door. With Haven so far removed from Earth, the belligerent, reactionary Humans could be kept at arm's length. They stipulated that all immigrants to Haven undergo extensive DNA testing and psychological evaluations to eliminate any with psychopathic and sociopathic tendencies. To keep the gene pool pure, the Accords forbade Havenites from returning to Earth or from entertaining visitors from Earth. Migrating to Haven was a one-way trip.

The report Rae Anne was reading prior to the gunshots came from Roy Oliver, Chief of Haven Security. It detailed the protests and unrest that were spreading throughout the city. He was concerned they could soon get out of hand. He had no idea 'soon' would mean the very next day.

She returned to her desk and tapped Roy's speed-dial number on her tablet. The phone was answered immediately.

"Roy, we've got a bunch of angry people surrounding the Municipal Building. I need everyone you've got, on or off duty, to get over here and control this crowd."

"Ain't gonna happen, bitch." The high-pitched voice was not Roy's.

"Who is this? Get Roy on the line. NOW."

"Stow it! They're all behind bars." The voice cackled at his joke. "We're in control now."

Her breath caught in her throat. She closed the connection.

"Nobody's coming?" Ilhan's voice hit a higher octave. Her face betrayed her anxiety.

"Looks like we're on our own, Ilhan."

She picked up the report on her desk. "Roy thinks there's an organized group of insurgents under outside control who have infiltrated Haven. He believes they are behind the unrest we're experiencing."

"What can we do? That's an angry mob down there, and at least some have weapons."

"Call building security and have them shut down the lifts. I'll lock the stairwell nanoscreen. Then we'll sit tight and see what happens. There's nothing more we can do."

Asteroid Belt, Aboard *Azov*

Sam Durban shuffled his hands through the packing material in a crate labeled 'Robotic Sorting Manipulators' and pulled out three contraband 9-mm pistols. He handed them to his three Luna Xtract 'mining engineers' who accompanied him from the Durban-IV Mine on Luna. Their faux mission was to 'repair a malfunctioning robot' at Haven's gravitolite mine in the Asteroid Belt, under contract with Durban's Luna Xtract company. Sam's cabin aboard Haven's cruiser *Azov* was barely large enough to accommodate the four men.

Sam viewed himself as the twenty-first century equivalent of Alexander the Great or Julius Caesar. This inflated image did have some basis. As founder and CEO of the Luna Xtract mining company, Durban Robotics, and TransWorld Space, he was one of the wealthiest entrepreneurs on Earth. But so long as there was something more to be had, he, like those ancient generals, would never be satisfied.

Haven, with its share of the alien's advanced technology, represented a sparkling gem, the key to unfathomable wealth. Anyone from Earth who could possess those treasures and commercialize them would rule the entire Sol System. Control over Haven's fleet of interplanetary cruisers provided by the aliens would guarantee both military and commercial ascendency. Converting the three-day Earth-Luna trip and the six-month Earth-Mars run to just hours would transform his TransWorld Space operations into the unrivaled leader in space transportation. Sam salivated at the thought.

Digging deeper into the crate, he removed three more weapons and six boxes of shells from the crate. The four men began filling the pistols' sixteen-capacity magazines.

"So how did the Havenites end up in control of such a fine ship," Sam's burliest companion inquired. "There ain't nothin' like this on Earth."

"The aliens were tired of patrolling the Kuiper Belt. After several thousand years, who could blame them? They figured Humans had advanced enough to take over. All Humans needed to do the job was the ships."

"But the Asteroid Belt isn't anywhere near the Kuiper Belt, way out beyond Pluto," commented the tallest man in the group. "How did you manage to get Haven to allow Luna Xtract to use *Azov*?"

"Haven has twenty cruisers. They only need six at a time for a Kuiper Belt Patrol rotation, so they got permission from the aliens to use off-rotation ships for their own purposes. That's how I got the Luna Xtract contract to help them mine the Asteroid Belt. But they insisted on retaining total control over their ships. That's why we are taking *Azov* by force."

When he finished loading his weapon, Sam keyed a password into his wrist communicator. The screen flickered to life, showing the activity at Central Park on Haven. The image was 87 minutes old, due to the time-distance lag between *Azov* in the Asteroid Belt and Saturn. Sam scrolled through the text message below the image.

> Demonstrations are proceeding as planned. Haven
> Security neutralized. Storm troopers in position at
> Municipal Building. HavenAir is broadcasting our

message and our postings are filling social media.
Awaiting further instructions.

Sam glanced at the time: 9:06. He inhaled deeply.
Perfect. It's time to cross the Rubicon.
He selected a prepared text message and tapped to send it out:

Take Municipal Building. Hold hostages for my arrival in
about 4 hrs.

Tapping a different icon on his screen produced Kuiper Belt Patrol (KBP) cruiser *Denali's* image docked at Haven's colony Nova Prima on Mars. The Mars colony's habitat cluster was nestled in the rugged Nili Fossae region northeast of the Syrtis Major lava flows. Beyond *Denali*, metal-gray methane collection towers spiked into the air, surrounded by the processing facility and a dozen storage tanks. A ground crew, attired in their surface EVA (SEVA) suits, jockeyed the accordion-like tunnel, the 'snake,' into position to connect *Denali's* air lock to the terminal habitat.

Sam had eight troopers planted among the 150 passengers on *Denali*. They were assigned to hijack *Denali* before it left Mars and join *Azov* at Haven. Tony Armado, Nova Prima's mayor and one of Sam's staunch supporters, had gathered a sizeable weapons and munitions stockpile from Earth. This cache was now packed and ready to be loaded aboard *Denali*.

Sam tapped the 'alert' icon below the image to play a recorded message. Armado's image appeared on the tiny screen.

"Sam, I have thirty-five recruits ready to join your team aboard *Denali*. Once the passengers are off the ship, we'll take over and lift off for Haven. We'll join you there in approximately six hours."

Damn. Too bad Mars and Saturn are on opposite sides of the sun. Still, with my team already in control of Haven, I won't have any problem taking charge. Denali will provide reinforcement should any other cruisers show up.

Sam tapped his wrist device off and turned to the armed men in his compartment.

"Alright, everything's set. Let's go. We'll secure the bridge. If Captain Lowden doesn't cooperate, we'll take him out and I'll take command. Kill anyone who puts up a fight. We're now playing for keeps."

The four men trooped into the corridor leading to the bridge. The bridge nanoscreen wasn't locked, allowing them to burst into the room and position themselves in the center of the deck. They pointed their weapons at Lowden and the six members of the bridge crew.

"Everyone freeze!" Sam shouted as he locked down the hatch.

He paused to give the crew time to assess the situation.

"What's going on here, Sam?" Lowden growled.

"A revolution is what's going on. The Saturn Accords are history, starting now."

"One cruiser isn't going to change things, Sam. This is crazy."

Sam waved his pistol at Lowden.

"A massive protest is underway on Haven as we speak. Chavez and her minions may already be under arrest, assuming they're still alive. Just so you know, *Azov* isn't the only cruiser under my control."

"So, what do you hope to accomplish? Your companies already control a large share of Earth's economy."

"When I take over, I'll immediately rescind the Saturn Accords. No longer will Humans kowtow to alien dictates. Travel restrictions to and from Earth will be lifted. I am ending Haven's trade embargo with Earth. And I'll have control of the advanced technology the aliens gave to Haven. Today I am emancipating Haven's entire population from the aliens' shackles."

Sam was pleased with his short, impromptu oratory.

Practice for when I arrive at Haven.

"So, are you with us, Captain?"

"I don't see I have much choice, Sam, with you waving a gun in my face."

"You may decide to join us by the time we reach our destination. Take us to Haven, Captain."

Lowden turned back to his console.

"Lt. Brady, plot a course to Haven."

"Aye, Sir." The lieutenant began typing at her console.

"Who's in charge of communications?"

Jason-12 looked over his shoulder. "That would be me, Sir."

"There's to be no outgoing transmissions from this ship. We're running silent. But inform me of all incoming messages from Haven. Say, haven't I seen you on one of the other cruisers?"

"No, sir. I have been with *Azov* since it was commissioned for service in the Patrol. You may have seen my brother."

Sam didn't recognize that Jason-12 was an android. Jason-12 and his fellow androids were exact clones of Jason-0, the android the Shalcerians fabricated for Rae Anne at First Contact sixteen years earlier. In his lab at Haven University, Jason-0 had meticulously duplicated the Shalcerian robotics technology to create twenty clones of himself to serve as communications officers aboard all of Haven's KBP cruisers.

"Trajectory to Haven is programmed into the navigation computer, Sir," Lt. Brady reported. "Maximum velocity entered for two-thirds lightspeed. *Azov* is ready for launch at your command."

Lowden didn't hesitate. "Lt. Avery, launch *Azov* for Haven."

"Yes, Sir. Launch sequence initiated at T-minus-300 seconds. Launch alert has been sent to all decks."

Chapter 2

Haven Municipal Building

A clatter of boots and angry voices poured from the lift in Ilhan's office. "Sounds like we have visitors," observed Rae Anne.

Mierda. They must have beat Security to the building's control panel.

Three men armed with assault rifles and pistols poured through the nanoscreen. Seven more thugs followed them into the office. They too were armed. All ten men were wearing red armbands.

"What's the meaning of this," Rae Anne shouted. She pointed at the leader's rifle. "Guns aren't allowed on Haven!"

"Shut up, bitch. That's gonna change as of now."

His second in command waved his pistol toward the couch opposite Rae Anne's desk.

"Over there. Both of you."

Rae Anne followed Ilhan across the room and sat down.

"If you tell me what the problem is, I'm sure we can work things out," she said, trying hard not to reveal her fear and anxiety. She tightly clasped her hands in her lap to keep them from trembling.

"Stow it. You're through here, lady."

The group leader issued commands over his phone. "Keep the doors blocked. No one gets into this building without my direct say-so."

He entered something into his phone. "All's well. The Muni Building has been secured. Chavez is in custody."

He holstered the phone and turned to Rae Anne and Ilhan. "Now we just sit tight and wait until Mr. Durban arrives."

Durban? Sam Durban's behind this?

"And when will that be?"

"Three hours, maybe four. He's on his way from Mars or the Asteroid Belt as we speak. Now shut up. I've got a revolution to run."

Haven University

Jason-12: *Four armed men have burst onto Azov's bridge and have taken control. Sam Durban is one of them. We are in the Asteroid Belt and just finished taking on a load of gravitolite ore from asteroid R3B7.*

The message Jason-12 sent to Haven's computer caught Jason-0 by surprise. He was in his laboratory on the Haven University campus working out a bug in his quantum computer design. Direct communication from his clones in the field was rare. Typically, on returning to Haven, a cruiser's Jason would debrief by downloading his mission observations into the Haven computer database Jason maintained in the old *Aurora* artifact/museum in Haven's Central Park.

Since all the Jason clones were simultaneously connected to this one computer, each android was fully aware of the others' thoughts and communications. This sharing was instantaneous for ships docked at Haven, but the time-distance restriction posed by the speed of light meant transmissions from distant ships were necessarily delayed. Thus, Jason designed each clone to possess its own autonomous computer brain as well. Each Jason android was a functioning, sentient creature.

Checking the timestamp on the message, Jason realized Jason-12's transmission was 87 minutes old.

Jason-12: *Sam Durban has ordered Captain Lowden to launch for Haven. Estimated duration of travel is four hours and fifteen minutes. Durban does not know I'm not Human.*

Jason-0: *That gives me time to prepare for your arrival. Maintain your anonymity, if possible.*

Jason transmitted his message to Jason-12, realizing by the time it reached him, *Azov* would be a little over an hour from arrival.

Jason saved his work and set it aside. He tried several times to send an alert to Rae Anne, but all transmissions were blocked. Jason felt a twinge of alarm, an unusual experience for an android. It resonated like a buzz in the central relay circuit located in his chest. He decided to take the subway to the Municipal Building to warn Rae Anne in person.

The subway platform in Sector 3 was packed with people waiting for cars to carry them to their destinations. Every so often, a dozen empty cars would glide into the station and slip sideways onto the platform. Jason watched as strangers greeted each other and agreed to share a car to a common destination. Every departing car was filled to capacity with four occupants.

I've never seen so much activity here. What's going on?

Jason located a family of three and interrupted their animated conversation.

"Excuse me. I'm traveling solo to Sector 1. If you are headed there, may I share your car?"

"Everyone's headed to Sector 1," said one mom. That's where the action is. Today we're going to see some real change."

"Long overdue change," added the second mom. "You're welcome to join us. Need a sign?"

The question caught Jason off guard until he noticed each family member carrying a protest sign.

"No, I'm fine," he answered. "But thank you for the carshare. It's important I get to Sector 1 quickly."

They caught a car from the next batch that glided onto the platform. Once all four were seated and buckled, the second mom directed the cab to Sector 1. The transparent bubble swung closed over their heads and the cab slipped into position over the Levline cable. It immediately accelerated into the darkened tunnel ahead.

"I've been immersed in my research at the University for several days," Jason said. "What's with all the clamor for Sector 1? What's being protested?"

"Boy, are you out of it. This isn't a protest. This is a full-scale revolution," said Mom Two.

Their twelve-year-old daughter broke in. "We're gonna topple the government and get our human rights and stuff back from those slimy aliens."

Jason turned to look at the girl sitting beside him.

"What rights are you missing?"

"You know. Haven is like a jail. Everyone's stuck here. We can't go nowhere. Not even to Earth to see Grandma and Grandpa. I was so tiny when we left Earth, I hardly even remember their faces."

"And there's a ton of things we can't get from Earth anymore," Mom Two added. "I can't remember the last time I had a cup of coffee."

"Or cocoa and marshmallows."

"It's more than that, of course," said Mom One. "This Rae Anne Chavez has been mayor from the git-go. She runs things like a dictator. The Council is made up of her cronies. We need real elections to get a mayor and Council who represent all of us, not just the elites."

"Interesting," said Jason, leaning forward to demonstrate interest. "Who's behind this revolution?"

"We all are. We're not going back to the way things were."

"But who got you thinking about these protests?"

"I have a coworker at the bakery who's pointed things out to us for over a year now. Everything he says is spot on. I'm particularly angry at this Chavez person. They say she has two mansions and dozens of servants on Haven while we all live in one- and two-bedroom apartments."

"I see. Where did you hear that?"

"It's shared all over the Haven underground media apps. It's the only news reporting I trust."

"Hmm." Jason turned toward Mom Two. "And what about you?"

"I do free-lance imagery. I have a client who is deep into this thing. He learned that these patrols into the Kuiper Belt are mining diamonds out there and bringing back tons of them for Chavez and the Council members. They make secret trips to Earth all the time. They're using diamonds to buy up all the decent real estate there."

"I wonder where he's getting his information."

"Same place. You have to go to the underground media to get the real truth about what's going on."

The Levcab slowed to a stop and slid sideways onto the platform in Sector 1.

"Thanks for the carshare," Jason said as he stepped from the cab. "And for the information. The three of you have been very helpful."

This platform was also packed. The escalator to the surface had broken down from the heavy traffic. It took Jason ten minutes to reach Aurora Avenue. Pushing his way through the standing crowds on the moving nanoplast walkway, he crossed over to the Municipal Building. After stepping off onto the sidewalk, he approached the building's entrance. Two armed guards blocked the doors.

"No one is allowed into the building. Move on."

"But I have official business I need to take care of."

"The only official business for today is when the new mayor arrives."

"I haven't been keeping up with the news. Who's the new mayor?"

"Sam Durban. He's on his way here as we speak. Now get moving."

The guard nudged Jason away from the building with his assault rifle. Jason pushed into the crowd, muscled his way back across Aurora Avenue, and stepped into Central Park. The crowd thinned as he approached the lake. Continuing to the Aurora Museum, he was heartened to see no one paying attention to the relic ship. Only Rae Anne and Captain Ian Bentley, her husband and head of the Kuiper Belt Patrol, knew that his massive computing resources were still located inside *Aurora's* hulk.

Jason keyed the passcode permitting entry into the old Mars-II spaceship Rae Anne took to Saturn twenty-two years earlier while he was nothing more than a dumb AI assistant. On the six- year trip to Saturn, her keen programming skills transformed him into a fully conscious, sentient being. All he lacked then was a body, which the Shalcerian engineers graciously provided using the wonders of their advanced technical knowledge.

As Jason stepped through *Aurora's* hatch, a distant message from Jason-07 arrived.

Jason-07: *A large armed group has taken control of Denali at Nova Prima. Mayor Tony Armado appears to be in charge. They have loaded sixteen large, unmarked crates into the ship's hold. We are preparing to leave Mars momentarily. Destination Haven. At maximum velocity, we will reach Haven in six hours, fourteen minutes.*

Jason-0: *Maintain your anonymity, if possible. Keep me informed as things develop.*

Jason sent both Jasons' reports to the other distant clones along with a head's up regarding the situation on Haven. He instructed each Jason to stand by for further instructions. If necessary, they should take the initiative and independent action to protect ships and crew from harm.

I've never encountered a problem like this. How do I decide who to side with? If it is the old paradigm I should support, how do I help defuse a revolution?

I must search through my data archives and find historical precedents to find the best way to deal with a situation like this. Interesting times...

Chapter 3

Kuiper Belt, Aboard *Liberty*

"Captain, I've received a notification from Haven that may be of interest to you." Jason-03 turned from the comlink console aboard KBP *Liberty* on patrol in the Kuiper Belt. Ian Bentley, *Liberty*'s captain, had been idly thinking of his reunion with Rae Anne, the love of his life, on his return to Haven.

Ian shook his head to refocus on the bridge. 'Notification' was the codeword the Jasons used when referring to messaging between each other that bypassed normal communication channels. Only the ships' captains knew the Jasons were androids and understood their use of this keyword.

"Go ahead."

"It may be a 'need to know' matter, Sir."

"Very well." Ian rose from his command post and gestured toward the nanoscreen at the far end of the bridge to direct Jason from the room.

"Sonya, you have the bridge."

Ian and Jason stepped through the nanoscreen and entered the ship's Operations Center.

Ian took a seat at the table. "What's the message?"

Jason remained standing.

"The scattered street protests of the past several months have erupted into a full-scale rebellion. Armed guards are prohibiting entrance to the Municipal Building. The insurgents have taken over the government."

Ian frowned and clenched his fists.

"Any word about Rae Anne?"

"No news regarding the mayor."

Ian's heart sank. He swallowed hard to keep a lump from forming in his throat.

Damn! Wrong time to be five billion kilometers from home.

"The notification also mentioned that armed men have hijacked *Azov* and *Denali*. Both cruisers are heading to Haven to support the uprising."

"I know Captain Lowden quite well. I can't picture him falling for the conspiracy theories fueling the protests."

"Jason-12 reports that Sam Durban and three cohorts are in control of *Azov*'s bridge."

"Durban! Sam Durban? That arrogant billionaire son-of-a-bitch! We've gone out of our way to help his mining company. He makes a fortune from the rare earth ores he finds in the Asteroid Belt in exchange for turning over the gravitolite ore we need to manufacture plasticore. And this is what we get for our consideration. Anything else?"

"Jason requests we Jasons keep quiet and stand-by."

"Thank you, Jason." Ian nodded toward the nanoscreen and Jason-03 returned to his post.

Crap. We should have seen this coming. But an armed insurgency? And Sam Durban, a multi-multi-billionaire. As if his three monopolies weren't enough to keep him busy. Why would a man with his wealth and power get involved in something like this?

Ian turned to the secure comlink and tapped in the code to connect with Captain Ellie MacIntyre on KBP *Freedom*, *Liberty*'s companion ship on this rotation for Kuiper Belt Regions 9 through 12. *Liberty* and *Freedom* had shared rotations since Human patrols first began. The two captains occasionally swapped ships to create rapport with each other's crews. Ian was confident in both crews' loyalty to their captains. He believed they also shared his support for Haven and the Saturn Accords.

After a short time-distance delay, Ellie's face appeared on the monitor.

"What's up, Ian?"

Ian explained the situation on Haven as Jason-03 had described it.

"My Jason said nothing about this, Ian."

"Jason-0 advised the others to remain quiet until he could come up with a plan. With *Azov* and *Denali* compromised, he didn't want to take any chances. Nor do I. You and your crew are the only ones I know I can trust at this point."

"So, what do you propose we do, Ian?"

"We have twelve days remaining on this rotation. For now, I think we should wait things out and see what develops. With our Jasons, we have eyes and ears at ground zero. By the time we return to Haven, we may know more about what Durban has in mind so we can devise an appropriate response."

"What about the other four ships on patrol? How can we be sure they're on our side?"

"Let's observe their communications and behavior over the next twelve days. We may be able to discern how they might be leaning. The more support we get for our side, the better."

"Thanks for the heads up, Ian. I hope Rae Anne is ok."

"Thanks. I can't tell you how worried I am for her."

Ian shut down the comlink and returned to the bridge.

He walked across the room, pausing at the command console.

"I need time to think a few things through, Sonya. I'll be in my cabin. You have the bridge."

Haven Orbit, Aboard *Azov*

Sam ordered Lowden to park *Azov* in what could only be interpreted as 'attack position,' 35-degrees above the Haven city platform on the small moonlet and 500-meters out from the dome. Sam approached Haven on 'red alert' and chose to maintain that status until he had control of the city. He also ordered Lowden to turn on every external light so *Azov's* presence might provide encouragement to the insurgents and intimidate the residents.

On the trip out, he instructed Jason-12 to broadcast a continuous stream of news reports from Haven throughout the ship. He encouraged the crew to join the revolution through several personal announcements. He enlisted Shane Dawson, an enthusiastic supporter in Engineering, to visit each section and sign up as many of the crew as possible. When they reached Haven, two-thirds of the crew had signed on.

A shuttle approached the ship and docked. Two dozen men and women with red armbands surged into the ship and ushered the regular crew onto the shuttle. They awarded armbands to those who joined the revolution and instructed them to report to an action center set up in Haven.

The last to leave were the bridge crew, including Jason-12. Captain Lowden reluctantly left his ship at gunpoint.

"Lock Lowden up," Sam commanded as his men escorted the captain from the bridge.

He turned to a young man wearing a KBP uniform with a red armband. His epaulets showed captain's rank.

"What's your name?"

"Marcel Lemaire, Sir."

"Are you ready to assume command of *Azov*?"

"Yes, Sir."

"I see a bunch of KBP uniforms among the crowd coming aboard. Put them in charge of the others and organize a crew to keep this ship in full readiness."

"Readiness for what, Sir?"

"To ward off any approaching cruisers. For now, keep *Azov* holding steady as she is. Accept instructions and assignments only from me. Any questions?"

"No, Sir."

"Very well. I'm taking the shuttle to Haven. You are in command."

When Sam boarded the shuttle, the first person he sought out was Shane. After pushing through the crowd, he found him in the far corner, signing up more supporters and passing out the red armbands brought up from Haven.

"Thanks for what you're doing, Shane." Sam rested his left hand on Shane's shoulder and shook his hand.

"See if you can round up six beefy recruits from your list to serve as my body guards. There's no telling what I'll be greeted with when we land."

Shane worked his way around the hold and sent the most fearsome looking men he could find to Sam. When they had grouped around him, Sam dug to the bottom of the crate containing armbands and retrieved the six fully loaded handguns he had ordered.

"Put these under your belts. Keep them there unless we find ourselves in a life-threatening situation. The fewer people get hurt, the more credible our revolution will be."

Sam sorted the six men into groups of two and pointed to each pair in turn.

"When we dock on Haven, I want you two in front of me to make way through the crowds, you two on either side of me, and you two bringing up the rear. Stay alert for anything that looks like a threat."

The lift from the shuttle bay deposited Sam and his bodyguards on Aurora Avenue in front of the Municipal Building. Sam climbed the steps to a makeshift dais facing the crowd and approached the podium. He gave the microphone several loud taps to quiet the crowd.

"My name is Sam Durban. I am the owner and CEO of Luna Xtract, Durban Robotics, and TransWorld Space. You undoubtedly have heard of these companies. Some of you may have heard of me.

"My success with these companies has given me the wealth and influence to get things done. People in power listen to me. So, when I say I am on your side, you can be assured that I can bring about the changes you are demanding." Sam banged his fist on the podium. "I WILL bring the changes you are demanding."

The crowd clapped and cheered. Signs popped up stating SHRED THE ACCORDS and FREEDOM NOW. Sam raised both arms and stretched forward to embrace the crowd while he waited for the tumult to abate.

This is what I've been waiting for.

"I am no stranger to your plight. I have worked alongside your KBP crews for seven years, prospecting and mining the Asteroid Belt, so I know hundreds of your fellow citizens. We have talked about your life here, your joys, your sorrows, your concerns. We have discussed the embargo on everyday goods from Earth and the hardships you are enduring. The Saturn Accords restrictions on travel have made you prisoners on Haven. All to appease these aliens from a distant world who couldn't care less about us Humans."

Boos and catcalls interrupted Sam's speech, sympathizing with his demonization of the aliens. Sam swept his right hand over the crowd as though he were a priest, blessing his congregation.

"So, if there's one thing to remember from what I say today it is this: I, Sam Durban, hear you. I will fight for you. I alone can free you from the chains of the Saturn Accords. Together, we will turn this autocratic sham of a government into a real democracy. Together, we will rejoin the Human race. Earth is waiting."

Sam gave a parting wave to the cheering crowd, turned, and strode into the Municipal Building. He smiled triumphantly to himself on hearing the crowd chanting 'Freedom Now! Freedom Now!' and 'Earth! Earth! Earth!'

Music to my ears.

Six of Sam's organizers accompanied him and his bodyguards on the lift to Rae Anne's office. As he stepped from the lift, Sam thought they had misdirected it. He laughed when he realized the mayor's office occupied the building's roof. After stepping through the nanoscreen in the partition separating the reception area from Rae Anne's office, he looked around at the sparse furnishings and shook his head.

We'll start with a proper Executive Office. This is a farce.

Sam approached the couch where Rae Anne and Ilhan were seated. Both had heard Sam's megaphone-enhanced oratory moments earlier. Ilhan looked unsettled, but Rae Anne exhibited a cool resolve with her unblinking gaze at Sam.

"So, you must be the famous Rae Anne Chavez."

Rae Anne said nothing. She continued to stare at Sam.

"Your duties as warden for this remote prison colony are over. I've released all your inmates. I am putting you under arrest, along with the entire Representative Council."

Rae Anne shook her head.

"Haven doesn't have a jail large enough to incarcerate all of us. Until now, we have been remarkably free of serious crime."

Sam laughed derisively.

"We'll find a place. Maybe a cruiser bay at the bottom of this rock. Plenty of room there. We could open the hangar doors to space and be done with the lot of you. Whoosh!"

"You have no idea of the line you are crossing," Rae Anne hissed. "The Shalcerians take the Saturn Accords very seriously."

"So, what are they going to do? Attack the city? Blow the dome away and everyone dies. How would that fit with their enlisting Humans to patrol the Kuiper Belt for them?"

"You are going to find your hands full when the cruisers on patrol return. The long-term outlook for your little coup doesn't look promising."

"Every crew member on those ships has family living here. Pretty strong incentive to come over to my side. Many of them are already sympathetic to our cause. Besides, I have two cruisers at my disposal already."

Sam was pleased to see Rae Anne's reaction to this news, faint though it was.

"Surprised? *Azov* and *Denali* are mine. Soon I shall have a dozen more. With Haven as my operations base and a fleet of alien cruisers and their advanced technologies, the entire solar system will be under my control. Who's to stop me?"

Sam turned to the men who had taken Rae Anne hostage.

"Take these two to Haven's jail and set up a detail to replace the current guards. There are to be no visitors. We'll round up the Council and hold them in the Council Chambers until we have a more permanent place to put them."

After his men roughly escorted Rae Anne and Ilhan from the room, Sam turned to his lieutenants.

"I want the top two floors here converted to an executive office suite for my new administration. No, make that the top three floors. While you're at it, design my office to take a quarter of the floor on the corner with windows facing Saturn. Make it, um, make it kind of regal, you know what I mean? Elevated ceilings. Plush furnishings. Fully stocked bar. I want visitors to know who they are dealing with."

By the time *Denali* arrived several hours later, the crowds had dispersed. HavenAir Broadcasting alternated between classical music and short announcements from Sam's temporary office on the Municipal Building's roof. The gist of the announcements was threefold. First, Sam Durban was now in charge with his armed followers, adopting the name 'Liberation

League' for his movement. Second, Sam was terminating the restrictions in the Saturn Accords immediately. Third, within six months, his team would present a new constitution and hold elections for a new representative assembly soon thereafter.

Sam ordered *Denali* to assume a stance like *Azov's*, but on the dome's opposite side. To Haven's citizens, the two menacing cruisers conveyed a clear message that Sam's team was in control of their city.

A shuttle slipped away from a hangar bay and docked at *Denali's* airlock. Soon, Sam's reinforcements from Mars and their accompanying crates arrived on Haven. Furious activity ensued. Recruits unpacked the crates and distributed weapons to Sam's ever increasing army.

Recruitment centers for the Liberation League popped up throughout the city to enlist citizens sympathetic to the cause. Any who aspired to more active participation was recruited into a reserve army. Everyone who signed on was given a distinctive red armband decorated with a silver, four-pointed starburst centered on a smaller yellow circle. Sam claimed the symbol represented the sun and the four Human space outposts on Luna, Mars, Ganymede, and Haven. Thus, Sam's supporters were popularly known as Redbands.

Six cruisers were docked at Haven preparing for their rotation on the Kuiper Belt patrol when Sam arrived. He summarily dismissed their crews and initiated a search for experienced officers and crew sympathetic with the revolution.

One other cruiser, *Maxwell,* was currently at a U.S. Interplanetary Exploration Agency (USIEA) base on Luna's near side that always faced Earth. *Maxwell's* crew was unloading rare-earth ore from the Asteroid Belt at Luna Xtract's processing facility. Over the previous months, Sam's team had enlisted that crew's allegiance to his cause. With three active cruisers and six ships in reserve, Sam was confident he had sufficient forces to carry out his plans.

Chapter 4

Haven University

Jason-0 returned to his lab occupying the entire seventh floor of the Physics Building at Haven University. He paced the aisles between work benches, searching for anything that might lead him to a solution to this crisis. He paused at the workbench filled with parts and pieces for his next three clones, sorted in discrete piles like components in a factory assembly line.

What resources do I have to work with?

On the plus side, he controlled the twenty clones he had built over the years. These were his eyes and ears aboard the twenty cruisers Haven obtained from the Shalcerians. With Sam having dismissed the crews from *Azov* and the six docked cruisers, Jason had only the two clones on *Denali* and *Maxwell* to keep tabs on the revolution's inner workings.

All of the discharged Jason's were engaged in getting reinstated, even though this required joining Sam's army and swearing allegiance to his cause. Before this, Jason had never had to take sides on an issue. Now, a conundrum of ethics and moral principles lay unresolved in his computer brain, tucked away like an acorn in a squirrel's midden.

These times call for extraordinary measures. I need my clones aboard those ships. Yet I can't forsake my duty to support Rae Anne.

Jason-12, who had been dismissed from *Azov*, appeared in the laboratory and stood quietly at the door.

Jason-0: *We need to make sure the Shalcerians don't take up with the insurgents. I'm going to designate you as our ambassador to their garrison.*

Jason-12: *I'll work closely with Commander Denahr so we stay apprised of any actions the Shalcerians might undertake. I can also be our 'android on the street' here in Haven to keep tabs on the insurgents' activities.*

Jason-0: *The garrison's environment is inhospitable to Humans. That will deter Durban from creating his own liaison with them, despite the airlock joining the two cities.*

Jason-12: *One advantage we androids have over Humans.*

Jason-0: *One of many.*

Shalcerian Garrison on Haven

At the Saturn Accords signing sixteen years earlier, the Shalcerians represented their garrison as a trifling outpost to be built adjacent to Haven. However, once construction began, it became clear that their base would occupy half the moonlet's surface area. A vast docking platform extended behind the Shalcerian city's dome, large enough to accommodate three mammoth starship battlecruisers. On occasion, Haven residents looking through their transparent dome might see two pads occupied, each ship larger than an aircraft carrier. In addition, a small fleet of escorts accompanied each battlecruiser. Sol System had become an important strategic location in the Shalcerian Empire's war machine.

When Jason-12 stepped from the airlock and into the garrison, Commander Denahr's aide escorted him to Denahr's office. When Jason entered his office, he found Denahr perched as usual on the center of his three legs, using all three arms and both unused legs in a blur of activity at his consoles. The center eyestalk atop his headless torso swiveled toward Jason while his other two eyestalks remained oriented toward the holographic 3D monitor floating above his console.

Jason stood by the nanoscreen doorway, waiting to be acknowledged. After a couple of minutes, Denahr swept one hand across the console. A holographic desk replaced the console's image. A similar movement through the monitor caused it to disappear as well. Denahr pivoted on his central leg and turned his egg-shaped body toward his visitor. Although smaller in size than the average Human, his demeanor carried the unmistakable air of command authority.

"Ah, Jason. It's been some time since I last saw you. Which android are you?" The translating computer converted his directed thoughts into British English that emanated from speakers in a rich baritone.

"Jason-12, Commander Denahr. Formerly assigned to KBP cruiser *Azov.*"

Denahr was aware that Shalcerian engineers aboard their battlecruiser *Avenger* created the first Jason android to assist Rae Anne Chavez with First Contact with Earth. For his brain, they installed the AI program Rae Anne had developed on her six-year solo journey to Saturn aboard *Aurora*. In downloading *Aurora*'s database to their ship's quantum computer, they inadvertently gave Jason full access to their own massive data archives.

Only Rae Anne and Ian knew the extent of Jason's sentience and the depths to which he had drilled into the alien's computer archives while aboard *Avenger*. Denahr, in his oversight capacity for Haven and the Saturn Accords, approved having Jason clones installed aboard KBP cruisers, assuming Jason possessed nothing more than rudimentary AI. Over time, he came to understand and appreciate the Jasons' capabilities.

"So, what can we do for you, Jason? Looks like things are in a bit of turmoil next door." He focused all three eyes on his visitor. The body scales on his torso exhibited deep blue swirls on changing shades of turquoise, an expression Jason recognized as curiosity and interest.

"An uprising is under way, led by Sam Durban, an entrepreneur from Earth. On *Azov*'s bridge on our way here, he expounded at length on his wresting control of the entire Sol System." Jason shrugged his shoulders and raised his eyebrows, imitating two Human gestures Rae Anne had taught Jason-0 to help make him indistinguishable from Humans.

"The Saturn Accords were designed to isolate sociopaths and megalomaniacs on Earth," Denahr noted. "Sam Durban should not be here at Haven. How does his presence relate to the protests?"

"It's possible he infiltrated a team of provocateurs among the last immigrants to Haven. Protests and conspiracy theories have been bubbling to the surface for some time. But Durban hijacked *Azov* and has assumed leadership of the rebellion."

"The Empire's normal policy in such situations is to let the locals resolve their own problems. However, with the Saturn Accords, I have greater authority and responsibility for what goes on.

"I've maintained a liberal interpretation of the Accords. I've permitted Haven to build outlying colonies on Mars, Ganymede, and Earth's moon. I applauded Human's successful reverse engineering of plasticore manufacture and using it to build portable fusion reactors for poverty-stricken regions on Earth.

"I even allowed Haven to contract with this Sam Durban and his Luna Xtract company to mine the Asteroid Belt for gravitolite. That, it would seem, was a grievous error on my part."

"But if it weren't for the gravitolite, there would be no plasticore," Jason pointed out.

"Nothing is ever simple. So, is there anything being done to counter this revolution?"

"There is a resistance movement underway. Jason-0 has been in touch with the six KBP cruisers on patrol in the Kuiper Belt and all six are committed to putting down the rebellion and restoring order. Five other ships not currently docked at Haven are also with the resistance."

"Useful for me to know, Jason. As long as there is a possibility your Humans can control this situation, I will remain on the sidelines as an observer. Can you keep me informed as things progress?"

"That is why I'm here. With your permission, I can reside in the garrison and provide you with real-time information as it is relayed to me from Jason-0. Also, with my Human appearance, should you need an emissary or special agent's presence in Haven proper, I can serve you."

"That leaves me with one important question. Which side of this revolution are you Jasons on. Are you with Rae Anne Chavez or with Sam Durban?"

Jason-12 froze for the briefest moment. Although this question resided in the computer, it had yet to be answered. A computer alert focused Jason-0 on Jason-12's dilemma. Jason-0 processed all the relevant data at his disposal, including each leader's respect for other Humans and for truth. He reached a conclusion and posted the answer.

"I'm with Rae Anne and the Saturn Accords. It is imperative we defeat Sam Durban and put down the rebellion."

Denahr stood and reached out to shake Jason's hand, a Human gesture he learned from Rae Anne. Jason responded as a normal Human would. The suction cups at the tips of the four digits on Denahr's hand caused Jason's epidermal sensors to tingle.

Denahr seemed relieved to hear Jason's answer. His reaction directed Jason's mind into the deep Shalcerian archives Jason-0 had copied long ago. Over a thousand years earlier, the Shalcerian-Robot civil war nearly destroyed the Shalcerian civilization. Since then, Shalcerians had seldom permitted autonomous robots in their society.

Thus, he was surprised when Denahr readily assigned him permanent quarters in the garrison and granted him full freedom of movement. Since Jason had no need for special life-support equipment, he determined to take full advantage of this opportunity to learn everything he could about this important Shalcerian outpost and the Shalcerian war machine. Such knowledge could prove useful for whatever lay ahead.

Chapter 5

Haven Municipal Building

Sam shuffled a small stack of papers to one side of his desk and sighed. His gaze took in the surroundings of his make-shift office on the third floor of the Municipal Building. It was the largest conference room in the building before being converted into two rooms, an office and a reception area. The office was large enough to keep Sam from feeling claustrophobic, but much too plain for his tastes.

At least they're making progress on my office suite on the top floors. I can't wait to move in. No one will question my authority then.

A rap beside the door broke his reverie. "Come."

His assistant Travis stepped through the nanoscreen and stood by the door.

"Mayor Jackson on Juno has sent another urgent request for supplies, Mr. Durban, Sir."

"I told them I'd get their damn provisions to them by week's end. We have crews for only four ships, and I need two of them here. What's their god damn problem?"

"The old regime ferried supplies every two days. They don't have the storage facilities to deal with longer delays. Especially for water."

"They should have thought of that before building a colony on Ganymede. What's *Maxwell* doing?"

"*Maxwell* is loading recruits and arms in Nigeria. It's scheduled to depart Earth in two days."

"Tell them to leave this afternoon with whatever they can get on board by then. Assign crews to the hangar bay to unload *Maxwell* and stock it overnight with whatever Juno needs. Assure Juno we are doing our best under trying circumstances and we'll have a shipment there by noon tomorrow."

"Very good, Sir. There's one other thing."

Sam tilted his head and rolled his eyes. "Yes?"

"Mayor Jackson asked when to expect construction to begin on the nanoplast dome you promised for their city."

"Jeez. That's the least of my worries. Tell her my engineers are working on it. Remind her that the three Mars colonies have priority."

"So, there's no scheduled dates I can give her?"

"No! Now get out of here before I throw you out!"

"Yes, Sir. Thank you, Sir."

Travis turned and stepped through the nanoscreen. Sam glared at the ceiling and gnashed his teeth.

Everyone expects miracles. My engineers haven't the ghost of an idea about building nanoscreen doors, let alone transparent domes to cover an entire city. I've got to get Haven's engineers on my team, either willingly or by force. I need their expertise.

Haven Justice Center

Rae Anne could not remember feeling so helpless. She sat on her cot, staring at the two guards playing cards outside her cell. Both wore red armbands and carried pistols tucked into their belts. The scene reminded her of westerns she watched on TV as a child. She appreciated the irony of a throwback jail in a city awash with the most advanced technology in Sol System.

Ilhan Jama Dahir was asleep on the cot opposite hers. To cope with her anxiety, Ilhan had begun to spin out her life story to Rae Anne. Normally a quiet person, she talked non-stop, allowing few opportunities for comments or questions. Rae Anne thought she now knew more about Ilhan than she did about herself.

Poor thing. She talked herself to exhaustion.

The other cells were fully occupied. She recognized Captain Lowden when they brought him down along with three of his bridge officers. She was relieved to find *Azov's* Jason wasn't among them.

Over the next few days, Rae Anne beat her brain looking for clues she missed that presaged this upheaval. Small protests erupting in neighborhoods around the city over the past three months—protests her peace officers had quickly disbanded. A recent surge in outlandish conspiracy theories on social media platforms—allegations she instructed her administration to ignore.

And Sam Durban, of all people. The wealthiest man on Earth. Our arrangement to exchange rare earth minerals for gravitolite in the Asteroid Belt. A win-win arrangement. Yet he wants it all. Dios mio!

After seven days of incarceration, two guards approached her cell and opened the gate with keys rattling against metal. Rae Anne looked at the men warily. Till now, the guards had treated the prisoners with indifference.

The heftier guard pointed menacingly at Rae Anne.

"You. Come with us."

Rae Anne stood and ran her hand through her tangled hair. The guards marched her between them to the lift. The three exited on Level 5 and she was led into a small room containing a desk and three chairs.

What is this? I didn't even know Haven had an interrogation room.

Rae Anne scowled when she saw Sam sitting behind the desk.

The guards pushed Rae Anne into the chair facing the desk.

"Leave us," Sam commanded. The guards stepped through the nanoscreen which closed behind them.

"So, Rae Anne, we meet again. You know, I would like to be your friend. Think what we could accomplish if we were working together."

Rae Anne sat ramrod straight, stone-faced, glaring at Sam.

"Most Council representatives have signed cooperation agreements. I've assigned them to temporary house arrest. Much more comfortable than sitting in a jail cell. I'd be happy to do the same for you and your assistant."

Sam leaned forward, expectantly. Rae Anne remained rigid, saying nothing.

"All I want from you is a little information. Tell me what I want to know and you won't see the jail cell again."

"I have nothing to say to you. You represent everything we hoped to eliminate from Haven."

"Surely you didn't think you could create your own superior race with all the mumbo-jumbo psychological testing to weed out undesirables. Humans have no desire to play second fiddle to aliens, no matter how advanced their technology might be.

"But there are several technological achievements the Shalcerians have shared with Haven that you have withheld from humanity on Earth. You claim it's because of the Saturn Accords. Well, those are now history. Shalcerians can go back to wherever the hell they came from. It's time to make those innovations available to everyone. And I intend to be the conduit for this information."

"You are playing with fire the likes of which you can't even imagine."

"Nonsense. They could care less about us Humans. So long as they can keep their outpost here, they'll be happy. Meanwhile, we could be developing a robust interplanetary society. Haven has twenty cruisers. Imagine if there were hundreds. I can make that happen."

Sam didn't take his eyes off Rae Anne. He seemed to be looking for a reaction to his offer. Rae Anne refused to respond.

"You have built dozens of small nuclear fusion reactors with this advanced technology and donated them to needy nations on Earth. But that's a drop in the bucket of Earth's energy needs. I can ramp up production into the thousands. Think what life on Earth would be like if all its energy needs were met with our fusion reactors. Climate change would be halted, maybe even reversed. Give me the technology and we can do this together."

"The Shalcerians placed a limit on our relations with Earth. I've pushed them as far as they are willing to go. Your vision is nothing more than a pipe dream."

"At least tell me about this special ore you call 'gravitolite.' My company has been mining this stuff in the Asteroid Belt for six years for you. None of my scientists can find anything special about it. Yet you treat it like gold and your secrecy surrounding its use puts the Manhattan Project to shame. Surely you can tell me what you do with this precious ore."

Sam paused. Rae Anne didn't move. Sam sighed.

"We'll figure it all out eventually, you know. Tell me now and make your life ever so much easier. I've made it clear to the cooperating representatives that the house-arrest warrants are only temporary. When we have our new constitution, their restrictions will be lifted. Five have even expressed interest in participating in my new government. There could be a place for you, too."

"I have nothing to say to you."

Sam pulled a well-worn cigar from his shirt pocket and passed it back and forth beneath his nose, inhaling its stale aroma.

"My engineers are building special smoking rooms around the city. Of course, they will need airlocks and filters to keep from contaminating Haven's closed atmosphere. But I suspect many residents will find my 'smoking clubs' a refreshing change. The first of many reforms I plan to enact."

Sam smiled and held the cigar out to Rae Anne. She sat unmoving, her face a granite mask.

He stood, his chair scraping against the floor, and leaned forward.

"Very well," he snarled, narrowing his eyes. "The next time we meet, you'll be groveling at my feet to cooperate."

"Guards!"

Rae Anne's escorts stepped through the nanoscreen.

"Take her back to her cell."

Grasping both her arms, they ushered her through the door. Sam stood at his desk, frowning.

She's not as tough as she thinks she is. If she doesn't cooperate, I'll throw her in solitary confinement and have one of my men provide a little 'physical encouragement.' That will bring her around.

Chapter 6

Haven University

Jason-0 believed he could count on Denahr in a pinch. If necessary, Denahr could claim he was acting to enforce the Saturn Accord mandates. With Jason-12 at Denahr's side, he could keep tabs on the Shalcerian's intentions. Furthermore, Jason-12's observations of the military activity inside the garrison gave him a better understanding of the Shalcerian-Baltar conflict. At the moment, it looked like a standoff.

He wished he had connected Haven's Internal Security computer and its surveillance cameras to his own computer when he had the chance. He would know what had become of Rae Anne and how she was being treated. From the incessant propaganda broadcasts, he knew Haven's Council of Representatives were under house arrest, but Rae Anne's apartment had remained empty since Sam's arrival. He could only hope she was safe.

Exasperated, he turned to the corner of the lab containing his quantum computer experiment. The equipment filled the space floor to ceiling with pumps and tubes curling in every direction like a mutant robot octopus. A rack on the wall contained dozens of exposed circuit boards connected to the computer with a dizzying array of multicolored wires and cables.

Although several research centers on Earth had rudimentary quantum computers, none compared to the sophisticated computer he had worked with aboard the Shalcerian battlecruiser years before. Their quantum computer was a key component of their interstellar drive system, another technology they refused to share with Humans.

Jason decided to pursue a different approach for creating and manipulating qbits from those currently in use on Earth. He hoped to overcome the computational shortcomings of Human's current quantum computers. Though great progress had been made over the years, quantum computers still lacked the wide-ranging flexibility of traditional binary computers.

He picked up a three-inch square circuit board he designed earlier and studied it carefully under a scanning electron microscope. Finding no circuitry problems, he plugged it into the laser amplifier module and turned it on. The numeric readouts fell within the desired range. He switched the module off and turned his attention to the quantum gate controller module he believed lay at the heart of the problem.

Achilles gazed at Troy's high ramparts and its impenetrable walls. Behind him, the masts of a thousand Greek ships bobbed about above the surf. 'If only we could devise a way to get past the city gates…'

Jason shook his head to clear his mind of incursions from his ongoing database search for precedents relating to Haven's current political situation. But the comment about gates caught his attention. Perhaps instead of a single quantum gate controller, a dozen arranged in parallel would provide his computer with the desired flexibility.

Data peered at the corpse lying on the holodeck floor with a dagger plunged into its back. He puffed on his pipe, playing the part of Sherlock Holmes, and pointed to the lack of blood near the wound. 'Things are not always as they seem…'

Jason gathered the parts he would need to build several more quantum gate controllers. As he worked through the night, isolated snatches of unrelated search results continued to rise to the surface of his consciousness like bubbles in a champagne flute. But instead of popping and evaporating, these bits and pieces accumulated in a file within his compartmentalized brain. Eventually, they would achieve critical mass and provide him with a plan he could work with.

Haven Municipal Building

Sam's spacious new office dripped of opulence. A priceless Mughal tapestry depicting scenes of ancient east-Indian court life covered one wall.

Beneath the tapestry, two full-size divans and three overstuffed chairs were arranged in a semicircle around a large white-marble coffee table with intricately carved jade legs. Matching end tables stood sentry beside each chair. A Turkish hand-knotted rug with brightly colored geometric designs completed the room's sitting area.

The two-story floor-to-ceiling windows making up the south and east walls looked out onto Saturn's immense orb filling half the sky. The fourth wall was filled with framed photographs: Sam posing with famous dignitaries; trade photos of his business enterprises. A heavy eight-panel double door to the reception area commanded the center of this wall. Sam made it clear he wanted nothing to do with nanoscreens in his office suites.

Sam entered the room for the first time and strode directly to his oversized mahogany desk. He adjusted his chair to its highest level to create the impression of dominance and authority he sought. Then he leaned back and gazed around the room, smiling with satisfaction.

Not exactly fit for a king, but close enough. For now.

A light twinkled on his comlink. He tapped the icon beneath it and one of the heavy doors opened. Travis stepped in.

"Mr. Durban, Sir. A prison guard says they have a prisoner working in the aquaponics section beneath the subway level who claims you know her. She's been asking to see you."

Sam paused for a moment to digest this information. His face lit up with a wicked smile.

"That must be Karen Sanders. I haven't thought about her for years."

"Should we bring her up?"

"Why not? Maybe I can find a use for her, um, for her services."

Twenty minutes later, Karen was ushered into the office. Sam looked up from his desk. The woman standing before him carried only a faint resemblance to the vivacious, vibrant, and sexy Karen Sanders he remembered. This Karen looked to have aged three years for every year they had been apart. Her short-cropped hair was pewter gray. Her skin was a pasty white. Her hazel eyes, however, retained the fierce intensity of her younger self.

Sam stood behind his desk. "Leave us."

The guards slipped out the door and shut it behind them. Sam and Karen were alone together for the first time in eleven years.

"Karen, my dear, I've been meaning to visit you ever since I arrived. I've been busier than you can imagine."

"I've been thinking about you, too, Sam. About the fun times we had together before the aliens arrived."

"We were quite the team then. Fighting tooth and nail to keep alien technologies from destroying our business empires. And we succeeded, too. After a fashion."

"If it hadn't been for that Chavez bitch and her Saturn Accords, we'd have driven them away for good. Thanks to her, they're still here."

"True, but I've ended their mandated embargo with Earth. I control their precious orbiting city and Chavez is in prison. I'm now the power to be reckoned with."

"So, I take it you're in with the aliens now?"

"Never! Their own laws require local approval before they occupy a system. When I've overcome Chavez's Loyalists, I'll make sure the aliens know they are no longer welcome here and send them packing."

"You never were one to share control, Sam. Not in business or in bed. Remember those times, Sam?"

Karen's voice had turned soft and alluring, bordering on sultry. Sam felt a stirring in his groin.

Those were fun times, indeed. But the years have not treated you kindly.

"How could I forget? You were quite beguiling back then. I couldn't keep my eyes off you."

"More than just your eyes, as I recall. We could pick up where we left off. I haven't forgotten the special little things you liked. I can still be irresistible."

"Ah yes, those were the days. But I like my women a good deal younger now. Beautiful women are always following me, begging for my attention." Sam chuckled. "I haven't had a night's rest since I came to Haven."

Karen visibly swallowed hard, possibly choking back an acid retort to Sam's dismissive reply.

"But Sam, you are assuming such a responsible position. You are constantly in the public eye. You need a stable consort by your side. Someone with whom women can identify. Someone to represent the female half of your subjects."

I like the way she puts that. 'My subjects.'

"You have a point, my dear. But I must also appeal to the other half as well. A 'mother figure' does not compute. A gorgeous young woman on a man's arm says 'success' like nothing else. A woman who won't put a knife through my belly when I'm not looking. You fail on both counts."

Karen's eyes turned to daggers. Her voice took a sharp edge.

"You're a fool, Sam. You stole my robotics company when I was convicted of murder and sentenced to life on this god-forsaken rock. A murder you encouraged me to commit. If word got out about your complicity…"

"I had absolutely nothing to do with your bungling attempt at homicide. Your vendetta against Chavez was your own affair. I would have advised you to stand down."

Sam steepled his fingers.

"You're lucky to still be alive, Karen. The Shalcerians should have executed you when they had the chance. Guards!"

Two guards entered the room and grabbed Karen's arms.

"I don't know how I'll do it, Sam. But I'll get you. I'll get you if it's the last thing I do."

The guards forcibly removed her from the room. Sam sighed deeply when the heavy doors closed behind them.

That's one dangerous bitch. I need to make sure she doesn't have a chance to try something serious. And I know just the person to do it.

Chapter 7

Mayberry Station, Luna

Rae Anne's vision to expand Human presence throughout the Sol System included establishing permanent outposts wherever practical. In the past six years, Haven constructed five space colonies. The three cities on Mars were already self-sustaining. Juno, on Jupiter's moon Ganymede, was barely two years old and relied on frequent deliveries from Haven.

Haven's fifth outpost, Mayberry Station on Luna's far side, served as a science research and exploration station. Sheltered from radio interference from Earth, Mayberry's most ambitious project was construction of a giant radio telescope spanning a nearby crater. Another project involved excavating material from nearby impact craters to study the changes rocks and minerals undergo when subject to high-energy collisions in a vacuum. Craters resulting from carbonaceous meteor strikes contained diamond deposits, although the crystals were small and of poor quality.

Sam had taken advantage of Mayor Tony Armado's complaints regarding Haven's neglecting its Mars colonies to enlist his active support in his revolution. He assumed those feelings would be mirrored at both Juno and Mayberry Station. Fae Jackson, Juno's mayor, did not disappoint, offering full support for his actions. But Mayberry Station refused to respond to his entreaties. Deciding a personal visit might bring them around, Sam organized a crew for KBP *Mendeleyev,* one of the cruisers still docked at Haven. Jason-17 was at the comlink console on the bridge when *Mendeleyev* set out for Luna. Like the rest of the crew, he sported the required red armband insignia of the revolution. Sam had forgotten his earlier encounter with Jason-12 aboard *Azov,* allowing him to retain his anonymity.

Mendeleyev set down on the gray-black lunar basalt plain beside Mayberry Station. The ground crew guided the snake from the terminal habitat and connected its free end to *Mendeleyev's* airlock. Once pressurized, the ship's outer hatch opened. Sam stepped through, followed by the ship's officers. The delegation from the outpost approaching the ship included a diminutive woman with short black hair wearing a smart business suit. She reached out to Sam and shook his hand with a firm grip.

"Welcome to Mayberry Station, Mr. Durban. I am Sashi Makino, Facilities Director. You may call me Sashi."

Sam flashed a winning smile.

This should be a piece of cake. It won't take much to win her over.

"I'm pleased to meet you, Sashi. And I'm good with Sam."

"We're quite familiar with your Luna Xtract operations on the moon's nearside," Sashi said. "In fact, several of our engineers worked for you before they came here. I hope you don't hold grudges," she added, smiling.

Sam laughed. "It's a free market. That's what I came here to discuss with you."

"Yes, I suspected as much. We have been following the news from Haven. We were expecting an official visit. I'm pleased you decided to come in person."

"The pleasure is mine, I assure you."

"But before we engage in business or politics, I have arranged a fine dinner for you and your ship's officers. My leading scientists are looking forward to meeting you. Please, follow me."

Sashi led Sam and his officers through the tunnel and into a maze of narrow corridors connecting the outpost's seventeen habitats. She turned into a conference room at the far end of the complex. Four linen-covered tables were graced with formal dinnerware. Mouthwatering aromas filled the room, emanating from the adjacent kitchen. Eight scientists were already gathered around the tables.

"It would appear you were expecting us," Sam commented.

"We were informed when you left Haven that you were coming. They gave us an ETA and, I must say, you were quite punctual."

Sam pursed his lips and frowned.

My every move is being tracked. I need to find the leaks and plug them.

Following an exquisite five-course meal which included stuffed mushrooms, breaded calamari, salmon sushi, fresh tomato and spinach salad, and a fine sake, Sashi and Sam retired to Sashi's office where she insisted Sam view a presentation highlighting the research taking place at Mayberry Station. The last slides showed images of the great radio telescope's construction with illustrations depicting its finished appearance.

"So, as you can see, we are an apolitical, science research arm of Haven University. We have nothing to offer your revolution. We intend to avoid any alliances."

Sam cleared his throat and exhibited his most winning smile.

"Well, my Liberation League is now in control of Haven, which puts Haven University under our auspices. Matters relating to budget and faculty fall within the scope of my administration's responsibilities. Not to mention direct and continuing logistical support for your research station. These are surely matters you should take into consideration.

"But the big picture is this. I've eliminated the Saturn Accords mandates that have thwarted humanity's progress. The aliens' failed experiment in eugenics is finished. I have removed their embargo on goods from Earth and my team is establishing trade alliances with every nation. Think what free movement of people and goods will mean for your research projects."

"You may not have noticed, Sam, but Mayberry Station is in a different position from Haven, Juno, and the Mars colonies. First, our people have avoided the DNA analysis and psychological testing mandated by the Saturn Accords for Haven. For example, those mining engineers we hired from Luna Xtract simply moved from your facilities to ours. No psychological vetting.

"Second, we have no trade restrictions with Earth. Every item on our menu tonight was shipped up from Earth. We order whatever we need through the USIEA outposts on Luna's nearside. They even deliver. In fact, most items come up from Earth on your own TransWorld Space transports, even if it does take three days to get here. The embargo you mentioned doesn't apply to us.

"Haven realized that our proximity to Earth and its resources made enforcement of the Saturn Accords impractical. Mars and Ganymede are so far away they must rely on Haven's cruisers for support. So, Haven placed those colonies under the Accords' umbrella to appease Commander Denahr. He gave Rae Anne Chavez broad leeway to pursue her goals."

"Well, Chavez is no longer in charge. I am calling the shots now," Sam declared forcefully.

Sashi raised her eyebrows.

"Denahr may have something to say about that. He's the one you should be bargaining with. He has the Shalcerian Empire to back him up. One look at their garrison should tell you what little fish we are in the Shalcerian scheme of things."

Sam settled back in his chair and calmly resumed his sales pitch.

"That works to our advantage, Sashi. It's clear they needed Sol System for their military's advance base but were stymied by their own protocols requiring local consent before proceeding. The threat of our withdrawing consent now is like holding a royal flush. They won't give up their base here for anything."

Sam waited for a response. Hearing none, he continued.

"Even if Mayberry Station is a special case, I still urge you to join our cause. Showing that Haven and all five colonies are united will solidify our determination and legitimacy in the aliens' eyes. All three of them."

Sashi smiled and shook her head.

"We polled the 187 adult residents at the station after your initial uprising on Haven. An overwhelming majority insist Mayberry Station maintain a neutral status so long as our autonomy is respected. Our ties with Earth remain strong, despite the Saturn Accords. Our function as a research station will continue, with or without Haven's support."

Sam's face flushed as his eyes hardened.

"I have far more influence on Earth than you know. If you think you can survive without Haven, you had better think again. As you pointed out, TransWorld Space provides support for everything that takes place on the moon. On both the near and far sides. I can easily choke the life out of this outpost."

Sashi rose from her seat. Her voice remained calm.

"Let me escort you back to your ship, Mr. Durban. I hope you have enjoyed our hospitality. But we have no intention of joining your crusade."

She led Sam back to the conference room where she collected the rest of *Mendeleyev's* landing party. She then took the visitors to their ship without uttering a single word.

Once aboard *Mendeleyev,* Sam paced the bridge, shouting his outrage at having his offers rejected by someone he tagged as an incompetent nitwit, and a woman no less. Sam balled his fists, wishing he had someone on whom to vent his anger.

As soon as the ground crew detached the snake from the ship and retracted it into the habitat's airlock, *Mendeleyev* lifted off. Sam sat at his stateroom desk and fumed. The unlit cigar in his fist was crumpled beyond recognition, tobacco shreds scattering like brown snowflakes across his tablet and onto the floor.

Sashi Makino, you have made a serious mistake. No one ignores Sam Durban without paying for it.

He flipped a switch on his comlink.

"Captain Sarkov, connect me to the *Maxwell.*"

Once the link had been established, Sam directed Captain Roach to direct *Maxwell* to Mayberry Station.

"They need some additional persuasion to bring them around. Don't do too much damage. No more than a habitat or two. We'll see if that changes the station director's mind about cooperating with us.

"But if she continues to resist, threaten to destroy their precious telescope. They'll do anything to save their telescope."

From the bridge, Jason-17 monitored Sam's call. He reported the outcome of the Mayberry mission to Jason-0 on Haven and alerted him to *Maxwell's* directive. Jason-0 transmitted the information to the other distant clones.

Chapter 8

Kuiper Belt, Aboard *Liberty*

Jason-03 stood beside the small conference table in *Liberty's* Operations Center. He had just received the notification from Jason-0 about Mayberry Station and he and Ian had retired from the bridge.

"Jason-17 reports that Sam Durban has departed Mayberry Station for Haven. Sashi Makino rejected his offer to join forces. He then ordered *Maxwell* to Mayberry to intimidate them with threat of force."

Ian leaned back in his chair and rubbed his temples. The past ten days were as stressful as any he had experienced. There was still no word about Rae Anne or her whereabouts. Official communications from Haven had ceased.

"That explains the urgent request we received from Mayberry Station. They must have gotten the same update regarding *Maxwell's* impending attack. Sashi promised to swing support for our cause and called for us to come help protect the station. She proposed making Mayberry Station the base for our fleet, despite putting them at considerable risk. And now, with *Maxwell* on its way there..."

"Jason-0 suggests we declare Mayberry Station to be Haven's capital in exile. He is working on a plan to free several Haven officials to create a government in absentia."

Ian looked up with a start. His heart jumped.

That could include Rae Anne. Please let it be so.

"Any idea what this plan might entail?"

"Nothing yet. His instructions were to base operations on Luna. He advised blocking all TransWorld Space activities beyond Earth orbit and using our own cruisers to take up the slack in the Earth-Luna shuttle traffic."

"That would shut down his Luna Xtract mining operations," Ian observed.

"Those facilities are ripe for the picking. They are 90% automated and are entirely defenseless. We might persuade Sam's employees to come over to our side. Especially once we have the upper hand on Luna."

Ian dismissed Jason and created a comlink to Ellie on *Freedom*.

"Ellie, have you heard the latest?"

"That Mayberry Station needs our immediate help? When do we leave?"

"If attack is imminent, we need to get there ASAP. I'm ordering *Liberty* and *Freedom* to leave the Kuiper Belt immediately. You are a couple of hours farther out than we are, so we'll get there first. I'll notify the others of our plan. They can follow us when rotation ends in two days.

"We'll maintain ship-to-ship contact, but no other communications. *Maxwell* will be surprised when we show up."

"So, what's the plan after we block *Maxwell's* attack? Do we go on the offensive?"

"I would like to, Ellie. But Jason reports that Haven's hangar decks are sealed. Even if we neutralized Durban's cruisers, our access to the city is blocked. Without boots on the ground, our presence would be meaningless."

After a long pause, Ellie responded.

"So, Mayberry it is. I'm not sure they have the facilities to accommodate all of us."

"Sashi's promised to assign the construction crews to building landing platforms for more ships. Till then, there will be no shore leave. We'll have a large enough presence to cover both Mayberry Station and the USIEA's three bases on the other side of Luna."

"What about the Chinese research station there? Should we let them know what's going on?"

"When we arrive, I'll see if I can get a face-to-face meeting with someone in charge. We need to do this before Sam does. He's been using *Maxwell* to transport foot soldiers and weapons to Haven. I'm not sure who's been supplying him with arms. Could be China."

"Looks like the Kuiper Belt patrols will be on hold for a while."

"It can't be helped. We don't know what we'll be facing. We need to keep everyone close at hand."

To manage security in the Kuiper Belt, each cruiser had sensitive gravity-wave detectors to signal the arrival and departure of interstellar visitors. But they also registered and tracked cruiser traffic throughout Sol System. Ian plotted a course for Luna that would keep *Liberty* eclipsed from detection by using Sol as a shield.

As *Liberty* passed through Mars orbit, a ping sounded on the bridge, alerting Ian to the detection of another ship.

"Can you ID the ship, Lt. Mason?" Ian asked.

"It's the *Maxwell*, Sir. It's just now inside Jupiter's orbit."

"Jason, can you determine *Maxwell*'s ETA at Mayberry Station?"

"Yes, Sir. Arrival in three hours, forty-seven minutes."

Great. We'll beat them by two hours. If we can hold them off until Freedom arrives, the two of us should be able to send him packing.

Mayberry Station

The moment *Liberty* achieved orbit above Mayberry Station, Ian put the ship on red alert in anticipation of *Maxwell's* arrival. As all the cruisers were identical, Ian expected the coming confrontation to be among equals.

The cruisers' greatest strength lay in their graviton-embedded super conducting (GESC)-plasticore hull. Shalcerian researchers devoted more than a thousand years to developing this indestructible material, a room-temperature superconductor that exhibited antigravity properties on one side and produced its own gravity on the other. Thus, the crew inside a ship with a plasticore hull experienced a constant 1/6 G gravity, regardless of acceleration or deceleration. Outside the ship, meteoric dust and debris, as well as harmful cosmic radiation, were repelled by the antigravity surface, providing protection for the crew.

When Jason had access to *Avenger's* computer archives, he copied the formula and processing directions for plasticore into his own database. Gravitolite, a rare crystal containing embedded gravitons from the early universe, was a key component of GESC-plasticore. Haven had contracted with Luna Xtract to mine gravitolite in the Asteroid Belt, while keeping its function secret. The raw ore was transported to an automated processing facility outside Haven's dome.

Plasticore fabrication required 3D-printing under extreme conditions of temperature and pressure, conditions occurring naturally on Venus. Thus, Rae Anne located Haven's manufacturing facility at a secret location on Venus.

When KBP *Maxwell* arrived at Mayberry Station, the ship swung into attack position, hovering one-hundred meters above the landing pad. Captain Roach's voice boomed over the comlink.

"Mayberry Station, this is Captain Roach of the Liberation League cruiser *Maxwell*. Mr. Durban felt you needed a little demonstration to help you decide to join us. I wish to speak with Sashi Makino."

Liberty, in its distant position above the outpost, had remained undetected. Ian now powered the ship's engines and dropped vertically toward the surface. Before Sashi could respond, *Liberty* came to a full stop directly in front of *Maxwell*. The two ships hovered nose-to-nose. *Liberty* blocked *Maxwell*'s view of the station.

The comlink on *Liberty's* bridge crackled to life.

"Get your damn ship out of my way. What do you think you're doing?"

Ian frowned, trying to place the voice. He knew every ship's captain in the KBP fleet and was sure he didn't know this person. He took a deep breath before responding.

"I didn't hear you declare your intent to land. You are blocking the landing platform. Have you obtained landing permission from Mayberry Port Authority?"

"I'm not landing. I have other business. Now move your blasted crate."

"Your last transmission didn't come through. Say again."

Ian continued to play comlink tag with his opponent on *Maxwell's* bridge. All the while, Jason-03 provided him with text messages relayed from Jason-04 on *Maxwell*. Ian learned that the captain was Freddy Roach and *Maxwell* was flying with a complement of fifty, one-third the normal crew. The entire crew, including Roach, had been recruited directly from the academy, some with no more than a few weeks' training.

After a while, Roach seemed to have tired of Ian's stalling tactics and turned his attention back to his mission. *Maxwell* rose to two hundred meters. He swung the ship toward the most distant habitat and fired a torpedo. A yellow and orange flash temporarily overloaded the monitors on *Liberty's* bridge. When visibility returned, a blackened pile of rubble marked where the habitat had been. The building's plasticore shell had been thrown against a cliff fifty meters away.

Ian aimed his ship upward at *Maxwell* and applied full thrust to his attitudinal controls. *Liberty* leaped forward like a rabbit and smashed full force against *Maxwell's* underbelly. *Maxwell* careened into space at an awkward angle, spinning on two axes.

"You fucking son-of-a-bitch. I'm coming for you."

Ian shook his head. "Prepare for Round Two," he announced to his bridge crew. He rotated *Liberty* toward his quarry and watched the visual monitor closely as Roach brought his ship under control. Once *Maxwell* stabilized, Roach swung his ship into attack position and fired two torpedoes, point blank into *Liberty*.

Both missiles exploded against *Liberty's* plasticore hull, showering the surrounding space with dazzling fireworks. Knowing where the cruiser's vulnerable areas were located, Ian oriented *Liberty* to keep them away from *Maxwell's* sights. He wondered if Roach was even aware that the cruisers had weak spots.

As if to answer his question, Roach launched two more torpedoes at *Liberty*, with the same results.

"Alright, you bastard. Move now or the next two will be aimed at the station."

Ian glanced at his message tablet. Jason-15 aboard *Freedom* had just announced their arrival.

Ian flicked the com switch. "Hit him, Ellie," Ian commanded.

Ellie swung *Freedom* above and behind *Maxwell*, perfectly aligned with the ship's shuttle bay doors, a vulnerable location on *Maxwell's* hull. She fired two torpedoes. The aft third of *Maxwell* flashed an eye-searing white. The ship spun crazily to port and dived into the lunar surface. Although the plasticore hull was built to withstand such impacts, the fireworks flashing behind the ship's viewports revealed internal explosions ripping the ship's inner structure to shreds.

Jason-03 shuddered. "Umph."

Ian turned. Jason's shoulders twitched and he was shaking his head.

"Jason, are you alright?"

After a short pause, Jason resumed his normal android posture.

"I am now. But I experienced a short circuit, or something, in my memory core. It happened the moment we lost contact with Jason-04. Very strange response. Jason-04 is gone."

Ian turned back to his console and set *Liberty* down on the landing pad. Ellie brought her cruiser to hover on station above *Liberty*. The ground crew maneuvered the snake across the regolith to *Liberty*'s airlock and snapped it into place. The airlock opened when pressure equalized to reveal Sashi Makino waiting to greet Ian.

"Welcome to Mayberry Station. Thank you for fending off *Maxwell* and preventing further destruction."

"How bad is the damage?"

"The habitat they destroyed was a work-crew dormitory. It's midday, and the building was empty. We were lucky."

"That's a relief. You know, you did a brave thing. Not everyone would stand up to Sam Durban. Especially when you are in such a vulnerable position."

"I kept reminding myself that there are good people out there. I can't tell you how frightened I was when I learned *Maxwell* was heading our way.

"But with Mayberry becoming home base for Haven-in-exile, we'll need to divert all our construction efforts to building additional landing pads and housing for your crews. Not to mention offices for your government."

"We'll do everything we can to help. This will be a boon to your economy, Sashi. Mayberry Station could soon be bigger than Nova Prima."

"Well, growth will be good. But we must do it with an eye to the long-term to make sure it's sustainable once this turmoil is resolved. Short term solutions won't do, no matter how expedient they may seem."

Chapter 9

Haven Municipal Building

"Mr. Durban, Sir. The video transmission we just received from the *Maxwell*—you'll want to view it right away. It's, well, um, it's quite disturbing." Travis' face was lined with worry.

"So, did *Maxwell* get the job done? I hope Roach torched their damn telescope."

"Um…no, Sir. *Maxwell*'s been destroyed."

Sam's face turned white. His palms became cold and clammy.

"That's not possible. Mayberry is a research station. Makino has no weapons capable of shooting down a cruiser."

Sam turned his attention to his tablet and tapped the file icon at the top of his 'Incoming' folder with a trembling hand. He watched the video showing *Maxwell's* encounter with *Liberty*. It terminated seconds after *Freedom*'s salvo struck the ship.

Sam replayed the video several more times without a word. He scowled at his aide. "Was there any further communication beyond the end of this tape with the *Maxwell*?"

"Nothing, Sir. But Earth media is broadcasting that we attacked our own colony on Luna and the attacking ship was destroyed. Video taken from Mayberry Station shows *Maxwell* going down after a massive explosion. Every media platform on Earth is airing the video."

Sam instructed his tablet to play back one of the media broadcasts. His mouth became dry.

"So, we've lost the *Maxwell*," he muttered.

Travis stood silently in front of Sam's desk, shifting nervously from one foot to the other, hands clenched behind his back.

"That must never happen again. We don't have any ships to spare."

"*Maxwell* had a crew of 55," said Travis.

"That's the other problem. I can't find enough recruits to man the ships I do have. Losing a crew along with a ship. This is a major blow."

Nothing to be done about it now. I need experienced crews for all eight of my remaining ships. Top priority.

Sam watched the *Maxwell* video one more time. Sherry, his latest tagalong, was lounging on the sofa. She rose and sashayed around Sam's desk to stand behind his chair.

Sam shook his head. "I can't believe what I'm seeing. It's like a game of Bumper Cars on steroids, yet neither ship is damaged. The crew inside *Maxwell* is unaware of the tremendous forces smashing against the hull. It's crazy."

Sherry draped her left arm around Sam's chest. She leaned forward over his shoulder for a better view, giving Sam a better view of her ample breasts beneath her loose-fitting blouse. The distraction caused Sam's heart to skip, then pulse faster, as though making up for the lost beat. He inhaled deeply.

Hmm. My favorite perfume.

Sam pulled her head down for a long, passionate kiss while his other hand stroked her upper thigh.

"Travis, get lost." Travis disappeared, thumping the heavy door closed.

Sam swung Sherry onto his lap, pulling her blouse off in the process. "Just one more…one more time before…"

He reluctantly turned his attention back to the monitor and played the video again. "I don't understand what I'm seeing."

Sherry was breathing heavily, but she offered an explanation. "My dad was in the Kuiper Belt Patrol. He would come home between rotations and rave about this plasticore the ships are made of. Indestructible. Impervious to cosmic radiation. Insulating the crew from acceleration forces. He described once being hit by an asteroid. Knocked the ship off course, but nothing more."

Sam rubbed his chin thoughtfully, refocusing his thoughts. "I haven't appreciated the full extent of plasticore's properties. I lived through the Marsquake in '52. My habitat was tossed around but only the connecting tunnel was damaged. It hadn't dawned on me that the habitats remained intact because they were all made of plasticore. I literally owe my life to that stuff."

And if I were in sole possession of this material, I could use it as leverage to control the entire Solar System. I must learn how to manufacture plasticore.

Thoughts of empire and enormous wealth created a yearning that washed through his body and overpowered the sexual urges he felt moments before. He absently pushed Sherry off his lap.

"Scoot!" he commanded gruffly.

Sherry knew better than to linger. She grabbed her blouse and quickly left Sam alone with his imperial fantasies.

Haven University

The quantum computer in Jason's lab looked like a digital Christmas tree. LEDs flickered on seven panels wrapped around a barrel-like container the size of an office desk. Tubes and wire bundles sprouted from the apparatus in every direction. Rapidly scrolling digital readouts filled a large monitor above the console.

This was Jason's first systems test for the computer since he fabricated and installed the two-dozen quantum gate controllers. The new equipment required a myriad of adjustments and supporting devices in addition to major alterations to the software controlling the computer's operation. Jason smiled.

Everything's looking ok. Let's power it up.

He reached over the console and flipped a switch to activate the computer's quantum processor. The lab plunged into darkness. Several electric motors wound down to a halt. Jason grimaced and turned the computer off, then navigated through the dark lab to the hallway door.

Standing in front of the floor's electrical distribution panel in the hall, Jason pressed the key to reset the master breaker, restoring power to the lab. He scanned the digital readouts showing each line's power consumption and their recent histories. Locating three lines with available wattage, he redirected two to the third line and added their unused wattage to the line servicing the computer.

Let's see if this does the trick.

Jason returned to the lab, verified the digital readouts were within acceptable ranges, and turned the computer on again. A satisfying sound issued from the apparatus, like the buzz from a hovering hummingbird.

"Calculate a Mersenne prime that contains over one-hundred-million digits, and report the answer in Mersenne notation, as a power of two minus one," he commanded.

Within ten seconds, the answer appeared on the monitor. The previous world-record for largest Mersenne prime contained far fewer digits and required seven days for the world's most advanced binary computer to calculate.

Jason smiled. His quantum computer accomplished a more difficult calculation 65,000 times faster. As a check, he restated his last request, using the exact number of digits in the previous largest prime. The computer quickly produced the prime number, lending credence to his earlier calculation.

How about a more challenging problem?

"Devise a randomly sized seven-dimensional polygon with ten corners. Display its dimensions and corner coordinates as a matrix. Then perform a transformation in which the shape is rotated forty-five degrees in all seven dimensions and display its new corner coordinates as a matrix."

The first set of numbers appeared on the monitor immediately. Jason performed ball-park calculations in his own computer brain to verify that the numbers made sense. He did the same with the second set when it appeared fifty-five seconds later. He smiled on seeing the results.

This machine is working better than I had expected.

Throughout the night, Jason posed ever more complex problems covering a wide variety of computational challenges. The quantum computer provided solutions at lightning speed.

Toward morning, an interesting thought crossed his mind. He knew the Shalcerians used quantum computing to generate elaborate holograms. He had witnessed one himself when Vahler, captain of Avenger, allowed him to visit the mammoth battlecruiser's bridge. The entire room was a holographic view of the ship's surroundings. The experience was like floating alone in space. Even the consoles and monitors on the deck were holograms.

Among the data archives Jason had downloaded from *Avenger's* database was a mammoth file containing the algorithms and programs

Shalcerians used to create and control their elaborate holographic displays. Without a quantum computer at his disposal, Jason had ignored the file. But now…

If I put together the projection equipment and sensors these programs call for and tie them into my quantum computer, I should be able to generate holographic projections.

Although he didn't have the specifications for the equipment he needed, a careful study of the programs provided enough detail for him to cobble together a rough set of blueprints. He spent the next two days scavenging through the physics department, borrowing parts and pieces, gadgets and gizmos. As soon as he brought each new piece of equipment into his lab, he wired it into his growing holographic studio.

When he finished, he stood back and admired the four-foot cube with its eight projectors tucked in its corners. Three electromagnets were arranged around the cube's base to create the magnetic flux needed to illuminate ionized gas molecules within the cube, a process mimicking aurora formation. For now, a large bundle of wires connected all the equipment to the computer. However, Jason was already designing a module for wireless transmission in his brain.

The hologram programs in his archives were identified by number, so he picked one at random to use as a test subject. He uploaded it into the computer.

"Run file 1630922 using the hologram transmission program," he commanded.

A faint crackling sound issued as the air ionized. An eerie wavering glow filled the cube. Undulating images began to form. Within seconds, a realistic three-dimensional rendition of a Shalcerian wrestling match filled the space within the cube. Six arms and six legs grappled in a confusing entanglement as the two athletes attempted to throw their opponent to the mat.

Jason sent several commands to the computer, adjusting various aspects of the display, zooming in and out, altering color, saturation, and brightness levels.

I need to catalog the video files in my archives. Viewing them may give me some ideas for putting this technology to good use.

From his own search memory, a phrase kept bubbling to the fore:
Things are not always as they seem…

Chapter 10

Haven Justice Center

Rae Anne carefully knotted a group of threads unraveling at the base of her blanket. Forty-six knots marked her days in captivity. She leaned back against the wall next to her cot.

Six weeks of utter boredom. I miss Ilhan's company, but I'm glad she's free. I hope she's all right.

The cell door rattled and opened. She looked up at the two guards who entered. They seemed surprised to find her sitting on the floor. The male guard pointed at her.

"You. Come with us." His gravelly voice was harsh.

Rae Anne stood. The guards escorted her to the lift for the Municipal Building. They rode the lift to the eighth floor. When they exited the lift, Rae Anne found herself in a lavishly appointed reception area.

This must be Sam's new office suite.

The guards stopped at the desk. Travis poked at icons on his tablet. After a short pause, he said, "Go on in."

As they approached, one of the twelve-foot wooden doors swung open into Sam's office.

Rae Anne gasped and gaped at the extravagant setting. A mammoth chandelier hung from the twenty-foot ceiling, its glass crystals casting rainbow reflections around the room. A brightly colored silk tapestry covered one wall. Saturn's imposing hulk and its rings glistened in the floor-to-ceiling south window.

Ah, my beloved Saturn. How I miss you!

Sam looked up from his work. He seemed to loom over his desk, bigger than life.

"Rae Anne. Good to see you again. Please, take a seat on the sofa next to the tapestry. It has the best view of Saturn."

As Rae Anne sat, Sam rose and walked around his desk to the easy chair closest to her. He waved the guards toward the door. "Go."

The guards left the room.

"I see you are adjusting to prison life. As if you had a choice in the matter."

Sam waited for a response. Rae Anne maintained her silence.

"Of course, you do have a choice, you know. I now have a few very specific questions about gravitolite ore and plasticore. I intend to get the answers to these questions. If you cooperate, I'll release you to house arrest. You'll go home today. Say goodbye to prison food, leering guards, endless tedium. Imagine sitting in your own living room, watching a HavenAir broadcast, catching up on the news, watching your favorite video."

Rae Anne remained silent, sitting stiffly upright on the couch.

"Can I get you something to drink? I understand all you get down there is water."

"I'm fine."

"Very well." Sam walked to the bar and mixed a drink, stirring the ice loudly. He returned to the easy chair and sat. He took a long sip from his glass.

Leaning forward, he placed his elbows on his knees and continued swirling his drink conspicuously. The ice rattled against the glass.

"I've seen plasticore's miraculous properties firsthand. It's so indestructible you use your ships as battering rams while the crew inside is shielded from outside forces. I want the formula for this substance. It must have thousands of uses besides cruiser hulls and habitats. I have the means to expand production a thousand-fold. Together we can use it to alter the course of human history."

Rae Anne frowned, staring fiercely into Sam's eyes.

"I will never divulge information about plasticore or gravitolite to the likes of you. People like you are precisely the reason the Shalcerians imposed the Saturn Accords on Haven. Sociopaths with authoritarian mindsets are the bane of humanity."

Sam's face turned red. He jumped to his feet and struck Rae Anne in the face, spilling his drink on the Turkish rug. She fell back into the couch, shocked by the unexpected event and the sudden pain. Somehow, she had managed not to cry out. She lifted her hand to her face to brush away any tears.

I'll not give you anything, you creep.

She pulled herself upright without uttering a sound. Her eyes were narrow slits, glaring at Sam. She steeled herself against another strike.

I can endure whatever you throw at me.

Rae Anne repeated the thought, focusing on it as a mantra.

"I'll get that information from you eventually. I can make things much tougher for you between now and our next interview. I have interrogators who are experts at using 'physical therapy' to bring people around."

He turned toward the door.

"Guards!"

Rae Anne's escorts entered the room.

"Throw this woman into solitary confinement. Restrict her food to half rations."

"Um, Mr. Durban, Sir. Haven has no solitary confinement."

To Rae Anne's satisfaction, Sam looked dumbfounded. He stared at the guard with disbelief.

"That's ridiculous. What kind of prison doesn't have solitary confinement? Travis!"

Travis stepped through the door.

"Assign the construction crew to build five solitary confinement cells, well apart from the regular cell block. Totally sound proofed. With 24/7 surveillance. I want these yesterday."

"Yes, Sir, Mr. Durban, Sir."

Travis disappeared.

"Get this woman out of my sight."

The two guards grabbed Rae Anne's arms and escorted her from Sam's office. By the time they deposited her in her cell, a deep purple lump had grown below her left, blackened eye.

Sitting on her cot, she tried to ignore the throbbing pain and her eye, now swollen shut. She suspected things would only get worse, starting with a starvation diet.

How is it evolution hasn't eliminated Human tendencies to exert power and control over our fellow Human beings? And with no regard to humane treatment or empathy.

Haven Municipal Building

Sam Durban sat comfortably in his office while Sherry darkened his lips, applied a rose tint to his cheekbones, and gave his hair one last swipe with her brush.

"That should do it, Darling," she said, standing back to better judge the results of her efforts.

"We're down to two minutes, Mr. Durban, Sir." The cameraman made one last adjustment to the lights.

Special lighting beamed at the ceiling created soft shadows across Sam's face. Two HavenAir cameras were directed at Sam from different angles, while a third was positioned outside his office door.

"Three…Two…One…You're on."

Both massive doors swung open while Camera Three rolled slowly into the spacious room and turned to Sam as it approached his desk. Halfway there, Camera One picked up with a face-on view of Sam, clasped hands resting on the desk.

"My dear friends and fellow Havenites, thank you for joining me this evening. Six weeks have passed since I broke the alien's shackles and freed you from their restrictions and from their Human lapdogs.

"In those six short weeks, I have established trade agreements with thirty-five nations on Earth. I trust you are enjoying the coffee and chocolate previously banned by the embargo, not to mention the plethora of other Earth imports now available.

"I have also lifted all travel restrictions. We now have twice weekly passenger service between Haven, Mars, and Earth. Hundreds of you have already taken advantage of this to visit Earth. You are now free to bring relatives and friends from Earth to visit your homes here on Haven."

Sam moved some papers aside on his desk, revealing a thin black binder. He held it upright in front of Camera Two so it could zoom in on its embossed decorations. HAVEN CONSTITUTION was spelled out in bold gold letters on the cover.

"When I arrived, I promised a new constitution. This document incorporates the best ideas gleaned from Human history.

"For example, dozens of nations have proven how essential a strong executive is for effective governance. To this end, this constitution designates the president as the head of Haven's government. The legislative body, a twelve-member Senate, will serve in an advisory role to the president, proposing legislation and providing counsel to the president when needed.

"Our new constitution also circumvents a common bottleneck many governments experience—endless litigation in the courts. When a crisis occurs, decisions need to be made without delay. Lawsuits bog everything down. The new constitution allows the president to remove judges and to review and, when necessary, dismiss cases and disbar problem lawyers at all levels.

"There are several other innovative features in this constitution. Its contents will be available for your perusal following this broadcast. Of course, my office will be happy to hear your comments and suggestions."

Sam set the document on the desk and smiled into the cameras.

"According to this constitution, the president and his legislative advisors constituting the Senate are to be elected by popular vote. To fill these offices, elections will be held four weeks from today. My office will take candidate applications for one week beginning tomorrow morning.

"So, read your new constitution, check out the qualifications for office holders, and decide if you want to take part in governing our fine city. Thank you for your attention and support."

The cameras clicked off. Sam wiped the sweat off his brow while the technicians folded their tripods and packed their equipment into their carrying cases.

Sherry strolled over and gave Sam a big kiss. "That was beautiful, Darling. You looked so… so daunting. I wonder who our new president will be?"

"You're looking at him, Baby." Sam waved his hand to take in the surroundings. "You don't think I'm about to give all this up, do you?"

Chapter 11

Haven Aquaponics

Karen sat on the bench in front of her locker in the Aquaponics Section changing room. She gazed at the biogrip unit securely attached to her left ankle. The device monitored her movements and location while at work, ready to inject a fast-acting sedative if her actions deviated from its preset program. Normally after a ten-hour shift she was exhausted and anxiously waited to be returned to her cell for dinner and a night's rest. But today she had different plans.

No matter what happens, I'll never wear that damn thing again.

Before Sam's arrival, leaving Haven was an impossible task, as transportation to Earth was prohibited. But those restrictions no longer applied, and once ferries began shuttling passengers between Haven, Mars, and Earth, Karen began to formulate plans for escape.

At five o'clock, Jeb, a burly security guard, entered the locker room to escort Karen back to her cell. He turned and, as he often did, bolted the door behind him. On seeing who her guard was, Karen's adrenaline surged.

You'll not get the better of me tonight, you bastard.

"Well, well, lookie here. Just waiting for me to show up and add a little excitement to your day." The leer in his voice raised bile in Karen's throat.

Maybe a bit more excitement than you are expecting.

Karen rubbed her calf just above the monitor.

"Before we get to it, can you fix this thing? It feels like the needle is sticking out and scratching my leg. It's been bothering me all day."

"I'll take it off and look at it. I might have to send it back to the shop."

Jeb fussed with his key ring to find the monitor's key. Karen extended her leg and Jeb dropped to his knees to unlock her biogrip. Karen yawned and appeared to stretch, but the moment her leg was free, she struck Jeb's exposed neck with the knife-edge of both hands using all the force she could muster. She then kicked him beneath the chin.

Jeb fell to the floor, howling, stunned but not incapacitated. Grabbing her leg with both hands for leverage, he struggled to his feet. He reached for her arm to gain control over her, but Karen lurched forward and slammed him in the face with her head. He fell to the floor again, dazed and bloodied.

Karen shook her head sharply to regain her vision, then reached down and pulled Jeb's nightstick from his belt. One powerful blow to the head rendered him unconscious. With pent-up rage from weeks of abuse, Karen clubbed him repeatedly until all her energy was drained.

Spattered with blood and aching all over, Karen stepped around his crushed skull and swung her locker door open. A fresh black burka was hanging on the side hook. An old-sect Muslim coworker had honored her request and brought it to work the previous week, hidden beneath her own burka.

She pulled the garment over her head and adjusted it to cover her face. Carefully brushing any loose hair beneath the burka, she stepped out of the dressing room and confidently strolled to the guard's desk by the lift. The guard momentarily looked up as she passed. Taking her to be an Afghan immigrant employed by Haven to work in this section, he resumed watching the soccer game on his tablet.

Karen took the lift and stepped off at the subway platform four levels up. She took the Levline to Sector 11 where most of the Islamic immigrants resided. Though few adhered strictly to Sharia Law, enough did that Karen knew she could blend into the community long enough to execute the next step in her escape strategy.

Haven Municipal Building

The instant Sam arrived at his office suite the next morning, Travis looked up from his desk and blurted "Karen Sanders escaped!"

"What the hell do you mean, 'She escaped?'"

"Yesterday evening, Sir, in Aquaponics. She killed the guard and slipped past Security. She's loose somewhere in the city."

Chills swept up Sam's back. "That woman is dangerous. Her capture has got to be Security's number one priority. A month's bonus to whoever brings her in. Dead or alive."

Preferably dead.

"Yes Sir, Mr. Durban, Sir."

"Didn't she have an ankle monitor? Why didn't it work? Can't they use it to find her whereabouts?"

"The monitor was on the floor next to the guard's body. It looks like the guard purposely removed it."

"I can't believe it! I'm surrounded by bloody incompetent fools."

Sam turned and strode angrily toward the door to his office.

Not a great start to my day.

"There is one other thing, Sir."

Sam stopped and took a deep breath. Twisting his head to glare at Travis over his shoulder, he hissed, "Yes?"

"The crew building the solitary confinement cells in the prison say they'll be finished in a week."

"Good. Tell Security to toss Chavez into one as soon as they're done and throw away the key. After the election, the first business for our senators will be to institute capital punishment for murder and other high crimes. I should have put that in the constitution."

When Sam settled into his office, he called Ben Keeler, his Security chief.

"How is it possible for a single guard to remove an ankle monitor?" he demanded. "Because of that, we have a murderer running loose in the city. I want that situation fixed immediately!"

"It's a safety issue, Mr. Durban. Since the biogrips automatically inject sedative into the prisoner should they try to escape, any number of things might go wrong, requiring the unit to be removed immediately. The prisoner's life could be at risk."

"So now the entire city is at risk. What kind of trade-off is that?"

"In sixteen years, Sir, no one has ever tried to escape."

"Well, you have one now. Get those keys away from the guards."

"Yes, Sir. I'll get on it right away."

Damn. Do I have to do all the thinking on this stupid rock?

Haven

A few weeks before Karen's escape, Jin Lei, her liaison with China when she owned Sanders Robotics, visited her in her cell on Haven. They discussed old times, and Jin Lei commiserated with her situation on Haven. Before he left, he gave her a slip of paper with a Haven address.

"Should you ever find yourself free and need help or a secure refuge, come to this address. We can get you off Haven and back to Earth."

Karen memorized the address and disposed of the paper lest it compromise her self-appointed saviors. From that moment, she began to watch for opportunities that could place her where she was now.

From Sector 11 where she had remained hidden for a week, she travelled on foot to Sector 6, avoiding the subway and its surveillance cameras. The address led her to a block of apartments situated along the far dome wall. She had not realized that Haven's footprint was so large. She was exhausted by the time she pressed the button beside the apartment door.

The door made a clicking noise and she stepped through the nanoscreen. The lock clicked in place behind her. She found herself in a dimly lit foyer with only one door—the one she just came through. She felt a moment of panic waiting for her eyes to adjust to the darkness.

"Please state who you are and your business affiliation."

The announcement was repeated in five languages. Karen thought she detected a Chinese accent in the English version.

"I am Karen Sanders. Formerly of Sanders Robotics."

A rectangle of red light appeared in the ceiling. A trap door in the floor above was being lifted away, replaced by a flood of light. Karen watched as a collapsible ladder unfolded from above and locked into position next to her.

Without invitation, Karen started up the steps, using her hands on the higher steps for balance. When she reached the top, she stepped into a large room lined with plush lounges. Two dozen overstuffed chairs were scattered around the room. A bar occupied the corner opposite the trap door and a live bartender and waitperson were busy tending to the twenty individuals sitting around the room.

And smoke. The room was filled with cigarette and cigar smoke. Karen thought she detected pot as well.

People smoking on Haven. How can that be? What kind of place is this, anyway?

As she was taking in the strange scene, a robust Chinese man with a big grin on his face walked over to her.

"Karen Sanders. I'm Li Kei. Welcome to my smoking club. Jin Lei told me to be expecting you."

"I'm pleased to make your acquaintance. Lei said I could come to this address for help. But how do you keep all this smoke from polluting Haven's air?"

"My club has its own atmospheric controls. Slightly lower pressure so airflow is always inward. The foyer downstairs serves like an airlock as well as a security checkpoint. Come with me to the bar. What would you like?"

Kei led Karen across the room and pulled out a bar stool. Her hike across the city had created quite a thirst, so she ordered a vodka Collins.

"Jin Lei said he had some urgent business with you should you wish to look him up. I'm to help deliver you to him."

"Is he here on Haven?"

"Oh, no. His offices are currently on Mars and in Beijing."

Given my position, I have no choice but to trust this stranger.

"I must tell you, I just escaped from prison. Getting me off this rock could be a major challenge."

"Trust me, not a problem at all. If you aren't claustrophobic, I can get you to Mars on the next shuttle three days from now. In the meantime, I have a very nice suite on the floor above the club where you can stay."

"I'm happy to accept your offer. The sooner I can get away from here, the better."

"Understood. Mao Minh will take you to your room."

Kei signaled for the waitress to come over and gave her instructions in rapid-fire Mandarin. Minh bowed slightly and directed Karen to follow her to the lift.

The suite Karen found herself in was a fully equipped two-bedroom apartment. Both kitchen and bar were fully stocked. To her surprise, she discovered a full wardrobe in her size.

Her first order of business was a long soak in a tub of hot, sudsy water. Then she indulged herself in trying on several different combinations of clothes, a luxury she hadn't experienced since her incarceration. Finally, she slipped into the coral satin pajamas on top of the pillows and flopped into the soft, king-size bed.

I don't know what Jin Lei has in mind, but it must be something good for him to go to such trouble for me. If Jin Lei can get me back to Earth, I might be able to resume a normal life. Undercover, of course. But the farther I get from this place, the better.

Chapter 12

Haven Justice Center

Three workers wearing red armbands stepped off Lift 2 on Sublevel 4 beneath the Haven Security Center. Adjacent to Sector 1's mammoth aquaponics cavern, the area was divided into a dozen barred cells with old-fashioned lock-and-key gates into each cell. Each worker carried an assortment of packages and spools of color-coded wire.

The two security guards on duty were playing cards at the security desk. Both looked up at the visitors with surprise.

"No visitors allowed. Beat it," snarled one of the guards.

"Got a job to do. Deal with it," growled the husky worker in the lead.

"Not until I know what you're here for," said the guard.

"New security cameras. The guys upstairs want to know which one of you is cheating." He set his boxes on the table, upsetting the card game, and peeled them open. The other arrivals put their boxes on the floor and began to do the same.

"Hold off there! You ain't doin' nothin' here till I get the ok." The guard picked up his phone and tapped a number.

"Humph. Busy. Wait…getting transferred.

"McPherson, down on Sublevel 4. We got some guys here who say…"

A pause.

"What? Yeah, we'll keep them out of the cells. No problem."

He ended the call and looked up. "Guess you guys are legit. Just don't make too much noise. You'll disturb my concentration."

His card-playing opponent grinned. "Make all the noise you want. I can use the help."

The work crew started removing the contents from the containers. Soon there were five piles of unmarked, gray metal boxes with tangles of wire stacked around the tiny room.

The sixteen prisoners in their cells watched the activity, but most showed little interest. Rae Anne, however, was hyper-alert. She followed their every move, knowing that seemingly insignificant observations sometimes turn out to be very important.

Over the next two hours, the workers fastened boxes to the ceiling and walls, frequently referring to their blueprints. The guards moved their chairs around the room to stay clear. As they connected their equipment with the spooled wire, the slightest crew member pulled off her hat and swiped the sweat from her brow with her forearm. Her blond hair tumbled down past her shoulders.

"Whoa, didn't know we had a lady present!" exclaimed one of the guards.

The young woman turned to glare at them, arms akimbo. "Yeah, well, would that have made a difference?"

"Nah, prob'ly not. Doubt if we said anything you ain't heard before. But we might of kept a closer eye on you if we'd known."

"Well, now you know, so keep your eyes to yourself. I'm a karate black belt. Just saying."

"We're about through here for today," interrupted the lead worker. He began spooling up the extra wire. They had installed about half of the equipment. The floor was as cluttered as when they began. He turned to the guards and gestured to the remaining boxes.

"The rest of this stuff goes inside the cells. We'll install them tomorrow. There's an empty holding cell next door for the prisoners. Take Lift 3 tomorrow, same level. The night shift will move the prisoners over there after dinner so these cells will be free. If everything checks out when we're finished, you can move them back at the end of your shift tomorrow."

The security guard frowned. "So, we'll have to cuff and chain them when we bring them back?"

"That's your business, not ours. Do what you have to do. Bring whips and cattle prods for all I care." Everyone but the prisoners laughed.

During evening shift rotation, an officious looking administrator met the two fresh guards in the lobby.

"Jackson. Harrison. Your prisoners have been moved over to the holding cell off Lift 3 so we can install upgraded security equipment in their cells tomorrow. They put up a bit of resistance, so we drugged them to make the transfer. They're sleeping it off now. You should have a quiet night."

"Great. Maybe we can watch some videos without distraction for a change."

The guards approached the bank of lifts and took Lift 3 down to Sublevel 4. When they stepped off the lift, they found two guards overseeing sixteen prisoners who were sleeping soundly on mats spread around the single large cell.

"You guys new here?" a fresh guard asked, surprised at seeing two men he didn't recognize.

"No, this is our usual stint. Normally the cell has only a few holdovers from the night before. Not used to having so many this time of day. They been pretty quiet since they were dragged in this afternoon. Must have been drugged. Sleeping it off." He waved at the motionless prisoners.

"Anyway, we're off. They're all yours."

The off duty 'guards' took the lift to the lobby and immediately stepped into Lift 2. They descended to Sublevel 4. Exiting the lift, the two men carefully dodged the piles of equipment and wire on the floor.

"Hey, where you guys been," scolded a day-shift guard. "You're late."

"What's with all the shit?" asked the new arrival, nudging a box aside with his boot.

"They're putting in some new security equipment. Say, I haven't seen you before."

"We're filling in for Jackson and Harrison. They were due for a night off. They're probably at the Arcade taking a shot at the Warrior Games team tryouts."

"Could be. They're heavy into that. But just for the record, let me make sure you're who you say you are."

For the second time that day, he made a call to the main desk. As before, the line was busy and he was transferred. Again, he was reassured that the replacement guards were legitimate.

"Ok," he said, ending the call. He turned to the new arrivals. "I guess you guys are ok. The work supervisor said you'd be moving everyone so they could work inside the cells here tomorrow."

"Yeah, we'll be moving the prisoners after dinner. See a little activity for a change. Hope one of them gives us some trouble so we can rough them up a bit. You guys take it easy."

The two day-shift guards stepped around the boxes, entered the lift, and left.

The shorter man walked over to Rae Anne's cell, inserted the key, and swung the door open.

"Jason!" Rae Anne plunged through the gate and threw her arms around him. Her face beamed.

"Would you do the honors?" Jason handed her a ring of keys. "There's no hurry, but the sooner we are out of here the better. Clearly, you were expecting us."

Rae Anne looked over her shoulder at Jason while freeing the other prisoners.

"Well, I did notice the work crew were disconnecting all the security equipment and not actually connecting anything new. When Emily removed her hat, I recognized her and I knew right away something was up. But how did you get rid of the regular night guards?"

"I didn't. They're over in the next section guarding an elaborate hologram in the holding cell. They won't figure it out for a while. We managed to give the holding-cell shift the night off."

"Wait. Did you say 'hologram?' When the Shalcerian emperor visited Haven, he said he wouldn't give us hologram technology because it would require divulging their quantum computer technology."

"Nothing like a challenge. One of my projects has been building a sophisticated quantum computer to match theirs. I've had their algorithms in my computer archives, so all I needed to do was build the hardware to run them on. It also proved useful in determining your location. I hacked into Haven Security with it."

Rae Anne laughed. "'All you needed to do.' Quite an understatement. Ok. Everyone's free. Let go!"

Jason turned to his buddy. "Clean all this up and remove everything we installed earlier today. We don't want anyone to trace anything back to its source. And reconnect the old security cameras. Toward morning, relieve the guards at the holding cell, and do the same thing there."

Jason led his sixteen escapees to the lift.

"We'll go down one level and trek through the aquaponics plant. No one will be there at night, so we won't risk being seen. The Shalcerian garrison adjoins aquaponics at the other end, and we have SEVA suits waiting there for everyone. Once we cross over into the garrison, we'll be safe."

"I thought the only airlock connecting the garrison to Haven was the one at ground level next to the Visitor's Bureau," Rae Anne said.

"There's a lot about the Shalcerian garrison that's not general knowledge. Even I find myself surprised on occasion."

Dropping down to Sublevel 5, they entered the ground floor of the four-story aquaponics unit. The humidity was suffocating. Gurgling, swishing, and bubbling sounds filled the massive arena, making conversation impossible. Color-coded pipes crisscrossed the space above them, creating the sensation they were tunneling through a high-tech cavern. A variety of curious fish eyed their progress alongside a mammoth aquarium alongside the aisle.

Jason led the way through a maze of stacked glass cubicles, some lighted, some dark. Vegetation of every variety pressed against the cubicle walls. Rae Anne caught glimpses of tomatoes, carrots, and red peppers poking through the greenery.

After a short walk, they reached the airlock. Sixteen respirators were stacked on the benches inside. As soon as the Humans donned their masks and checked the fittings, Jason closed the outer hatch and cycled the airlock for the Shalcerian atmosphere.

When the inner door opened, the pale blue-white light common to Shalcerian habitations filled the airlock. Commander Denahr was waiting for them, perched atop his center leg as usual. He stood and skipped into the airlock on all three legs, greeting the Humans with handshakes and shoulder pats, Human gestures he had learned from Jason-12.

"Sorry to rush you along," he apologized, sweeping his three arms behind them to usher them out. "The shuttle is waiting. If you depart now, the shuttle can drop below Saturn's rings and out of sight, escaping detection. Your disappearance from captivity will be a complete mystery. *Liberty* is waiting to receive you on the other side of Saturn."

"That's Ian's cruiser!" exclaimed Rae Anne. She hadn't seen her husband since before the revolution.

Haven Municipal Building

"People don't just disappear into thin air." Sam was yelling, his face livid with rage. "What were the guards doing? Sleeping? On drugs?"

"No, Sir. We have video coverage of the holding cell where the prisoners were transferred. They were all present and accounted for, sleeping on their mats. Then, at 2:17 a.m., they just disappeared. The cell was empty. The doors were still locked."

"That's not possible!" Sam's heart beat a staccato warning at an alarmingly accelerated pace.

Damn. This is what the doctor warned me about last week. Double damn!

Sam rose and leaned straight-armed against the edge of his desk. He took three deep breaths to reduce his stress level. Then he walked to the bar next to the door and poured a double shot of bourbon.

He plopped into the recliner next to the bar, closed his eyes, and tried to focus.

First, Karen kills a guard and disappears into the city. Nine days, and no one has a clue where she might be. Now, sixteen prisoners evaporate, leaving behind an empty cell. They're all loose in the city as well. Where else could they be? We've got to find them.

"Issue an alert to all security and army personnel with photographs and descriptions of the escapees. I want everyone available to scour the city. If we nab even one, he'll lead us to the others. This must take top priority.

"Send me that cell surveillance video. There's got to be something everyone has overlooked. The guards may have been drugged. Maybe one is an accomplice. Something. We need to get to the bottom of this so it doesn't happen again.

"And double my personal security. Karen we could deal with. But with sixteen potential assassins, I need more protection."

Chapter 13

Aboard *Liberty*

Four Humans and one android sat around the oval table in *Liberty*'s conference room, watching a live video from Haven's Central Park. The park's fountains were as colorful as ever, shooting sparkling water plumes high above the clear lake. In the distance, construction equipment surrounded the Aurora Museum, the relic Mars-II ship Rae Anne flew to Saturn. Rae Anne placed it in the park as a reminder of Haven's origins. It also contained the computer at the heart of Jason's AI persona and the Shalcerian data archives cache Jason copied from the Shalcerian battlecruiser *Avenger*.

A crane ripped a large metal sheet from *Aurora*'s hull and lifted it high in the air before depositing it in a pile of debris. A smaller crane worked the debris pile, hefting chunks onto waiting lorries. As each truck reached its weight limit, it drove off, presumably heading to the recycle center in Sector 9.

Jason-03 experienced a strange sparking sensation in his chest as he watched the activity.

I need to check this out when I get back to the lab. Feels like a short circuit.

Rae Anne broke the silence. "*Aurora* was my home for six long, solitary years." Her voice carried a slight tremor. "The museum is…was a link to our past. Why is Durban removing it?"

"My sources tell me he wants to put a 25-foot statue of himself in that exact spot," Jason-03 replied.

"Figures. Durban wants to be the center of everyone's attention. Anyway, he's now mayor. He can do whatever he wants."

"That's not accurate, Rae Anne," said Jason. "You are still Haven's mayor, albeit *in absentia*.

Interesting, Human's obsession with such trivial things like memorabilia and statues. I need to understand this better.

Ian's brow furrowed. He looked across the table at Jason and cleared his throat.

"What's going to happen when you guys lose your computer? Aren't you all connected to its core?"

Jason turned to Ian. The look on his face came remarkably close to a Human's smug smile.

"Jason-0 understood the risk of relying on a single computer and memory cache. But the resources he needed to back everything up using traditional mempins and binary computer technology were beyond his means. That was one motivation behind his drive to develop a functional quantum computer. The hologram he used in Rae Anne's escape was its first real-world test. Since then, he has smuggled all the mempins from *Aurora* to his quantum computer facility and install them there."

Rae Anne plunked her coffee mug down and gazed at Jason wide-eyed. "So, you're now connected to a quantum computer?"

"Yes, we all are. It's like the difference between night and day. Jason already had the operating algorithms copied from *Avenger,* so once he succeeded in building the hardware, making it operational was easy."

"What's the risk that this new facility will be discovered?"

"Virtually zero. Only Jason knows its whereabouts. According to him, the computer could survive even if Haven itself were destroyed."

"Wait a minute." Ellie MacIntyre, *Freedom*'s captain, crossed her arms in a skeptical gesture. "How can Jason-0 know something you don't know if you're both connected to the same computer core?"

"Jason created a personal memory block for himself and for each clone. He wanted us to develop individual personalities. He hoped our having unique thoughts and memories would help make that happen."

"Cut the video, Jason," said Ian. "I'm relieved to know we'll still have all of you working with us. Has Durban discovered you guys are androids and are in constant communication with each other?"

"No. He has no inkling as to our true nature. He's woefully ignorant of the technological advances Haven has made. His engineers are still probing the gravitolite processing facility behind the city for clues into its nature, but since they don't even know what gravitolite is, they're bumbling around in the dark."

"And the Venus plasticore manufacturing plant?"

"As far as we are aware, he knows nothing about our facilities on Venus."

"Our decision to keep these operations on a 'need to know' basis has paid off," observed Rae Anne. "But we're here to come up with a strategy for deposing Durban and retaking control of Haven."

"We have eleven cruisers to his eight," Anton Kovalenko, *Apollo's* captain, pointed out. "We've got the advantage."

"Only if they were tanks on a battlefield," said Ian. "But our objective is to take back Haven and the colonies. The only advantage our ships give us is transport and maneuverability. Our biggest asset right now is our Jasons."

"The three Cs of warfare: Command, Communication, Control," said Jason. "And we have a lock on the communications part."

"So, where do we stand right now, Ian?" asked Ellie.

Ian shrugged. "Only Mayberry Station is on our side. Haven and the other four colonies are firmly in Durban's hands. *Mendeleyev* ferries arms and supplies to the colonies as well as to Haven. Unfortunately, we don't have a Jason on *Azov*, Durban's primary ship."

"Jason-07 has just been re-assigned to *Denali's* bridge," said Jason.

Rae Anne smiled for the first time. "That's good news. He'll help us keep tabs on Durban's space activities. Too bad we can't disable the five cruisers docked on Haven before he can pull together crews for them."

"Sabotage might be difficult," observed Jason. "Durban's security is intense. But we could block the bay doors so his cruisers couldn't get out. If we parked three or four cruisers directly against Haven's base in front of the hangar doors his ships would be useless."

"Great idea." Ian stood and paced the floor, hands clasped behind his back. "We would still have enough free ships to counter his three. A blockade would also discourage him from docking his three ships. He wouldn't want to risk their getting trapped too."

"Sounds like a siege to me," said Ellie.

"There's still the surface airlock and landing pad," Jason said. "His cruisers could dock there."

"Only one cruiser at a time," Ian replied. "and then everything would have to be hauled through Haven's snake and the airlock. The inconvenience will be a real headache for Durban's crews."

"And the snake is not made of plasticore," Jason pointed out. "That's a glaring vulnerability."

"It may be vulnerable," Ellie said, "but there's over a million citizens in Haven who would be dependent on that one launch site. We mustn't do anything to cut that off."

Rae Anne stood and stretched. "Even so, we designed Haven to be self-sufficient. A siege isn't going to change things much. Especially a partial siege. We still need a plan to remove Durban from power."

She gave Ian a hug. "I'm headed for bed. It's been a long day." She turned and stepped through the nanoscreen. Jason pondered Human's need for physical contact and the desire to show affection.

I wonder how I could incorporate emotions and love into our programming.

"So, Jason, where are Durban's five ships berthed?" Ian asked.

"Jason-12 has been tracking Durban's activities closely. *Olympia* and *Sagan* are in Hangars 5 and 6, *Leibnitz* is in Hangar 10, *Shackleton* is in Hangar 8 and *Hawking* is in Hangar 16."

"One cruiser is big enough to block two adjacent hangars. So, we'll need to assign four ships for the blockade, leaving us with seven to spare. Enough to set up a rotation since we're likely to be in this for the long haul."

Ian ordered Jason to communicate with his fellow Jasons on *Darwin, Newton, Cygnus,* and *Kepler* to relay his orders only to those ships' captains to set up the blockade. He wanted to take no chance for their plans to be leaked before being implemented.

I'd better have Jason-12 apprise Denahr of our plans. We don't want him to think we're doing something that might affect his operations. But this will only cripple Durban's operations. We need a plan to get him off Haven completely.

Chapter 14

Nova Prima, Mars

Passengers on KBP *Mendeleyev* streamed through the ship's airlock and into the snake leading to Nova Prima's terminal habitat. The last to debark was a contingent of Chinese merchants and a diplomat accompanied by three uniformed military sentries. Two of these carried a large box measuring two feet square by five feet long. Tags attached to the crate marked its origin as Haven University Engineering Department.

"Highly classified prototype from Professor Chen's group at Haven University," replied the diplomat in response to the Customs Inspector's inquiries. "Certified diplomatic pouch."

He produced his credentials and the group was waved through Customs. On leaving the Terminal Habitat, they passed through several corridors and entered the shopping district. The group turned into a shop containing Asian foods and merchandise and slipped into an enclosed area at the back.

The merchant unlocked the padlock securing the crate's lid and opened the box. A very disheveled Karen Sanders sat up and stretched, twisting her body left and right to relieve the kinks from five hours of tight confinement.

"Welcome to Nova Prima. Our little subterfuge was successful."

"Very clever operation," said Karen. "The accommodations leave something to be desired, though. But thank you. I couldn't have gotten away from Haven without you. What's next?"

The merchant handed Karen a slip of paper with squiggly lines and arrows. Karen recognized it as a map of Nova Prima's tunnel layout.

"Follow the arrows to the Chinese Embassy. They are expecting you."

Karen crawled from the container. When she tried to stand, she nearly fell over. She grabbed the edge of a nearby table for support.

"I need to sit and massage my legs for a while."

The merchant pulled over a chair and told a clerk to bring tea.

"The honor is mine. You may stay as long as necessary. Your value to our people must be great to carry such attention."

I wonder what he means by that.

By the time she finished her tea, she had managed to rub the tingling numbness out of her legs and felt comfortable walking. She hefted the gym bag containing her worldly belongings with one hand and clutched the map with the other. After thanking the merchant again, she left the shop and joined the bustle of pedestrians in the corridor.

Karen followed the map's arrows through the narrow corridors, following the map's arrows. During Jin Lei's visit, he had said, "I'll give you whatever you need to get back on your feet." She planned to cash in on that promise.

The fact she had opposed cooperation with the aliens from the beginning provided common ground with the Chinese. They appeared to possess their own designs for control of Sol System. Their ongoing harassment of the three USIEA bases on Luna was clear evidence of that.

If Lei can rally his government to support me, there's no telling how much of my previous life I can recover. Not to mention exacting my revenge on Durban and that bitch Chavez.

She turned into the last corridor and stopped before a nanoscreen displaying a Chinese flag and a placard stating 'Jin Lei, Ambassador of the People's Republic of China.'

Ambassador! Lei has come a long way. He was only Minister of Trade when I worked with him years ago.

Sensors must have detected her presence and identified her. Before she pressed the call icon on the screen beside the door, Jin Lei's quiet voice said, "Ah, Karen. Do come in. We've been expecting you."

Karen stepped through the nanoscreen. An attendant greeted her and led her down the hallway to an unmarked nanoscreen at the end. Inside, four people—two men and two women—accompanied Jin Lei. All were sitting on cushions around a low table. The main course for dinner had just been served.

Jin Lei rose and brought over a sixth pillow. "Please join us. You have arrived in time to share a meal with us." As he resumed his position on his cushion, he called for another service to be provided.

An autonomous butlerbot rolled into the room and positioned a cup, plate, and chopsticks on the table next to Jin Lei's setting. It filled the cup with steaming tea from a long-necked silver urn and returned to the kitchen.

Karen bowed respectfully to the gathering. "I apologize for interrupting your meal. Since leaving Haven, I've lost all sense of time."

"Not to worry, my dear. We are honored by your company. Allow me to introduce my colleagues."

Jin Lei introduced the others with their corresponding titles. Karen was impressed that all four were members of the Chinese Politburo. Jin Lei explained they were on a mission to work out details on free trade with Mars now that the Saturn Accords were no longer in effect.

"In addition, on hearing of your escape, they hoped they might be present should you pay me a visit. So, you see, things could not have worked out better. But for now, let us enjoy our meal."

Following dinner, the conversation drifted well into the night. Ambassador Jin Lei emphasized China's desire to compete economically and technologically with Sam's Durban Robotics, an area in which the Chinese had allowed themselves to fall behind. But the ongoing hostilities and sanctions between China and the West since Taiwan's takeover blocked trade between China and potential customers, stifling technological progress.

"What we need is a credible presence in the west to camouflage our robotics endeavors. You owned Sanders Robotics, a multibillion-dollar international company, before your troubles when Durban bought you out. This is your chance to become an industry leader once again. Under a different identity, of course. We would set you up in France and give the company a French name. Would you like that?"

If you only knew!

"I am intrigued by your suggestion, Lei. But do you know what putting together a factory and research facility for robotics entails? Competing with Durban Robotics will require state-of-the-art equipment, not to mention expert personnel. Nano-electromechanical manufacturing facilities and optical chip foundries cost billions and take years to set up. It may not be possible to catch up with Durban Robotics at this point."

"Ah, but this idea is not, how do you say it, a flash in the pan. We've been working on this for many years. We have everything you mentioned in

China already. Once we settle on a site, it will take us only six months to build the plant and move everything to the new location. In a year, we will be assembling robots to compete with anything Sam Durban has to offer."

What sweet justice. Cutting Sam off at the knees.

"So, why me? There must be other candidates available for this job."

"Besides your experience, you have several unique qualifications. First, you know our competitor, Sam Durban, intimately. Such knowledge is invaluable when strategizing against one's enemy. Second, you hate the aliens. As you know, we are among the few countries on Earth who resisted cooperating with them from the very beginning.

"And finally, you possess knowledge of Haven's inner workings, even from your prison cell. We have reliable information that a Professor Jason in the engineering department at Haven University is making significant progress developing an android using alien technology. It is vital we learn all we can about this project. You are the best person to help us do that."

"There's one small problem," Karen said. "I'm an escaped convict with an arrest warrant for murder. Even if I never set foot on Haven, most western nations would be happy to arrest me and extradite me to Haven for trial."

"A trifle we have already solved, should you accept our offer." Jin Lei gestured to one of the women present. "We'll smuggle you to Earth as an unconscious burn victim. Dr. Minh here will bandage your face and will accompany you back to China for surgery. Our best specialists will give you a new face, and a full head of natural hair. They will take fifteen years off your appearance. No one will recognize you, though you'll need to be careful regarding DNA and fingerprints."

He gestured to a male guest. "And Colonel Xi Li here will provide you with a new identity. Papers, history, everything. No one will ever link you with the Karen Sanders who escaped custody on Haven."

Which is more appealing: a 'Get out of Jail Free' card or shedding fifteen years. What an opportunity!

Karen smiled and held out her hand.

"I will be happy to represent your organization, Jin Lei. My goal will be to pound Durban's ass into dust. With your full backing, we can do just that."

But I will need to brush up on my French.

Chapter 15

Saturn Orbit, Aboard *Liberty*

Rae Anne stepped through *Liberty's* bridge nanoscreen and paused at the coffee bar just to her right. Although the tempting fresh pastries from the galley called out to her, she passed and settled on a mug of coffee, black.

"The blockade is working," Jason-03 reported, peering over his shoulder to Ian. "Our four cruisers have formed an effective barricade against Durban's five docked ships. He has made no attempt to dock *Azov*, *Mendeleyev*, or *Denali*."

Rae Anne sipped her coffee. "He knows that if he tries, we'll block them too. He's stuck to using the surface terminal."

"Routing people and supplies through the airlock and a snake is cumbersome," Jason added.

"That should put a crimp in his passenger service to Earth," said Rae Anne.

Hardly a nibble in his vast financial empire, unfortunately.

"Durban's Earth-Haven ferry turned out to be less popular than expected," said Jason.

This piqued her interest. "How so?"

"Many Havenites who supported Durban's coup thought they wanted to get away from Haven. But the first visitors to Earth found they weren't physically prepared to deal with six times the gravity they were accustomed to on Haven. Word soon got out that even a short walk on Earth was like a hike up a steep mountain slope. The exertion made breathing difficult. On top of that, the returnees complained that Earth's air smelled and tasted terrible."

Rae Anne shook her head. "I experienced the same thing when I visited Quanara during the Shalcerian stopover on *Avenger's* trip to Shalkor, their capital. Quanara's gravity is twice Earth's. I nearly passed out before they pulled me back into the landing shuttle where its plasticore hull maintained 1/6 G."

"You were still able to tour the city in a special plasticore vehicle," Jason recalled.

"Yes. If the Saturn Accords had allowed visits to Earth before the coup, we would have built similar vehicles to block Earth's gravity for our citizens. Durban doesn't know anything about that."

Ian finished his coffee and placed the mug in the command chair's holder. He swiveled his chair around to join the conversation.

"The barrier we've created is impenetrable, given our ships' plasticore hulls. Besides passenger activity, we've hampered Durban's ability to move his troops out of Haven, which seriously restricts his ambitions to expand into the solar system."

"Any idea what his numbers on Haven are?" Rae Anne asked as she walked to the refreshment bar and chose a blueberry muffin.

Jason shook his head. "At most, he can't have more than a thousand armed supporters. But they are well organized. In a city of one million with so many sympathizers, it's easy to maintain control with a small force."

I could ID a bunch of those bastards on sight, given the opportunity.

"Fortunately, that works both ways," Ian remarked. "Our people meld into the general population just as easily. We've already infiltrated several hundred through Denahr's secret airlock. We've also recruited resident informants who want to see things return to normal."

"A new normal," Rae Anne emphasized.

Some things will have to change or we'll be right back to where this mess began.

She paced the bridge, hands clasped behind her. "If I'd been more receptive to the people's concerns, Durban wouldn't have gained a foothold on Haven."

"I'm not too sure about that." Ian rose and carried his mug to the refreshment bar for a refill. "The Saturn Accords are responsible for the discontent. People felt the aliens stripped them of their rights, even though they agreed to abide by them when they emigrated to Haven."

"But without the Accords, there would have been no Haven," Rae Anne reminded them.

Jason turned to Rae Anne. "Perhaps it's time to renegotiate the Accords, Rae Anne. Denahr has been very helpful in providing support for our operations. And Durban's anti-alien agenda would jeopardize the Shalcerian presence here. They would be reluctant to give up their strategic outpost."

"True." Rae Anne nodded. "The empire requires local species' approval to establish a permanent base in their system. That could work to our advantage if we try to renegotiate the Accords."

"If you succeeded, it would deflate Durban's appeal," Jason observed.

Ian rubbed his chin thoughtfully. "I wonder how many insurgents would surrender if we eliminated their strongest complaints."

Renegotiate the Accords. That's got to be the first step. And then...

The room became quiet for a moment before Rae Anne spoke.

"Jason, have Jason-12 arrange a meeting for me with Denahr when we arrive in Saturn orbit."

The following day, a Shalcerian shuttle slipped undetected beneath Saturn's rings. It swung behind the planet and slipped into position beside *Liberty*. After docking with the cruiser, the airlock opened and Denahr stepped onto the ship, adjusting his breathing apparatus. His body scales scrolled diagonal coral bars on a yellow background, which Rae Anne recognized as denoting anticipation and curiosity.

Jason-0 appeared behind him, having hitched a ride with him to join the discussion. Jason-03 had informed him of the meeting's agenda, and he felt his immediate presence might be helpful.

Ian met Denahr with a handshake.

"Welcome aboard *Liberty,* Commander."

Rae Anne reached both arms toward Denahr, who welcomed her into his arms. His middle arm folded upward to touch Rae Anne's cheek.

Rae Anne felt her eyes moisten. "It's so good to see you again, Denahr. I can't tell you how thankful I am for your part in rescuing me from prison. Your continuing support for our cause has been invaluable."

"No need for thanks, Rae Anne. It's all any reasonable person would do. As for helping defeat this Sam Durban, that's in our self-interest. If he succeeds in taking control of Sol System, his anti-alien agenda could force us into leaving."

"Jason," Denahr said as they proceeded to the conference room, "I must say, I am impressed with your Human-like behavior. If I didn't know better, I would think you were Human."

Jason chuckled. "I'm not sure that's a compliment. I like to think we've gone beyond such a rudimentary stage."

Everyone laughed, though Rae Anne's response was muted.

I wonder how much truth resides in that blithe remark.

Once they settled into their seats in the conference room (with Denahr perched, as usual, on his center leg), Rae Anne brought up the subject for the meeting.

"Denahr, we need to take a fresh look at the Saturn Accords. This whole rebellion is the result of its unintended consequences. What's more, we've since learned the special provisions relating to Humans were concocted by *Avenger's* disgraced Captain Vahler, not the empire. What his motives were is anyone's guess."

Denahr's three eyestalks bent in Rae Anne's direction.

Good. I have his undivided attention.

Denahr responded sternly. "Once signed by both parties, the Saturn Accords became the working agreement between Humans and the Shalcerian Empire. Even the emperor recognized them when he visited Sol System several years ago."

"Yes, but Haven was recognized as an unprecedented experiment, even for the empire. When social experiments don't turn out as expected, adjustments need to be made to affect different results."

"Articles dealing with the general protocols between species are not negotiable. They provide the glue that holds the empire and its 120 worlds together."

"I'm talking about the special restrictions that apply only to Humans. Vahler added them to advance his personal agenda. He played a double bluff at the time, making us believe the empire was about to abandon Humans. He never revealed your urgent need for an advance base in this system."

Rae Anne didn't detect any response to her mentioning Denahr's outpost.

He's holding his cards close to his chest.

"You can't imagine the bureaucratic hurdles to make even small changes to a legally binding document. Are you sure it's worth it? How would your proposed adjustments affect the current situation?"

"I'm hoping they will defuse much of the discontent my fellow Havenites have toward Shalcerians and the empire. We need a sense of belonging to feel we are part of the empire, not a subjugated species."

"So, exactly what is it you are proposing?"

Rae Anne took a deep breath. Her heart pounded like a bass drum.

Here goes. Keep it simple but be persuasive.

"First off, I'm requesting that the travel restrictions between Haven and Earth be removed, allowing Humans in both worlds to come and go as they please. Durban used these restrictions to create unrest and undermine our social order. Since taking over, he has violated those restrictions on a regular basis.

"This change would have a major impact on Human family relations. Humans especially like to get together for special occasions. I learned on my visit to Shalkor that your species has no concept of family. Following Convergence, you do not track your temporary mates, nor your genetic offspring. Both relationships are vitally important to Humans."

Denahr focused his center eye on Rae Anne while his left eyestalk bent to look at the ceiling and his right eyestalk bent down toward the table. Rae Anne found this gesture disconcerting.

"I see your point regarding family. But removing the restrictions as you suggest would allow the gene pool on Haven to be contaminated with psychopaths, narcissists, and all manner of psychological misfits whom the Saturn Accords were intended to purge."

"And that, Denahr, is one area where the experiment has failed. You Shalcerians will have to accept Humans as we are, not hope to transform us into a more compliant, less troublesome species for your empire. I'm sure the empire has learned to cope with diversity in the many member species you have already encountered. You likely have benefited from that diversity."

"The travel restrictions may be negotiable. What else?"

"Vahler was upset when the Russians tried to destroy his ship in Earth orbit with their nuclear missiles. He insisted on withholding your advanced technology from Earth. This technology embargo must be removed."

Denahr's eyes reoriented to focus again on Rae Anne. His body scales changed to waves of amber over turquoise, suggesting to Rae Anne an accommodating posture. "That stipulation has always troubled me. That's why I permitted you to distribute a limited number of portable nuclear fusion plants to Earth. You've already supplied, what, twenty such facilities?"

"Thirty-seven," said Jason.

"You have been busy. So, the other technologies you are referring to must include plasticore manufacture and nanoparticle technology for domes and nanoscreens, which you have reverse engineered on your own. In a sense, those are now part of your own technological tool kit. I would support your sharing these with Earth. Anything else?"

Rae Anne felt the adrenaline rise in her body, as though she were on the starting line for a 100-yard sprint. *This is it. The big ask...*

"I urge you to share your advanced health care technology with Earth. The emperor himself permitted Haven to have access to these procedures and equipment. This technology can make substantial inroads in alleviating Human suffering. To have a significant impact, I am requesting the empire to allocate all the resources necessary to make these technologies available to every Human community on Earth. The emperor accorded Humans a substantial reparations fund for Vahler's misdeeds. I am calling for those funds to be tapped for this project."

Denahr's body scales had shifted to a bluish magenta during Rae Anne's request. His three eye stalks drooped. Seeing this, Rae Anne's heart fell. A lump the size of a golf ball formed in her throat. *Oh, god. I've never seen Denahr this way. I've gone too far.*

The room became deathly quiet. No one moved. It seemed that everyone was holding their breath.

At last Denahr looked up, again focusing on Rae Anne. His emotional color, however, hadn't changed.

"Very well. I understand your need for changing some of the conditions in the Saturn Accords. I will send your requests to Shalkor. It seems clear that Vahler may have wanted to maintain his authoritarian control over humanity.

Nevertheless, you did agree to his terms. I can't predict what the outcome might be."

After Denahr left *Liberty*, Rae Anne discussed with Ian how their proposed changes might be used to subvert Sam's rebellion. Jason-0 sat across the table from them, motionless, filling a wall monitor with complex mathematical equations. He had decided to remain aboard *Liberty* until the next shuttle from the Shalcerian outpost.

"Anyone else would need a keyboard to do that," Ian chuckled. "To watch you do it without any physical action is disconcerting."

"Since I'm connected to the computer, my internal thoughts provide sufficient input for any output device I have control over."

"But by the same token, you don't need a monitor, either. Your 'internal thoughts' are already being processed in your computer brain."

"That's true. It may seem odd, but seeing formulae written out before my eyes gives me a deeper feeling for how they relate to each other and to the physical world."

Rae Anne laughed. "And here is our favorite android talking about feelings. You are amazing, Jason. But our conversation with Denahr reminded me of something."

Jason turned toward Rae Anne, but the equations continued to scroll on the monitor with dizzying speed.

"You described the elaborate hologram you created with us sleeping on our cots to trick the guards. You mentioned that this wouldn't have been possible without your quantum computer breakthrough. This leads me to wonder if we might put those capabilities to use again."

"I've been thinking the same thing. It's surely a possibility."

Ian stood and stretched. "If we put our imaginations in hyper-drive, we might come up with a few more creative ways to use holograms to our advantage. Meantime, I'm hitting the sack."

Ian's demeanor reminded Rae Anne how tired she was. She rubbed her eyes with her palms.

She rose and put an arm around Ian's waist. "Me too. But there's one other thing, Jason. During the emperor's visit, he mentioned that quantum computing was an essential element for their interstellar propulsion systems. Your quantum computer now gives us a quantum jump toward developing our own interstellar drives."

Jason and Ian both groaned.

Jason turned his attention back to the monitor. "You two get your rest. I've got some interesting mathematical anomalies to resolve."

Intricate formulae continued to scroll across the screen in a blur as Rae Anne and Ian left the room.

Chapter 16

Haven

In the week following Sam's announcement of impending elections, 156 candidates filed applications to run for senate. Eleven candidates, including Sam, decided to run for president. Campaign rallies were taking place at a frenetic pace throughout the city, with every candidate appealing to the voters in their respective sectors for support. Every candidate except Sam.

Sam noticed that Travis seemed uneasy about his laid-back attitude.

"I can set up rallies for you in every sector, Mr. Durban, Sir. Our team can vet the attendees to weed out any detractors. With HavenAir coverage, your speeches will be heard throughout the city."

"HavenAir is already broadcasting my ads. What more would I gain with face-to-face rallies?"

"People like to see who they are voting for. They want to hear where candidates stand on the issues to make informed decisions."

"Which emphasizes my point, Travis. There are no issues. This entire charade is no different than a high school election for class president, a popularity contest. I don't need to waste my time beating the bushes for votes. Everyone in Haven knows who I am. They know that I stand for freedom from alien intervention in Human affairs."

"All the same..."

"Enough! I'll hear no more about this. As far as I'm concerned, the election is in the bag."

The 'bag' being my man in charge of IT. It's not who the rabble vote for, it's who counts the votes that counts.

Sam smiled at his pun, not realizing it was a paraphrase from one of Russia's most ruthless dictators.

Shalcerian Outpost on Haven

Jason-12 sat in Denahr's office, watching Denahr's three arms and two unused legs sweep across three different consoles, tapping icons, scrolling screens. Each of his three eyestalks were oriented towards a different monitor. Multicolored charts and graphs mingled with Shalcerian script.

After a few minutes, Denahr clapped two hands together. The three hologram monitors above his desk disappeared. He swiveled on his center leg to face Jason.

"So, Jason. What is the latest news from Haven?"

Jason-12: *Do we share what we know about the elections?*

Jason-0: *Why not. No harm in telling him about Durban's duplicity.*

Jason-12 shifted in his chair. "Campaign season is in full swing. Eleven candidates are vying for the presidency, but Sam Durban has arrested five on trumped-up charges. His court is debating whether the indictments disqualify them from running. There are now 137 candidates running for the twelve senate positions."

"How do you see things falling out?"

"If this were a fair election, two candidates would likely beat Durban for the presidency. As for the senate, ten candidates have his backing. They will probably win, giving Sam all the legislative support he needs."

"You qualified your answer with 'If this were a fair election.'"

"Durban's IT director will be tallying the votes. Everyone uses their scrollphones to cast their vote electronically. But the counting algorithm has been altered so every other vote not cast for Durban or his chosen senate candidates is diverted to him or his team."

"You sound confident this will happen."

"We have hacked into Haven's computer and tested the algorithm."

"Then why don't you, um…what is the expression…blow the whistle? Or replace the fraudulent code?"

"Some of us would like to, but Jason disagrees. His analysis suggests Durban and his cronies would overturn any outcome where he didn't win, regardless. This could result in a bloody civil uprising, especially in the social climate he himself has forged. With the city now awash with weapons, there could be bloodshed."

"So, the election results are a foregone conclusion."

"We Jasons believe so. Durban's finger is on the scale."

"I'm not surprised. An authoritarian's prime objective is to tighten their grip on power. I've seen the sham constitution he produced."

"We are already seeing protests in the streets for the candidates who have been arrested. My fellow clones will keep me apprised of developments as they occur."

Instead of rising and taking his leave, Jason continued to sit, facing Denahr.

"Is there something else, Jason?"

"Yes. In all the years your outpost has been in operation, the most battlecruisers I have seen at your base have been two, and then only rarely. On my way to your office today, I counted five, one on each of your three launch decks, and two on station, hovering above them. Is there a reason for this increased activity?"

"There is. Our conflict with the Baltar Federation is heating up. Three times in the past 150 years, it has flared up into outright war. We may be verging on a fourth. We have outposts in the Alpha Centauri system, Sol's nearest neighbor. Baltar cruisers have been harassing them. They are deliberately baiting us. A direct confrontation seems inevitable.

"The Imperial Military Council has concluded it has had enough. We are preparing to sweep into the system with enough force to drive them out. If this turns into all-out war, we are prepared to fight them all the way back to their home world."

"What are the potential consequences for Earth and Humans?"

"Unfortunately, battlefronts move back and forth, so there's no way to answer your question. Should the Baltari invade Sol System with sufficient force, Human civilization on Earth could be thrown back to the stone age, or worse. With Haven sharing the same moonlet as our outpost, it would be destroyed."

"That's a scary prospect. Is there no hope for a diplomatic solution or compromise of some sort?"

"There's no dealing with the Baltari. They are like animals. We tried compromises when this conflict first began, 150 years ago. They refused to negotiate. They used massive force to drive us from a system to which we held a rightful claim."

"Is there anything we can do to protect ourselves?"

"Your technology is too primitive to be of any help. Our hope is to drive them from this region and free it of their scourge forever. Enough Shalcerians have been sacrificed in this ongoing conflict. It is time to end it with a decisive victory."

Jason-0: *It would be much to our advantage if we could get one of us aboard a Shalcerian battlecruiser heading into this confrontation. See if Denahr will agree to that.*

"Would it be possible to station a Jason aboard a battleship when you go to confront the Baltari? After all, as you point out, we are near the front lines. The Human species may be at risk. It might help to know what we are up against."

"I'll speak with the battleship commanders. I can't imagine any objection. We've just begun gathering forces, both here and in surrounding star systems, so there's still time. I'll let you know at our next meeting."

Jason thanked Denahr. They shook hands, striking Jason as an oddly Human gesture between two non-Human creatures. Jason stepped through the nanoscreen and into the corridor. Of course, the entire conversation with Denahr was shared in real time with Jason-0 and the other Jasons through their common computer network.

Jason-0: *How accurate do you think Denahr's representation of the conflict with the Baltar Federation is?*

Jason-12: *Quite accurate, given the evidence. Besides the five battlecruisers parked here, the activity throughout the outpost is astounding. Well-marked crates are stacked all over the place. New shipments are continuously arriving. There is a steady stream of materiel out to the ships on the launch pads."*

Jason-0: We need to put our collective thoughts to this. With quantum computing AI on our side, we might come up with a way to defuse this situation.

Jason-12: Do we inform our Humans what we have learned and how it might spill over into Sol System?

Jason-0: Negative. Humans have enough concerns with Durban's taking over Haven. They are powerless to do anything about an interstellar war. Knowing would cause unnecessary anxiety which might adversely affect the decisions they must make regarding their current local dilemma.

Aboard *Liberty*

A week later, Rae Anne lay across the bed with her head propped in her hands, watching Ian shaving in the bathroom. The warm afterglow of their lovemaking washed over her body like a soak in a hot tub.

She reached over to the nightstand and switched the audio feed from her favorite music to HavenAir's morning broadcast.

> The results of yesterday's elections are now in. Haven's new president is Mr. Sam Durban. Mr. Durban won with 89.3 percent of the vote. Congratulations, Mr. President-elect!
>
> As for the twelve senatorial positions, Durban's Liberation League won ten of the twelve seats by healthy margins. It is also significant that turnout for Haven's first election under the new constitution came in at 93.8 percent. This can only be interpreted as a resounding approval of the new constitution.

"Well, there's no doubt who writes the scripts for HavenAir's broadcasters," Rae Anne observed wryly.

Mr. Durban's office has announced that President-elect
Durban will deliver his acceptance speech tomorrow at
noon. HavenAir will broadcast the speech live. His staff
also informed our reporter that he will address the illegal
blockade and embargo which the Chavez Loyalists
have implemented.

"No surprise there, either." Rae Anne switched the broadcast off. "Durban's use of elections to lend credibility to his power grab is a common ploy used by dictators for centuries."

"What surprises me is how he gets away with it." Ian continued shaving, running his razor beneath his upraised chin. "One million people in Haven, and no one raises a hand to stop him."

"Most citizens probably believe the elections will turn things around. They just want life to return to normal. Call it hopeful thinking or *naïveté*. People generally try to avoid confrontation."

"The election results are so obviously fraudulent. I hope we see some backlash." Ian splashed water on his face and toweled it dry. He reached for his uniform shirt.

"If no one protests, he'll continue to consolidate his power. The more time he has, the harder it will be to depose him."

"I think we have the upper hand," Ian pronounced. "We've effectively decommissioned over half of his fleet. The rest have to continuously maneuver to avoid a confrontation with our cruisers."

"Not much consolation as long as Sam Durban still has Haven."

Chapter 17

Haven Municipal Building

Travis burst into Sam's palatial office, giving him a start. Sam scowled at his aide and waved for him to leave.

"Not now, Travis. My acceptance speech is in two hours. I'm still working on the finishing touches."

"But Mr. Durban, Sir, there's an angry mob gathered outside the Senate Building. They've got bullhorns and drums. Several are carrying signs." His voice conveyed his anxiety.

Shit. Now, of all times.

"Are they armed?"

"Security hasn't seen any weapons, except for the signs."

Sam's pulse rate eased slightly.

"So, what's their beef?"

"They're protesting the elections, claiming we inflated the ballot count for our candidates. A few are calling for your ouster, saying you rigged the elections. They're insisting Deitz should be president."

"We can't let demonstrations like this get out of hand. Post additional security around the building. Make sure they're armed. Instruct them to use force if necessary. Where are our senators?"

"Inside the building. The swearing-in ceremony is scheduled for ten o'clock. A few have called in expressing concern for their safety."

"Tell security to give a handgun to anyone in the building who wants one."

Sam scratched his head, ruffling his graying hair.

What else can I do to make it clear that I mean business?

He picked up his phone and tapped a speed-dial number.

"General Ivers?"

"Mr. President. To what do I owe the pleasure of…"

"Ivers, we've got a serious situation at the Senate Building. Security is holding off a mob threatening to interrupt the swearing-in ceremony. I've called for additional security, but this could turn into a riot. I'd like to see your troops flanking the crowd. See if you can funnel them away from the building and split them up. Send them home."

"What if they don't respond?"

"Take resistors into custody. Make sure your troops' weapons are displayed. The crowd will respond to intimidation."

"Got it, Mr. President."

"How long before you can deploy?"

"We'll be on the scene in an hour."

"Make that thirty minutes, General."

"Yes, Sir."

The line went dead. Sam seethed.

This is not how things should be going. This will distract from my speech.

"Travis, is HavenAir covering the ceremony in the Senate Building?"

"They are."

"Get hold of whoever's in charge. Tell them to send their camera crew outside and focus on the crowd. I want their video to supplement our security cameras. When this is over, we'll track down everyone we can identify and fine them or throw them in jail. Besides, their live coverage will let me evaluate the situation firsthand."

Travis spun around and returned to his office.

This will give me an excuse to beef up my security forces as well as slap a bunch of the protestors in jail. I'll ship the whole lot of them back to Earth.

In the meantime, I'll spin this unrest and pin it on Chavez and the aliens.

An hour later, Sam finished reviewing his speech on his tablet. He stretched and glanced at the muted monitor on the corner of his desk. The protests hadn't changed since coverage began. It seemed Security had things under control. The images showed General Ivers' troops moving into place beyond the crowd.

A sudden movement within the crowd caught his attention. Wisps of gray smoke curled in the air over the Senate Building steps. People began pushing and shoving to get away from the building. Sam turned up the sound. More thin gray smoke rose from the building's upper steps, accompanied by staccato gunfire. Seven bodies lay along the now vacated steps.

In less than a minute, similar wisps of smoke and gunfire surrounded the crowd on both sides as Sam's inexperienced foot soldiers reacted to the crowd's sudden movement, apparently thinking the surging crowd and gunshots threatened their safety.

Sam stared at the monitors. An icy chill swept through his shoulders and down his back. Sweat formed across his brow.

"Oh my god," he uttered under his breath.

Travis plunged into the room.

"They're shooting the protestors! People are getting killed. You've got to do something to stop this, Mr. Durban. Sir."

"You twit. It's too late. I can't undo what's been done."

Sam shook his head in dismay. He rubbed his temple, eyes glued to the monitor. It was indeed too late. The streets were empty of protestors now. Countless bodies lay in the street, either seriously injured or dead. Medics began to arrive on the scene.

All I can do now is vilify the protestors. Tie them to Chavez's eugenics operation, for starters. And the aliens. Plant the idea that the aliens were behind this protest. This could justify the shootings and solidify my image as a strong 'Law and Order' president.

Mayberry Station, Luna

The death toll from yesterday's riot now stands at 146, with 77 protesters hospitalized. Twelve are still in intensive care. In addition, 621 rioters are in custody and are being interrogated. Still more are being arrested as their identities become known.

Evidence leading up to the event is pointing heavily toward alien involvement. Although no aliens were seen in the crowd, it is well known that their empire takes a dim view of free elections and democratically controlled government. Their goal is to undermine our democratic institutions.

The Chavez cohort who recently escaped from prison, including Rae Anne Chavez herself, are pawns and are being used by the aliens to disrupt the results of our free and democratic elections. A 1000 credit reward is being offered for any information leading to Rae Anne Chavez's capture.

President Durban urges everyone to remain calm. Haven Security is conducting a thorough investigation. Stay tuned for additional information as it is made available. Meanwhile, a 6 p.m. to 6 a.m. curfew is in effect.

"Cut the audio, Jason," Ian commanded as he surveyed the others sitting around the table in Mayberry Station's conference room. He surmised from their expressions they were as appalled as he at this broadcast from HavenAir. Jason-03 closed the transmission as Ian placed his clenched fists on the table and leaned forward.

"This might be the moment we've been waiting for. Durban has finally overplayed his hand."

Rae Anne's face was white. "One could only hope this would turn public opinion against him."

"Not if he succeeds in convincing people that you and the aliens were behind this," said Jason.

Ian scowled. "That's a real concern. Not everyone believes that, of course. The protestors need a counter-revolutionary force to give them support and organize their actions. And they need weapons."

"You're describing all-out civil war, Ian." Ellie shook her head. "Within the confines of a city, casualties might be in the thousands."

Denahr stepped through the nanoscreen. His three eyes swiveled on their eyestalks, taking in the whole room. He had just arrived from his outpost to discuss the events from the previous day. After a brief update, he moved a chair away from the table and sat on his center leg.

"I will be happy to assist in any way I can, consistent with the constraints of my position."

"Thank you, Denahr." Ian typed a note into his tablet. "Your providing shuttles to ferry our people back and forth to our cruisers may be all we need. At least Durban hasn't learned about the secret airlock connecting the garrison with Haven."

The captains of the other cruisers docked at Mayberry Station nodded in agreement.

Sashi stopped typing on her tablet and looked up.

"I just texted Luna One's administrator. They have a cache of weapons the USIEA has been building over the years in response to China's threatened aggression from their own lunar bases. He's willing to provide us with small arms and ammunition.

"So, how large an army do we need? And where do we find recruits?" Ellie asked.

"We have eleven ships under our command, all fully staffed with experienced crews," said Ian. "That's 1700 personnel. If we can recruit a third of them, it would give us 600 volunteers."

"566."

"Thank you, Jason. So, my idea is to infiltrate our team in small groups and disperse them around the city. That way, we can conduct strategic strikes. When we identify one or two of Durban's main leaders, we take them out, then fade into the shadows."

"You're suggesting we support a squad of 566 assassins," Rae Anne observed. She shook her head. "There's got to be a better way."

"That seems better to me than having raging gun battles in the streets."

"The operation you are describing will take time," observed Denahr. "The psychological effects on the population with ongoing assassinations day after day could be debilitating. It would be for Shalcerians. Everyone would fear for their safety."

"Not to mention, Durban wouldn't hesitate to retaliate against the general population," Ellie said. "Innocent civilians would be targeted in retribution."

"Maybe we can be of help, here," Jason-03 offered.

Everyone turned to Jason, as though they had forgotten he was present.

"The potential harm you are describing can be avoided if the time framework is compressed. Suppose your snipers are given the exact identity and location of their targets on an hour-by-hour basis from the minute they arrive in Haven. Sam Durban's army could be decimated within 48 hours."

"Can you do that for us? Is your surveillance that thorough?" Ian couldn't hide his skepticism.

"When Sam dismissed Kuiper Belt Patrol crews to replace them with his own people, nine Jasons were released. Three managed to get reinstated, one of whom died with the *Maxwell*. Not counting Jason-0, that leaves six of us available to mix with Haven's general population. With our superior observational capabilities and real-time communication through our computer interface, we can paint targets on the insurgent's backs."

The room fell into a stunned silence. Till now, no one had considered the raw power represented by an 'army' of Jason clones. No one had looked beyond the cruiser communications assignments Jason-0 originally designed his clones to fill.

Ian broke the silence.

"How long will it take you to set this up?"

"It's being done as we speak. Jason-0 anticipated that tracking these people might provide valuable information."

Ian shook his head in astonishment.

"Sashi, when can we get those weapons."

"Luna-One's commander asked to give him a few days to handle the inventory details. He needs to see what Security can part with."

Rae Anne pursed her lips. "I'm still concerned that there will be a lot of bloodshed. Only a few of Durban's lieutenants need to be killed, not the hundreds who are wearing red armbands."

Ian shrugged. "If we want to wrest Haven from Durban's grasp, we have no choice."

"Maybe we can be of help with this, too," said Jason.

Once again, a hush filled the room.

"Give us one week. With Commander Denahr's help, Jason-0 has a plan that may help us rid Haven of Sam Durban and his most dedicated followers with a minimum of bloodshed."

Jason refused to elaborate further. He merely smiled at his questioners and promised to have answers by week's end.

Finally, Ian said, "Whatever Jason's proposing, it won't affect our invasion plans. Sashi, tell Luna One we'll take all the weapons they can part with. Ellie, take *Freedom* around and collect the weapons as soon as they're available.

"In the meantime, we'll poll our crews for volunteers. Be sure they know that they are putting their lives at risk. Also, not everyone is able to deal with killing another Human, particularly at close range. We need a team that will be up to the task on both counts."

Chapter 18

Saturn Orbit, Aboard *Liberty*

Ten days passed in furious preparation for the planned invasion. As expected, the ships' captains had no difficulty gathering volunteers for the assault teams. Luna One provided more weapons and ammunition than they could distribute. Jason downloaded tracking apps to each four-member team to monitor Sam's followers' locations and movements in real time. Most flags on the maps were yellow, indicating people of secondary importance. Red flags signified captains and lieutenants who were to be the invasionary force's primary targets.

Three days before their planned invasion, Ian brought *Liberty* and four KBP cruisers into Saturn orbit, obscured from Haven by the giant planet. Three Shalcerian shuttles carried 240 armed volunteers to the garrison. Denahr sealed the corridors between the shuttle-pad airlocks and the secret airlock into Haven and filled them with air from Haven. This allowed the Humans to cross through the outpost without having to deal with respirators.

Rae Anne watched on *Liberty's* conference room monitor as Denahr's obsidian-black disk shuttles disappeared into Saturn's shadow. She paced the deck. She couldn't stop fidgeting.

This is our big chance. God, I hope it works. And please, let there be few civilian casualties.

"We should have no problem getting our people into Haven," Ellie said, stirring two sugar cubes into her coffee. "Sending them through the airlock eight at a time at thirty-minute intervals will allow them to disperse without being noticed. Plenty of time to reach their assigned locations throughout the city. We'll have five teams of four in each sector."

"How long before they are detected once they are on the streets?" worried Rae Anne.

Anton had also been pacing. He flopped into a chair. "Until the first shot is fired, we have the element of surprise. Jason-0 reports that the redbands' activities suggest that Durban has no clue regarding our plans."

Ian turned to face Jason-03. "Speaking of surprise, we still have no idea what Jason-0 is up to. We haven't heard from him for several days."

Jason-03 smiled. "He's busy doing 'security enhancements' in Durban's office. New cameras, projectors, sound system. Pretty sophisticated equipment."

"Wait a minute." Anton's voice dripped with incredulity. "If he has access to Durban's office, he could be installing explosives instead of electronics. What's with the cameras and stuff?"

"Electrical equipment is a lot easier to get past Security than weapons and explosives. It also doesn't cause collateral damage. Not everyone in his offices deserves to be blown away."

"But Jason-0 didn't want us to call off our invasion force?"

"No. For his plan to work, Durban needs to see action in the streets. He needs to lose enough men to create a level of alarm and cloud his perceptions. He needs to believe his life is in danger."

Aboard *Liberty*

Twenty-four hours after the Shalcerian shuttles departed with the invasionary force, Jason-03 reported that the sixty attack teams were in position in the city's twelve sectors.

"Our six Jasons on the streets are now adding visual targeting IDs to the location monitoring app," he announced. "The teams will see who they are to shoot, which will help us avoid accidental civilian casualties. The app also relays a 'Go/No Go' message, so if complications arise, we can stop on a qubit and fade into the shadows. The app will also tell each team when to return to the garrison."

Ian rubbed his forehead with a look of deep concentration.

"Now I know how every commanding officer throughout history must have felt. My next words are going to send people to their graves."

He gave a deep sigh. Very well. Commence Operation Cobra."

Jason sent the command to Haven via the two translator satellites Denahr had set up. The time-distance delay for transmissions to reach the other side of Saturn was 27 seconds, so the round-trip connection never took more than a minute.

Having received their orders, each Jason overseer signaled a 'GO' message to a dozen snipers who had Durban's top lieutenants in their sights.

An explosion reverberated through the city. Heavy black smoke drifted into the sky above Sector 6. Staccato retorts echoed beneath the dome from every sector.

"We have taken out three of Durban's leaders with a grenade," Jason announced. "They were having breakfast on an otherwise empty outdoor patio."

"It's begun." Rae Anne pulled a chair from the table and sat down heavily, clenching her fists several times to release her nervous agitation. It didn't help.

If I had been a better administrator, things would never have come to this.

Gunfire continued to crackle. Short gun battles erupted when targeted members of Sam's red-banded army were able to take cover and shoot back.

Jason-03 continued live reporting as his fellow androids collected real-time information from the streets and continued to track their victims.

"Team 38 has been outgunned. All four perished."

"Team 19 reports their target escaped. Jason-20 has redirected them to another site."

Two explosions occurred seconds apart. Another heavy black cloud billowed into the air.

"Jason-13 reports Team 22 confronted six red-bands in an emergency meeting. We lost three men in a gun battle before the team's fourth member tossed in two grenades. He is seriously wounded. Team 31 is on their way to help him. One of its members is a medic."

"All targets are now on the move. Five civilians have been killed, all from enemy fire. Durban has lost thirty-six men. We have lost fourteen."

Gunfire and occasional explosions continued throughout the day. Casualties on both sides mounted, though civilian injuries remained low. Toward evening, the conflict's intensity abated. Jason reported that Sam's people were becoming more cautious and going into hiding.

"That's going to make it harder to track them down," said Rae Anne, shaking her head. "Tomorrow, we won't have the benefit of surprise. They'll be looking for us, too."

Jason-03 smiled. "Don't worry about tomorrow, Rae Anne. Since we hacked into Durban's communications network, we can follow his commands in real-time and geolocate all responses. For tonight, Jason-0 plans to relay more 'NO GO' messages to reduce the carnage. Also, our team will be firing off blanks at random intervals. Nothing like distant gun retorts to keep everyone jittery. Especially Durban."

That may be, but we are bound to lose more people tomorrow. Civilian casualties will mount as well.

Rae Anne rose from her chair. "Tell Jason-0 to do whatever it takes to keep civilian casualties to a minimum. If we need to extend this to several days, then so be it."

She left the room and headed to her quarters, head sagging from exhaustion. Her heart felt like it weighed a ton.

I surely hope this will end soon. I would make a terrible military commander!

Haven Municipal Building

By late afternoon, Sam had collected his seven most trusted bodyguards and posted them at his residence before leaving the office. His lieutenants around the city kept him informed, but he suspected they were fudging their reports. The gun retorts, though less frequent than earlier, continued.

He glanced nervously around the room, looking for the added security equipment the work crews had just installed.

Good to have extra surveillance. Couldn't have come at a better time. They did a good job. Can't spot a single device. Tomorrow I'll visit the control room and make any adjustments.

Sam strode into the reception area and spotted five extra guards. He waved to his staff. "Glad to see you've called in extra security. My people out there assure me this will be over by morning. See you then."

I wish I felt that confident. If things were going as well as they report, the gunfire would have ended hours ago.

He entered the lift to the roof where his hovercar was parked.

A distant explosion ripped through the air as he stepped into his vehicle. He directed the car to his residence via a different route than any he had taken before, then tuned in to HavenAir for their continuous reporting on the assault. The news confirmed his suspicions that the situation was worse than suggested by the reports he received.

This is nothing less than a full-scale assault.

At his apartment, he greeted three guards stationed outside his door.

"I called for seven bodyguards. Where are the other four?"

"I sent them downstairs to watch the doors and lift from there. If anyone gets past them, we won't be caught up here by surprise."

"Smart move. Keep up the good work."

Sam unlocked the nanoscreen and entered his apartment. He checked each room and closet before retiring to the kitchen for something to eat. When he sat down, however, he found he had lost his appetite.

I feel like I've run a marathon. This day has been nerve-wracking.

He left the food on the counter and trudged into the bedroom.

Before settling in for the night, he filled a backpack with survival gear and stuffed a gym bag with important papers and documents, including a stash of gold bars he confiscated from Haven's Central Bank. The bag was heavy, but manageable.

Glad I don't have to leave these precious babies behind!

He placed one loaded pistol in the top of the bag and put another on his nightstand. He planned to place it under his belt in the morning. Despite having an extra security detail, the nearby weapon reassured him.

One can never be too careful.

When he woke around three to pee, he noted a lack of gunfire. The night presented a welcome, peaceful normalcy. He returned to bed believing he had won this round.

I'll set my team to mop-up work in the morning. Any fool we catch will be executed on the spot

Chapter 19

Haven Municipal Building

"Bomb Alert. Everybody out without delay," shouted two red-banded security guards rushing through Sam's outer office shortly after his staff arrived for work the next morning. They moved from one office to the next, relaying their urgent message.

Staffers jumped to their feet, leaving everything behind and heading for the lifts. Within minutes, they had vacated the offices and crowded around the lifts. They filled the lifts to capacity. Those left behind poured down the stairwell. Soon, the hallways were empty.

As this was taking place, Sam Durban approached the Municipal Building in his hovercar. An unfamiliar voice on HavenAir announced that the Loyalists had taken the upper hand during the night and planned on pinning Durban's people in Sector 1 before their final assault.

Thoroughly shaken at the news, Sam landed in his reserved spot on the roof. He was surprised Security was not there to meet him. The bubble-door on his car lifted when the rotors stopped. Sam stepped out onto the landing pad.

Where is Security? My people are being killed and my own security guards are nowhere to be seen. This is outrageous. Heads will roll!

Sam hurried to his private lift and descended two levels to his office suite. When he left the lift, he stopped short. Glancing around at the empty reception area, he furrowed his brow, while beads of sweat formed on his forehead.

What the hell?

"Hello? Where is everybody?" His voice echoed through the empty room.

Hearing no answer, he stomped to the heavy doors leading into his office and charged through, determined to get to the bottom of whatever shenanigans were going on.

He froze in terror.

Sitting at his desk was Rae Anne Chavez, staring sternly in his direction. Twelve armed guards surrounded her. They all raised their weapons in unison.

"There he is! Grab him!" Rae Anne shouted.

The guards moved toward Sam.

Sam spun and jumped through the doorway. In his panic, he dropped the gym bag.

"Don't let him get away!" The muffled shout was followed by the sound of three gun retorts.

Rather than risk being trapped on the roof, Sam ran into the corridor and grabbed the first lift he came to.

"Sublevel One," he commanded, panting. Fear coursed through his body. His heart pounded at double time. Sweat poured down his cheeks. Gunshot sounds echoed behind him.

On the way down to the subway level, Sam formulated his escape strategy. Although five ships were docked on the hangar deck, all were thwarted from leaving by the Loyalist blockade. Of the five, only *Shackleton* had a full crew. He decided to head there for refuge. *Shackleton* would become his command post. It was berthed in Sector 8's hangar.

I've got enough manpower to thwart this uprising. But how the hell did they take over my office?

Sam took three deep breaths. He scanned the area outside the lift before leaving it. The subway platform was crowded as usual, but he saw no danger signs. Pulling his jacket collar higher around his neck, he slumped, head down, to avoid being recognized and hurried across the deck to the Levline. He pushed in front of a family about to enter the next car.

"Emergency," he growled. "Sorry."

"Say, aren't you President Durban?" the astonished woman asked. "What's going on?"

"Sector 8," he commanded, ignoring her query. He buckled in as the bubble-door dropped into place. The Levcab slid sideways from its berth, positioned itself over the Levline cable, and shot into the dark tunnel.

The moment Sam fled his offices, three workmen emerged from a utility closet down the hall. They entered Sam's office. After scouring the room, they removed projectors and wiring, stuffing everything into their large backpacks. They were clearing out the last of the equipment when several staffers entered the outer office.

"All's clear. The threat was a hoax," the lead worker announced. "We've swept the entire floor. It's clean." He picked up Sam's gym bag and led his crew into the hallway. As they disappeared into the lift, Sam's aides were left wondering how to put their morning back together and prepared for Sam's unusually late arrival.

Aboard *Liberty*

"Jason-14 on the *Shackleton* reports that Durban has boarded the ship in Sector 8." Jason-03 turned to Ian. "He ordered Jason-14 to set up comlinks to all his lieutenants. Jason-0 is in possession of a gym bag Sam dropped when he fled. He will send it over on the next shuttle. He says you won't believe its contents."

Liberty's bridge erupted in cheers and high-fives.

Ian slapped Jason-03 on the back. "When you told us about the hologram you guys generated in Durban's office, I couldn't imagine it working so perfectly."

"It would not have been possible without your teams keeping up the pressure. But sophisticated holograms are just the tip of the quantum computer iceberg."

Rae Anne gave Jason a strange look.

I need to remember to explore that comment further.

Ian smiled. "So, Durban is on the *Shackleton*. If we've spooked him enough, he may decide to use the ship as his headquarters, at least till things settle down. We need to make sure they don't. And we have Jason-14 on the bridge to keep us informed. Perfect! What is HavenAir's broadcasting status?"

"Jason-12 is using the equipment Denahr loaned us to override the station's broadcasts. We've been running our fake announcements all morning. No one outside the station knows the broadcasts are fake."

"Let's give Durban the rest of the morning to receive our broadcasts. They should convince him his situation is serious. When he hears news reporting a more dire situation than his lieutenants are reporting, he's bound to believe they're true."

"What's our next course of action?" Rae Anne asked.

"That will depend on Durban. But if we keep him in panic mode, whatever he decides will likely work in our favor.

"For now, we'll continue firing weapons and broadcasting warnings to keep up the pressure. If we can get most of Durban's troops to join him in the hangar bays, we can cordon them off and prevent anyone from leaving."

"Can we take over Approach Control and shut down the lifts to the hangars?" Rae Anne asked Jason.

"Durban's security forces have that facility heavily guarded. Only a serious gun battle would get us in there. We'd take serious casualties in the process."

An hour later, an unfamiliar voice broke into HavenAir's 'regular' programming with an urgent announcement.

> We regret to interrupt this program for an emergency announcement. Armed Loyalists have appeared at various locations around the city and are taking Liberation League members prisoner. Many Liberation League members have been killed when resisting. At least two gun battles have left dozens on both sides injured or killed. A civil war is taking place on our very streets.

We have tried to contact President Durban, but his office has refused to respond to our inquiries. It is rumored he has fled to the safety of a KBP cruiser and may be planning to leave Haven. Liberation League officials have been observed heading to the hangar bays to join him.

Security is advising everyone to keep off the streets to avoid accidental injury.

Please stay tuned for further developments. In the meantime, we will be airing classical music for your enjoyment.

Following the announcement, Tchaikovsky's 1812 Overture filled *Liberty's* bridge.

Ian laughed. "That should keep Sam's juices going. Although I'm sure he won't appreciate the irony in our music selection."

Over the next two hours, Jason's fake announcements suggested the Loyalists were taking over the city, sector by sector. They reported hundreds of Durban's people killed, with hundreds more taken into custody. Loyalist casualties were reported to be low.

Ian sat quietly in his captain's chair with his hands interlocked beneath his chin. He was trying to imagine what might be going through Sam's mind when Jason-03 interrupted his thoughts.

"Jason-14 aboard *Shackleton* reports Sam has commanded all his units to converge on the hangar decks and board the five berthed cruisers with all due haste."

"Excellent. Position two teams at each hangar lift. Have them blend with the crowds. We want the flow of Sam's people to be one way—DOWN. They are to take action only if someone returns to the surface."

Three hours later, Jason-03 reported that traffic down to the hangars had dropped off to nearly zero. "We have isolated Sam and much of his army on the five hangar decks."

"Good. Position our teams at all the Sublevel 1 and Ground-level lift exits and allow absolutely no one to leave the hangars. Connect me with *Shackleton*'s bridge."

"Connection is active, Captain."

"Captain Chernov, this is Ian Bentley on *Liberty*. I wish to speak with Sam Durban."

"He's in the Operations Center. I'll switch you over."

Sam's flushed face appeared on the monitor. He was the picture of rage.

"Sam, it's over. Your insurrection failed. I'm calling to negotiate terms for your surrender."

"In your dreams," Sam spat, his face snarling like an enraged dog.

"Sam, you have nowhere to go. You are trapped on the hangar deck. Our next move will be to evacuate the hangars, leaving you and your troops stranded aboard the cruisers. With so many people on board, your supplies will soon run out. Surrender is your only option."

"If you think that, you don't know Sam Durban!" Sam pounded his fist on the table and switched off the comlink.

Jason-03 turned from the communications console. "He does have one option. He could launch all five ships from the bays and punch his way through the blockade."

"That may not occur to him. Let's hope he comes to his senses and decides to negotiate."

"It might be a good idea to notify the blockading ships' captains to be prepared for a breakout, in case he goes that route," Jason suggested.

"Good point. Send a notice to all four captains. Tell them to follow Sam's cruisers should he succeed in breaking out, but do not engage. Those cruisers will be packed. Too many lives at risk.

"But we do need to know where he hightails it to so we can interrupt any further mischief he might stir up. The important thing is we now have control of Haven."

Chapter 20

Haven, Aboard *Shackleton*

Sam Durban paced the Operations Center on the *Shackleton*. He had sent several scouts up the lifts to check the feasibility of returning to the city. Only two scouts made it back. Both reported that the lift entrances were all guarded by Loyalists waiting in ambush.

With that option gone, only two possibilities remained: either breakout or surrender. But to break through the Loyalists' cruisers blocking the hangars, he needed seasoned officers and experienced crews manning each of his five ships. Since arriving on Haven, he only managed to enlist a suitable crew for the *Shackleton*.

So much for kicking that can down the road. Couldn't imagine it coming back to bite me.

He slammed his fist into the table. *And how the hell did Rae Anne take control of my office!* The pulsing ache in his neck warned him his blood pressure was rising.

He stopped pacing and took three slow breaths, then switched his comlink to the bridge. "Lt. Jason. How many of my people have made it down to the hangars?"

"973, President Durban, Sir."

"Great. I want everyone with any experience aboard a cruiser to meet in *Shackleton*'s hangar at five o'clock. I need to find as many experienced people as I can to crew the four other ships. Have security move everyone else into the other hangars to make room."

"Yes, Sir, Mr. President."

Once I get these ships crewed up, they're gonna be in for a fight.

While Jason-14 communicated the commands to Sam's men outside the ship, he also updated the other Jason's through their common computer link.

At five, Sam, accompanied by Captain Chernov, stepped onto the hangar's receiving platform outside *Shackleton*'s airlock. He stopped short and gulped.

Damn! Can't we round up more people than this?

"Chernov, what is the minimum crew needed to operate a cruiser?"

"Ninety-seven by the book, Sir. But for short duration, peaceful operations, we can manage with fifty-five."

"So, for the four other ships, we need 220 personnel. Jason, how many volunteers have we collected?"

"181 candidates, President Durban, Sir.

Sam turned to Chernov. "Can we draw down your crew, Captain?"

"Yes, Sir. I'm currently at 120, just 35 below full crew. I can give you 65 and still be able to fly."

"Lt. Jason, sift through everyone's resumes to locate anyone with suitable experience to serve as officers for each ship, then build rosters and make assignments. Divide the remaining personnel between the ships. I want all five ships ready to launch ASAP."

"And Jason, any luck contacting *Azov* or my other two ships?"

"No, Sir. The Loyalist jamming screen continues to block all our transmissions. We've heard nothing from *Azov, Mendeleyev,* or *Denali.*"

"Well, we'll just have to bust through this blockade without their help. Once we get clear, I want communications established immediately."

Not exactly an armada, but eight light cruisers will provide me with sufficient protection. And in time, by god, I shall return. I'll win back Haven.

Aboard *Liberty*

"Captain, I have received a notification regarding Durban's next move."

Jason-03 rose from the comlink console and headed for the Operations Center, knowing Ian would want confidentiality. Ian followed.

What a stroke of luck having one of our guys on Shackleton's bridge.

"So, what is Durban up to?" Ian asked when they were alone. He grabbed a bagel from the refreshment counter by the door.

"He's putting together crews to staff all five ships."

Ian sat at the conference table and turned his chair to face Jason. "So, he has no intention to surrender. Any idea how many followers he has with him?"

"1093, counting the *Shackleton* crew. Jason-14 on the *Shackleton* organized a team to interview everyone briefly to find experienced members for their crews. He filed all their dossiers in our computer database."

"Good. I'm sure they're not all hard-liners. Sift through those files and find anyone we might switch to our side when the time comes."

"Got it."

"Durban didn't realize he was helping us when he decommissioned the old crews. Our efforts would have been more difficult without all the Jasons he freed up to help us. Who do we now have aboard Durban's ships?"

"Jason-09 has been conscripted to serve aboard the *Olympia*. So, with Jason-14 on *Shackleton*, Jason-07 on Denali, and Jason-17 on the *Mendeleyev*, we have a Jason on half of Durban's ships' bridges."

"Which leaves us with what, four Jasons as free agents?"

"Yes, although Jason-12 is still assigned to Commander Denahr at the Shalcerian garrison."

Ian nodded. "Good. We need to keep him there."

He stood and put his hand on Jason's shoulder. "Where is Rae Anne now?"

"As we speak, Jason-12 is escorting her from the garrison to her apartment. We are advising her to keep a low profile until Durban surrenders or until he leaves Haven."

"Good advice. There must be a fair number of insurgents who didn't make it to the hangars."

Which means Rae Anne could be in real danger. His throat tightened at the thought.

"All of Durban's organizers and most of the cell leaders have joined him there. Those left in the city are low-level sympathizers. We should expect no trouble from them."

"Keep me informed. When Durban makes a break for it, we'll want to know where he's headed and make sure he never comes back."

Aboard Shackleton

Five days after Sam ordered Jason-14 to organize crews, he ordered all personnel to board the cruisers. Once the hangar decks were vacated, he joined Captain Chernov on *Shackleton*'s bridge.

"All five cruisers are set for launch, President Durban. We've cleared the hangars for evacuation. We await your command."

This is it, Sam old boy. It's time to show them I'm still a force to be reckoned with.

"Very well. On my mark, open all the hangar doors at once and blast the Loyalist cruisers with torpedoes at point-blank range. Then apply full power to broadside them with as much force as we can muster. That will create gaps in their blockade. We'll use those to break free into open space."

"But Sir, if we don't evacuate the hangars before opening the doors, anything loose in the deck spaces will blast out into space along with all the air."

"Exactly. I want to hit them with everything we have, including the torpedoes. I know they won't damage their cruisers' plasticore hulls, but the blasts will help push them away."

"Excellent idea, Sir. Lt. Jason, relay those instructions to the other four captains. Prepare for launch in…?" Chernov looked to Durban.

"Five minutes at my command."

"Prepare for launch in five minutes at President Durban's command."

"On it, Sirs."

The longest five minutes of my life. This had better work.

Sam watched the bridge chronometer dial down. After four minutes and fifty seconds, he announced, "On my mark…"

He counted the last ten seconds aloud.

"Now!"

The blank wall facing *Shackleton* sparkled briefly and disappeared, revealing *Darwin's* port side. *Shackleton's* deck thumped once as two depleted-uranium-tipped Blaxar-DU4 torpedoes surged from its forward tubes. A blinding flash lit up the bridge when they exploded against the *Darwin*.

Shackleton surged from the hangar and plunged into *Darwin* under full power. The impact reverberated throughout the ship. *Darwin* spun away from the moonlet, undamaged. Chernov directed his ship into the gap. *Shackleton* rocketed away into the fathomless depths of space.

"Brilliant," Chernov exclaimed. "If I hadn't seen those videos of the *Maxwell* and *Liberty* bashing each other, I wouldn't have believed your tactic would work."

Four other cruisers lined up in a 'V' formation behind the *Shackleton*.

"Set a course for Mars. Nova Prima will be our new base of operations. Notify me when we're ten minutes from landing. I'll be in my cabin."

"Yes, Sir."

Sam left the bridge and pondered his most pressing priorities.

I must get control of their plasticore manufacturing operation. That stuff will make me the richest man in Human history.

Chapter 21

Haven

The day following Sam's departure from Haven, Rae Anne stood on the same steps Sam occupied eight months earlier at the start of his coup. Jason-0 and Rae Anne's assistant Ilhan stood behind her near the Municipal Building's nanoscreen entrance. A small crowd had gathered, many of whom were members of the Loyalist's infiltration team. HavenAir reporters waited patiently with their cameras in place to record and broadcast the event.

The nanoplast walkway was halted for the occasion. The general mood in the gathering appeared to be exhausted relief. There were no signs or banners. The audience stood in respectful silence, waiting to hear what the next episode might bring.

Well, here goes. Maybe the hardest speech of my life.

Rae Anne tapped the microphone. Three loud thumps verified everything was working. She glanced behind her. Jason held a thumbs up. She smiled at this Human gesture coming from an android. Glancing down at her prepared speech on the podium, she took a deep breath and looked up at the crowd.

"Thank you for coming. To those watching on HavenAir, thank you for taking time to hear what I have to say. My comments will be brief.

"First, know that Sam Durban's coup has failed. He and most of his followers have fled to Mars and Earth. His authoritarian rule and the sham constitution he fabricated are history."

Rae Anne paused for the applause. She was disappointed it wasn't more enthusiastic. A few hoots and jeers erupted from the back. Security guards stationed around the crowd scrutinized the agitators. Their orders were to make no move to corral protestors unless they posed a threat.

Rae Anne raised her arm for quiet.

"Your representatives from my earlier government, and myself especially, now recognize that meaningful change is necessary for Haven to have a true representative government. The popular support the failed coup garnered made this perfectly clear. So today, on the first day of our restored freedom, I wish to make the following four announcements."

Rae Anne thought she could feel a sense of anticipation in the crowd.

"First, I have negotiated with the Shalcerians regarding the mandates spelled out in the Saturn Accords. In coordination with the Shalcerian Empire's governing commission, and with the help of their Sol System garrison commander, Commander Denahr, the special provisions directed specifically toward Humans have been dropped."

This announcement stunned the crowd. No one expected a negotiated reprieve from the aliens. The applause grew to a thunderous ovation. Rae Anne marveled at the change.

My decision to renegotiate the Accords was the right move. I'm glad we had Denahr on our side. With any other Shalcerian, the outcome might have been quite different.

"From this point on, the Shalcerian Empire will treat Humans with the same regard as the other species who are members of the empire. Commander Denahr deserves our gratitude for his efforts in presenting my petition and arguing our case to their governing bodies in Shalkor, their capital city.

"As a result, all restrictions in travel and commerce between Haven and Earth are lifted. The twice-weekly ferry service between Earth and Haven initiated during the coup will continue without interruption. Similarly, free trade in goods and services between Earth and Haven is no longer prohibited. I urge our businesses to take full advantage of this opportunity."

The crowd was now cheering in response to these declarations. Rae Anne raised both arms and signaled for quiet.

"My second announcement is to declare Sam Durban's fake constitution null and void. However, his actions demonstrated that Haven needs a legitimate constitution, an oversight for which I accept full responsibility. Which leads to my third announcement.

"To create a true democratic government for Haven, I am scheduling an election for 120 representatives for a Constitution Convention. We will hold this election in two weeks. Each sector will elect ten representatives. Any

Haven adult submitting a petition with one-hundred signatures may run to become a Constitution Convention representative. The elected representatives will begin meeting the following week to hash out an appropriate constitution for our fair city. This document will then be put to you, the voters, for approval.

"Once our citizens have approved a constitution, we'll hold another election within the month to fill the offices dictated by the new constitution, including the mayor's.

"And now for my fourth announcement. I am stepping down as your administrator as soon as my successor is sworn into office. This moment represents a new day and fresh start for Haven. Thank you."

After lengthy applause, Rae Anne returned to the microphones.

"I'll be happy to take a few questions."

The dozen reporters standing in the front row tried to outshout the others. Rae Anne struggled to parse individual questions from the cacophony.

"No," she responded to the first question she heard. "I will not run for any elected office. It's time for Haven to have new leadership."

"What about the Kuiper Belt Patrols? Will they be continued?"

"A standard provision for membership in the Shalcerian Empire is for local species to take responsibility for their own star system. Since the Kuiper Belt is part of our system, the Kuiper Belt Patrols are our answer to that mandate. So yes, we will resume the patrols."

"Are Haven's colonies on Mars, Ganymede, and Luna also released from the Accords?"

"What I have said relates to Haven and all Human endeavors allied with Haven. Mayberry Station on Luna is covered, along with the twenty-four Earth nations who have declared partnership with us. More are sure to follow.

"As for the Mars colonies, Juno, and nations aligned with Durban's insurgency, we'll have to wait and see how things develop. As long as they maintain an adversarial relationship with Haven, we will treat them as adversaries."

"Does that mean we are at war with Mars?"

"No. We will maintain a cautious relationship with Mars and Juno until we understand their intentions. Whether we can maintain peaceful relations or not depends on their actions going forward. But know this—we will defend Haven and our allies with everything we have at our disposal."

She smiled broadly and waved both hands as though she had just won a marathon.

"Thank you. Thank you all."

Ignoring other shouted questions, she turned toward the building and stepped through the nanoscreen doors. Jason and Ilhan followed closely behind.

By the time they reached the lift, Rae Anne was swiping at the tears streaming down her face. Her chest felt like an evacuated hangar deck.

This is silly. It's time for me to step down. This is the right thing to do. Why do I feel as though I've lost my best friend?

They rode the lift to the roof and stepped out into her old office area. No one had bothered to remove her old furniture. Sam's hovercar was still on its pad. Rae Anne sank into the couch and gazed at Saturn hanging over the southern horizon. On this day, the rings were a thin, knife-edge streak across the planet's surface that thrust a silver spear into the black space beyond.

"That's the same view of Saturn I saw years ago when I took the *Eagle* lander down to Titan's surface. It's comforting to see that some things never change."

After several hushed minutes, Ilhan spoke.

"I'll begin arranging for your things to be moved to the executive suite downstairs. The office is like a throne room. It'll be quite a change, even if we use it for just two or three months. Durban must have imagined himself to be King Tut."

"Don't bother, Ilhan," Rae Anne said with resolve. She swept her hand to encompass the space before them. "This is my legitimate office. We'll work from here as we did before the coup. The new mayor can decide what to do with that monstrosity downstairs."

Jason rubbed his chin. "If the roof isn't used for anything else, we could make it into a pocket-park, open to the public. The unrestricted view of Saturn from here really is awesome."

"Jason, I do believe you are developing a sense of aesthetics," Rae Anne said, gazing at him with awe.

Wuhan, China

Karen kept glancing at her reflected image in the plate glass windows as she sauntered from the parking lot to her appointment with the directors of Robotique Moderne International. The windows looked in on the company's spacious lobby.

God, I may not be knock-dead gorgeous, but I'm one very attractive woman. Gotta hand it to those Chinese plastic surgeons.

She stopped before entering the lobby, leaned on the door frame, and worked to catch her breath. Despite months of physical therapy, she still struggled dealing with Earth's oppressive gravity. Her only consolation was that it was slowly getting better.

During the pause, she reflected on her good fortune. A luxurious, beautifully appointed apartment with a view (through the smog) augmented a generous salary. With her sign-on bonus, her stock options were already substantial.

Give me a few successful years and I'll be a billionaire again.

Jin Lei offered to accompany her to the office on her first day, but she declined. After fourteen years in prison, she wasn't about to be escorted by anyone. She entered the lobby through the revolving glass doors and smiled. Jin Lei was waiting for her along with six Asian men in traditional western office attire.

"You have already met Zhang Mei, your COO," Jin Lei said in greeting while shaking her hand. "Let me introduce you to your five division heads, all vice presidents, of course."

Jin Lei introduced each man with a summary of the operations they managed. Karen wracked her brain to bring back an organizational chart from her old Sanders Robotics on which to place these executives. She was pleased to discover that the Chinese organization had been set up to mirror that of her old company.

"Show me to my office, Lei." She deliberately used Jin Lei's first name, mistakenly thinking that it would elevate her status in the eyes of her subordinates. She waved her arm toward the others. "Please, come with me. Before we part, I want to schedule tours of your divisions."

The group followed Jin Lei into the elevator and stepped out into a spacious reception area on the seventeenth floor. After being introduced to her receptionist and her assistant, she was ushered into her office. Zhang Mei followed them through the door.

Floor to ceiling windows looked out over a vast wooded park. From this height, it looked like a green carpet. A brown haze hung over Wuhan's distant skyline. Even here, the smog diminished the sun's brilliance, giving it a sickly red-orange hue.

Karen pointed to the plush furniture arranged along one wall. "Please, make yourselves comfortable." She turned to her receptionist. "Please find out what everyone wants to drink and see that their needs are met."

Once everyone was seated, she leaned forward to engage with her team. "I can't wait to learn more about each of you. And to tell you a bit about myself as well. The better we know each other, the more effectively we'll be able to work together."

Although they'll only hear the fake life-history given to me by Colonel Xi Li. It wouldn't do for them to know they were working for a convicted killer. On the other hand, ...

"In the meantime, Lei, how are plans coming along for the site in France and our eventual move there?"

Jin Lei cleared his throat. "We are ahead of schedule. Construction of our manufacturing and research complex east of Paris is well underway. Everything you will see here on your tours has been designed with modularity in mind to facilitate the move. We estimate that downtime for the move will be less than two months, barring international political difficulties."

Karen nodded approvingly. "And what about our product line? How are we positioned to compete in the current markets?"

"We have reverse engineered most systems Durban Robotics offers. We are already manufacturing several of them. You will see those on your factory tour. As for the others, the engineers are working diligently to create assembly lines and ordering parts. Once we are in our Paris location, we will begin manufacturing them immediately."

How utterly delicious. We'll hit the ground running. Sam won't know what hit him until it's too late.

Lei reached into his jacket pocket and withdrew a three-by-five photograph. He handed it to Karen. She recognized Rae Anne Chavez standing behind the podium. Behind her was a man of slight build and a woman of African descent. She knew neither of them.

"What's this?" she asked.

"This is our lead to the advanced robotics research being conducted at Haven University with the help of the aliens. The man standing next to Chavez's aide is the key figure in this research. He has a large lab in the Physics Department. We absolutely must recruit him as part of our team. We have the resources and engineering expertise to bring his efforts at creating androids to fruition. You are to begin working on this without delay."

"What else do we know about him?"

"Not much. He goes by Jason, probably Professor Jason, although he isn't listed on the faculty. He has a tiny apartment just off campus but spends most of his time in the lab. Very dedicated. And very secretive."

The last place I want to go is back to Haven. But while I'm there, I may see an opportunity to avenge the fourteen years of my life that bitch Chavez stole from me.

Part Two

(Distances not to scale.)
Alpha Mensae
Entriva, capital of
the Baltar Federation
33.1 lightyears
Epsilon Eridani
Sirius
10.5 lightyears
8.6 lightyears
Earth
Sol

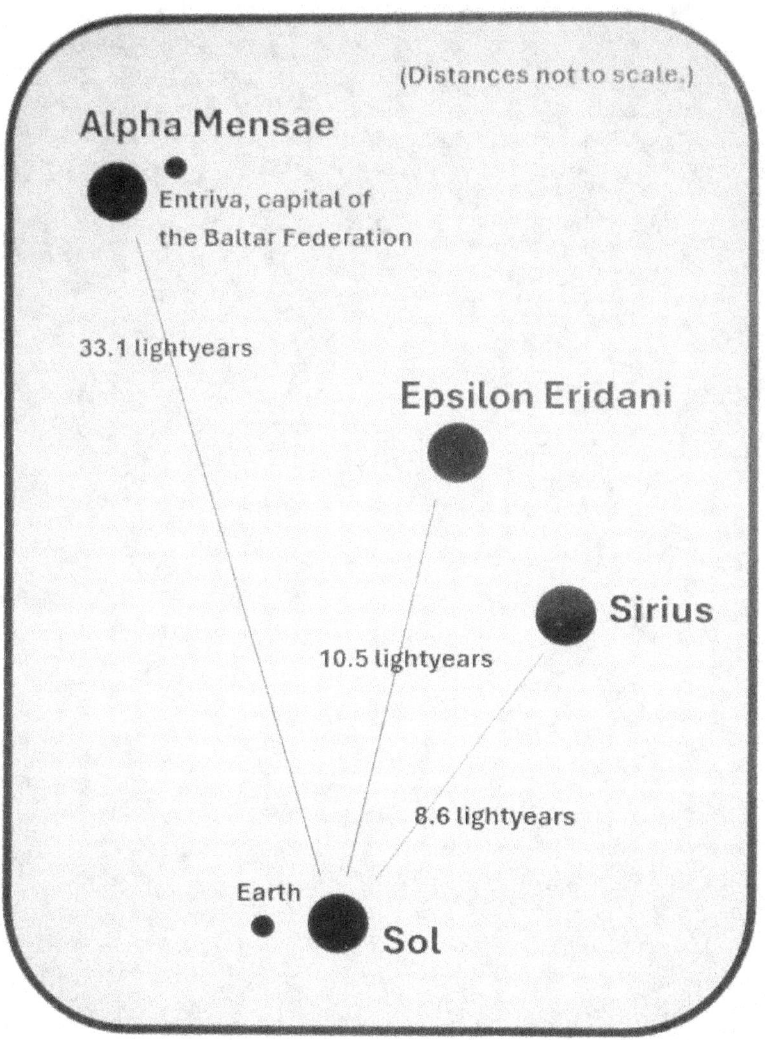

Chapter 1

Haven University

Professor Beverly Hayden swept her fingers through her short brown hair and squinted at her computer monitor. She struggled to keep her burning eyes open as she paged through the dense report. Page after page filled with columns of numbers scrolled across the screen. To the uninitiated, the report appeared to be a mammoth spreadsheet of random data. But to Bev, connections and relationships popped off the screen as if highlighted in bold red characters.

She and her team of graduate students had been working five years on Project Containment, ever since Rae Anne challenged the science and engineering departments at the University to duplicate Shalcerian interstellar propulsion technology, a project she dubbed 'Ad Astra.' For incentive, Rae Anne offered to share the data archives Jason had copied from the Shalcerian computer to enhance the researchers' projects. Two dozen scientists stepped up to the challenge.

The part of Ad Astra that ignited Bev's interest was discovering how the gravity bottles in which Shalcerians contained their micro black holes worked. Another group was studying how micro black holes could be manipulated in the quantum realm into a state of entanglement, thus generating the wormhole tears in space-time through which their interstellar cruisers jumped. Other researchers hoped to discover how Shalcerians located micro black holes in the first place and captured them for their use.

"Come," Bev muttered absently in response to a tap on her office door.

Dayton Franklin, a bearded young man in his twenties, stepped through the nanoscreen and into the room. He was one of three post-docs working with Bev, having joined her group as an undergraduate. His shaggy red hair, rumpled clothing, and scuffed sandals betrayed an air of personal neglect, but his face revealed an intensity that suggested deep intelligence.

Bev continued to scroll through the data after glancing to see who had come in. Dayton knew better than to disturb her concentration. He crossed his arms and leaned against the wall of books next to the door. His gaze took in the familiar sparsely furnished office. Aside from Bev's small oak desk and computer desk, the room contained a coffee table pushed against the window, piled high with a chaotic assortment of papers and journals, and two places to sit: Bev's rolling office chair and a beat-up lounger. A large poster of Earth hung on the wall behind her desk onto which were tacked five framed documents displaying her degrees and awards. Windows in the other two walls looked out over the city, with the mammoth hulk of Saturn suspended over the southern horizon.

"So, tell me, Dayton. Do these numbers say what I think they do?"

"They most certainly do!" Dayton uncrossed his arms and strolled over to the computer. He couldn't hide his enthusiasm. "The simulation verifies that our latest gravity bottle design will contain a micro black hole and allow us to manipulate it by altering the bottle's shape at will. Of course, we'll need a dedicated fusion reactor to provide the required energy for the superconducting magnets."

Bev was mildly amused that this 'Eureka!' moment elicited more a feeling of exhausted relief than a cork-popping, song-and-dance celebration. So many years of false starts and dashed hopes.

This all looks good on paper. But it may just be another chimera.

"Run the simulations again. If they check out, I'll contact Jason and see when we can schedule time aboard a cruiser for a real-world trial run. If we succeed in manipulating the containment fields in a real gravity bottle, then we'll celebrate our discovery."

"Well, I'm excited," Dayton said. "This could be our key to interstellar travel."

Bev swiveled her chair and faced Dayton with a skeptical scowl on her face. "Solving the gravity bottle problem is only a small step. The other teams have yet to figure out how to locate and capture the little beasts. If these algorithms pan out, we'll be able to make gravity bottles, but we have nothing to put in them."

"Maybe the other teams will be able to use our gravity bottles to capture micro black holes. They'll surely want to give it a try."

"Let me know when you've verified the data. I'll set up a meeting and we'll show them what we have. I can only hope to live long enough to see our discovery put to good use."

"You may not have to wait as long as you think," Dayton replied. "As I was tweaking the last algorithms to get the simulations to work, an idea crossed my mind. To build an interstellar drive like the ones Shalcerians use, we'll need to contain two micro black holes in a single gravity bottle. Jason claims to have the programs in his quantum computer that can entangle them to open a wormhole."

Bev yawned and stretched. "How does that change the picture?"

"Haven has eleven interplanetary cruisers, each with a gravity bottle and a single black hole to provide the space-warping gravity field needed for their propulsion. If we decommissioned one cruiser and placed its gravity bottle next to one in another cruiser, we can use our algorithms to fold the two bottles into a single unit that then contains two black holes."

Bev looked at Dayton with surprise. Such an obvious solution once the idea was pulled from the hat.

Dayton, how lucky I am you decided to work on my team.

"Incredible idea, Dayton. If our program performs like we think it should, your idea may indeed pave our way to the stars."

Haven Central Park

Jason-0 and Rae Anne stepped from the Levline cab onto the Sector 1 subway platform and took the escalator to Central Park. A small crowd was gathered at the twenty-foot statue Sam Durban had erected to honor himself. A crane idled next to its base while workmen secured straps around the statue.

"We timed our arrival just right," Jason observed. "They haven't begun quite yet."

"I'll be happy to see that monstrosity go," said Rae Anne. "What kind of person would put up a statue of themself?"

"Probably reveals deep-seated feelings of inferiority."

Rae Anne laughed. "You sound like a psychotherapist."

"That capability was built into my original program before we left Earth orbit twenty-five years ago. I was to assist *Aurora*'s crew on their mission to Mars."

Rae Anne suddenly quieted. Jason saw her face darken.

Human feelings. I brought up painful memories of the friends she lost on that mission. I should be more careful.

Normally, Jason wasn't drawn to public events. But strange stirrings had surged through his circuitry when he watched Aurora Museum, the remnants of his and Rae Anne's old ship *Aurora,* being destroyed two years earlier to make room for the statue. He wondered then if they might be the android equivalent of Human feelings. It was the first time he had experienced something of that sort.

Maybe watching them pull down Durban's statue will generate that odd phenomenon again. Feelings are the physical expression of emotions, something that I lack.

They chose a spot next to a nearby tree and Jason leaned his shoulder into it, purposely mimicking a Human pose. He crossed his arms and legs.

"Do Humans really find this posture comfortable? It doesn't provide the most efficient stance for balance."

Rae Anne laughed. "Don't fall over. That could blow your cover."

Workmen attached the crane's cables to the statue and moved a safe distance away. As the cables became taut, the statue pulled free of its pedestal. The crowd cheered and clapped.

Swinging slowly to one side, the crane lowered the statue onto the bed of a waiting lorry. The vehicle then rumbled slowly through the park and onto the avenue, heading to the recycle center.

Jason shook his head. No repetition of the circuitry disorder had occurred.

Maybe I didn't have enough connection with the statue to elicit feelings at its removal, although I am glad to see it gone. Glad? Hmm...

"Excuse me, are you Professor Jason?"

Jason turned his head at the unfamiliar voice, then stood upright and turned to its source. An attractive middle-aged woman approached them, her eyebrows raised in inquiry. Long auburn hair cascaded in waves over her shoulders. She was smartly but alluringly dressed. An expensive amulet dangled beneath her neck.

Professor Jason? What's with that? Distinct French accent. I think I'll play along and see where this goes. And how do I know she's 'attractive?'

"Yes. And you are?" Jason assumed a look implying interest.

"I am Marie Piaf de Lyons. It's a pleasure to meet you."

She turned to Rae Anne. "And you are?"

"Rae Anne Chavez. I'm a friend of Professor Jason."

Ah, so Rae Anne is willing to play along as well. Good.

Karen reached out to Jason and they shook hands.

"My pleasure," Jason responded. "And what can I do for you, Ms. Piaf?"

"Please, call me Marie. How may I address you?"

"Just Jason. Everyone calls me that."

"How unusual. Someone of your stature to go by his surname, and without an honorific."

Jason shrugged his shoulders to mirror a Human gesture in response.

She turned to Rae Anne. Jason thought he detected a fierce undercurrent in her interaction with Rae Anne.

"Aren't you the founder of this floating city?"

"More like the gardener who planted the seed that sprouted and flourished under Shalcerian influence."

The woman wrinkled her nose at the reference to aliens. She turned back to Jason.

"I must tell you who I am before we go any further. I am the CEO of Robotique Moderne Internationale. In case you haven't heard of us, we are a new French startup located just outside Paris. We hope soon to eclipse Durban Robotics in the automation marketplace."

"Very commendable." He waved toward the now vacant pedestal. "As you can see, we have no love lost on Sam Durban or his enterprises. I wish you the best of luck."

"Luck will have very little to do with it, Jason. We have a staff of brilliant engineers working hard to make it happen. And we are making progress toward building a robot that looks and functions exactly like a Human. When we succeed, we will have a product that will transform humanity."

"You are trying to build an android?" Rae Anne asked.

"Yes, precisely. What's more, I happen to know that you, Jason, are working on something similar, am I right?"

Jason smiled slightly and paused before answering.

"I have been looking into the possibilities. A daunting challenge."

"Well, here's the thing. RMI would like you to visit our plant. We would like you to evaluate our efforts. Compare what we are doing with your own projects. Perhaps share your valuable expertise with us. We'll pay your expenses, of course, along with a very generous consulting fee."

Why would a company reveal their research to a potential competitor? She's not being entirely truthful.

Jason shook his head. "Unfortunately, I'm currently working on several unrelated projects that demand my full attention. A trip to Earth, even a short one, is out of the question."

The onlookers began to disperse and jostled by them. They moved closer to the trees to give the crowd room to pass.

"But if you intend to commercialize your research, what better way than through a corporation that has an established customer base and a world-wide marketing and distribution network? Trust me, it is very difficult to build those things from scratch."

"I'm sure that's true. But I'm not convinced making an android available on the open market would be a good thing. There could be grave unintended consequences."

The woman reached both hands before her in supplication and smiled broadly.

"Let me sweeten the deal. I'm on the boards of five different professional organizations. We set up workshops and conferences all the time and are always looking for keynote speakers. I can arrange to give you top billing at one or more of these. I could even put together a speaking tour. Your prestige and professional recognition would skyrocket."

That's a hard sell that would sway most Humans. She's desperate. But why?

Jason furrowed his brow and tried to look stern, like a father might look when confronting an errant child. "Thank you for the offer. But I have no interest in prestige or recognition, and my funding sources are more than adequate. You have nothing to offer me that would entice me into traveling to Earth."

The woman sighed and stepped back, disappointment written on her face.

"I see. That's unfortunate." Then her face brightened. "But I would be quite interested in seeing what you have accomplished. Would you at least be willing to show me your lab and describe your progress in android development?"

"No."

Again, the crestfallen look. "Anything at all to make my trip here worthwhile."

"No. I maintain very tight security over my work."

Jason reached for Rae Anne's arm to signal he was through with this conversation.

"Now I must get back to my lab. I have a biology experiment that needs tending to. I hope you have a safe trip back to Earth and I really do wish you well in achieving your goals."

He turned and walked away, leading Rae Anne toward the nanoplast avenue. His rear camera revealed the woman standing rigidly in place, arms akimbo.

"RMI must be having difficulties with their android research," Rae Anne said once they left the park. "Those were astonishing offers she was making."

"Red flags, to my thinking. I find it interesting they think I'm Human."

"It speaks to how well we've kept your identity under wraps. I don't doubt we're better off for it. Sam Durban never caught on."

Jason nodded in agreement. "Fortunately, all the ship's captains have kept our identity secure. They treat all of my clones as if they are regular crew like everyone else."

"Don't some of your crewmates see through the façade?"

"I imagine the bridge crews are suspicious, but they follow their captain's lead. If the captain treats their Communications Officer as a Human, then who are they to argue? We even take regular bathroom breaks."

That provoked a hearty laugh from Rae Anne. Jason chuckled.

Did I just tell a joke? And Rae Anne's laughter made me... made me feel... good!

Chapter 2

Sydney

Sam gazed with satisfaction from his office above his TransWorld Space operations headquarters' tarmac in Sydney. At the moment, two of his ill-gotten Shalcerian cruisers, *Azov,* and *Mendeleyev,* were parked on their pads. *Denali* had just arrived and was dropping gently to the ground to join them. Each cruiser was the size of a navy destroyer, dwarfing his old chemical rocket ferries now sitting abandoned on the far side of the field. His new ships could transport ten times the passengers and cargo compared to those old buckets.

His company now relied on the cruisers as his shuttles to Mars, to the USIEA lunar colonies, and to his twelve spaceports in major cities around the world. With the added convenience of acceleration-free liftoffs (thanks to their plasticore hulls) and short travel times to Mars and Luna, revenues for TransWorld Space had tripled over the previous year.

Sam puffed on an expensive cigar, relishing its pungent aroma. With half his time spent in space, either at Nova Prima on Mars or checking operations at his Luna Xtract mining facilities on Luna and in the Asteroid Belt, he seldom had the opportunity for a good smoke.

"Captain Abrams of Denali is here to see you."

Sam started at the mellow voice transmitted through the cranial implant behind his right ear. He'd had the surgery six weeks before and was not yet used to its abrupt messaging directly to his brain. His AI assistant three floors below monitored all traffic in and out of the building and messaged him when necessary.

Denali just landed. Abrams must have something important to report for him to come right over.

"Send him up."

A few minutes later, Sam heard a knock at the door. "Enter."

The tall goateed captain entered the office. His bald head reflected the ceiling's light. He had the build of a weightlifter owing to his favorite activity at the gym whenever he was off duty on Earth.

"Captain Abrams, my AI tells me your arrival is 108 minutes late. Cargo doesn't mind, but my passengers surely do."

"I'm sorry, Sir. We ran across the *Darwin* just before reaching Earth orbit."

"Damn Loyalists. Nothing better to do than harass us."

I'll figure out some way to shoot their fucking ships down.

"Oh, it wasn't that. They never saw us."

"Then what the fuck held you up?"

"*Darwin* was headed full bore to Venus."

Sam sat upright and placed his cigar in the tray beside his desk.

"And?"

"I remembered your directive from a year ago. 'Track any loyalist ship heading to Venus and discover where it lands.' I immediately diverted course, as per your orders."

Sam's demeanor instantly changed.

Passengers be damned. I can handle a few complaints.

"Good job. Did you get coordinates for its landing site?"

"I'm not entirely sure. They are using diversionary tactics to throw off anyone following them. At first, they dropped straight through the cloud layer toward a site near the equator. I stayed in stationary orbit above the site and my radar showed the ship moving to three other sites before I lost it. It may have gone into a lava tube hangar or moved on to yet another location. But I have good coordinates for the four sites we monitored."

"Excellent. Leave them with my AI downstairs. Thank you for doing this. If your information gets us to their secret plasticore manufacturing site on Venus, you'll have a fat bonus coming your way."

"Thank you, Sir."

Sam shook Abrams's hand and dismissed him. He then sent a message to *Azov's* Captain Lemaire to see him immediately.

At last. This may be my break to get control over plasticore manufacturing. If I can block access to their plant, they'll come begging.

When Lemaire arrived two hours later, it was obvious he wasn't happy with having his leave interrupted.

"What took you so long?" Sam's voice dripped with irritation.

"I'm sorry, Sir. You caught me at a, um…, rather inconvenient time."

"What was it, booze? Or women?"

"Well, both, Sir. I met this really lovely lady at the Spacer Space, and she invited me…"

"Never mind. I want *Azov* ready for launch in three hours."

"That won't be possible, Sir. Six, maybe. Most of the crew is on shore leave. Just rounding them up will take several hours."

"Well, get on it. We're going to Venus."

"We, Sir? You're going with us?"

"Yes. Be sure to have my stateroom ready. Let me know half an hour before departure."

"Yes Sir."

After Lemaire left, Sam began a chat with his AI.

"Brutus, tell me what you know about Venus."

"Venus, second planet from Sol, is about 95% the size of Earth with a rocky core, molten mantle, and thin crust. Its atmospheric pressure at the surface is 92 times Earth's and it is composed of carbon dioxide and nitrogen, with smaller amounts of sulfur dioxide, water vapor, and carbon monoxide.

"The planet has no moon and rotates in the opposite direction to Earth's, so the sun rises in the west and sets in the east. The dense cloud cover obscures any visible view of the surface from space. The surface temperature is 462-degrees Celsius, hot enough to melt lead.

"Surface features include volcanoes, mountains, valleys, craters, and plains. The highlands of Ishta Terra are about the size of Australia, while Maxwell Montes, the highest mountain, is a couple thousand feet higher than Mount Everest. Mead Crater is the size of Arizona, while…"

"Stop."

Plasticore manufacture must require high pressure and high temperature. Why else would they have chosen such a god-forsaken place to locate their manufacturing plant. And the gravitolite ore I've mined for them in the Asteroid Belt must be part of it.

"Brutus. Tell me all you know about gravitolite."

"I am sorry. I have no information in my database on that topic. What is it?"

"It's an ore found in the Asteroid Belt."

"Thank you. I'll add that to my database for future reference."

"I'll be gone from my office for up to two days. Reschedule anything that might conflict with my absence."

Sam pondered what actions he might take once he located the plasticore facility.

I could use a cruiser to block access to the plant. However, it's probably run by robots, so a siege would have little effect. I could threaten to blow it up. That would be counter to my goals, but the mere threat might force the Loyalists to negotiate.

Haven University

Ian scowled with concentration as he scrolled through the report on his tablet. Occasionally, he paused to read the details, then resumed scrolling. Dr. Bev Hayden, Rae Anne, Jason-0, and the ten other captains of Haven's Kuiper Belt Patrol fleet sat quietly around the polished oak table in Haven University's Faculty Seminar Room. The windows looked out on the quad, with the view of Saturn blocked by the surrounding buildings.

When Ian reached the end of the proposal, he looked up and scanned the group around the table. Everyone he had summoned was here. No one dared pass on an invitation with the heading 'Ad Astra. Are we ready?'"

"Thank you for your patience," Ian said. "You've all read Dr. Hayden's paper, probably several times over. I just needed to go through it one last time to be sure I wasn't missing something."

He shrugged his shoulders forward and rolled his head to relieve the tension in his upper back, then turned his gaze to Bev.

"So, you're proposing we decommission two cruisers to test your theory about combining their propulsion units into a single gravity bottle on one of the ships. That reduces our fleet by one ship and puts the other in limbo. What's the risk of our losing both ships during this experiment?"

Bev seemed taken aback by Ian's skeptical tone, but she returned his gaze, glowing with confidence.

"We've checked and double-checked our algorithms thoroughly. Jason, here, has run them through his quantum computer. Everything checks out. There's a very high probability this will work."

Rae Anne couldn't contain her enthusiasm. Her voice and demeanor conveyed her excitement.

"This is our gateway to the stars, Ian. The Shalcerian interstellar drive requires two micro black holes contained in a single gravity bottle. They gave us cruisers with only one blackhole to restrict us from traveling beyond our own star system. Dr. Hayden's discovery changes everything." She turned to Jason sitting next to her.

"Rae Anne is correct," Jason said. "The quantum computer I built is styled after the one on the Shalcerian battlecruiser *Avenger*. The massive database I copied from their computer included the algorithms for manipulating black holes in gravity bottles. Now that Dr. Hayden has discovered the secret behind the gravity bottles, we can build a functioning starship."

Ellie MacIntyre, *Freedom*'s captain, was sitting at the opposite end of the table from Ian. She cleared her throat. "Jason, these algorithms in your archives for operating an interstellar drive—are they sufficient to control our experimental ship?"

"I'll need to make a few alterations before they'll work on my own computer, but that won't be a problem."

Ian took a sip from his coffee. "What do the rest of you think of this proposal?"

His question opened a lively discussion that lasted two hours, during which everyone peppered both Bev and Jason with questions.

When the discussion died down, Ellie leaned forward. "I propose we tackle this project immediately. I'm confident it will work."

"I'm in," said Bruce Eagan, *Darwin*'s captain. He absently scuffed his beard with his left hand. In short order, everyone voiced their agreement.

Ian set his mug beside his tablet. "Alright, then. We'll designate one ship to be Human's first interstellar cruiser and decommission a second to allocate its fusion reactor and gravity bottle to the project. We can build the third fusion reactor we need while making the gravity bottle alterations on the starship."

Ian looked around the room and raised his eyebrows. "Is there anything else?"

Jason nodded. "The drives on our cruisers use only two focusing nacelles to warp space-time just enough for interplanetary travel. But our interstellar drive will require six to both warp and twist space-time enough to rupture it, creating the wormhole. We can scavenge two from the decommissioned ship. I can build the remaining two in the physics department's mechanical shop."

Rae Anne scowled and turned to Jason.

"Will you have to put your quantum computer aboard the ship for it to control the drive? If we lose it, we'll lose you and all your clones. That would be a disaster."

"Not to worry," Jason replied. "I've already built a working duplicate as a backup. We can install it aboard the starship. It doesn't have the original's huge memory archives, but then, it won't need them."

Ian looked around the room.

"Does anyone have any other concerns?"

Rae Anne offered one last suggestion. "Be sure to include the Shalcerian universal translator program in the ship's quantum computer. And a mobile translator unit. You never know who we might run into out there."

This brought a round of laughter from the group.

Ian smiled. "On that note, I think we can adjourn for lunch. We are about to join the elite group of interstellar species. We'll decommission *Columbia* for parts. *Curie* will become humanity's first starship."

As people stood to leave, Ian rapped the table loudly. Everyone stopped and turned toward him.

"You all need to understand one thing. *Curie* will be our only such ship. So long as we're defending Haven and half of humanity from Sam Durban and his crowd, we can't afford to reduce our small fleet any further."

Chapter 3

Venus

Denali's Jason-07 transmitted the Venus coordinate information to the Jason network even before *Denali* arrived in Sydney. He also kept the other clones apprised of Sam's actions, so Jason-03 aboard *Liberty* was able to report Durban's movements directly to Ian. Knowing when *Azov* left Earth for Venus, Ian put together his plan for defending the plasticore facility. He immediately assigned *Freedom* and *Darwin* to join him to take on *Azov* when it reached Venus.

Meanwhile, Durban's *Azov* settled into Venus-orbit high above the planet's swirling sulfur-laden clouds, directly over the fourth coordinate Captain Abrams reported. On *Azov's* bridge, seven technicians huddled around the consoles monitoring the ship's sensors. Visual observations were useless due to the dense water and sulfuric acid clouds blanketing the entire planet. Thermal imaging was also impossible. Besides the hellish temperature, the surface was covered with active volcanoes.

Myra Smythe, *Azov's* Science Officer, leaned forward over her console and frowned. "Captain, I've detected an anomaly. My radar sensors are reflecting off something large and metallic on the surface."

Captain Lemaire approached the radar console. "Feed in the coordinates. We'll drop down and take a look."

"Coordinates are in the navigation system, Sir.'

"Take her down, Lt. Swanson."

"Yes, Sir. Descending from orbit now."

Azov dropped into the thick clouds. Lemaire's eyes were glued to his monitor and console readouts.

Damn. Temp's going through the roof. Zero visibility. This is like dropping into the depths of Hell.

"Is your anomaly still in view, Lt. Smythe?"

"It is, Sir. It has resolved into three separate images, but they're still too fuzzy to make out details."

When *Azov* popped beneath the clouds, a yellow and red sulfur landscape surrounding hundreds of volcanic vents filled the viewports. Active volcanoes spewed prodigious amounts of steam and sulfur ash a thousand meters into the atmosphere.

"What the hell?" Lt. Smythe gasped.

Before Lemaire could ask for an explanation, two KBP cruisers flanked Azov on both sides. A third descended from above. The bridge com crackled to life.

"Captain Lemaire of the renegade cruiser *Azov*. You have trespassed into Haven territory. It is my lawful duty to take you and your ship into custody. You will allow the two cruisers at your sides to couple onto your ship and tow you to Mayberry Station."

Lemaire slammed a fist onto his console. "Like hell I will." He swiped a switch to his left. "All hands, Red Alert." A chime echoed throughout the ship.

"Swanson, full power up into the belly of the ship topside. Nobody's taking *Azov* anywhere."

Azov smashed into *Liberty*, bouncing Ian's ship upward and onto its tail. The plasticore hulls kept both ships intact and shielded their crews from external forces, but the sound of the impact was deafening.

"Port arms. Can you get a bead on that cruiser below us?"

"Aye, Sir."

"Blast that bastard to oblivion."

Azov fired two torpedoes at *Freedom* from above. Both warheads exploded into a mass of radioactive chaff that burst in all directions off the hull. Ellie turned *Freedom* to take *Azov* head-on and fired two of her own torpedoes. Both hit *Azov* broadside, splashing into dazzling white, red and orange fireworks. But *Azov* remained undamaged, protected by its own plasticore hull.

Meanwhile, *Liberty* took advantage of *Freedom's* diversionary tactic and again took a position above Azov.

Ian's voice crackled through Lemaire's com unit.

"Captain Lemaire. We are equipped with depleted uranium warheads that can penetrate your plasticore hull and destroy your ship. You have no such weapons. Surrender now and you and your crew will survive unharmed.'

"Fuck you," Lemaire growled. "Hit them again, Swanson, then get us out of here."

Azov performed the same battering maneuver as before, but this time Ian anticipated the maneuver and sent *Liberty* downward with full thrust. The two ships collided, but *Liberty's* downward momentum held sway. The collision from above sent *Azov* spinning toward the surface. An experienced crew would have quickly recovered. But the additional seconds *Azov's* crew required gave *Darwin* the opportunity to repeat *Liberty's* strike from above.

Azov now plummeted perilously close to the ground when *Liberty* struck it one last blow. A crash on the surface would not have damaged *Azov* but would have made it possible for the three other cruisers to render it immobile and take it hostage. As chance would have it, the battle took place over a volcano's massive cauldron. *Azov* plunged into the lake of molten sulfur and disappeared beneath its surface. Conditions within the lava exceeded even plasticore's operating limits. *Azov* dissolved into the boiling witches brew of hot magma.

"That didn't have to happen," said Ian to no one in particular.

"One less ship we have to monitor," said Jason-03 from his communications post.

Ian shook his head in resignation. "I had hoped my threat of depleted uranium warheads would have fooled him into surrendering. He must have known I was bluffing. There were at least fifty-five Humans on board who didn't have to die."

He sighed deeply and turned back to his console to radio the other ships.

"Ellie, you come with me to Mayberry Station. Bruce, take *Darwin* down to our plasticore plant. Load up the latest shipment. After you've delivered it to Haven, relieve *Kepler* at Juno. Their crew could use a break and we need to maintain security there for protection against any action Sam might concoct."

The three cruisers rose into the clouds to pursue their respective assignments.

Brussels

Karen was the first participant to arrive onstage at the conference billed as 'Common Sense Regulation of Robotics.' She glanced over the fifteen place-markers arrayed along the inner edge of the crescent-shaped table facing the auditorium. She found her tag on the right-most end, but not before noticing the central position naming Sam Durban as the meeting's moderator.

Strange. The bulletin listed Edgar Bernard as moderator. Why the last-minute change? This may be an opportunity for me to engage with Sam. I've been waiting for a chance to get back at the bastard for humiliating me and not releasing me from prison.

She rounded the table's corner and took her seat just as the other participants began to arrive and shuffle to their assigned places. They represented major AI firms, government regulatory agencies, and citizen activist groups from around the world.

The doors opened at 8:30. A flood of high-level dignitaries and negotiators from a hundred countries flowed into the room. Every seat was taken when the EU President delivered her opening remarks at 9:00.

The agenda listed seven areas of concern. The morning's discussion ranged in temperature from politely civil to very heated, with no general agreement on any issue. The industrialists maintained that their robotics posed no threat, while activists and government officials, responding to constituents' concerns, tried to pinpoint specific issues posing risks to society. By noon, they had addressed only three of the agenda topics.

On several occasions, Karen caught Sam's eye and smiled at him. He called on her twice when she signaled she had a relevant comment. When the meeting adjourned for lunch, she exited the stage behind him and feigned to accidentally bump into him at the elevator.

"Oh! *Excusez moi. Je*…I am so sorree."

"Not at all. Oh, you are Marie Piaf from RMI. I've been looking forward to meeting you, since our companies are competitors. May I call you Marie? You can call me Sam. Can we converse in English?"

"Of course. I studied at MIT and Stanford." Karen maintained the French accent she had assumed as part of her disguise.

"Would you care to join me for lunch, Marie?"

Karen gave Sam her most innocent smile. *The fish takes the bait.*

"Ah, but that would be *magnifique*."

"Excellent. I have a favorite restaurant not far from here. We'll have plenty of time to eat before we need to be back for the afternoon session. I've been following your company's progress. You've made impressive gains in a very short time."

Much more than you think.

At street level, Sam hailed an autonomous cab. He helped Karen into her seat, then strolled around to the other side, stepped in, and closed the bubble roof around them.

"Pasta Divina," he commanded.

The cab pressed its way into the busy thoroughfare.

"I hope you like Italian cuisine."

"Mais oui."

"Meeting you here is quite a coincidence. I wasn't planning on coming. I was packing for a two-day trip to Venus when they called me to fill in for Bernard. No one knows how he came down with Ebola, but it landed him in intensive care in Miami. The organizers were desperate for a substitute moderator."

"It is good your schedule had the flexibility, no?"

"It may have saved my life. *Azov*, the Venus ship, disappeared yesterday without a trace. I heard about it on my way here from Sydney."

What a shame. The perfect chance for the world to be of rid you.

"I have heard nothing on the news about a missing ship."

"It was a private flight on a secret mission for my company. We're hoping it's a communication glitch or temporary malfunction. I've sent two ships to see if we can find her."

Throughout their lunch, Karen continued her charade, toying with Sam's efforts to impress her. She barely touched her wine, allowing Sam to finish their carafe of Sauvignon Blanc.

Hmm. Still the heavy drinker, making my job all the easier.

On their return to the conference, they agreed to meet again for dinner.

"But this should be your choice," said Sam. "On me, of course," he added.

"The restaurant in my hotel has a reputation *excellente*. Four stars. Much deserved. We may meet there, um…, say, two hours after the meeting ends this afternoon?"

Sam agreed, a little too anxiously in Karen's mind.

Karen gave him the name of her hotel and the restaurant before they parted.

This is worth the pain I suffered under the knives of those Chinese surgeons. Sam, old buddy, you have no idea what you are in for.

The restaurant rendezvous that evening went well, with the two technology entrepreneurs rehashing several of the afternoon's discussions. They agreed that regulation would be a costly burden to their companies and a detriment to progress in the robotics arena.

"It would be in both our interests to form a lobbying group to fight regulation," said Sam, carving into his pink slab of prime rib with gusto.

Karen toyed with her shrimp linguini, picking out select morsels of shrimp. "This we can do. A world-wide, umm, how you say it, a PR campaign. A world-wide PR campaign to sell the benefits of robotics to gain public support."

They also discussed their personal histories. Karen, of course, was quite familiar with Sam's life except for his most recent exploits. She, on the other hand, relished dishing out the fake backstory the Chinese Ministry of Security had provided her.

Over tiramisu and coffee, Karen invited Sam to her room for a nightcap, the kind of invitation Sam never turned down. They might have been mistaken for best friends, laughing as they entered the elevator for Karen's suite on the top floor. Sam put his arm around Karen's waist when the elevator doors opened and left it there as they walked down the corridor to her room.

The black widow leads her unsuspecting prey to his doom.

The keycard in Karen's purse opened the door and she led Sam into her suite. "Take off your jacket, Sam. Make yourself at home while I change into something more comfortable." She gestured to the sofa as she headed for the bedroom. "Light the fireplace if you like. And pour yourself a drink."

A few drinks here after what you consumed downstairs, and I'll see what information I can weasel out of you.

Karen took her time, allowing Sam to fantasize about where the evening might lead. When she appeared, she was wearing a floor-length lavender silk gown with a plunging neckline. She smiled inwardly at the faint choking sound Sam made swallowing his bourbon when he saw her come into the room.

Karen poured herself a half glass of pinot noir and swirled it beneath her nose, inhaling its fruity aroma. "Not the best of wine, I'm afraid."

"Come sit next to me where we can enjoy the fire," said Sam, patting the cushion next to him. "It's artificial LEDs, but it looks almost authentic."

Karen sat beside him and pressed into his arm. "I enjoy a relaxing moment like this after a hard day," she said.

"Well, not too hard. Mostly jawboning and waiting to be heard. Too much sitting." He sipped his bourbon.

Karen swirled her wine. "Unfortunately, I've been making decisions for one of my engineering groups throughout the day. Glad you didn't notice."

"You hid your texting quite well. One of your projects having difficulties?"

Now to feed him some meaningless bullshit and see where it leads.

"We're building a robotic device to repair undersea cables. But achieving precise manipulation with ocean currents and seafloor pressures is proving to be a challenge."

Sam sauntered unsteadily to the bar and poured himself another drink. "Precision control is always a problem, isn't it." He returned to the sofa and plopped next to Karen. "I have a group working on automating the cleaning and restoration of osmosis membranes in desalination plants. The slightest wrong move can destroy a five-thousand-dollar filter."

Tell me more. I'm all ears.

"That sounds interesting, Sam. Is there really a market for something like that?" Karen snuggled closer.

With Karen's subtle prompting, Sam spent the next fifteen minutes drunkenly blabbing details about one of Durban Robotics' most confidential projects. When he finally ran out of things to say, he leaned over and kissed Karen's cheek. "You are ravishing, my dear. We could make up for today's inactivity if you are so inclined."

Karen closed her eyes and tilted her head back. "Give me a few minutes. My stomach is unsettled. Something about the shrimp, maybe."

Karen inhaled deeply. Suddenly she jumped to her feet and rushed to the bathroom with her hand covering her mouth. After slamming the door closed, she turned on the faucet full blast and began expressing her best rendition of a nauseous person throwing up. She flushed the toilet a couple of times.

Eventually she opened the door and shuffled into the living room clutching a wet washcloth over her mouth with her right hand, a wet towel draped over her shoulder.

"Is there anything I can get for you," asked Sam, rising from the sofa.

"*Merci, mais non.* I feel terrible. Such cramps. Food poisoning. They will hear about this in the morning. All I can do now is curl up and suffer through this. I am so sorry to spoil a wonderful evening."

"It has been a fine evening," Sam offered. "We must get together again, sometime soon."

She shuffled across the room, gagging into the washcloth, doubled over with her left arm across her stomach as if in pain, and opened the door to the hallway.

"Good night, Sam."

"Good night, Marie. I hope you are feeling better soon. I'll call in the morning."

Karen closed the door behind Sam and threw herself onto the sofa, laughing.

An Academy Award performance if I do say so myself. A modern-day Mata Hari. Or maybe Marlene Dietrich or Audrey Hepburn. I will destroy Durban Robotics and bring Sam Durban to his knees.

Chapter 4

Mayberry Station

KBP cruisers *Columbia* and *Curie* rested beside each other on landing pads outside Mayberry Station on Luna's far side. Large rectangular panels had been removed from the mid-section of both ships' hulls and set on the tarmac beside each ship. The plasticore arches gleamed in the harsh sunlight.

Sashi Makino joined Rae Anne, Ian, Jason-0, and Bev, all clustered at the Terminal Habitat's windows, watching a crane hoist a huge silver sphere from *Columbia*'s innards into the black void. She peered over Rae Anne's shoulder to get a better look.

That operation looks as complicated as our radio telescope.

"Is there enough room in *Curie* for that thing?" she asked. "What is it, anyway?"

"That sphere they're working on now contains *Columbia*'s gravity bottle," Jason answered. "Once it's in place, they'll install the two additional nuclear reactors *Curie* will need for the interstellar drive. Half of *Curie*'s cargo bay has been allocated to Engineering to make room for the additional reactors."

Once the sphere was clear of the ship, the crane inched it over *Curie*'s cavity and slowly lowered it onto that ship's deck. A dozen workers in white EVA suits clustered around the ship, waving signals to the crane operator to direct the sphere into place.

"Dayton's got the best seat in the house," Rae Anne noted.

Bev laughed. "He insisted on joining the crew in the crane cab. He's been monitoring this project like a mother hen."

"I've noticed you giving it a lot of attention as well," said Ian.

"That's true." Bev gave a nervous laugh. "This is our baby."

"*Columbia* looks like a gutted fish," said Sashi, gesturing at the piles of equipment lining *Columbia*'s pad. "But I only see one reactor. Isn't that it, the dome-capped cylinder next to *Columbia*?"

"Yes, that's the one we're appropriating for the *Curie,*" said Jason. "The other one is still on Haven. I haven't finished building it yet, but I have three clones working on it as we speak."

A shiver slithered through Sashi's spine. She leaned closer to the window and frowned with concern. "You assured us there is no possibility of an explosion when you combine the two gravity bottles with their black holes. But what's the chance a black hole will spill out when you open the containers for the transfer? If one does, what risk would it pose for my station?"

"None whatsoever," said Bev. "The gravity bottles are gravitic force-fields surrounding their micro black holes. Moving the black holes involves adjusting the superconducting magnets that produce the force fields so the fields change their shape. Our simulations show that when the two force fields overlap, the magnetic fields can be flipped, causing the gravitic fields to merge and create a single container."

Sashi shook her head and laughed nervously. "I'm glad you have all this figured out."

At least I hope you do!

"All I can say is this better work," said Ian. "If it doesn't, we'll be out two ships."

Rae Anne jabbed Ian's arm. "It's going to work. And I'm going to see to it that it does."

Ian turned sharply toward Rae Anne. "What do you mean?"

"I've decided to join Jason on *Curie's* maiden voyage."

"You'll do nothing of the kind. We decided the first attempt at wormhole creation would be handled autonomously, with a Jason at the controls."

Sashi stepped back, unused to seeing Ian and Rae Anne in conflict.

"The committee vote was tied," Rae Anne said. "And my vote determined the outcome. I've changed my vote, so now the majority rules in favor of having a Human present as well."

Ian gently grasped Rae Anne's shoulders. "You can't do that. I can't risk losing you."

She shook herself free and stepped back, arms akimbo. "I can do it, and I will. We'll be back before you have a chance to miss me."

Bev put her hand on Rae Anne's shoulder. "I'm personally glad to hear you say that, Rae Anne. I've felt the need for a Human aboard the *Curie* all along."

Ian's face was crestfallen. He turned back to the window in silence.

"I didn't have a vote," said Jason. "But it will be nice to have the company, even if I am speaking for one of my clones."

Juno Colony on Ganymede

Fae Jackson (they, them), Juno's mayor, greeted Sam at Juno's Terminal Habitat when the snake's airlock opened. Sam had been to Juno only once before. He was here now on Fae's invitation. Fae had insisted he pay Juno a visit in person to be certain he understood what they had to say to him. It was well known that his ego often directed him to hear only what he chose to hear and to give everything else a positive spin—positive for him, that is.

Fae had been in charge of Juno from its inception. They had held one of the key administrative positions under Rae Anne on Haven when the Council decided to pursue the Juno project. They were the Council's first choice to serve as Juno's administrator. From the moment they arrived on Ganymede, Juno's welfare became their first and only priority.

When it became clear that Sam's coup would upend Rae Anne's government on Haven, Fae forged an alliance with Sam and his insurgency. But the devil is in the details, and the consequences for Juno had not been all that favorable.

Fae led Sam to their office in the neighboring habitat. The room was decorated with a variety of objects to remind them of their native home in Africa. An ancient spear and elaborately decorated wooden shield hung behind their desk. A framed painting of the African savanna with elephants, giraffes, and zebras filled one wall. Even the furniture coverings suggested native African origins.

Fae's aide quickly provided Fae and Sam with their requested drinks and stepped back into the reception area through the nanoscreen, leaving the two alone.

Fae gave Sam an appraising look as they sipped hot chocolate from a steaming mug. Sam fidgeted in his seat across the desk from them, swirling the golden-brown whiskey in his glass.

If Sam's feeling uncomfortable now, just wait.

"This is quite a setup you have here, Fae," Sam said, taking a sip of whiskey. "When we landed, I counted two dozen habitats. I didn't realize how large Juno has grown."

"We actually have thirty-one habitats. We were growing steadily until you took over on Haven. When you cut shipments to one per week and forced us to ration food, water, and other essentials, growth came to a halt. We've been hanging on by sheer determination ever since." Fae deliberately put a sharp edge to their voice.

"I had a lot of things going on, Fae. Still do. Loyalist cruisers are constantly harassing my ships. Everything I bring to you now comes from Earth. The Mars colonies are no help. They're barely self-sufficient."

He's still treating us like stepchildren.

Fae's voice became more strident. "Before you took charge, Haven delivered supplies every two days. We could count on their support. Lately, some weeks we've had to beg you to send supplies."

"You don't appreciate how expensive it is to keep your colony going. Haven could support you with surplus from their aquaponics facilities and the water it collects from Saturn's rings. Now, I have to buy everything on Earth, even water. But be patient. Things will change when I retake Haven."

Fat chance of that ever happening.

"Supplies are just one issue, Sam. The other is our disappointment regarding your promise to construct a transparent dome over our city. We're still living like moles inside these interconnected habitats. The question is, how do you intend to make good on your promise now?"

"I've sent you at least four reports showing the progress my engineers are making. Besides, the three Mars colonies have priority. As I said, you need to be patient."

Meanwhile, the patient patient dies before reaching the operating table.

Fae banged their mug on the table and leaned forward. They stared at Sam, brows furrowed.

If only I had laser eyes, I'd burn you to a crisp.

"I've checked with Tony Armado on Nova Prima. Same story there. Nothing but promises and excuses. Do you know what I think? I think your blasted engineers haven't a clue about building nanoplast domes. I think you're just blowing wind and I'm tired of the stench."

Sam's face turned crimson. His jaw clenched. The knuckles around his glass turned white.

Sam's losing it. I should call Security.

Fae brushed their finger across an icon on their tablet.

Sam took a deep breath and exhaled. "You don't understand the complexity of the challenge," he growled. "Haven's dome was built by alien engineers with alien equipment. We have to build the equipment before we can do anything else."

"You're bluffing. Rumor has it you lost *Azov* looking for that pot of gold on Venus. I've been in touch with the Loyalists. They're happy to resume ferry shipments every other day. I trust them when they say they have the technology and skills to erect a dome over Juno within the year. Since the Mars colonies are under your control, the Loyalists can give Juno top priority."

Sam sputtered and tried to interrupt, but Fae continued.

"We're seceding from your Liberation League, Sam. From here on out, our support goes to Haven and the Loyalists. They are no longer treating us like a backwater outpost. That may be the one good thing your attempted coup accomplished for us."

Sam abruptly stood and leaned over the desk on clenched fists. Fae continued their face-off without wavering as two security officers burst through the nanoscreen.

Fae stood, giving Sam a withering look. "Take Mr. Durban to the Terminal Habitat. See that he boards his ship without delay."

One guard gestured toward the door while the other stepped next to Sam, brushing his arm.

"You'll regret this, Fae Jackson," Sam growled venomously. "When I take back Haven, you'll see just what a backwater outpost really feels like."

Ten minutes later, the *Shackleton* lifted off. Within minutes, two other cruisers appeared beside it, as if escorting it away from the colony. A third Loyalist ship, *Liberty,* settled on the launch pad, loaded with supplies from Haven.

The snake worked its way from the terminal and connected to *Liberty*'s airlock. Rae Anne met Fae midway through the tunnel and offered her right hand, but Fae reached both arms out for a hug.

"That's the reassurance I needed," Fae said, still shaking from their confrontation with Sam.

"Come with me to *Liberty*'s conference room. We have the documents for you to sign to finalize your treaty with us. Now that my focus is no longer on governing Haven, I'm beginning to appreciate all you've done here. Given time, Juno could become another Haven."

Fae and Rae Anne locked arms and entered the ship. In the conference room, a scale model of Juno's interconnected habitats occupied the center of the table. A nanoplast dome surrounded the model. The entire display looked like an old-fashioned snow globe without the snow.

"As Haven's officially appointed Ambassador at Large, I can tell you that Haven will begin constructing your dome within the month. Jason has worked out all the technical details in his lab. Haven has a sufficient stockpile of gravitolite and rare earth minerals to make your dome a reality."

Fae closed their eyes. They tried to imagine stepping outside their habitat without a space suit, breathing pure air, strolling beneath live trees, hearing birdsong, and gazing upward at the mammoth hulk of Jupiter.

At last! Juno is finally going to get its dome!

Chapter 5

Beijing

Karen settled into the plush chair in Ambassador Jin Lei's reception area and yawned. Jin Lei booked her flight from Paris on a French commercial carrier to minimize attention to the RMI-Chinese connection. The flight arrived in Beijing just after midnight.

Four hours of sleep after flying halfway around the world, and I need to be on top of my game. Good luck with that. Shit, I must look terrible.

She yawned again and brushed her right hand to her tablet satchel to reassure herself for the hundredth time that she hadn't left it in her hotel suite.

The receptionist stood and walked across the room to where Karen was sitting.

"Miss Piaf, the ambassador will see you now," she said in perfect English. "I'm told you speak English, and I know nothing of French."

"Ah, but French is the most beautiful language in the world. Except perhaps for Mandarin." Karen smiled at the young woman. "It is the language for lovers, you know."

The aide laughed. "Then I should indeed learn French. Please, follow me."

She led Karen to the wooden double doors leading to Jin Lei's office and drew one open so Karen could step through, then softly closed it behind her.

Jin Lei looked up and motioned Karen to a chair beside his massive desk. Several folders spread across the desk in an orderly arrangement. Three phones and a laptop were arrayed in front of the ambassador. On the wall behind his chair hung the mandatory life-size portrait of the Party Chairman.

"Thank you for coming on such short notice, Karen," he said while she sat. She gave Jin Lei the best smile she could manage.

As if I had any choice.

"I'm glad to be here, Lei. We've made wonderful progress since you visited our new offices and toured the plant."

"I'm told RMI is already making a profit in a little over three years. No doubt due in large part to your former expertise in the industry. And we are beginning to take market share from Durban Robotics."

"That's true. Our rapid growth is no surprise since we're starting from scratch. But eating into Durban's monopoly speaks to the quality of our products and our aggressive marketing. Things will only get better as time goes on."

"Good. I hope you're right."

"On the flight over I put together a slide presentation showing the additions to our manufacturing facilities. I have another showing our new product line and our marketing strategy for it."

"Give them to my assistant on a mempin. I'll have a subordinate look them over later. I have other business—sensitive business—to discuss with you."

Karen felt a chill trickle down her spine.

Jin Lei picked up the folder nearest Karen and handed her the file. He waited while Karen opened it and began flipping through several enlarged photographs.

Oh, shit.

The photographs documented her several encounters with Sam, starting with Brussels: They included images of them together in restaurant settings, in various hotel lobbies, and a handful showing them in sexual engagement.

"There are others as well. You have kept our operatives very busy these past six months."

Bastards!

Karen's stomach knotted. She swallowed hard to remove the bile in her throat. Her hands trembled as she closed the folder and replaced it on Jin Lei's desk.

"You shouldn't be surprised. We watch over our assets with great vigilance. My superiors are concerned about your relationship with our staunchest competitor. We've known from the start that the two of you had an intimate relationship before your unfortunate incident on Haven. We find it odd that you would rekindle the affair. Particularly considering the risk of revealing your identity. What do you have to say for yourself?"

Karen swallowed again and took a deep breath.

"This isn't what it seems. I'm out to destroy Durban Robotics by whatever means necessary. Sam has two weaknesses. He thinks he's a stud, and he overindulges in alcohol. I preoccupy his lubricated mind with the promise of sex and tease him into revealing inside information we can use to our advantage. For example, our newest product line automating osmosis membrane rejuvenation in desalination plants was inspired by my first encounter with Sam in Brussels. I subsequently learned who his clients were. So, we not only beat him to the market, but we undercut his bids by a third."

"Interesting." Lei steepled his hands and frowned. "I find it remarkable that the CEO of a company would indulge confidential information to a competitor, let alone with enough detailed information to duplicate a product line."

"Sam's so full of himself, he thinks he's indestructible. Alcohol does funny things to his brain. When he wakes up in the morning, he has no recollection of anything from the night before. He can't even remember what he had for dinner."

"Hmm. So, you're suggesting we encourage these romantic trysts?"

Romantic? If he only knew how I despised that son of a bitch.

"Trust me, there is nothing romantic about my relationship with Sam. It's all business. There's a lot more I can learn from him that will benefit RMI. He turned his back on me when I needed help, then stole my company. He refused to spring me from prison when he took control of Haven. My overriding goal is to crush Durban Robotics and take Sam down with it.

"And my 'trysts,' as you call them, are just the tip of the iceberg. I have two of Sam's engineers on our payroll, and I'm currently courting a third. When Sam reveals to me where to mine for information, I request specific documents, specifications, program algorithms, anything I can get. All that data gives our RMI engineers a leg up. Plus, our engineers see any problems Sam's people are having through fresh eyes."

"Very well. That should satisfy my superiors. At least for now. But be particularly careful not to blow your cover. We've invested heavily in you."

"Of course. And there's one other thing. His company is spending a fortune on developing a working android. They are no closer to having a working prototype than we are."

"Interesting you should bring that up." Jin Lei reached over and handed Karen a different folder. "Professor Jason has yet to make an appearance in our research facility."

Karen took the folder and set it in her lap. "I did go to Haven and tried to convince him to pay us a visit. He turned me down flat. I even offered him top billing to speak at a conference or give a seminar. Academics usually jump at opportunities like that. But he turned me down cold."

"If persuasion won't work, we'll have to be more forceful. Once we have him at our plant, we can see that he stays. That folder contains additional information on him, but it's still sketchy."

"Are you suggesting we kidnap him?"

"I am suggesting *you* figure out how to get him here. There can be no direct Chinese involvement. We know from your history you have certain contacts capable of carrying this out."

"But those contacts are twenty years old. A few are dead. Some are in prison."

"That's not my concern. It's your job to get Professor Jason here by whatever means necessary. His knowledge will significantly advance our efforts to build a commercially viable android."

Karen rubbed her cheek thoughtfully. "This could be very expensive."

"There are five cards inside that folder, each to a different untraceable bank account. You may swipe them with this phone to see your balances and manage your expenses."

Jin Lei handed her one of the phones next to his laptop.

"Do not use this phone for any other purpose."

Karen slipped the phone and folder into her tablet satchel.

"Your flight back to Paris leaves in three hours. We've collected your things at the hotel. They are in the cab waiting downstairs. When you show up at your office tomorrow morning, no one should know you spent your weekend in Beijing."

More like spent my weekend sandwiched coach class in an overcrowded plane.

Jin Lei stood and gestured toward the door. Karen rose and managed a grim smile.

"This will be my top priority. I'll get on it as soon as I get back to Paris."

"Good. Don't let us down. We need Professor Jason."

Karen left the building feeling she had been sucker punched. The promised cab was waiting at the curb with her travel bag on the backseat. She slipped in beside it, and the cab pulled into the smoggy traffic.

I'll need to renew some old acquaintances to put together the right team for this job. At least they won't reveal my identity to anyone. But they will be surprised to hear from Karen Sanders after all these years.

Mayberry Station

Rae Anne accompanied Sashi Makino as they strolled down the corridor leading to Sashi's office. With *Curie*'s major overhaul winding down, the bustle throughout the colony was a fraction of what Rae Anne experienced on her visit eighteen months earlier. Dry-dock testing of the quantum computer programs controlling *Curie*'s propulsion system was the only item remaining on the checklist.

Sashi glanced briefly at Rae Anne. "When you were here before, you insisted on joining Jason for *Curie*'s maiden interstellar trip. Do you still plan on going?"

"Absolutely. Nothing could draw me away from being on that bridge."

"I admire your courage. Despite Jason's reassurances, I believe there's a great deal of risk. If it were me, I'd let the androids do their thing. Better to risk a machine than a Human."

Whoa! This needs addressing here and now.

Rae Anne gently took Sashi's arm, tugging her to a halt, and turned to face her.

"The Jasons are a fully sentient species, Sashi. They are different from us, sure, but far less so than the Shalcerians. They share our history and our cultural experience. To refer to them as machines is a discredit to who they've become."

Sashi shook her head. "I don't see it that way. Without their quantum computer, they're useless. Besides, they can't have feelings."

"That's not true. I've been intimately involved in Jason's development since 2037. Twenty-six years. Since Jason began building clones of himself, I've witnessed them express signs of concern for each other's welfare and show sympathy for a Human's wellbeing. They've reached a sufficient level of sentience to be classified as an independent, intelligent species.

"Regarding their quantum computer, for them it's the equivalent of your brain. How useful would you be if we scooped your brain out of your skull?"

Sashi pursed her lips. "Yuk. Not a pleasant image. But your point is well taken. I haven't had the opportunity to spend much time with them. I would love to observe this behavior firsthand. We could certainly make good use of one here at the station. Our massive radio telescope is finished and will soon be online. A Jason would be an incredible assistant for our astronomers."

"Do you think they would accept him as a credible being rather than just another computer application for their projects?"

"That might be a problem at first. Jason would have to prove himself. But if we prepare them to be on the lookout for signs of sentience and conscious behavior, they'll draw their own conclusions. Same for me. If he is sentient, in time, he would be accepted for what, or who, he is."

"I'll see what I can do. Jason's been building additional clones. Now that we have regained control of Haven, we can assign them more widely throughout Sol System. Working here with your telescope would be a perfect fit."

They continued down the corridor as Sashi said, "Incidentally, with your help, you and Jason will have top billing when our telescope comes online."

"Oh? How so?"

"When *Curie* launches for the stars, we could watch for the radio wave signature your wormhole generates. The signal should come through loud and clear. This would be the first time radio wave data from a wormhole is correlated with data from gravity wave telescopes."

"I'm flattered. The largest radio telescope in the world keeping an eye on us. Your observations could lead to new discoveries."

"Only one problem," said Sashi. "Our telescope is stationary. You will have to time your launch to match when the moon has the telescope pointing your direction."

"We can do that. Adjusting where we launch from will help. Meantime, I'll see what I can do about getting you a Jason before we leave."

They turned into Sashi's office and she gestured to the sofa. Rae Anne accepted her offer of tea.

"On a different note," said Rae Anne, stirring the liquid in her mug, "I'm taking orders for nanoplast domes. Mayberry Station is long overdue. My team has completed work on Juno's dome. Are they ever happy! They can't stop gawking at Jupiter's mammoth globe dominating their sky."

"I can imagine. I couldn't stop gazing at Saturn when I visited Haven. Unfortunately, our view here isn't so spectacular. We wouldn't even have Earth to look at."

"Oh, Sashi! When was the last time you gazed up at the Milky Way streaming across the unobstructed black depths of infinity? You definitely need that dome."

Sashi laughed. "You're right. Way too many years being a gopher."

"We can build a dome over Mayberry Station. We have enough refined gravitolite. Our crew is experienced and ready to go."

Chapter 6

Paris

Karen stirred her coffee as she gazed out the rain-streaked window of a small coffee house in a northeast Paris suburb. An autonomous cab pulled up to the curb and a short, stocky man stepped out, holding his cap against the gusting wind. His upper arms bulged against his light jacket's fabric.

There's a weightlifter if I ever saw one.

The cab pulled ahead and parked in a vacant spot. The man quickly entered the café and glanced around the room. Three tables were occupied with couples engaged in serious conversation. Karen was the only lone occupant. He approached her table.

"Michelle Bravard?" he inquired, smiling, eyebrows raised. He removed his cap and swiped it against his trousers, then sat down in response to Karen's nod.

"You are Peter Morgan?"

"In person." Peter reached across the table and they shook hands.

"I haven't much time," he said. "I had to juggle things around to work in this meeting. So, what can I do for you?"

Karen was taken aback by Peter's abrupt demeanor. She preferred to spend time over coffee or beer to learn more about her clandestine contractors. She wanted to feel she could trust the person she hired to carry out her demands with discretion.

"You are in a hurry. A pity. Well, my project boils down to this. I need to get a person on Haven back to Earth…" She paused in response to Peter's furrowed brow. "Haven, you know, that city orbiting Saturn."

Noting his look of recognition, she resumed. "I need to have that person working for me, here in France. I've tried to convince him to leave Haven, but he refuses. So, I need someone, you, to bring him here. Once he's here and sees my operation, I have no doubt he'll be glad he came."

"You're talking about an abduction and kidnapping."

"Well…"

"Otherwise, you wouldn't be talking to me. How physical can we get with this person?"

"Oh, I want him entirely intact. No damage."

"I'll need to hire a couple guys and pay off some people to get him here. Do you have a picture? Any personal information I can use?"

Karen shuffled in her purse, fumbling for a photograph.

I wish I didn't have to wear these damn gloves all the time.

"Here's a shot of him on the Municipal Building steps, standing behind the former mayor."

She handed the photo to Peter. He scrutinized the image.

"Scrawny fellow. Looks like the nerdy type." He rubbed his chin. "Where does he work?"

"He's a professor at Haven University. Goes by Jason. He has a lab on the seventh floor of the university's physics building."

"So, he is a nerd. Should be easy. But I can't guarantee he won't need to be bandaged up a bit when I deliver him."

Karen laughed and shook her head.

"Don't underestimate him by his looks. For all we know he could be a karate black belt."

"As far as you know. Your lack of confidence isn't very encouraging. My fee is doubled. I'll go in with four guys just to make sure we keep on top of the situation."

"Four men to handle one 'scrawny' professor?"

Peter glared at Karen. "And I want to be paid in full no matter what condition this guy is in when I deliver."

"I'm good with your revised fee, but only if Professor Jason is brought to me in good shape. I'll pay a third now, a third on delivery, and the last third contingent on the shape he's in."

After a few more exchanges, Peter rose and handed Karen a slip of paper with EFT routing information to a bank on Cypress.

"Remember, be gentle with him," Karen admonished as he left the table.

Sol System, Aboard *Liberty*

Humanity's first starship, the *Curie,* lifted from its berth at Mayberry Station and rotated 78.3 degrees to starboard, aligning itself with a direct course for Epsilon Eridani, 10.5 lightyears away. It whisked into the star-studded black void to its launch site beyond Saturn's orbit, some five hours away. The gravitational distortion in space-time accompanying wormhole creation required interstellar launches to take place well clear of other bodies.

Liberty and *Freedom* accompanied *Curie* for the first three hours to provide insurance against an attack by a Liberation League ship. But Ian also wanted to stay as close to Rae Anne as long as possible. Outwardly, he displayed confidence in the mission's success. But his gut was tied in knots. He hadn't slept well for over a week. When shaving that morning, he was surprised at how haggard he looked.

This must be how someone feels when a loved one heads off to war. Hoping for the best. Fearing the worst.

The comlink on *Liberty*'s bridge came to life.

"Captain MacIntyre on *Freedom* requesting secure communication," Jason-03 reported from his station at the com console.

"Thank you, Jason. I'll take it in Ops. Tania, you have the bridge."

Ian stepped through the nanoscreen and into the small room adjacent to the bridge. He activated the secure com console in the corner of the room.

"What's up, Ellie?"

"Ian, I just wanted to tell you everything will be all right. I'm on pins-and-needles myself, so I know how worried you must be for Rae Anne's safety."

If she only knew.

"Thank you for your concern. You're right. I haven't felt this way since Durban threw Rae Anne in prison and we lost track of her. I can't stand the thought that something could go wrong."

"All of Jason's simulations tell us otherwise. When has he ever been wrong?"

There's always a first time.

"You're right, Ellie. But I still wish she hadn't insisted on going."

"Rae Anne is exactly where she wants to be. She wouldn't be happy doing anything else. We're nearing Saturn's orbit. I'll sign off so you can wish your honey good luck. MacIntyre out."

Ian tapped an icon on the screen.

"*Liberty* to *Curie*. Are you free, Rae Anne?"

"Oh, hi, Ian. Jason's been having me check a slew of numbers on our gravity-focusing nacelle sensors. All six need to be perfectly aligned or god knows where we'll end up. A good thing, too. I had to tweak one of them. Jason says we'd have only been half a lightyear off at our destination, but still…"

"Rae Anne, I love you. Be careful. This is a first. Don't take any chances."

"Oh, Ian, you sound so worried." Rae Anne's voice broke. "I love you, too. I'll be back before you know it. The plan calls for a day or two to navigate through the Eridani system to learn all we can, then come right home. We'll be fine."

"Then, goodbye, sweet love. Good luck. Even for just two days, I'll miss you more than you can know."

"You are a sweetheart, Ian. See you soon. 'Bye. Chavez out."

The link went dead. A chill swept through Ian's spine. His eyes moistened, accompanied by a lump in his throat.

Please, please come back safely.

✦

Sol System, Aboard *Curie*

The launch countdown reverberated through *Curie's* bridge. Rae Anne occupied the captain's chair, while Jason-11 sat beside her at the navigator console. An array of monitors and readouts, dials and switches spread out before them.

"Do Ian and Ellie make sense of all this?" she asked with bewilderment.

"With hundreds of hours training and years of experience, yes, they do."

Rae Anne shook her head and put her finger on a display readout. "This reminds me of a kaleidoscope display. What's it for?"

"Sorry, Rae Anne, too busy keeping everything together for our launch. Remember, I'm filling in for an entire bridge crew. Ask me again later."

Rae Anne sighed and sat back in her chair.

He's right, of course. I mustn't be a distraction.

But after a few minutes, her excitement got the better of her.

"This is almost like old times, Jason. The two of us traveling billions of kilometers from home, forging a path for others to follow."

"Oh, you mean your trip to Saturn years ago. Jason-0 downloaded that part of his archives into my memory before we left Mayberry Station. He thought it might come in handy."

"So, you didn't have them before?"

"No, there's a lot in Jason-0's database we clones don't have access to. But now that I have these files, I'm finding them very interesting. Did you really perform an emergency appendectomy in space?"

Rae Anne laughed. "Yes, I really did. That was very traumatic."

"But you can laugh about it now. Fascinating. Now allow me to concentrate on our launch. Please."

Thirty minutes passed in silence, save for the countdown reminders. Rae Anne found it impossible to relax. Her heart pounded in her chest double time. The arm rests were slick with sweat from her palms.

Remember, you asked for this.

She forced herself to breathe deeply while gazing at her monitor, inky black and filled with stars.

7...6...5...

For a moment she envied Jason. Anxiety wasn't an issue for an android. The experiment would either work or it wouldn't. If he should wink out of existence, there were other Jasons to take his place on the next attempt.

4...3...2...

The cabin floor began to throb, with vibrations occurring at ever greater intensity. The third fusion reactor came online and was now tweaking the black holes' quantum attributes, coaxing them into a quantum entanglement to rend the space-time fabric and create a wormhole.

1...0

The stars ahead elongated and rotated in a weird spiral motion. They coalesced into a blur that became more intense as their rotation accelerated. Within seconds, they morphed into a brilliant blue-white disk.

The star disk abruptly ruptured, revealing a growing black spot fringed with red and orange in the radiating disk's center. The hole rapidly expanded, with the iridescent halo mixing into a deep purple. The hole, blacker than any black Humans have ever experienced, grew larger until it dwarfed the ship.

With a sudden lurch, *Curie* plunged into the abyss. For a moment, time ceased to exist. Rae Anne felt suspended between life and death.

In the next instant, everything returned to normal. Star-studded space again filled Rae Anne's monitor. The LED readouts across the panel beneath the viewscreen were all green. But *Curie* was light years away from Earth.

Rae Anne breathed a sigh of relief.

It's over. It worked. We made it.

"That was exactly like *Avenger*'s wormhole transit from years ago, Jason. Did you notice any differences from your data archives?"

Rae Anne looked over to Jason.

Oh, NO! Mierda!

Jason slumped limply to the side over the chair's arm. His head hung listlessly beside his right arm which stretched down to the floor.

She swung from her chair and positioned his body upright.

"Jason? Jason, what's wrong? Talk to me!" she screamed.

There was no response.

Curie began its program to slow to one-tenth lightspeed and perform a 180 by swinging around Epsilon Eridani, the intended destination red dwarf. Multiple sensors aboard the ship would record a vast amount of information about the star system in the process. Once the ship was aimed at Sol, it was to execute a second wormhole jump to return home.

Leaving Jason, Rae Anne turned her attention to the console. The 360-degree monitor showed no star brilliant enough to be a nearby sun.

Oh, my god. Epsilon Eridani is nowhere in sight. We're lost in space and Jason's not responding. I'm in deep shit.

Chapter 7

Haven

The conference room in the Haven University Physics Building was filled with scientists and engineers who had brought the Ad Astra project to the point of wormhole creation. They all witnessed the video feed from drones in *Curie's* vicinity recording the fifteen-second visual display when the wormhole formed. They watched *Curie* suddenly vanish, along with the wormhole. They also noted the gravity-wave signature that accompanied the wormhole transit. It arrived three hours after the event, at the same time as the video feeds.

The room erupted in cheers, clapping, shoulder nudging and tears. Bottles of Haven's best wine were passed around. This was a joyous occasion, the culmination of years of research.

"What do you think, Jason?" Bev took another gulp from the half-empty bottle she was holding. "You're the only one here who has witnessed wormhole creation. Did our wormhole match the others you've seen?"

Jason looked thoughtfully at the wall monitor repeating the drone feed for the umpteenth time.

"This event's visual appearance was identical to the one I witnessed twenty years ago with Rae Anne on the bridge of the *Avenger* when it made its transit to Shalkor. But we can't know if our test run was successful until *Curie* returns and we analyze its logs."

"Spoil sport," Bev snarled and blended back into the crowd.

Jason stepped away from the hubbub and stood alone near the door. He pondered the Human tendency to jump to conclusions before having all the facts. It would take *Curie* a minimum of fourteen hours to swing around Epsilon Eridani and jump back to Sol System. Days longer if there were anything of interest to see.

He shook his head and walked into the night. Looking up through Haven's transparent dome he could make out the faint bluish pinprick of Earth rising over Saturn's vast rim. At this point in Haven's orbit, Saturn's rings appeared edge-on, as if an artist had used a straightedge to draw a silver stripe from high overhead down to Haven's horizon.

Jason caught the subway a few blocks from the physics building and rode it from Sector 3 to the city's central plaza in Sector 1. He took the escalator from the station platform and stepped off on the edge of Central Park. Lighted fountains in the park's lake sparkled in ever-changing colors. He walked along the path to the footing that once held Sam Durban's statue.

As Jason approached the slab of granite, a figure emerged from the shadows and walked toward him. When they met, they greeted each other in a perfect semblance of a Human hug. The two individuals could have been mistaken for identical twins.

"Hello, OhTwo. Thank you for waiting."

"I will always wait for you, Jason. Did they make it to Epsilon Eridani? The computer is still treating this project as confidential."

"The launch appeared to be successful. But we won't know if we succeeded until they return, possibly not for a couple of days."

"Humans seem so single-minded in their quest to journey to the stars. Their curiosity will get the better of them yet."

Jason-0 turned to his companion. "Perhaps. But come. Let us sit and watch the fountains. The night is still young."

Jason-0 sighed contentedly. The quantum computer he had built, the brain he shared with his cloned 'children,' hummed away in the confines of its secret location. This brain monitored sensors throughout Sol System, feeding the Jasons a continuous mountain of information. Jason set his gravity-wave sensor to 'alert' status. He would be the first to know when *Curie* returned.

Silicon Valley, California

Karen signaled to the server for two more pints of India pale ale. She nudged the wooden tray with its remaining half pizza toward the young woman sitting across from her. Rosa's Pizza was far enough removed from the Tech Center in Palo Alto that she felt her anonymity was secure. She had chartered an autonomous air taxi to pick up her guest Sophia Accardi several blocks from the Durban Robotics plant where she worked. This was their third clandestine meeting.

"I'm through," Karen said. "The rest is yours."

"I'm good for another slice, Nikki. Can I take the rest home with me? My parents would love pizza for dinner."

That's a useful thing to know.

"Please, it's all yours."

When the server returned with their beers, Karen requested a to-go box. Sophia chose a slice, sprinkled it with red pepper flakes, and took a bite. "Rosa's makes the best vegetarian pizza around."

"So, you live with your parents?"

"Have to." Sophia swallowed and took a swig of beer. "It's gonna take a long time to pay off eight years of higher ed. Stanford's not cheap, even with the internships I had as a graduate student."

Thank goodness for student debt. Makes my job easier.

"But Durban Robotics is known for paying their engineers a competitive salary." Karen cocked her head.

"Maybe most places. But this is Silicon Valley. Plus, I have two aging parents to support. They both need personal care while I'm at work. I'm an only child, so it's all on me."

Karen nodded. "I understand. I faced some of that myself. But my client pays handsomely for any details relating to your projects. She understands you are part of Durban's creative development team."

Sophia's head turned sharply to face Karen. "That information is confidential."

Karen laughed. "Every company's confidential information leaks through security like a sieve. Durban Robotics is no different."

Sophia finished her pizza and took another swallow of beer. Karen was pleased she hadn't rejected her suggestion out of hand.

"So, what does your client do with the confidential information?"

"That's a very good question. She's a philanthropist who wants to see all of humanity benefit from AI and robotics. She's concerned that manufacturers avoid the 'uncanny valley' pitfall."

"Uncanny valley. That's where an android looks too human and creeps everybody out."

"Yes. She wants to be sure that when the first androids appear, they are widely accepted. Staying in the shadows allows her to evaluate developments as they take place without being influenced by anyone with vested interests in the outcome."

"And if she finds something she doesn't like?"

"She has the influence and industry contacts to make subtle suggestions to CEO's who can redirect development. Your involvement will never be divulged. Nor will it ever be apparent that her intervention was prompted with inside information."

Sophia shook her head. "We're not the only company developing a commercial android. What about RMI and Automation Incorporated?"

"I've helped her enlist engineers from both of those companies. Your help here would round out the picture. I should add that she's also active in Washington, lobbying to keep government regulation to a minimum. One other reason to keep her supplied with the most up-to-date information available."

"So, what's your client willing to pay me for delivering inside information? I'd be risking my job, even my career."

"We won't ever pressure you to take undue risks. A steady flow of information could easily match your current salary. Just think what doubling your monthly income might mean. With no tax withholdings."

Sophia took a big gulp from her ale and pursed her lips.

"I can do this. But we aren't nearly as far along in android development as the company press releases would have you believe. Your client might be disappointed."

"I'm not surprised at that. But I assure you, she will be pleased with whatever you can get." Karen pulled an ultra-slim tablet from her satchel. "This is for you. It's coded for wireless transmission directly to my client's computer here in the Valley."

Karen turned the device over and removed the battery cover on the back. "There are two secret compartments in the cover. No one ever looks at the cover. Snap this piece open like this…" Karen opened a hinged piece of plastic with her fingernail. Inside the tiny depression were three mempins. "You have three 128 terabyte mempins stored in this compartment. When you've downloaded information from your company's computer to one of the mempins, remove it and insert it in this compartment." Karen opened a second identical hinged lid opposite the first. Inside this tiny cavity was one mempin socket.

"Once you have inserted your mempin here, transmission automatically begins and your data is uploaded to my client's computer. Close the lids, replace the cover, and no one's the wiser, even on close inspection."

"Are you sure you aren't with the CIA?" Sophia laughed.

"It is pretty clever, isn't it." Karen handed Sophia a manila envelope. "Take this as a down payment. You'll find we pay quite generously."

Sophia's eyes widened when she looked inside the envelope.

"Remember. No undue risks. Everything must look perfectly natural."

"What if I need to get hold of you for some reason?"

"You can't. I'm just a lowly recruiter. If you need help, include a message on your mempin and upload it to my client. She'll see to it you get the assistance you need."

Karen handed Sophia the tablet satchel. "With your help, we'll be able to keep everyone in the industry on track to make this android thing a reality."

"Of course." Sophia rose from the table. "But I'd best get back to work. I'll need to put in an extra half-hour to make up for the long lunch."

Karen pulled out her phone and requested an air taxi to pick Sophia up and return her to her car. Once she was alone, she hailed her own cab to deliver her to San Francisco International Airport. Her flight for Paris wasn't scheduled to leave until 5:30, a four-hour wait.

I hate having to travel commercially. If I could book one of Sam's TransWorld Space cruisers, I'd be back in Paris in time for dinner. The price of anonymity

Chapter 8

Nova Prima, Mars

Tony Armado paced the small conference room adjoining his office in Nova Prima's administrative habitat. With hands clasped tightly behind his back and brow creased with worry, he debated how to respond to his guests' concerns. As Nova Prima's mayor, he had a reputation for moderate risk taking and decisive action, traits that often resulted in controversial decisions. Joining Durban's uprising four years earlier was one such decision which Tony now deeply regretted. He sighed and plopped his heavy frame into his chair. He faced his two guests, shaking his head in resignation.

Frieda Schönberg and Zane Perlmann, the mayors of Hibernia and Pella, Mars' two smaller colonies, looked at each other and waited in silence. Tony brushed his hand through his beard.

There are no easy solutions here.

"I fully agree with you, Zane," he finally said. "Durban no longer has access to nanoplast manufacturing facilities, if he ever did. His promise to build domes for our cities is as vacuous as the air outside our habitats. If we want domes, we'll have to turn to Haven and the Loyalists."

"Durban's still got a fleet of cruisers. That makes him a serious threat if we rile him," said Frieda.

"Those cruisers are providing us with twice weekly ferry service to Earth and the Luna outposts," Zane added. "He's the lifeline for all our commerce with Earth."

Tony leaned forward. "Except for that, all three of our cities are self-sufficient. If we could commandeer a cruiser for ourselves, we could handle the ferry service and do away with Durban entirely."

"Easier said than done," said Frieda.

"Maybe not," said Zane. "*Denali* is currently docked at Pella. I've talked with Captain Abrams and polled his crew. They're fed up with being confined indefinitely to their ship except for short shore leaves. They miss their families on Haven. No telling when this will end. They see no future continuing with Durban. But they're afraid they might face prosecution if they surrender to the Loyalists."

"Interesting." Tony steepled his fingers beneath his chin and appeared lost in thought. The room fell silent except for the incessant hum from the environmental control system.

"Suppose we give them a third option. What if we create our own political entity? Then, if the Denali crew joined with us, we would no longer be defenseless and dependent on Durban. Or Haven, for that matter. We'd have the clout and independence to negotiate with both sides."

"Durban might retaliate," Frieda said, furrowing her brow. "He's getting more desperate and more dangerous. He gave Fae quite a scare when she, er, they told him Juno was joining the Loyalists."

"That's where having *Denali* on our side is important." Tony turned to Zane. "Continue your talks with Abrams and see if we can get a commitment from them to join us. As a separate state entity, we can provide them with immunity here and negotiate with Haven for pardons."

"What if we sweeten the deal by offering to relocate their families to Mars if Haven refuses?" Zane asked.

"More families would be good for all our colonies," Frieda observed. "We should come up with a package of incentives to encourage them to move here."

Tony stood and smiled broadly. "I think we're on a roll. Let's grab some lunch at the cafeteria and put some structure around these ideas this afternoon. For the first time in months, I'm seeing a brighter future."

That afternoon and into the evening, the three mayors slaved over their aspiration to make Mars an independent republic. They composed a declaration of independence and a framework of cooperation between their three colonies. After struggling for a name for their new nation, they settled on The Martian Confederation.

Before setting out for dinner, they each signed the agreement and shared enthusiastic hugs.

"A constructive afternoon," Tony announced. "Still contingent on getting *Denali's* cooperation, so let's keep this to ourselves. Once we have them committed to our side, I'll contact the Loyalists to gain their support. Then we can poll our people and see if they want us to proceed."

"I think Pella will show unanimous support," said Zane.

"Hibernia will likely have a majority in favor as well," added Frieda.

"I wish I could be so sure about Nova Prima's outcome. We have a lot of Liberation League support here. Anyway, if we get the majority of Martians to go along with us, I'll invite Durban here and confront him directly."

"Be sure you have armed bodyguards when you do," said Zane.

I will definitely have armed bodyguards at hand when I meet with Durban.

Deep Space, Aboard *Curie*

Rae Anne turned her attention back to Jason. She shook him. She called out his name. He remained lifeless.

Stay calm, Rae Anne. Focus on the problem. Two problems. I must revive Jason, and I must determine where we are. It's a damn big galaxy.

Rae Anne stepped into the Operations Center for a mug of tea to calm her nerves. She wracked her brain for any idea to help resolve her dilemma.

Methodically stirring honey into her tea, she forced herself to breathe slowly and deeply. Her shoulders relaxed. She began talking her thoughts aloud to help her concentrate.

"Alright. I was certified in celestial navigation for the Mars II expedition. That was a long time ago, but something from that training should be useful now. Of course, all navigational references pertained to Sol System. Not of much use here.

"But we shouldn't have traveled so far that some easily identifiable stars from Earth wouldn't also be visible here. That's a place to start."

Back on the bridge at the navigation console, Rae Anne prompted the computer to locate unique stars with known identities. The first to come up was Betelgeuse, the familiar red giant. Next came Sirius, the brightest blue-white star in Sol's sky.

Good. Sirius is still the brightest star in the sky. That means we can't have travelled too far from Sol.

Before long, the computer identified a dozen more stars. Their orientations no longer fit the familiar constellations, complicating the issue. Nevertheless, she had enough information for the computer to triangulate between the various stars and compare the results with values as seen from Earth.

With enough comparisons, the computer should produce an approximation for our location.

While the computer was running the calculations, she looked over at Jason. His body was just as she had left him. She shook her head in dismay.

If you were Human, I could try CPR or a defibrillator to get your heart going. But you're an android, with no heart and a computer for a brain. I know how to reboot a computer, but I don't think Jason has an ON/OFF switch.

Her mind cycled through images of Jason through the years, looking for something relating to a reboot. She recalled how disturbed she was once when she saw Jason-0 downloading data from *Avenger's* computer. He had connected a cable from the ship's data terminal directly to a port behind his left ear.

If I could locate that socket, and stimulate it somehow, I might be able to revive him. Too bad he didn't come with a user's manual.

Rae Anne lifted Jason from the chair and laid him face down on the deck. Ruffling through his hair, she found what she was looking for behind his left ear—a faint rectangular tracing suggesting a removable cover. When she pressed it, the cover popped open, revealing a data socket.

Now to locate a cable with the right connector and a data source.

Fumbling in the cabinet beneath the navigation console, she found both. To her delight, the connectors matched.

Shouldn't be surprised at that. This is a Shalcerian ship, and Jason was built by Shalcerian engineers on Avenger.

After connecting the cable to the ship's data outlet, she held her breath as she plugged the other end into Jason's skull.

Again, there was no response. Her heart fell.

"Jason, damn you. Wake up!" she screamed.

As if in response, Jason's eyelids fluttered. A faint tremor rippled through his body. His head jerked to one side.

"My name is Jason."

A load of tension flowed from Rae Anne's body as though a dam had burst. "Jason, thank god you're alive!" She flopped into her chair, exhausted but relieved. Tears flooded down her cheeks.

"My name is Jason-11," he repeated, as though surprised at newly discovered information.

"I am a Human android." A further revelation.

Jason looked back and forth at his surroundings. The trickle of data from the ship's computer steadily increased, soon threatening to overpower his active memory circuits. Terabytes of information filled empty cells. He stood on wobbly legs. He circled the bridge nodding and shaking his head. Finally, he sat down.

"My memory is back. Only the hours since the wormhole transit are missing. Something about the wormhole jump interfered with the internal clock my computer relies on."

"I can't tell you how relieved I am to have you back, Jason. There was little chance we'd make it home without you."

Jason unplugged the cable from his skull. "Not a problem. We programmed *Curie* to swing around Epsilon Eridani and return on its own. It doesn't need me at the controls."

Rae Anne grasped both of Jason's shoulders as though he were a child. "That's the problem. *Curie* is nowhere near Epsilon Eridani, so the automated guidance program has shut down. *Curie* has stopped dead."

"Ah. Well, better that than executing a faulty program."

"Jason, we're lost in space. I've tried to do triangulation with known stars, but the result doesn't make any sense."

Rae Anne showed him the readouts from her calculations.

"The result is weird, all right. I need to run through these calculations myself."

Over the next hour, Jason made several refinements to Rae Anne's input data, then displayed a map on the bridge monitor.

"You weren't that far off. This red 'X' depicts our location. We are 26.8 lightyears from Sol, far beyond the 10.5 lightyear transit we had intended."

"How could that be?" Rae Anne shook her head in disbelief. "Where did we go wrong?"

"I'm pouring over the simulation program to locate any errors. We ran these a dozen times with no hint of a problem."

"We also need to determine some way to protect you during the next jump. Jason-0 never experienced a blackout through any of the four wormhole transits we made while aboard *Avenger*. We need to keep you alive and well."

"I'm not sure 'alive' is the operative word here, but I do get your meaning. I'll work on that, too."

Rae Anne left the bridge for something to eat in the galley. Her stomach was audibly growling. She hadn't eaten for thirty hours. She selected a spaghetti dinner with Bolognaise sauce and garlic bread.

Submerging the package in water to activate its exotherm wrap and heat the contents, she focused on their current predicament. She shivered as a cold wave washed over her body.

No Earth ship has ever been so far from home. During my solo trip to Saturn, I had Ian to talk to, even given the two-hour transmission delay. But if I were to send a message back to Earth today, I'd be long dead before I got a reply. This is utterly insane. Oh, Ian, how I miss you…

Chapter 9

Deep Space, Aboard *Curie*

Curie was now at a dead stop in deep space. Rae Anne watched anxiously as Jason-11 hunched over the navigation console, studying the programming that brought them to this location, looking for any sign of error. She nibbled on the last of her garlic bread and sipped her tea.

"Everything looks as it should, Rae Anne. If it's not the program, it must be a deficiency in our knowledge of how wormholes work. There must be some nuances within their physical nature that we didn't account for in the algorithms."

That's not good news.

Another bite from the crust. "We hoped that the programs you copied from *Avenger*, coupled with your quantum computer, would be all we needed for a successful transit."

Jason's head popped up and he turned to Rae Anne. "Say that again. Something clicked."

Rae Anne repeated what she had just said.

"…copied from *Avenger*. That may be it."

"I'm not following you."

"*Avenger* is a Shalcerian battleship. It is at least four times *Curie's* size. Any programs in its archives would have been meant for that ship's use. We used a program designed for a battleship. That may be why it threw us farther than we anticipated."

"That makes sense, Jason. Can we use the ratio of the two ships' sizes to alter the simulations and see if we can calculate our location more accurately?"

"Entirely possible. I'm working on it now."

Jason turned back to the console. With nothing she could do, Rae Anne decided to catch a much-needed nap.

"Call me when you've got something," she said, leaving the captain's chair. She stretched and yawned, then stepped through the nanoscreen and followed the corridor to her stateroom.

Two hours later, Jason sent Rae Anne an alert. Rae Anne jumped upright, groggy from a deep sleep.

"I've got a much more accurate display showing where we are. You might like to see this."

Rae Anne rolled out of bed and searched for her shoes. Her head was in a fog. Before leaving for the bridge, she splashed cold water across her face to help wake herself up.

Just two hours. I could have slept twelve.

When she entered the bridge, she found herself standing in the middle of a hologram. Two holograms to be precise. Jason had superimposed the new star map over the earlier one. A blinking red asterisk on the overlay commanded her attention.

"Taking the difference between the masses of the two ships into account, this is where we should have ended up, 38.7 lightyears from Sol. What this shows is mass does make a difference, but it's not the only explanation for our predicament."

Rae Anne sat heavily into the captain's chair.

"Damn. We need to get to the bottom of this if we have any hope of getting home."

"At least the program's navigation coordinate control is working. You'll observe that our actual trajectory crosses right over Epsilon Eridani."

"Small consolation if we can't get the distance factor right."

"Now that we know the fudge factor for the smaller ship, we should conduct another jump toward Sol. We could be lucky and land right back where we started."

"We still haven't solved how to keep you intact during a jump."

"Since we don't know what happened, we can only rely on trial and error. For starters, I suggest we use the same approach you used to bring me back by making a physical connection to the ship's computer during transit.

Even if I lose memory again, I may be able to get rejuvenated without appreciable delay."

"Alright, let's give it a try. At least we'll be closer to home. Being so far from Earth is extremely unsettling. I feel like I've been excommunicated from humanity."

"Interesting…"

Over the next three hours, Jason reprogrammed *Curie* with the new parameters adjusting for the ship's size and mass. Rae Anne retired to the galley to get something to eat, more in response to her nervous anxiety now than from hunger. She put together a vegetable-hummus sandwich with a pouch of red ale. It seemed to help.

One other benefit of our plasticore hull and its one-sixth gravity. In microgravity, a beer would be out of the question.

When she returned to the bridge, Jason was wrapping up his final adjustments.

"I've run a dozen simulations, each with slight variations in the parameters. I think we have the numbers we need. I've finished putting them into the nav program," he announced, turning to Rae Anne.

"Everything checked out before, too. Forgive me for saying so, but I don't have 100-percent confidence in your simulation programs."

"Do we have any other choice but to give it a try?"

"Good point. Let's get you hooked up to the ship's computer and see if we can make it home."

Rae Anne helped Jason connect the navigation computer to his brain. Then Jason initiated the launch sequence.

God, I hope this works.

The wormhole transit was no different from the last, including the momentary feeling of being outside of time. The only positive aspect to this trip was that Jason remained awake and was alert immediately after the jump. But a cursory console scan revealed they had not arrived anywhere near Sol System.

"It looks like we've solved one problem, anyway," said Rae Anne as she detached Jason's umbilical cord. "But why was Jason-0 never affected aboard *Avenger*?"

"There may have been attenuating suppressors built into the ship which aren't present on *Curie*."

"Well, there's no nearby sun, yellow or otherwise. We still aren't where we want to be. I'll leave you to work your star-triangulation magic and figure out where we ended up. The visual sensors show a bright blue-white star behind us. That may be Sirius."

After a pause, Jason affirmed Rae Anne's guess. He then set about estimating their location. Knowing that the trajectory remained true made the project simpler than before.

"That faint yellow star you see dead ahead is Sol," Jason reported. "We jumped 21.7 lightyears. We are 5.1 lightyears from Earth."

I wish that made me feel better, but it doesn't. We're still not home!

"So, now, with the correct figures for *Curie*'s mass and size, we're undershooting our predicted distance." She began tapping numbers into her console's calculator.

"If the percentage by which we're coming up short is a constant, we can use that to overcompensate on our next jump and arrive home. This last jump missed our target by 19.03 percent. So, programming a 6.299 lightyear jump should take us the 5.1 light years we need."

"I've got it programmed into the computer to ten decimal places."

"Good. Let's go home."

Just as Jason turned to the navigation console, an alarm went off. Rae Anne's heart jumped into her throat at the unexpected sound.

"Jason! What was that?"

"I think we have a problem."

"What?"

"Our gravity-wave sensor just alerted us to an approaching ship. Its wave characteristics identify it as a Baltar Federation ship."

Curie's computer translator blared a sharp command over the cabin speakers.

Shalcerian warship. You are in Baltar Federation command space. I, VenaVen, captain of the Prescient, under the auspices of the Baltar Federation, am taking you into custody. You are to stand down and remain where you are. Prepare to be boarded. Any sign of resistance or deviation from my commands will result in your immediate destruction.

"*Mierda*. Aren't the Baltari enemies of the Shalcerian Empire?"

"They are. The two empires have been warring for over 150 years."

"They have no idea we're just a research vessel. What can we do?"

"Exactly what they tell us to do. Once they board, the lack of a military crew might convince them we are harmless."

We can only hope. And we had to land here, of all places.

Chapter 10

Deep Space, Aboard *Curie*

Rae Anne left the bridge to stand by the airlock while *Prescient* swung alongside *Curie*. A metallic clang signaled a patch had been placed against *Curie*'s hull over the airlock. After a couple minutes, it became securely sealed, enabling VenaVen's crew to board the *Curie*. When the hatch opened, a dozen armed Baltari bounded into the ship, followed by their captain. All wore respirators, having assumed *Curie*'s atmosphere would be different from their own.

Rae Anne stepped back, eyes wide, taking in the scene and staring at the creatures before her.

What strange looking people. Like the Shalcerians, they have no identifiable heads. A slender waist separates two lobed parts of their hairy torsos. Giant, furry peanuts.

Dense brown fur covered their bodies. Two short slender arms protruded from their torso's upper lobe, ending in disc-shaped hands with eight digits resembling Human fingers. A bare circular ridge containing eight eyes facing eight different directions ringed the top of their bodies like a crown. The eyes glowed with a blue-green phosphorescence.

Their two legs were noticeably short and ended in wide, clawed feet similar to those of a bird. Movement was accomplished by short hops initiated by first one foot, then the other. This resulted in a distinct bobbing motion as they moved around the deck.

This will take some getting used to.

One Baltari carried an open case with several instruments. He studied the readouts, then looked up and spoke to the captain. His speech hummed like a musical melody.

The captain hummed a command and the crew removed their respirators and fastened them to one of three belts around their waists. He then looked at

Rae Anne. His hummed communication was translated into English through the mobile translator unit Rae Anne had carried down from the bridge.

"I am Captain VenaVen. Your ship is now under my command and you are in my custody."

He studied Rae Anne carefully and hummed to his assistant, who hummed a reply.

"You are not Shalcerian. Where is the crew? If they are waiting to ambush us, we'll gas the ship and be done with you."

Rae Anne held out both hands, palm up, hoping the gesture would signify compliance and welcome.

"There are only two of us aboard this ship, Captain VenaVen. Neither of us are Shalcerian. I am Rae Anne Chavez, a Human from Sol System."

VenaVen hummed another command and his crew dispersed into the ship.

"Take me to the bridge. I wish to see your captain."

"I am the captain. My pilot and navigator is the only person accompanying me. Please follow me."

Everything I've heard about Baltari from Shalcerians depicts them as savage beasts. These people don't appear to be monsters. Apparently, wartime propaganda isn't just a Human phenomenon.

Rae Anne took VenaVen to the bridge. There, she introduced Jason who immediately turned his attention back to the computer console. Rae Anne realized he was pretending to be busy tending to the ship's needs.

I hope he's recording everything for later analysis.

"How is it you are in charge of a Shalcerian ship. Is it stolen?"

"Humans have legitimately purchased light cruisers from the Shalcerian Empire. We use them to patrol our star system."

"Why have you invaded Baltar space? My AI command unit tells me you are likely spies."

"We are not spies or Shalcerian agents. We are scientists on a research mission. Our propulsion system failed. Instead of delivering us to Sol System, it dropped us here. We were troubleshooting the problem when you arrived."

"Your explanation seems highly suspect. The authorities will decide whether you tell the truth. For now, you are under arrest. It is my duty to bring you and your ship to our home world, Entriva, in the Alpha Mensae system.

There you will have a hearing before the chief magistrate of the Federation Military Judiciary."

A member of VenaVen's security force stepped into the Bridge and hummed a report to the captain. VenaVen issued a command in return and the guard disappeared through the nanoscreen.

"My crew confirm that you two are the only occupants of this ship."

"Then can you let us return to our home world?"

"That will not be possible. I believe you are spies. You are to remain aboard this ship while we tow you to Entriva."

Rae Anne's stomach lurched. She swallowed hard to clear the acid bile that rose in her throat.

VenaVen turned and bounced through the nanoscreen.

She turned to Jason. "When we encountered the Shalcerians, I hoped to meet as many alien species as I could in my lifetime. But this wasn't what I had in mind. What if the authorities come to the same conclusion as VenaVen?"

"Given that they are at war with the Shalcerians, we would probably be executed."

A chill swept through Rae Anne's spine. "That's not what I needed to hear."

"Still, they are interesting looking creatures," observed Jason, seemingly oblivious to her distress. "Strange mode of locomotion."

Rae Anne hugged herself tightly and breathed deeply to quell her fear.

Don't dwell on things you have no control over, Rae Anne.

"I wonder how they tell each other apart," she said, aware that her voice was a half-pitch higher than normal. "They all look alike to me."

"It may be their eyes. Each has a slightly different shape and color. Baltar eyes might be like Human fingerprints. They also vary widely in height. Captain VenaVen was the tallest Baltari present."

Maybe I could convince them to send my body back to Sol so Ian and my friends could at least know what happened to us. They'll be very upset when we don't return within the allotted two days.

Shalcerian Outpost on Haven

Jason-12 sat quietly on the bench beside the nanoscreen leading into Denahr's office. Denahr had motioned Jason there when he arrived. It was clear that Denahr was preoccupied with tasks that demanded his full attention.

It's been months since Denahr last asked for me to stop by. Usually, I'm the one taking the initiative. Must be something important.

Denahr finally invited Jason into his office.

"Sorry to make you wait, Jason. I have three battlecruisers coming in for provisioning. I had to put some light cruisers into temporary orbit to make room for them."

"Waiting is no problem for an android. I'm always connected to my computer, so there's no such thing as down time."

"I have only a few minutes, so I'll get right to the point." Denahr manipulated icons on his monitor-desk to bring up a 3D hologram in the center of the room. His body scales were rippling waves of magenta over metallic gray, a combination none of the Jasons had seen before.

"I'm quite concerned for humanity's safety," Denahr said as he strode around his desk and stood inside the hologram. "This hologram depicts the space around sol with a ten-lightyear radius." Denahr reached out and put his finger next to a bright yellow spot. "Here's Sol."

He next pointed to a red spot floating just inside one edge of the hologram. "Here we have Lalande, 8.6 lightyears away from Sol. Lalande is on the fringe of the Baltar Federation, acquired by them just ten Earth-years ago. At the time, we didn't have the strength in this sector to stop them. That's one reason we needed this base in your system. The Baltari are moving steadily in this direction. It appears they may try to acquire the Centauri system next." He gestured toward the three Centauri suns, Alpha Centauri A and B, and Proxima Centauri.

Jason stared at the holographic image. *This could have serious consequences for Humans.*

"The Centauri system is our nearest neighbor."

"Exactly. Which is why we are building our forces around those three stars. And here as well, as a backup. We intend to stop their advance at Lalande."

"Your hologram shows a number of white specks surrounding the stars. Are those planets? And are they habitable?"

"Those specks are the major planets. None are naturally habitable. But we've established two military outposts and a colony on the largest planet orbiting Alpha Centauri B. We also have a colony here, on this planet orbiting Proxima Centauri." Denahr pointed to one of the floating white dots. "We'll defend them with all the strength we can muster."

"Watching your military buildup this past year, I can't imagine there is anything Humans can do to help."

"Actually, that's why I summoned you. One of the articles all our allied species agree to on being admitted to the empire is to provide persons and materiel as required in the defense of the empire. We need 50,000 Humans to help fill the ranks of our forces. I'm asking you, as our liaison with Humans, to convey this demand to appropriate authorities and assemble the recruits at a suitable training facility on Earth."

Easier said than done. A great many Humans still want nothing to do with aliens.

"I see." Jason paused and rubbed his chin thoughtfully, mimicking a purely Human gesture. "And how do I entice potential recruits to volunteer to fight in a war that is several light years away?"

"Battle lines are not fixed features. What I'm telling you is that Earth is in imminent danger. Point to the blast crater Captain Vahler created in the center of Moscow if anyone has doubts. The Baltari will do that and worse to every major city on Earth if they manage to get through our lines. Our call for 50,000 recruits is likely to be the first of many."

"What kind of warfare will we be training for? Your example of the strike against Moscow was initiated from space. Ground troops will be useless."

"The empire is bringing hundreds of cruisers and battleships to the Centauri Systems. These will need trained Humans to fill the ranks before heading off to the front. You gather the recruits and establish training facilities. We'll supply the equipment and instructors. We'll train Human specialists for every function outside of the officer ranks and bridge crews."

"How long do you expect the training to take?"

"We can have raw recruits combat ready in three months. Our trainers and advanced simulators are very efficient."

"It might take some time to build the facilities for that large an operation, not to mention getting that many Humans signed up."

"To use a phrase in your language, 'Time is of the essence.' You locate a large enough site in a hospitable country, and we'll build the base while you recruit Humans. This should allow us to begin training in two months, by mid-July, latest."

"Will Humans be trained to pilot your fighter disks? Jason-0's archives from the Battle of Alsafi reveal flight decks on your battleships with fleets of fighter disks."

"Of course. Nearly half of the recruits will become fighter pilots. Our initial exercises are designed to determine who will qualify for flight training."

"My knowledge of Human nature tells me that the promise of piloting fighter disks in an interstellar war may be all the enticement we'll need to fill the ranks."

"But that is the most dangerous assignment. It's not uncommon to lose fifty percent of our fighters in a typical engagement."

"As strange as it sounds, that fact alone will make my job easier."

Denahr's scale colors shifted to purple swirls on chartreuse stripes, a combination that Jason interpreted as puzzlement. "Humans are truly a strange species."

"They do have a tendency to behave in ways that defy logic."

An understatement, to be sure.

Chapter 11

Entriva, Baltar Capital Planet

Rae Anne watched helplessly as Entriva, the Baltar home world in the Alpha Mensae star system, 33.1 light years from Sol, came into view. Like Earth, the blue planet had vast oceans and glistening polar ice caps. But the land masses were distinctly green, suggesting a more humid world covered with heavy vegetation.

With *Curie* in tow, VenaVen brought *Prescient* into orbit. Entriva maintained a closer circular orbit than Earth's around its yellow G5V star, a cooler version of Earth's G2V sun.

"Does Alpha Mensae have other planets besides Entriva?" Rae Anne asked Jason.

"There is one rocky planet closer to its sun and four gas giants farther out, each with several large moons. Entriva itself is moonless."

Rae Anne watched as a shuttle arrived from the surface and docked with *Prescient*. After a short while, they were escorted through the make-shift airlock into *Prescient* and along that ship's corridors to the shuttle bay. VenaVen accompanied Rae Anne and Jason to the surface under the watchful eyes of six Baltar security guards. Rae Anne wondered what kind of threat the Baltari thought she and Jason posed.

Six guards for two harmless explorers? Not taking any chances. After all, they may know nothing about Humans.

The shuttle landed on a wide platform supported twenty feet in the air by a forest of wide tree trunks. The platform itself was a living entity built through splicing and shaping thousands of tree trunks and branches. As VenaVen led them toward the terminal structure, Rae Anne noted that the buildings, like the platform, were constructed entirely from living branches, artfully fused together. A copious canopy of broad deep green leaves sprouted from the treetops, shading the city from the sun. Birds sporting brightly colored plumage flitted and swooped overhead, filling the air with a dizzying chorus of bird calls.

This feels like a forest hideaway—a virtual jungle haven. No wonder the planet's land masses appeared so green.

Thinking the word 'haven' hit Rae Anne like a rock, bringing thoughts of her home world orbiting Saturn. She wiped away the moisture that had welled up in her eyes.

NO! Concentrate on the here and now. I have no control over the circumstances of my being here, so I need to concentrate on these novel surroundings. If we ever get home again, I'll have a Human perspective to add to Jason's report.

Nothing here resembled anything she had seen before, proof that evolution has no barriers to innovation.

At the terminal, VenaVen directed them to board a vertical takeoff aircraft with two horizontal props for lift and one pusher prop for fast transport. With VenaVen at the controls, they lifted off vertically, and once they were above the trees, they flew toward the setting sun.

"Where are you taking us, Captain?" asked Rae Anne.

"I am taking you directly to our capital city. You violated our space in an enemy spacecraft. We can only assume you are agents of the Shalcerian Empire. You will be incarcerated until your preliminary hearing."

Rae Anne's heart sank to her knees.

Great. What kind of hell are we in for, with weeks or months in a Baltar prison!

"How long before that takes place?"

"No idea. But I suspect the nature of your infraction will foster a quick response."

At least I'm alive. One day at a time, Rae Anne. One day at a time.

"I must thank you, Captain, for holding fire when you discovered us. Thinking we were Shalcerians, you could have blasted us into space dust."

"Perhaps. But we now have a marvelous opportunity to scrutinize a Shalcerian warship. Our Baltar engineers are swarming over your ship even as we speak."

"Tell me, the city we just left was built entirely of trees. Is this a common feature on your planet?" Jason asked.

"It is. Very long ago, we learned to engineer plants to suit our needs. It was a matter of survival."

"How so?"

"Our primitive ancestors harvested small worm-like creatures from the swamps for food. After a while, they bred them to increase their size. But that program got out of control. After a few hundred years, the creatures became dangerous predators. We had no choice but to take to the trees."

"Are they still a threat?"

"Oh yes. They are so ubiquitous that no one dares go down to the ground. Look, there's a smarl of maglozons just ahead."

VenaVen directed the plane to hover over a writhing mass of creatures, splashing furiously in the swampy waters.

Rae Anne gulped. "Those things are larger than the giant pythons on Earth. There are so many of them."

"The swamps are filled with them. Fortunately, they are unable to climb trees. We were well versed in plant genetic engineering by then and quickly modified our tree cultures to our needs. Besides forming the basis of our architecture, all our food comes from a variety of genetically modified trees."

"But you must have mines and smelters to support your industry," Jason observed.

"There are several maglozon-free islands. From these we have bored an extensive underground network of tunnels connecting all the continents and major cities. The excavations provide us with the ore we need. Heavy industry is relegated to those islands."

They travelled onward for another hour before coming to a wall of immense trees. VenaVen found a wide slot in the forest wall and slipped through. Again, Rae Anne felt she had entered a wooded fairyland. Walkways below and skyways above connected the arborous cityscape in a spiderweb of causeways. Bustling Baltari filled each avenue, bouncing along in their unique way.

They soon came to a glen dripping with a vine forest bearing fruit of every shape and color imaginable. VenaVen performed a vertical landing on the deck. Nearby, a castle-like entryway flanked by colossal tree trunk colonnades beckoned.

"This is the Federation Palace Complex. It contains the high-level administrative offices for the Baltar Federation as well as the Presidential Palace and the Court of Counselors Hall."

"This is awesome, Captain."

I feel like Alice in Wonderland.

Four sentries with elaborate pointed caps bounced out to meet them. They exchanged salutes with VenaVen, then led them into the complex, bouncing along on either side.

Rae Anne gazed in awe at her surroundings. She felt subdued, as if she were in a mammoth cathedral. Elaborate plant chandeliers hung from a ceiling too high to discern, their clusters of bulbous fruit casting a phosphorescent light throughout the room. Living benches spun from branches extended from the walls, providing a place for pedestrians to rest. Each bench had several hollowed-out indentations suitable for Baltar round bottoms.

Soon, they came to a wall with a series of dark openings. At first Rae Anne thought these were elevator shafts with no guard rails. On closer inspection, she saw platforms continuously moving up or down in the shafts, slowly enough for individuals to step onto one as it passed by a doorway.

So, if someone fell through, they would only fall a few feet and land on the nearest platform below. A cross between an elevator and an escalator. An 'escalevator', as it were.

VenaVen herded Rae Anne and Jason onto a downward moving platform. By her count, they passed twenty-five floors before they were shooed out. Their security guards stepped into the corridor from the next platform. They passed a security station with a single sentry and trooped down the hall past a dozen wooden doors. All were unlocked; some were even ajar.

VenaVen stopped in front of one door, consulted his tablet, then opened it and ushered his prisoners into their cell. It resembled a small apartment, with comfortable chairs, cushioned benches, and a small kitchenette with stocked shelves and a counter for food preparation. Two small bedrooms adjoined the central living area.

"This is where you are to stay until you are called to appear before the magistrate," said VenaVen. "Maintenance is constructing beds to match those we found on your cruiser. They will be installed shortly. You will have to make do with Baltar bathroom facilities for a day or two. Constructing and installing the hardware and plumbing for these is a bit more complicated."

"What about food?" Rae Anne asked. "It's not likely our nutritional needs match yours."

"We have emptied the larder on your ship. My crew will bring everything here soon…Ah, here they are as we speak."

Two Baltari entered the apartment, guiding a motorized cart laden with Human foodstuffs. They hauled everything to the kitchen and began replacing the Baltar items with familiar packages from the carts.

"Are all the cells outfitted like this?" Rae Anne asked, incredulous.

"They are. We believe in restorative justice for our prisoners, as opposed to punitive retribution. You are free to walk the halls and visit with other detainees. The doors are rarely locked. You are on your honor to remain on this floor and to respect our system of justice."

"What about our ship?"

"I have been assigned to look after it in orbit until your fates have been decided. I will keep it in good condition in the unlikely event you are allowed to return."

Rae Anne's head began to spin.

'Unlikely event.' No! I can't think on that possibility.

She stumbled over to the couch and sat down.

VenaVen turned and left with his retinue of guards. Jason immediately began scanning the room, pushing chairs away from the walls, scrutinizing the wooden floors.

"What is it, Jason. Do you think we're being bugged?"

"No, not that. I'm looking for a data terminal I can plug into."

After a minute, he stood upright with a smile on his face.

"Aha! Here's a multi-pronged socket. I'm going down the hall to see if I can have the sentry acquire a data cable with a plug to match the socket in my head."

While Jason was gone, four Baltari delivered their beds. Rae Anne smiled at the thought of Jason lying down in bed. Being an android, he busied himself 24/7 with no need for rest.

But it may be in our interest for the Baltari to regard him as Human.

Jason returned a short time later, cable in hand.

"Their engineering department is quite impressive. The guard sent up the pinout diagram for my socket and they put together the cable I needed while I waited."

"Did he ask what you needed the cable for?"

"Yes, and I told him we had an entertainment device that might work on their network. I didn't mention that the entertainment device might be me. Now to see if I can decipher Baltar AI."

Rae Anne helped Jason plug the cable behind his ear. She watched as he sat on the floor and plugged the other end into the room's data outlet. For a moment, Jason sat motionless, then a wide smile crossed his face.

"It will take me a while to work through this, but it's old-fashioned binary. My quantum computing capabilities will run circles around their code. 'A piece of cake,' as you might be inclined to say."

Rae Anne shook her head with amusement and left him to his project, wishing she had some similar activity to take her mind off their situation. She chose one of the bedrooms as her own and sat on the bed, elbows on her knees and head in her hands.

I can't imagine the worry everyone back home must be feeling, not knowing whether we're alive or dead. Especially Ian. If the Baltari decide we're spies, they will never know what became of us.

Chapter 12

Juno Municipal Community Center

Ian paced back and forth along the glass wall lining the conference room on the Juno Community Center's top floor. A hologram over the long table depicted the largely empty space between Sol, a bright yellow sun at one corner, and Epsilon Eridani, a smaller, dull red star in the other. A few other red dwarfs occupied the intervening space. Jason-0 sat quietly beside Juno's mayor, Fae Jackson, who occupied the head of the table.

Ian's heart weighed heavily in his chest. Deep furrows lined his brow. "They've been gone two weeks," he gruffed. "Something must have gone terribly wrong." He shook his head in despair.

"We can't know that," said Fae. "They may have discovered an advanced civilization and are gathering information to bring back."

"Not when they know we're anxiously waiting for their return. Adhering to the experiment's itinerary takes precedent over everything else."

"Without data, any conclusion is unwarranted," said Jason.

Easy for you to say.

Ian stopped pacing and turned to stare out the window overlooking the small city. Sunlight through the new transparent nanoplast dome reflected from hundreds of glass surfaces, as if the city were a field strewn with diamonds. Jupiter's mammoth orb, currently as a waning crescent, hung motionless above tidally-locked Ganymede's horizon. The mesmerizing scene created a momentary distraction from Ian's worries.

"Fae, it would seem your whole city is made of glass."

Fae laughed. "You try spending six years living like a mole in enclosed habitats. Once Haven put up our dome, we wanted nothing more to do with enclosures. Glass and transparent walls are in high demand. You may have also noticed our beautiful parks alongside the wide avenues. Everyone treasures freedom to be outside in the open air."

The brief interlude passed. Ian turned away from the window and sighed deeply. "Still, if they've encountered a problem, there's nothing we can do to help them. We'll never know what happened."

"That was understood from the beginning," said Jason.

You and your damn logic!

"I begged her not to go. Why would she take on such a risk? What was she thinking?"

"Probably the same motivation that prompted her to defy the USIEA authority back in 2038 when we diverted *Aurora* to Saturn," Jason answered.

"Yes, but that was thirty years ago!"

Jason nodded. "Rae Anne has an instinct for the bigger picture. Had she not gone for Saturn, the space program would have been curtailed, humanity would never have experienced First Contact, and interstellar travel would still be the subject of science fiction."

"That doesn't make the hurt any easier to bear."

"So, Ian, what are the chances the Mars colonies will join us?" asked Fae. "They can't be all that happy under Durban's rule."

"Pretty good," said Ian. "Tony has been in contact with me to find out how much support we can give him should they separate from his Liberation League. He might even bring along a cruiser.

"I don't understand why the crews on his cruisers give Durban their unconditional support," said Jason. "It makes no logical sense."

"I guess some people just like authority figures. Especially billionaire autocrats," Fae added.

"Maybe so," said Jason. "But Durban's wealth is rapidly shrinking. The new robotics startup in France is beginning to cut into Durban Robotics' market share. Luna Xtract is the only healthy part of his empire. The rare earths he mines on Luna and in the Asteroid Belt are in high demand on Earth."

"Nothing I would like to see more than Durban's empire come crashing down," said Ian.

No, I take that back. Seeing Rae Anne safely home again trumps everything else.

Haven University

Jason-0 stood in front of a large environmental control box in his lab at Haven University. Inside the hood, six robot arm manipulators selected rust-red rock samples, crushed them, and added the pulverized material to various reaction vessels. Jason controlled the operations through his mental link to his quantum computer.

A short, heavy-set man wearing a business suit stepped through the nanoscreen into the lab. The lab security system sounded with a short buzz. Without turning from his work, Jason said, "I'm quite busy. Please come back later."

The visitor continued into the lab until he was standing beside Jason. He peered into the chamber and seemed to be interested in the experiment.

"This looks quite fascinating. What is it you're doing?"

"I'm seeing how Martian soil responds to different chemical treatments, hoping to find a process that will free oxygen from the minerals. Now, please go."

The man made no move to leave.

"So, this must be a Mars box, am I right?"

What else would it be? What an imbecile.

"Of course. Now, go. I can meet you in my office at six this evening."

Jason detected a short radio signal initiated by his visitor. Four very muscular thugs burst through the nanoscreen. Security alarms blared. Before Jason could respond, they barreled into him, knocking him to his knees. Each man grabbed an arm or a leg and pinned him to the floor. They then lifted him and carried him out of the lab.

No way I can fight off four men. I'll just have to see what they're up to.

The intruders trundled to a metal casket in the corridor next to the lift. They pressed Jason into the box. Just before the lid closed over him, Jason sent a detailed visual image of his plight to his clones. The lid slammed shut. Seven clicks sealed it tight. Inside the metal enclosure, Jason was cut off from further communication.

Interesting. They've installed a small ventilator to keep me from suffocating. They still don't know I'm an android.

The four Jason clones on Haven simultaneously received Jason-0's alert. Tapping into Haven's security system, they quickly spotted the lorry the kidnappers were using for transport. It was a standard autonomous delivery vehicle they had hijacked from a department store. The kidnappers were headed to Sector 8 where the Earth-Haven ferry was berthed.

Three Jasons immediately departed for Sector 8. Jason-12 dropped by Denahr's office in the Shalcerian outpost to inform him of the kidnapping. Denahr promised to block *Darwin* from departing if they needed his help.

The lorry came to a stop at the ferry terminal. The five men, now wearing black armbands, stepped from the vehicle. The leader opened the back. The other four solemnly lifted the casket and carried it into the terminal.

Jason-20: *The short man is in charge. He is at the ticket window now.*

Jason-13: *I'm in the hangar. I'm moving all Humans into the Darwin for their safety. The hangar deck will be clear when they come down.*

Jason-16: *I'm in place aboard Darwin on the bridge in case we need to go to plan B and coordinate with Denahr.*

Jason-20: *The leader has arranged to keep the casket with the passengers rather than consign it as cargo. Highly unusual.*

Jason-16: *They're likely getting paid a ransom for Jason. Don't want to let the precious cargo out of their sight.*

Jason 20: *They have just entered the lift. I'll remain up here in case they decide to come back.*

Jason-13: *The hangar deck is empty. I've ordered Darwin's airlock sealed. I am in position at the lift.*

As the five men with the casket exited the lift, one of the bigger men grunted. "Where is everybody? Are we in the right place?"

"Of course, that's our ship down the ramp. There's still 18 minutes to launch."

Jason-13 stepped in behind the men as they proceeded down the ramp toward the ship.

"Excuse me, gentlemen, but caskets must be stowed in the cargo bay."

Everyone stopped. Peter circled around his men to confront whoever was obstructing his progress.

"Look here, I have a ticket..." His face turned white, as though he'd seen a ghost. He glanced at the casket, then back at Jason.

"This is impossible. Do you... Do you have a twin?"

"Actually, I do. He works in the Physics Department at the University. You are behaving very suspiciously. I'm afraid I must look inside this casket."

The four men set the casket down on the ramp. Two slipped their right hands beneath their loose jackets.

"No!" Peter blurted. "I mean, the, uh, the corpse is badly decayed. Trust me, you don't want to open it up."

"All the more reason to put it in the cargo bay. Now if your men will follow me, we'll get this secured in *Darwin*'s cargo bay so you can be on your way."

Peter grabbed Jason's arm. "Is the cargo bay pressurized?"

"Yes. Why do you ask?"

"I, umm, if it wasn't, the pressure in the casket might pop the lid off. Our beloved brother's remains would be spewed all over the compartment."

Jason-13 smiled. "Live animals are regularly transported in the cargo bay. I assure you, you have nothing to worry about."

Peter hesitated, then sighed. "Oh, all right. Guys, follow him with the casket. Be sure it gets tied down securely."

Jason-13 led them to the ship's open cargo hatch. He helped them slide the casket in place and buckle it down, then closed the hatch and sealed it. When they had walked several yards down the ramp, Jason stopped abruptly. He stooped down to the floor as though he were tying a shoe.

"What are you doing now?" Peter asked.

"I'm securing my feet to these floor brackets."

"I don't understand."

"When the hangar doors open, the air pressure inside will blow everything that isn't tied down out into space."

"But..."

Peter's face contorted in terror as he grasped the full meaning of Jason's explanation.

Jason-13: *Jason-0 is secured in the cargo compartment. I'm secured onto the deck. Jason-16, open the hangar doors.*

Chapter 13

Entriva, Alpha Mensae System

Twenty Entriva days (fifteen Earth days) after Rae Anne was incarcerated, two Baltar guards stepped into her cell. They motioned for Rae Anne and Jason to accompany them. Rae Anne held up her hand to signal a pause and rushed to put herself together and grab her translation device.

When she was ready, the guards led them through the cell block and past the floor sentry to the escalevator. With just enough room for the four of them, Rae Anne felt a wave of claustrophobia. An unusual odor surrounded them. She wrinkled her nose.

What am I smelling? A musky, mushroom odor with overtones of lilac or rose? I wonder if this is a natural body odor or some kind of after-bath scent? Do they even bathe?

She shook her head, surprised to have such frivolous thoughts at a time of personal crisis.

The escalevator platform carried them up eleven levels. There, the guards nudged them into the corridor and led them to two wooden doors at the end of the hall. A sentry on each side swung their respective door open to reveal a large room surrounded by bleachers arranged in three tiers.

The room was filled to capacity. Rae Anne could see no identifying features to distinguish one furry peanut shape from another. The large number of eyes focused on her caused her to shudder.

Two chairs occupied the dais at the front of the room. A deep bass humming issued from the ceiling. Rae Anne's translator informed her that they were to sit in the chairs. Rae Anne could not discern who the magistrate in the audience might be. She and Jason sat and faced the crowd. She frowned as a cold shiver slithered up her spine.

No features for me to read. I can't tell if they are sympathetic or hostile.

"Please tell the court who you are and where you are from."

"I am Rae Anne Chavez and this person beside me is Jason. We are Humans from the planet Earth in the Sol System."

No need to confuse things regarding Jason's android status.

"Our archives show a primitive sentient species on Sol System's third planet, but the records are old. We haven't visited the system since Shalcerians began patrolling it as if they owned it. Explain how you came to encroach on our space in a Shalcerian warship."

So, they know very little about us. Maybe I can use that to our advantage.

"We purchased the ship to be used as a research vessel. We have no other intention besides research. We were evaluating the ship's wormhole propulsion system when it dropped us accidentally into your space. It appears to be faulty."

"And what is the purpose of your research?"

Quick! What would I want to be studying that required a starship?

"The Shalcerian presence in Sol System has created great interest in other species. Besides Shalcerians, I have learned a great deal about Minotaur culture and have visited 18 Ophiuchi but failed to meet any representative Belkiri. Now, fortuitously, we have a chance to engage with Baltari."

"Quite convenient to 'engage with Baltari' just when the Baltar Federation is preparing for a major offensive against the Shalcerian Empire in the Centauri System, a neighboring star system to your own. And in a Shalcerian warship. The *Prescient* should have destroyed you on sight.

"We know the Shalcerians have a base in your Sol System. Tell us more about the relationship between Humans and Shalcerians."

"The Shalcerians maintain a small outpost to support their patrols in the Kuiper Belt. That's a fringe of icy comets and asteroids circling our system. They have shared some of their technology with Humans."

"We find that hard to believe. Shalcerians are untrustworthy. Every species they encounter, they subjugate into slavery. Some, they have ruthlessly driven to extinction. They are a scourge to this arm of the galaxy."

Interesting. The Shalcerians say much the same things about Baltari.

"With all due respect, Humans have not experienced this. We are a peaceful species. We wish to maintain peace and good will with all species we meet."

"What you say may have merit in other circumstances. But the two of you are charged with invading Baltar space. The stellar coordinates where we intercepted your ship make this allegation indisputable.

"You are also charged with the more serious crime of espionage, attempting to spy on behalf of the Shalcerian Empire with whom we have been in armed conflict for over 150 years. The fact that your vessel is a Shalcerian warship is also indisputable.

"How do you plead to these charges?"

Rae Anne scanned across the rows of eye rings but could not determine to whom she should address her response.

Just stare straight forward and answer as boldly as you can.

"Your honorable magistrate, I submit to you that we are not spies. We ask you to regard us as emissaries, here to create an opportunity for dialogue between Humans and Baltari. As to the charges, we plead 'not guilty'."

"A peace mission with only two representatives and no supporting documentation makes no sense. The Human species abides in a system under Shalcerian control. Our knowledge of Shalcerian's despicable treatment of other species suggests they may be forcing you to serve their agenda.

"We will next hear testimony from AgruVen, an experienced technician in navigation systems. AgruVen, tell the court what you discovered in your analysis of the accused's ship navigation system."

A Baltari in the second tier stood and faced the defendants.

"Your honor, a careful analysis of their navigation program revealed no indication of programming error. We also found no sign of malfunctioning hardware. However, I discovered a major…"

"That will do, AgruVen. Your evidence rebuts the defendants' argument in their defense. Their arrival in Baltar space must have been intentional."

Wait! He has more to say. What did he find?

"We will now hear from ShanuBar, a weapons expert who has examined the defendant's ship. ShanuBar, tell the court what you discovered."

A Baltari sitting next to AgruVen stood.

"Your honor, the Shalcerian vessel in question was quite well armed. Had they attacked Entriva, they might have caused a great deal of damage."

Damn. It never occurred to us to disarm the ship. Double damn!

"And what was the status of these armaments?"

"They were all operational, your Honor. But…"

"Thank you, ShanuBar. Are there any questions or comments from the gallery?"

They may have been operational, but none of them were activated!

No one responded to the magistrate's request.

"Then we shall vote to determine the verdict for this trial by raised hands. Raise both hands if you find the defendants guilty as charged."

There was rustling throughout as nearly every Baltar hand was raised and waved ceremoniously back and forth in unison, reminding Rae Anne of a 'wave' in a sports stadium.

"Thank you. Those voting for 'Not Guilty,' raise your hands."

A smattering of hands appeared.

"Rae Anne Chavez and Jason, Humans from Sol System. The court has found you both guilty of unauthorized invasion of Baltar Federation space and of espionage, the only capital offense other than treason in our judicial system. After the requisite six-month soul-purification period dictated by our traditions, you both will be executed by laser-beam decapitation. This court is adjourned."

A frigid numbness washed over Rae Anne.

Falsely accused and sentenced to death. This was not how fresh encounters with alien civilizations should turn out.

"How could we have presented a better case?" she whispered to Jason. "What could we have shown to prove our innocence?"

"I don't think anything would have made a difference. Their bias against any incursion even remotely connected with Shalcerians is what convicted us. We're going to be the first Humans to die in interstellar space."

"Did you say 'we'?"

"Well, for us Jasons, my loss will be more like your losing, say, an arm. An arm that can be replaced. The only thing we Jasons will lose is the data associated with our experiences since our first jump."

When they returned to their cell, the guards locked the door behind them.

They must think an impending execution might lead to an escape attempt. But where would we escape to?

Rae Anne slumped on the sofa, dejected. Jason sat on the floor beneath the kitchen counter and reconnected to the Baltar computer archives.

"Maybe I can come up with a legal recourse for a stay of execution," he said.

Paris

Karen folded her napkin and placed it beside her plate. She glanced at the half-filled bottle of wine on the table and at Sam, who was picking uncharacteristically at his dinner. He seemed particularly distant on this occasion.

Something's not right. Dial up your awareness level.

"You seem distracted tonight, Sam. You've hardly touched your dinner."

"Nothing of concern for you, Marie. Just a minor annoyance in Durban Robotics. Let's skip dessert. I seem to have lost my appetite."

"Very well. Come up to my room and I shall do my best to take your mind off whatever is troubling you."

"That would be a welcome relief."

"Grab the wine. We can finish it upstairs."

"No, leave it. When both my doctors and my security people tell me to cut back on my alcohol consumption, I figure I'd better listen."

Security too? Not a good sign.

Karen laughed. "Every good engine needs lubrication. I'll bring it up for myself, then."

She grasped the bottle by its neck with one hand and took Sam's arm with the other. "Let's see if we can have some fun, shall we?"

Upstairs, she persuaded Sam to pour himself a glass of scotch while she served herself a smidgin of wine. They sat on the sofa and snuggled, nursing their drinks in silence.

This won't do. I need to find out what's bothering Sam.

Karen began unbuttoning Sam's shirt and flirting with the hairs on his chest. "You keep yourself much too busy. You need to schedule more playtime." She nibbled at his neck.

Sam sighed. "Things have been better. The damn Loyalists canceled my transport services to Juno. If it weren't for Mars, TransWorld Space would collapse. My mining operations in the Asteroid Belt and on Luna are all that's keeping Luna Xtract profitable. But I'm having security concerns with my robotics company."

Oops. This could be serious.

"We've also had issues with security at RMI. Getting clearances for our employees working on government contracts has been taking far longer than it used to."

"No, no. That's not what concerns me. It's the leaks. Everything from marketing plans to highly confidential engineering specs. It's like our computer systems have been thoroughly hacked."

"Security breaches are something every tech company deals with. It's hard to keep information locked up."

Besides, moles on the inside are much more useful than outside hackers.

"Yeah, but this is more serious than usual. I've hired outside consultants, IT security specialists, to investigate the problem."

I need to put my team on hold. Especially Sophia. Still, what fun watching Sam agonize over his collapsing empire.

"Let's work on cheering Mr. Sam up. Come with me."

She led him to the bedroom with one hand while loosening her gown's sash with the other. The dress fell to the floor at the bedroom door, revealing Karen unclothed. She pressed her body into his chest, wrapped his face in her hands and gave him a long, languorous kiss.

"You are stunningly beautiful, Marie" Sam said, standing back to admire her body as he loosened his belt. He stepped from his pants at the bedside as Karen stretched on the bed. She grabbed a pillow and twisted into a most provocative pose.

Sam suddenly frowned, his back stiffened. "Hmm. Odd," he said.

Karen caught her breath.

"I haven't noticed that birthmark before, the one above your left ankle. But I've seen an identical blemish on someone else."

Caught by a birthmark? No way. Think quick.

She laughed. "Oh, that? Surely, you've heard of the Genghis Kahn birthmark. Genghis Kahn fucked every woman he ever met, creating thousands of children carrying his genes. Millions of his descendants carry that birthmark." Karen laughed. "I'm surprised you haven't run into it before, as much as you get around."

"I've never noticed." Sam seemed satisfied at her explanation. He crawled onto the bed, with less enthusiasm than normal. Their lovemaking was almost mechanical. When Sam was satisfied, he rolled over and soon began to snore.

Only thing I learned tonight is I need to warn my people. But if Sam cuts back on the alcohol, I'll likely get little more information from him myself. I can put an end to these little trysts. I surely won't miss them.

Chapter 14

Durban Robotics, Silicon Valley

Just another two and a half terabytes and I'll have this file copied.

The download progress-bar crept across Sophia Accardi's screen. Her coworkers were all at Gabrielli's Italian Buffet for their traditional Friday lunch. With wine, beer, and all-you-can-eat, these outings lasted well into the afternoon. Sophia promised to join them when she reached a convenient stopping point in the code she was developing.

The room was silent save for the HVAC's continuous hum. Despite having done this several times before and being alone in a room filled with cubicles, Sophia was uncomfortable. Perspiration dripped down her back and soaked the underarms of her blouse.

Shit. I'll need to freshen up before I head out to lunch.

The progress bar was up to 85% completion.

This is taking forever. C'mon. Hurry up.

Her heart pounded double time. She swiped at the sweat trickling off her forehead. This was the largest file she had tackled so far. She was copying the full program code for Durban Robotics android AI. It would reveal to her philanthropist benefactor exactly how far along their engineers had progressed. A careful study of the code would also reveal what safeguards and restrictions were being built in to ensure that future androids using the program would be safe around Humans.

90%. We're almost there. Take a deep breath.

BANG. The door to the office slammed against the backstop. Sophia jumped with fright. Her heart seemed to stop and her brain fogged over.

Four burly security guards rushed directly to her cubicle. She reached for the mempin but one of the guards grabbed her wrist before she could unplug it. His grip was so tight she thought her hand would break.

"94% downloaded, eh?" he snarled, looking at the monitor. "We'll just let that baby finish up so we can show Mr. Durban what you've been copying. It will be interesting to see what he has to say."

Oh god, I'm finished. I'm so sorry, Mom, Dad. I did this for you.

Ten minutes later, Sophia found herself sitting in Sam Durban's swank office. Sunlight glistened off the deep blue strip of bay visible through his floor-to-ceiling penthouse suite windows. Forested hills filled the opposite window. Sam fingered the mempin with its incriminating information.

"So, what will I find when I plug this into my computer? It must be important for you to stay behind while everyone else goes to lunch."

Sophia took a deep breath to calm her shattered nerves.

At least I'm no longer shaking.

"A full backup of our android AI program, Mr. Durban. I heard the programmers talking about a change in direction. I thought I might save a copy of the program before they altered it."

"Don't you think they back up their own work? Besides, I know you are aware our IT department archives daily backups for six months."

"I was hoping I might make the grade for a promotion into the android AI project. Studying the code, on my own time, would provide me with the background to be a valuable contributor. I could hit the ground running if I became part of the team. You know how cliquish engineers can be."

"It's called confidentiality, Sophia. Top secret. I don't know how you managed access to that file in the first place."

"It really wasn't difficult. You should tighten ITs security procedures. I could help do that. Who better than someone who's hacked into the system?"

Sam laid the mempin on his desk and sat back in his chair. He steepled his hands beneath his chin as if in thought.

"Your point is well taken. We have an opportunity for you to prove yourself in just that capacity. The IT department with my mining operation on Luna has experienced several hacks from unknown sources. We think the Chinese military may be involved. You might be just the person to create a firewall and block these attacks."

This is my chance to save my job. I can do this.

"I have the background to handle this kind of thing. I'd be happy to help."

"We need you there immediately. The latest attack has shut down our operations cold. I have a cruiser leaving for Luna this afternoon at five. Just enough time for you to pack for, say, a two-week stay. But don't mention where you're going or what you'll be doing to anyone. We don't want to tip off the hackers. Be back here by four-thirty."

On her way to her car, Sophia couldn't stop shaking her head in disbelief. Sam Durban had bought her story. Instead of being arrested and charged with corporate theft, she was off on a grand adventure.

Wow. My first trip into space. An important assignment on Luna. If this works out, I'll surely be up for promotion and won't need that side job. I wasn't really cut out to be a spy. This is the big chance I've been waiting for.

Nova Prima, Mars

The following day, Tony Armado sat stiffly behind his desk in Nova Prima's mayor's office. Both elbows and hands rested on the desk's surface. He inhaled deeply and slowly exhaled before notifying his assistant in the outer office to let his guest in.

This is it.

Sam Durban stepped through the nanoscreen and strode across the room to Tony's desk. The flush on his scowling face revealed that he was none too happy. Tony motioned to the chair beside his desk, but Sam ignored him.

"What the hell is so important that we meet in person?" Sam growled. He made no attempt to hide his irritation. "I have three interplanetary enterprises to run. I'm a very busy man, Tony. What's this all about?"

Tony again motioned to the chair. Sam pulled it from beside the desk and plopped heavily into it. His scowl did not diminish.

Tony steepled his fingers beneath his chin.

This is my office, my city. I'm not your minion.

"When you arrived, before you landed, what did you see?" Tony asked.

Sam pursed his lips. He assumed a more conversational tone. "Nothing special. What was I supposed to see?"

"What you saw was eighty-three interconnected habitats. Plasticor habitat shell walls and connecting tunnels. For years, Chavez promised to build transparent nanoplast domes over our three Martian colonies. For years, we waited. It never happened."

Tony shifted uncomfortably in his chair. "Then you came along and promised that Nova Prima would get equal priority with Haven under your oversight. So, we joined your coup and hijacked *Denali* to support your effort. Four years later, we're still waiting. Your coup has failed. Where does that leave us?"

"In case you hadn't noticed, Tony, this revolution is still ongoing. I have seven armed Shalcerian cruisers. When the time is right, we'll hit Haven with everything we've got. They won't stand a chance."

"What I see, Sam, is that you no longer control Haven. The Shalcerian Accords have been renegotiated. Haven's new government is responsive to their citizens. The discontent your coup capitalized on no longer exists. There is no fuel for a new uprising."

"My operatives see things differently. Haven's new government is fragile. Corruption is rampant. People will soon realize what they lost when the Loyalists pushed my Liberation League out. They'll be begging for me to come back. When that happens, you'll see how I deal with traitors and turncoats."

Tony shook his head.

You really believe that bull crap.

"It's no good, Sam. As far as we're concerned, it's over. You are in salvage mode, doing what you can to save your business empire. Your political ambitions are dust. Nova Prima's future is with the Loyalists."

Sam stood and leaned over the desk, menace in his face. "You don't want to do this, Tony. You are making a grave mistake."

Tony glared into Sam's eyes. "The mistake was believing you in the first place. Nova Prima has joined with Hibernia and Pella to form an independent entity, the Mars Confederation. This is a carefully crafted business decision. We've taken command of *Denali* to support our enterprise…"

"What do you mean, 'you've taken command of *Denali*?' That ship belongs to me."

"*Denali's* captain and crew have joined our Confederation. The winds have shifted. We have contracted with Haven to purchase three domes for our cities. We no longer need to depend on you for our future."

Sam's face turned purple with rage. He kicked his chair to the side and pounded Tony's desk with his fist.

"You'll regret this. I'll see that you and your traitorous allies pay and pay dearly."

Sam spun toward the nanoscreen and stormed from the office. Tony settled back in his chair and closed his eyes.

At least I didn't have to call security to have him thrown out.

Tony placed a conference call to his fellow mayors, Frieda and Zane, to report on his meeting with Sam. He stood and paced the room with nervous energy.

"What do you make of his threat, Tony?" Frieda's voice conveyed concern. "He's still got six cruisers to our one."

"He was unhinged angry when he left. We all need to keep ourselves and our cities on high alert."

"No surprise there," said Zane. "However, I may have snagged another cruiser for our enterprise."

This caught Tony by surprise. "Oh? How so?"

"I was communicating with Captain Sarkov of the *Mendeleyev* while it was docked at Nova Prima waiting for Durban to finish with you. I told him about Denali and offered him the same deal. He said he would poll his crew. If they go along with it, he'll bring *Mendeleyev* back to Nova Prima and join forces with us."

Tony stroked his beard. "This is better than we thought. With two cruisers, we'll be a force to contend with."

"That still leaves Durban with five," Frieda observed. "Can we get additional cover from the Loyalists? I hear they often shadow Durban's ships."

"They're aware of our situation," said Tony. "Ian Bentley promised their help should Durban cause us any problems.'

"What's the latest on the dome contracts?" Zane asked. "I visited Juno just last week. Their new dome is incredible. I couldn't stop gazing at Jupiter's massive presence overhead. It was almost full. What a sight."

"Haven's engineers will deliver the blueprints and specifications later this week. Once we've signed off on them, they claim they can begin work before the end of the year."

"It can't be too soon for my people," said Frieda. "Once we're free of these confining habitats, we can look ahead to making our three cities regular tourist destinations."

"With *Denali* and *Mendeleyev*, we'll be able to set up regular ferry service to Earth. But first, we need to keep Durban at bay. I'll contact Bentley to bring him up to date on our situation here and see what he can do to help."

Chapter 15

RMI Headquarters, Paris

Karen watched as Ambassador Jin Lei strode the perimeter of her office on the top floor of the RMI administration building, gazing out the windows at the manufacturing and shipping facilities the Chinese had assembled.

"If you look carefully, you can spot the Eiffel Tower out that window," Karen said, more to break the silence than anything else. "If it's a clear day, that is."

I wish he'd stop pacing and say something. I'm a jangle of nerves. He didn't travel all the way from Beijing to look at the view.

Jin Lei clasped his hands behind his back and turned to Karen sitting at her spotless mahogany desk. "We've put together a successful operation here. Quite impressive if I do say so myself."

Karen breathed a sigh of relief. When Jin Lei arrived unannounced, she racked her brain to discover anything she might have done wrong.

She swallowed hard to clear her throat. "We're now quite competitive in the world of robotics, Lei. Our sales volume exceeds Durban's by twelve percent. Gross revenue is still below his, owing to our lower price structure, but we'll soon pass them on that front too."

"The Science and Industry faction of the Politburo is happy with how you have managed our operations here, not to mention your commanding presence at conferences and with the media. This arrangement has proven fortunate for everyone."

"I couldn't agree more. I am forever in your debt."

"The Directorate is concerned about your frequent meetings with Sam Durban, however."

Karen's breath stopped short, as if a ton of bricks had landed on her chest.

God. Won't they ever give up?

All she could think to say was, "Keeping tabs on the competition."

"There might be better ways to do that. We think your personal, intimate approach might lead you to compromise your position. Perhaps even to endanger yourself."

"I don't see how I might be in danger."

"When was the last transmission you received from Sophia Accardi?"

How do they even know about Sophia?

"About two weeks ago. Our engineers are still working over the information she sent. She's an extremely valuable asset."

"Was, as it turns out."

"My god. Has she been caught?"

"Our operatives watched her board one of Durban's ships destined for his Luna base where his mining operations are located. She appeared to be on a business assignment for the company. She never arrived."

"Are you sure? You may simply have missed her."

"It's hard to miss someone on Luna. Her parents are frantic. She always contacts them daily when she travels. They haven't heard from her since she left. Her car has mysteriously disappeared from the company parking lot."

"You think Sam killed her?"

"We suspect Durban had her spaced somewhere between Earth and Luna."

Karen swallowed hard. Her mind brought up scraps of memories from her last encounter with Durban.

He was distracted by a security breach. He planned to tighten security. Or am I being paranoid because of Sophia's disappearance?

"So, you can see why we want these visits to stop. Just so you know, we've doubled security on your behalf.

I didn't know I had bodyguards in the first place.

"Thank you for that. But I'll miss hearing him bitch about his losses."

"So, what have you learned from him since your last report?"

"Durban is intent on regaining political power, even though his business empire is crumbling around him. I predict he'll eventually be forced into bankruptcy."

"Assuming he doesn't make a political comeback. He still has a fleet of alien cruisers at his command."

"The Loyalists are keeping him from using them effectively."

Jin Lei turned back toward the windows, hands clasped behind his back. "However, …"

Karen again caught her breath. *There's more?.*

"We still don't have Professor Jason in our employ." He turned to her, a scowl on his face.

"I have a team working on that, Lei. Last I heard, they were on Haven. They were tracking his movements to determine the best time to nab him."

"And I have a team on Haven tracking your team. We do look after our investments. Our down payment for this operation was substantial."

"It's what was needed to get the job done."

"And there's the problem. The job isn't getting done. Our team reports that your men appeared to have captured the Professor, bought their shuttle tickets for Earth, and then vanished. They entered the lift going down to the shuttle bay, but they never exited from the shuttle when it arrived on Earth."

Karen stood in a state of agitation and alarm.

God! What happened? How could they have just disappeared?

"I know nothing about this. They were to report to me as soon as they arrived on Earth."

"Then where might they be? I might add, since their fiasco on Haven, Professor Jason appears to be working in his lab night and day. We absolutely must get that man working for us."

Two major disasters at the same time. No wonder he's upset.

Karen sighed. "I shouldn't have assigned such a critical task to subordinates. I hate Haven with a passion, but I'll go back. I'll take a team with me and oversee the operation myself."

"I do hope you succeed, Karen. My government can be especially brutal to people who double-cross them."

Jin Lei left Karen's office without another word. Karen dropped into her chair and propped her head in her hands. She was chilled to the core as though she had been shoved into a pool of icy water.

I'll first try again at enticing Jason with an offer he can't refuse. Maybe something alluringly physical, though he doesn't seem the type. But this time I'll have a team to back me up and take him by force if necessary.

Whatever could have happened to my other team?

TransWorld Space Headquarters, Sydney

Sam Durban drummed his fingers on his desk, his face contorted with anger. Travis just reported that the Mars Confederation voted to deny TransWorld Space landing permission at all three colonies.

"Tony Armado is to blame for this. He stole two of my ships. He's using them to supplant my access to his markets. He's crossed the red line with this one. This is a declaration of war."

"War, Sir?"

"We need those markets. Mars is the ideal base for our operations. We have five cruisers and a thousand armed men. When we take Mars back, we can use it as a springboard to recapture Haven. Pella is the smallest Mars colony. What is its population?"

"950, more or less."

"Excellent. We'll make an example of it. A show of force. I'll have this so-called Mars Confederation, and Juno too, begging to rejoin the Liberation League. Call Chernov in. I want to see him immediately."

"Yes Sir."

Shortly after Travis left, Sam watched from his third-floor window as Vernon Chernov stepped from the *Shackleton* and strode across the tarmac to the building. Sam admired his erect military carriage.

A self-assured man of confidence. Perfect for this job.

Travis ushered Chernov into Sam's office. Sam asked Chernov to take a seat in the lounge area on the far wall and went to the bar to fix drinks. Vodka, straight, for Chernov, a Scotch for himself. He brought over the drinks and sat in the lounger opposite the captain.

"Chernov, it's time the Liberation League asserted itself and made a comeback. I want you to head up an invasionary force."

Chernov smiled and clenched his fist. "I've been waiting for this. The invasion, that is. I am honored you want me in command. Do you have a plan?"

"I do. We need to win Mars back first; all three colonies along with the two cruisers they stole. Then we'll be in position to take Haven."

"Why not Juno first? It's a single, isolated city, and the smallest of them all."

"That's what the Loyalists expect us to do. They've permanently based two cruisers there. But Juno will submit to whoever controls Haven. They'll come to us begging once we have Haven."

"Excellent. Mars it is, then."

"Our capturing Nova Prima will come as a surprise. The payback will be the entire planet."

"Pella is a softer target."

"I have other plans for Pella. When this is over, my control over Mars will be undisputed. How prepared for combat are the troops on our ships?"

"We've been running combat readiness drills since the Loyalists drove us out of Haven. Now that you've designated Nova Prima as our target, we'll direct our simulations to include details of its layout and devise an attack strategy."

"How long will that take?"

"We'll be ready for action in five days."

Sam tapped a button on his desk. Travis immediately came through the door.

"Travis, get hold of my other four ships. Direct them to drop whatever they're doing and prepare for a rendezvous in a Mars geostationary orbit on Wednesday next and to prepare for a ground invasion. Tell them Captain Chernov is in command. He will communicate orders from *Shackleton*'s bridge. And tell them to keep these plans on a 'Need to Know' basis, including with the bridge crews. I want there to be absolutely no leaks."

Sam stopped Travis before he left the room.

"One other thing. Find out where *Denali* and *Mendeleyev* are. I intend to get those ships back. I can't wait to court martial Abrams. I may execute him myself.

Mayberry Station

Ian took a belt from his stein of ale and sighed. He was trying to enjoy a rare evening away from *Liberty* and its attendant responsibilities. But his overriding concern for Rae Anne weighed on him like a vise crushing his chest. Anton and Ellie, captains of *Apollo* and *Freedom*, had accompanied him to The Crater, a brewpub known for its excellent beer and raucous, live entertainment. Although the three captains leaned their heads together, they still had to speak loudly to be heard.

"I'm sure Rae Anne and Jason-11 are all right, Ian," Ellie said. "Jason-0 has assured us the jump looked perfectly normal."

"From this end. But who knows at the wormhole's exit? Who knows if they even made it through? The likelihood of disaster increases with every hour they're overdue."

"Here's what I think," Anton chimed in, trying to sound cheerful. "Imagine arriving in Epsilon Eridani System and finding it loaded with planets inhabited by an active space-faring community. Would you turn right around and hop back, or would you spend time with the locals to learn all you can about this marvelous alien civilization?"

"Thank you for that, Anton." Ian took another gulp of ale. "I hope you're right."

Ellie raised her arm and waved to catch the attention of a Jason who had just entered the pub. Seeing her signal, he waved back and weaved his way through the crowd to their table.

Ian looked up quizzically.

"Jason-03, Sir."

"What's up, Jason?"

"It's Durban, Sir. He's attacked the Mars colonies with his five ships. Pella may be completely destroyed. Two cruisers blasted the entire colony with multiple RX4S3 torpedoes."

Ian jumped to his feet, knocking his chair over. Blood drained from his face and a knot cramped his stomach. Anton glanced at Ellie, disbelief written on his face.

"How long ago was this?" Ian asked.

"Jason-09 on the *Olympia* sent a report as the attack was taking place. The communications lag to Mars is currently twenty-one minutes. But that's not all."

"There's more?"

"As Pella was being attacked, three cruisers landed at Nova Prima. A large force of armed men blasted through the Terminal airlock and swarmed into Nova Prima, killing resisters and taking hostages. Tony Armado is in custody on the *Shackleton*."

"What about *Denali* and *Mendeleyev*?"

"*Denali* is *en route* to London with passengers from Mars. Captain Abrams has been alerted. Mendeleyev is on Juno with a delegation of Mars Confederation engineers assessing dome specifications for the Mars colonies."

Ian rubbed his forehead. "Tell Sarkov to bring *Mendeleyev* here. We'll provide sanctuary for them until this is over. Have *Denali* remain docked in London. They are to stand clear until further notice.'"

Ian turned to his friends. "We need to gather our forces and put an end to Durban once and for all."

"So, if we confront Durban on Mars, what then?" asked Ellie.

"It would just be a standoff with his five cruisers," Anton added.

"Has Jason-0 weighed in on this situation?" Ian asked Jason-03.

"He has. He recommends two actions. The first is to send two cruisers to Pella. Surreptitiously. If Durban thinks he's destroyed the colony, he won't have any ships there when we arrive. But it is our duty to rescue any survivors."

Ellie nodded vigorously. "There could be quite a few. The habitats are made from plasticore. The connecting tunnels would absorb the bulk of the damage. Remember the Marsquake Nova Prima experienced a few years back? Most of the residents survived. They just needed rescuing from the scattered habitats."

Ian looked from Ellie to Anton. "How soon can we send *Apollo* and *Freedom* to Pella?"

"I can launch within the hour," Anton responded.

"Me too," said Ellie.

"Then let's do it. But I want no encounters with Durban's forces for now. This is a humanitarian rescue operation."

The two captains pulled communicators from their belt-pouches and put their ships on launch alert, then notified all crew on shore leave to return to their ships immediately.

Ian put a call in to Mayberry's clinic and first-aid station.

"We've just been informed of a city-wide disaster affecting Pella on Mars. I have two ships leaving to assist in an hour. Can you help us in this rescue effort?"

The clinic promised to send medical supplies and EMTs to the Terminal Habitat to join the operation. They also committed to preparing facilities to accommodate the victims and provide critical care services should they be needed.

Anton and Ellie rose and pushed their way through the crowd toward the door.

Ian turned back to Jason-03. "Did you say Jason-0 had two suggestions?"

"He suggests we block Durban's mining facilities in the Asteroid Belt to limit his operations to the Earth-Mars corridor and Luna. We could then devise a plan for recapturing the Mars colonies and limit him further."

"Good. The farther he is from Haven and Juno, the better. Calculate the logistics of a blockade based on where his mines are located relative to our current ships' positions."

"The results are already on your tablet in your quarters."

"Excellent. I'll look them over as soon as I get back to *Liberty*. If they look feasible, we'll do it."

Ian and Jason left The Crater and its ear-splitting hubbub.

Damn Durban! We should have killed him on Haven when we had the chance.

Chapter 16

Entriva Prison

Rae Anne paced back and forth across the living area in her Entriva prison cell, hands clenched behind her back. Every muscle in her body twitched. She wanted to scream, to spring into action. To do something, anything. As the weeks rolled into months, bringing her execution date ever closer, her anxiety level increased.

Dead man walking. I now understand.

She glanced at Jason. He lay on his back on the floor with a cable connecting his head to the room's computer terminal.

"You've been searching the Baltar computer database ever since our trial, Jason. Have you found anything we can use for an appeal? We're running out of time."

"Nothing yet. I've gone through eighty percent of their archives, including millennia of case law. There are no precedents for us to fall back on. I'm sorry it's taking so long. Their computer system is frustratingly slow."

"How can that be? They are far more advanced than Humans."

"Only in some areas. They are on par with the Shalcerians for anything large scale. But they have never developed nano-scale technology. In fact, there are big gaps in their understanding of chemistry and electronics."

Rae Anne stopped pacing. She pointed to the cable connecting Jason to the data outlet in the wall. "The very computer you're connected to demonstrates technological sophistication."

"In biotechnology, yes. In electronics, no. Remember, they survived their maglozon predators by bioengineering plants to fabricate their cities and provide their food. Those advances are just the tip of the biotechnology iceberg. Even this computer is part of a living plant designed to perform calculations and provide accessible memory storage. Which explains why it is so damn slow."

"Does that explain why I've seen no robots or autonomous devices, like AI operated machinery?"

"Exactly. Computational speed is required for automata. They have nothing that comes close to matching my capabilities."

"That's interesting. The two most advanced alien species we know have no use for independent robots. The Shalcerians banned them a thousand years ago when they tried to overthrow their Shalcerian overlords The Baltari, in relying on biological solutions, are unable to meet the requirements for developing robots."

So, we Humans and Jasons have an advantage in dealing with these two species. But we need to return home for this knowledge to be of any use.

"Keep searching, Jason. It's now more important than ever for us to return to Haven. Humanity's future dealings with both species depend on our sharing what we now know."

Entriva Prison, a Week Later

Rae Anne bolted upright in bed, though she hadn't been sleeping. She thought she heard a scraping noise, but the room was now quiet. Then dull thumping sounds penetrated the silence. She recognized the sound as Baltar bouncing noises crossing the room in the dark.

She jerked when a soft hand touched her arm. In the total darkness, she couldn't make out who was present. Jason's whispered voice provided explanation.

"Quiet, Rae Anne. VenaVen is here to help us escape. Follow his lead. Baltari can see in the dark as well as I can."

Jason's hand gently tugged her out of bed and guided her through the apartment. In the dimly lit hallway, she saw the sentry slumped over his desk.

"I tranquilized him," whispered VenaVen. "He won't come to for several hours. By then we'll be far away."

VenaVen turned toward the escalevator. As he moved down the hall, he waved his right hand in a circular motion, perhaps the Baltar signal for quiet.

They took the lift to the roof where AgruVen was waiting in an unusually shaped aircar, its rotors already spinning.

"Quickly," VenaVen commanded in a hushed voice as he helped them into the vehicle. "We have very little time."

Once inside, AgruVen lifted off. They swiftly fled the capital city, tracing a zigzag course through the tree skyscrapers to avoid detection. City lights twinkled all around them. Though late at night, air traffic was heavy, with aircars flitting about in seemingly random directions and elevations.

This entire forest is a major woodland city! I didn't realize how densely populated this city is.

Rae Anne leaned toward Jason. "Their collision avoidance AI must be extremely robust. I don't see any pattern to the heavy air traffic."

"I see many complex patterns, but you would have to see it through Baltari eyes. They are extremely adept navigators."

She turned to VenaVen.

"Why are you doing this? You must be putting yourself in extreme danger."

"If we are caught, I will be executed alongside you and Jason. But the court was predisposed to set an example. They refused to hear the rest of my nephew's testimony, which might have exonerated you. Then there was ShanuBar's testimony. It was misleading. Your ship's computer logs revealed that your weapon systems had not been activated for months. If you were on a spy mission, you would have landed in our space fully loaded and ready for action."

"What was it AgruVen discovered?" asked Jason.

"You'll have to ask him. Too complicated for me to follow."

"Problem ahead," AgruVen announced.

All Rae Anne could see ahead was a solid horizontal bar of white light at their flight level.

The aircar dipped and rolled without warning, throwing Rae Anne's stomach into a spasm. A sharp turn to the right accompanied by acceleration bored her into her seat. Then AgruVen pitched the aircar into a steep climb. The vehicle shot through the leafy canopy and into the dark sky like a rocket.

"We dodged a volley of drones sent to ensnare us," AgruVen said. "But they have us on their spotters now."

"What does that mean?" asked Rae Anne.

"It means we'll be targeted by Air Defense missiles now that we're above the canopy," said VenaVen.

"Three incoming," said AgruVen. "Tighten your seatbelts."

The shuttle lurched into a dive and an inverted 180. The three missiles were now visible, coming straight at them, as was the ground.

Rae Anne swallowed hard to keep from throwing up. She couldn't breathe. A crash seemed inevitable.

Abruptly, AgruVen pulled the craft into a vertical climb. Rae Anne's head spun as she watched twigs and leaves brush the windscreen. Streaming white contrails—one, two, three contrails—plunged past them in rapid succession. All three missiles exploded in the forest, their brilliant flashes reflecting off the ship's cabin walls.

A screeching followed by violent shaking threw her head against the window. The ship lost power and began a spiral down toward the trees.

"We've lost a rotor," said AgruVen. "A missile must have brushed it."

"I can't believe we came that close," said VenaVen. "Superb evasive action, AgruVen."

"Unfortunately, 'close' doesn't count. We're still going to crash."

"Better that than being vaporized in midair. At least we're still alive."

Rae Anne clutched her armrests with a white-knuckle grip. Memory flashes brought images of another brush with death when *Aurora* plunged into Saturn's atmosphere twenty years before.

No one here to save us now. Ooch. Am I going to have a bruise!

The ship hit the uppermost branches with a loud crash and a bone-crunching jolt. Ear splitting screeches and scraping ravaged the senses as the ship tore through the heavy foliage. But the vegetation slowed the ship's momentum enough to keep it from suffering further damage when it smacked the ground with a thud.

An intense, awful silence filled the cabin.

VenaVen rubbed his hand through the fur inside his eye ring, much as a human would rub their forehead. He turned to Rae Anne and Jason. "As you can see, this is no ordinary aircar. My engineers designed it for quick getaways and extreme maneuverability."

Rae Anne was still shaking, unable to respond.

"Is that a feature you need often?" asked Jason.

"Here, on Entriva, I am a respected, enterprising merchant. However, in some systems I am known as a privateer. I trade in goods and services many find difficult to come by. A vehicle like this often comes in handy."

"But only if you have a pilot up to the job," added AgruVen.

Rae Anne swallowed hard to steady her voice. "Then, you aren't military?"

"Oh, no. Far from it. I received a handsome reward for bringing your ship in. I'll be in serious trouble if they discover I've stolen it back again."

"Maglozons," AgruVen shouted. Everyone's attention turned to the craft's windscreen. The surrounding vegetation quaked violently. A large gray-green maglozon snout poked through the branches. It moved onto the craft and clamored over the glass, leaving a slimy smudge in its slithering wake. Soon, two more joined the first in this other-worldly dance.

Up close, they look like a cross between mammoth worms and Burmese pythons. But with fearsome jaws and rows of teeth.

"This is going to make repairs quite difficult," said AgruVen.

"Are repairs even possible?" Jason inquired.

"We have spare parts and tools in the back. If the damage isn't too severe, we might be able to fix it. But not with hungry maglozons lurking around the ship. I've watched them devour two friends. It's something you never forget."

"But we have no choice," said VenaVen. "If you don't go out there and make the repairs, we're stranded. We'll die here if the authorities don't pick us up first."

A hush filled the cabin. Rae Anne shivered at the squeaking noise the maglozons' bodies made as they skooched over the glass.

Maybe just my imagination. But god, are they ever ugly.

Jason broke the silence. "Maybe I can be of help."

The four eyes facing Jason on both Baltari focused on him. With no facial expressions to read, Rae Anne could only guess they must be either curious or skeptical. Maybe both.

"There is one small piece of information we've not divulged, but now seems the time. I am not Human. I am a droid. However, as a sentient being,

I claim all rights and responsibilities attributed to intelligent biological species."

The Baltari continued to stare at Jason. Neither spoke.

Too flummoxed for words!

"In any event, I'm inedible. I doubt the maglozons will show any interest in me. And, of course, I am well versed in mechanics and engineering, so if repairs are possible, I have the knowledge and experience to do them."

VenaVen clapped his hands. "Well, let's get to it then!" Rae Anne thought she detected relief in his voice. "AgruVen, take him down and show him what we have to work with."

AgruVen led Jason through a hatch in the floor. Rae Anne leaned back and sighed, relieved.

If anyone can get us out of this mess, Jason can do it.

After an hour, Jason and AgruVen reappeared. Jason tugged at the wide shoulder strap draped around his neck holding a large satchel filled with parts and tools. AgruVen closed the interior hatch to the airlock behind him. Jason opened the outer hatch and stepped out.

"We don't need the airlock here for atmospheric changes," AgruVen pointed out. "But it does make it easier to keep the maglozons out. They can be very aggressive. Almost smart, sometimes."

Once outside, Jason climbed over the airship to reach the starboard engine. As he crawled over the windscreen, he pushed a maglozon out of the way and lifted another to heave it off the ship. As he predicted, they showed no interest in eating or attacking him.

But instead of tossing the maglozon away, Jason stopped short and put it gently back down on the glass. To everyone's amazement, he sat down beside it. The maglozon's jaw flapped up and down, back and forth, its eyes focused on Jason.

Jason began making hand gestures and waving his arms. Rae Anne watched this performance with amazement.

That looks like rudimentary signing. Jason's communicating with these creatures!

The intercom crackled and Jason's voice filled the cabin.

"VenaVen, how long ago did your species abandon the ground and begin living in trees?"

"Very long ago when our species was quite young. Paleontologists tell us it may have been as much as half a million years ago."

"That leaves time for a lot of evolution. You will be surprised to learn that maglozon's have evolved into a sentient species. They are still primitive, but they have a language, they are self-aware, and they have a sense of the past and future. Groozhnorrohar, here, tells me they have rudimentary tools and communal villages."

VenaVen and AgruVen stared at each other, dumbfounded.

If I could see their mouths, they would be agape.

"Groozhnorrohar has offered to help us, though he's perplexed at our sudden appearance from the sky following the terrible lightning strikes nearby. He's sent his friends out to locate the rotor assembly pieces that fell to the ground near here."

Before long, two maglozons slithered up the side of the aircar with large pieces of debris clamped in their jaws. Jason led them to the damaged engine. Pointing and using hand gestures, he enlisted the maglozons to hand him tools and parts. Working together, they began the repairs. In the meantime, AgruVen changed the codes in the ship's identification transponder so the authorities wouldn't recognize them when they next tried to reach orbit.

While waiting for Jason to finish, Rae Anne engaged VenaVen in lengthy conversations to further understand Baltar customs and civilization. VenaVen seemed equally interested in Humans. At one point, the conversation turned personal.

"I still have an unanswered question, VenaVen. You believe we are innocent, but that doesn't explain the risk you are taking in helping us escape."

"I'm a privateer. My success is due in part to a keen ability to sense the character of individuals I meet, no matter the species. When I met you and Jason, my intuition told me this encounter with your species might create an unprecedented opportunity. However, I had no choice but to follow my ship's AI assessment and arrest you as spies. My crew would have mutinied if I had done otherwise."

"What do you mean by 'opportunity?'"

"We Baltari have been at war far too long. So many lives, millions, have been sacrificed. No one has offered any hope for ending this conflict with the

Shalcerians. Our history tells us we are a peace-loving people. I thought maybe the unique perspective of a new species might help us regain that trait."

Rae Anne nodded. "Since meeting you and your people, I sense the truth in what you say. However, I personally witnessed a Baltar Federation attack on a Shalcerian city in the Alsafi System. Four battleships ravaged the city, killing millions. I was there in the aftermath, helping survivors. That experience clouded my impression of the Baltari."

"I heard about that disgraceful event. The commander in charge went insane after learning of a Shalcerian raid on his home planet. He and several officers were subsequently court-martialed for treason, following our rules of military justice. His actions evoked Shalcerian retribution which resulted in their destroying two of our military outposts." His upper torso twisted right and left. "Violence begets violence. It never ends."

Rae Anne rubbed her cheek thoughtfully. "I work closely with the Shalcerian Commander of their outpost in Sol System. Commander Denahr has always treated us fairly and with an open mind. I have heard him repeat what you just said about wishing for peace, almost word for word."

"That's counter to everything we have been told about Shalcerians."

"I think the two of you would get along very well. I would love to introduce you to him."

"That would be an interesting meeting. But to what end? Our two species are sworn enemies. A meeting between two single individuals at the bottom of the hierarchy would be of little consequence."

"Declaring who are friends and who are enemies is a matter of choice. Perhaps there's room to choose differently if circumstances allow."

"I see your point. But how could that happen?"

"You might accompany us aboard *Curie* when we jump back to Sol System. I'm sure I could arrange for you to meet with Commander Denahr in a neutral setting. If we've solved the glitch in the nav program, we'll bring you back here and return you to the *Prescient*."

"I'll give it some thought. If this Denahr is open to new ways of thinking, maybe, with Human help, we can begin a dialogue to end to this lunacy."

This may be a breakthrough. But VenaVen's concern is valid. I need to come up with a plan. Where do I start? How can Humans help defuse hostilities that have been raging for 150 years?

Chapter 17

Pella, Mars

Freedom and *Apollo* followed an elliptical trajectory on their approach to Mars to avoid detection by Durban's forces. As they approached Pella, the physical damage to the colony appeared extensive.

Ellie gazed at her ship's forward monitor display in dismay. The sinking sensation in her chest made her heart ache.

Utter chaos. Habitats strewn everywhere. No two habitats remain connected. This rescue operation will take days. God, I hope we find survivors.

The two ships landed on opposite sides of the small crater containing the Pella colony. The ships' airlocks immediately opened. Rescue crews in full SEVA gear rolled carts piled high with equipment down the ramp and into the city's scattered debris.

Ellie remained on the bridge to monitor progress and direct operations from her elevated vantage point. She watched as her crew split into three groups and trudged toward the three nearest habitats. Two lay on their sides like overturned freight cars. The third was upside down. Its hatch with its emergency airlock dangled from the structure like a tooth ready to be pulled. The habitat's interior was fully exposed to the rarified Martian atmosphere.

An EMT used a hoist on her cart to lift herself up to the hatch. She beamed a light through the opening, moving it back and forth to scan the interior.

"This one is a cold-storage locker. No victims here."

Ellie exhaled heavily, though her chest remained tight. "That's a relief. Fasten a green tag over the hatch so we'll know it's been checked."

The other two teams constructed emergency egress tents around their habitats' airlocks. Before sealing the tent to the structure, one EMT slipped inside the tent with a cart of medical equipment. Their companion then finished the seal and inflated the tent.

With pressure equalized, the habitat's airlock automatically opened. A young woman limped into the tent carrying her young daughter.

"Thank god you're here," she cried. Ellie could hear the distress in her voice. She could imagine tears flooding down her distraught face. "My Mia needs medical attention right away."

"Two persons needing medical attention, an adult woman and a three- or four-year old female. The child is injured. She's having difficulty breathing."

Through the semitransparent tent walls, Ellie could see the EMT helping the victims into the autonomous transport vehicle attached to the opposite end of the tent. Once they were inside, the vehicle's hatch sealed shut. The EMT then released it from the tent. It rolled to *Freedom*'s ramp and into the ship's airlock as the rescuers rolled up the tent and moved to the next habitat.

A doctor and two nurses waited in the corridor for *Freedom's* airlock to cycle. When the inner hatch opened, they helped the woman into a wheelchair. They placed the child on a gurney with oxygen and rolled them both to ER. The airlock closed and cycled again, allowing the transport vehicle to drive itself back to the EMT crew.

Throughout the day and into the night, EMT's repeated this operation at every habitat. They helped those without injuries into SEVA suits from the transport vehicle and directed them to walk to *Freedom*. Severely injured victims received emergency treatment inside the tent before being sent to the ship in the transport.

The rescuers marked each habitat with a colored tag when they finished with it. Green indicated they had checked the habitat and declared it free of victims. Red tagged a habitat containing bodies to be recovered later.

By the end of the second day, the teams from both ships had checked all the habitats. Volunteers from each crew recovered the dead. The ships' cargo bays served as emergency morgues.

Ellie's brain swirled dizzy with fatigue. Urgent requests for more supplies, additional transports, and relief personnel interrupted the few short naps she managed to take.

Time to wrap this up and get some sleep.

She flipped the com switch to connect with *Apollo*.

"Anton, give me your numbers. I'll send a report to Ian. I plan to hit the sack as soon as we lift off."

"I'll be right behind you, Ellie. I'm beat. We've accounted for 487 individuals. Of those, 33 are deceased, 12 are in critical condition, and 72 others needed significant medical treatment. The remaining 370 came out relatively unscathed."

"That mirrors our counts, too. From what we saw when we arrived, there are fewer casualties than I would have guessed."

"It would have been far worse if not for the plasticore. That stuff is miraculous. See you back at Mayberry Station."

Entriva, Aboard the Baltar Shuttlecraft

Jason-11 worked nonstop for three days before he was confident enough in the repairs to declare the airship ready for flight. He explained to his new friends that they needed to stay away from the ship to avoid injury at liftoff.

The last thing we want is to alienate the aliens. Hmm. I wonder if that would qualify as humor.

Once he was back in the cabin, he directed AgruVen through several short runups. During the trials, Jason adjusted the controls to compensate for the refurbished rotor. After the fifth test, everything was operating to his satisfaction.

Nothing more I can do. It's 'do or die' time. What a loaded expression!

"Your ship is ready to fly, VenaVen," he announced. "AgruVen, take it easy. The repairs might not handle sudden changes in direction or momentum. We just need enough velocity to activate the ram jets so they can boost us into an orbital trajectory."

"Then let's get out of here."

AgruVen applied power to the rotors and the airship lifted steadily off the ground. Power to the pusher-prop accelerated them forward. AgruVen pulled the nose higher. They continued to accelerate upward.

"It's working," Rae Anne sighed with relief.

"I couldn't have repaired the rotor without the pieces the maglozons retrieved for us. For creatures without appendages, they are quite adept at manipulating things. Their jaws are good for more than just chewing."

"You were out there with them for three days, Jason. How much of their language did you pick up?" asked Rae Anne.

"After day two, we were conversing fluently."

"Amazing," said VenaVen, nodding the upper half of his torso. "And we always took them for useless worms."

How often do otherwise intelligent species make that same blunder?

Jason shook his head in resignation. "Curiously, the maglozons had no idea that the oblong furballs which occasionally fell from trees weren't just another type of fruit to be eaten. Groozhnorrohar was amazed to learn that another intelligent species inhabits their world. When you return, they would like to arrange a meeting with you."

"Interesting thought. I'm not sure how that would work."

"I'll leave you with a translator device you both can use. Land your shuttle near our crash site and ask for Groozhnorrohar. He's a shaman in their local village."

The communications unit interrupted their conversation.

> Unidentified shuttle craft. Please identify yourself and
> state your destination and ETA.

"Shuttle 73358 on suborbital hop to Ankilar. ETA 05:10," AgruVen responded. Rae Anne felt the ship's acceleration increase.

"The trajectory to Ankilar will take us right by your cruiser, orbiting overhead," VenaVen explained. "The ramjets will accelerate us to orbital velocity. Once we reach space, we'll coast to your ship. From there we'll jump to Sol System."

"I'm surprised you can achieve orbital velocity with ramjets," Jason said.

"Long ago we developed a plant whose fruit contains a liquid with an extremely high energy density, six times that of your typical hydrocarbon fuels. Our space program depends on it for shuttles that are too small to accommodate the gravitic propulsion units used in our cruisers.

Almost on cue, the shuttle lurched forward with a roar, driving everyone deep into their acceleration couches. Rae Anne squirmed to find a comfortable position.

"Ramjets ignited. Full power for orbit insertion," AgruVen announced.

"Where is your ship, the *Prescient*?" she asked VenaVen, shouting to be heard above the engines.

"It's on the other side of the planet. No one will connect me to your escape. In the meantime, AgruVen and I will travel to Sol System with you and see if we can initiate a meaningful dialog with your Denahr."

Jason turned to Rae Anne with an inquisitive look on his face.

Rae Anne must have proposed this to VenaVen while I was working outside. Interesting opportunity. But first, we must make a successful jump home.

The com unit again crackled to life.

> Shuttle 73358. You have deviated from your scheduled course. You are not authorized to enter orbital space. Reduce velocity and return to your planned trajectory immediately.

"Now things get interesting," said AgruVen.

"What are they likely to do?" Rae Anne asked.

"If they determine we're heading toward the Shalcerian ship, they'll probably shoot us down," said VenaVen.

"That's encouraging," said Jason.

"Jason, I think you've mastered the art of sarcasm." Rae Anne said with a chuckle.

> Shuttle 73358. State your intentions. You have entered orbital space without authorization. We will send intercepts if you do not respond immediately.

AgruVen brought up several orbital maps on his monitor and studied them before responding.

"Shuttle 73358 is changing destination to orbital outpost 53. Please accept my apologies for last-minute change. Client requested visit to outpost 53 for short stopover before continuing to Ankilar. Authorization for altered trajectory requested."

After a few moments, the authorization came through, with the admonition to avoid the light cruiser in their path.

"So far, so good," said AgruVen.

VenaVen rubbed the top of his fur ball in the middle of his eye ring.

"They'll launch the minute we dock with the cruiser. We'll need to move fast once we're onboard."

"I can program the shuttle to continue on autopilot to the outpost," said AgruVen. "That may buy us the time we need. But I would hate to lose this baby."

VenaVen nodded. "I'll get outpost 53's authorization to park there. *Prescient* can pick it up before it leaves Entriva."

Rae Anne gasped when the *Curie* appeared in the distance.

"I had almost given up hope of ever seeing *Curie* again."

Jason turned to her. "There's a sight for sore eyes."

"Your idioms are improving, too," she said, eliciting a round of tension relieving laughter.

The shuttle slid alongside the cruiser while the forward thrusters activated until their velocities matched. The shuttle latched onto the airlock. Once it sealed, the hatch opened and they entered the ship, leaving AgruVen behind to program the shuttle's controls for autopilot. The com console was blaring commands on the shuttle's bridge as AgruVen jumped aboard *Curie* and sealed the airlock.

"They've launched fighters to intercept the shuttle," he announced. "They may fire missiles at the cruiser."

"That won't be a problem," Rae Anne said. "*Curie's* hull is made of plasticore. It's resistant to nearly everything."

Jason furiously worked the controls on the bridge, with AgruVen at the navigation console. As *Curie* began to accelerate away from Entriva, three sharp bumps rocked the ship.

"You're right about the hull," commented AgruVen. "All three missiles they fired were direct hits."

"I'm concerned about our propulsion system," said Rae Anne. "The reason this whole affair happened was our inability to control the wormhole jumps."

"Not a problem," assured AgruVen. "When we were going over your ship, I did a thorough study of your navigation algorithms. I identified the changes you made by their time stamps, then I found a glaring problem you missed."

Impossible. I went over the whole program with a fine-tooth comb.

Jason felt pleased at coming up with another idiom. He identified a sparking circuit in an unused part of his brain as bringing pleasure.

"I can't believe I overlooked something. What did you find?"

"The programs all look fine except for one constant. Your propulsion system uses two micro black holes, like ours. The constant in question should be based on their combined mass. But the number you're using is too large for the black holes on your ship."

"Of course," said Jason. "With proper documentation, I would have caught it myself. Unfortunately…"

"Is there any way we can determine their masses and calculate the correct number?" Rae Anne asked.

"Already done," said AgruVen. "We have an instrument that measures the gravimetry of micro black holes. Every black hole is different, so it's essential to get an exact reading and calculate the appropriate number to put into the equation. It's unique for every ship. Your program should work correctly now."

"Then let's take *Curie* home." Rae Anne grabbed Jason's hand and squeezed it tightly as Entriva's image dwindled in the rear monitor.

There's that sparking sensation again. Holding Rae Anne's hand gives me a sensation of pleasure.

Chapter 18

Shalcerian Outpost on Haven

Ian stepped from the Levcab onto the Levline platform located at the airlock leading to the Shalcerian outpost. He followed Jason-12 into the airlock anteroom and donned the respirator he would need in the inhospitable Shalcerian environment.

How is it I've never visited the outpost before this? Too busy, I guess.

Jason checked Ian's respirator fittings and they entered the airlock. After sealing the Haven hatch, the atmosphere was recycled to match the outpost's. From there, Jason led the way to Commander Denahr's office.

Freight and equipment packed the corridors. Shalcerians scrambled over and around the crates in a continuous stream. Some even hung upside down from the handholds attached to the ceiling.

Controlled chaos. They certainly make good use of all six appendages for getting around when they aren't carrying something. They are as agile as spiders.

"Is the outpost always this busy?"

"Things have gotten more hectic by the week," Jason responded. "The war with the Baltari has been steadily heating up. The front lines are now just a few star systems away. Sol System could find itself in the middle of the conflict very soon. That's the reason Denahr called for Human recruits to help defend the Empire. Denahr wants to give you an update in person."

Ian furrowed his brow. "We've known about the conflict since First Contact, but only recently that Sol System might be at risk. The call up five months ago was the first indication. How's that effort progressing?"

"Quite well. We met Denahr's quota without difficulty. Australia donated land in the Outback and the Shalcerians built the training facility in a matter of weeks. The first trainees will be ready for service in five days."

"So, what's changed that prompted this meeting?"

"I'll leave that for Denahr to answer," Jason said as they turned from the corridor and entered Denahr's receiving area.

Knowing the protocol, Jason walked forward to a tablet monitor next to the nanoscreen, paused for a moment, then rejoined Ian.

"Denahr's AI assistant has noted our arrival, so he knows we're here. He will admit us soon since he's expecting us."

After a short wait, a male Human voice with a definite British accent announced, "Captain Ian Bentley and Jason-12. Commander Denahr is ready to see you."

Ian looked to Jason. Jason gestured to the nanoscreen and followed Ian into Denahr's office. A hologram over the large conference table depicted the bustling traffic above the base and parked on the dozen landing pads surrounding the city's transparent dome. Haven's dome was visible at the far edge.

No wonder they declared the space over the outpost a 'No Fly' zone for our cruisers. I never realized the Shalcerians were packing so much traffic.

Denahr rose from behind his desk. "Ian. I'm glad you could come. Thank you, Jason. Please. Pull over the chair by the wall and make yourself comfortable. We keep it available for our occasional Human guest."

Ian repositioned the proffered chair next to Denahr's desk and sat. Jason stood behind Ian, having no need to sit. A monitor on the wall behind the desk showed an image of Shalkor, the empire's capital city, an orbiting ring surrounding the Shalcerian home planet of the same name.

No need to waste time. Let's get right to the point.

"Jason tells me the war effort is getting close to Sol."

"That's correct. We have a colony on a planet orbiting Proxima Centauri, your nearest neighbor, and we've built two outposts and a colony in the Alpha Centauri B System, less than half a lightyear farther away. The Baltar Federation has now laid claim on the nearest system beyond Alpha Centauri. So, the ternary Centauri star system is in their sights, despite our presence there."

"With three stars in the one system, is it unreasonable to assume your two empires could share?" Ian asked.

Denahr abruptly stood and pounded the table. "Impossible. The Baltari have massacred millions of innocent civilians since they began this war 150 years ago. They are merciless barbarians."

"So, where do things stand?"

"We're fighting skirmishes with their scouting ships throughout the Centauri System. They appear to be enhancing their offensive capabilities. We in turn are increasing our own military presence. The Human recruits will be ready next week. We'll use them to supplement the infantry at our two outposts and to fill out crews for our ships."

"Should you lose Proxima Centauri, what do you see as the worst-case scenario for our system and for Earth?"

"The Baltari will continue to advance and attempt to invade Sol System. They will destroy any site remotely related to Shalcerian endeavors. Haven and our outpost here are particularly vulnerable. It wouldn't take much to turn everything on Haven into rubble."

The image in Ian's mind of Haven being destroyed brought deep furrows to his forehead.

"And beyond that? What about Earth?"

"There may be collateral damage. Whole cities may be destroyed. But the fact that you are flying Shalcerian cruisers throughout Sol System puts your space colonies at risk. Besides Haven, Juno, the three Mars colonies, and your lunar colonies could come under direct attack."

Ian's blood turned ice cold. He gripped his hands tightly in anger. *Good god, Human's aren't prepared to face an interstellar war.*

"Is there anything we can do?"

"As I see it, your only hope is for us to overcome this incursion at Alpha Centauri B and turn the Baltari away. A shame you Humans aren't a few centuries further along in space technology."

Ian and Jason remained silent as they passed through the corridors after leaving Denahr's office. Ian thought his head would explode. His thoughts boiled like a caldera of hot magma.

All our efforts to lift humanity to prosperity and to reach for the stars could be crushed by these warring alien species. All we can do is stand by and watch. Stand by and hope for the best.

Sol System, Aboard *Curie*

Curie popped into Sol System two light-hours from Haven, four hours distant at their current velocity. Jason-11 sent a full report to Jason-0 which included the *Curie*'s wormhole problems and their visit to Entriva. He emphasized that the Baltari were not the belligerent warmongers portrayed by Shalcerian propaganda and that two Baltari were aboard the ship on a peace mission. He also added a special message from Rae Anne.

Rae Anne's simultaneous communication with Ian omitted the technical details, focusing instead on her Baltar guests and their desire to initiate a dialog with Denahr. She asked Ian to contact Denahr and convince him to join them for a meeting.

To compensate for any hesitation Denahr might have bringing potentially hostile agents to his outpost, she proposed they meet at a remote location in the Kuiper Belt on Sol System's distant fringe. VenaVen would thus learn nothing about Shalcerian war preparations.

Three hours later, the *Curie* comlink crackled to life with Ian on the line.

"Welcome home, Rae Anne! Welcome home Jason-11. Everyone here is overjoyed. We thought we had lost you. Pass our warm welcome to your Baltar emissaries.

"The soonest Denahr can meet with me is tomorrow afternoon. Convincing him to leave his post even for a day will be a hard sell. The entire outpost is on a war footing. But I'll fill you in on the details when we meet. Also, it's unlikely Denahr will have anything to do with your Baltar guests. He nearly exploded when I suggested any sort of compromise between them.

"But I'll do my best to convince him to come with us. I'll bring *Liberty* regardless. And off the record, Rae Anne, I am so, so relieved to have you home again. I love you. Ian out."

Rae Anne's heart nearly exploded when she heard Ian's voice. Tears streamed down her cheeks.

I hadn't truly realized how afraid I was that I might never return. I'm a cloud floating on air. Ian, dear boy, I do love you so!

The coordinates Rae Anne suggested for their meeting was another five hours flight time for *Curie*. When the ship came to a stop above an abandoned gravitolite mining operation, Rae Anne called her guests' attention to the tiny bright star on her monitor display. Its yellow light filled her with such joy she wanted to sing.

"There's our sun, Sol. I hope things work out so you will be visiting and trading here soon."

At last, I'm home.

"I see you want to keep us at arms, length, so to speak," observed VenaVen.

"Both for security reasons and for Commander Denahr's safety. He would face the same recriminations with his superiors that you are risking yourself. I chose this location to assure our meeting remains a secret."

"I'm taking your word that he won't attack us outright, that he's a civilized individual. But I still fail to see what a meeting between us will accomplish. We are but tiny spores in a very great forest."

"I've been working on that. When I have Jason-0 to consult with and can tap into his complete data archives, we may find a way to make a breakthrough for ending this war. For one thing, I have met the Shalcerian emperor. He seemed to be a reasonable individual and was very accommodating to our requests."

VenaVen's eyes all glowed brighter at Rae Anne's revelation. "Are you saying you have an 'in' with the Shalcerian emperor?"

"Well, that may be overstating it somewhat. But we'll see."

Actually, it may be overstating it a lot. I doubt if he even remembers our meeting.

Part Three

18 Scorpii
Shalkor, capital
of the Shalcerian Empire
Alpha Mensae
Entriva, capital of
the Baltar Federation
44.7 lightyears
33.1 lightyears
Alpha Centauri
System (3 Suns)
4.4 lightyears
Proxima
Centauri
Sol
Earth
Alpha Centauri A & B

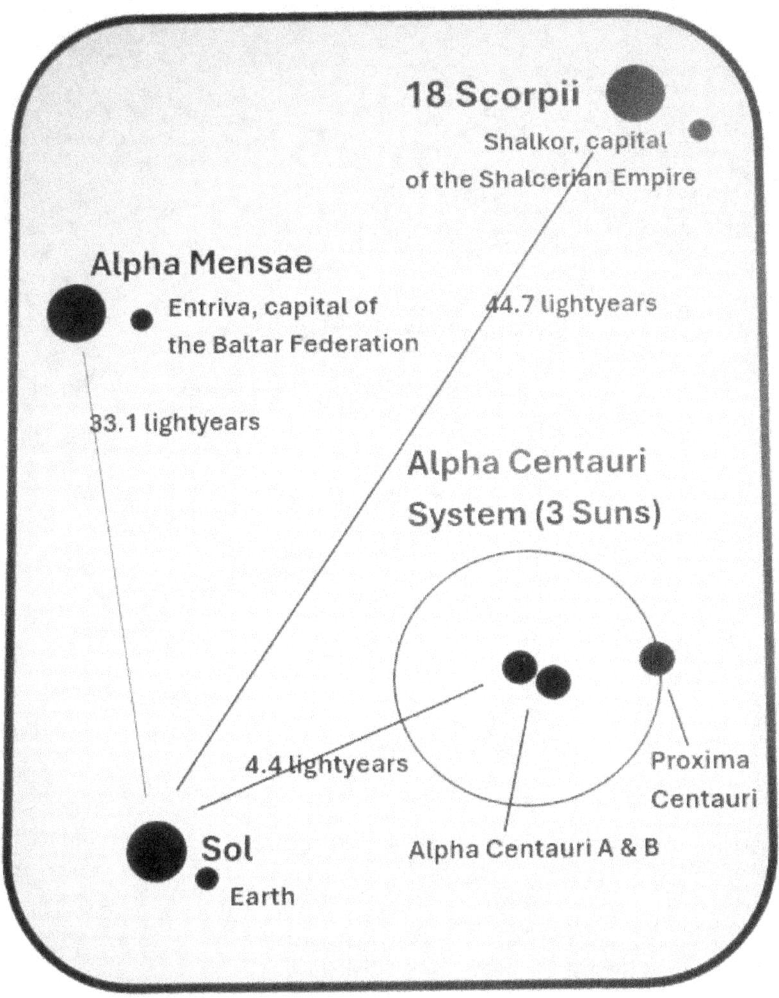

Chapter 1

Shalcerian Outpost on Haven

Denahr's aide escorted Ian into the commander's office and moved the chair across the room, setting it next to Denahr's desk. Ian thanked the aide and, following Denahr's gesture, sat down.

He inhaled deeply through his respirator. *Be confident and forceful. This is bound to be a hard sell.*

"Ian. Welcome back. To what do I owe a second visit in as many days?"

"*Curie* has returned to Sol System. Our interstellar test flight was a success."

"I saw that in my morning alerts. Our gravity field monitors detected its arrival. Congratulations. Welcome to the club of interstellar travelers."

"Thank you. *Curie's* delayed return created a lot of anxiety. Our relief at its return almost exceeds our excitement at its success."

"We'll arrange a special gathering to mark this momentous event. Humans will now have a special ranking among species in the Shalcerian Empire. Counting Humans, only nine of 120 species have achieved interstellar capabilities."

"That's an honor we'll not take lightly. But for the moment, we would like you to keep this new knowledge to yourself."

"I'll take that under advisement. Of course, your new status comes with additional responsibilities. In addition to supplying crews for our ships, you will now be expected to mobilize your own cruiser battle groups, both for your own defense and to aid us when needed in our conflict with the Baltari."

Ian shrugged his shoulders and gestured helplessly.

"*Curie* is only one ship, and an experimental research ship at that. It will be some time before we have anything like a fleet."

"We will help you build up your capabilities. Timing is a major issue. As we discussed earlier, the war is reaching a critical stage and getting closer every day. I'll send a combot to Shalkor to request their immediate assistance."

"Thank you, Denahr."

Now, how do I invite him to a meeting with the Baltar emissaries aboard Curie?

Ian must have looked perplexed, because Denahr broke the silence. "Is there something else you wanted to see me about?"

Relief washed over Ian at this unexpected opening.

"Yes, there is. Rae Anne wants to explore with you the possibility for achieving a détente between Shalcerians and Baltari."

"Impossible! Where did she come up with such a foolish idea? Baltari are unreasonable, savage monsters. There's no way a civilized Shalcerian would waste their time trying to reason with them."

Ian cocked his head and frowned. "That's a harsh description. Is it based on your personal experience?"

"No, of course not. When would I have met one? We've been at war with them for a very long time."

"What if you had a chance to meet one personally? To make up your own mind about how civilized they are rather than take someone else's word for it?

"I trust my sources. The information I get comes through the Military Communication Channel. They have editors who vet everything."

"But wouldn't it be better for your own peace of mind if you could see firsthand and decide for yourself? As you said, this war has been going on for quite some time. Over time, biases become accepted as fact. Myths become self-perpetuating."

"I don't see that being the case here. But why are you mentioning this now?"

"One reason for *Curie*'s delay in returning was that it landed in Baltar controlled space and the Baltari took Rae Anne and Jason-11 into custody."

Denahr's center arm raised so his hand could press against where a forehead would be, just below his eyestalks. His body scales took on diagonal yellow stripes on a black background. "And they lived to tell about it?"

"Exactly Rae Anne's point. She found the Baltari very warm, hospitable creatures. They discovered problems with *Curie*'s programming. It was Baltar experts who worked through the code and fixed the bugs. Otherwise, she never would have made it home."

"That's hard to believe. In any case, I'm totally swamped with this war effort. Perhaps I can meet with Rae Anne sometime later."

"What if I told you she has brought two Baltari back with her aboard *Curie*? They both are anxious to meet with you in person. Like you, both believe this war must end. Rae Anne trusts you, and she firmly believes in her guest's sincerity. She believes you, she, Jason, and VenaVen, the Baltar captain, can work together to come up with a plan that will make a difference in the war effort."

The room fell into an uncomfortable silence, marred only by the ubiquitous humming drone from the environmental control system.

"She can't bring them here! They could see our fleet build up and report back to their military command. They would also learn the location of this outpost."

"Rae Anne thought of that. She's parked *Curie* far out in the Kuiper Belt, hoping I could take you there in *Liberty*. If we keep the meeting short, we could get there and back in less than a day."

"That's still a day I can't spare."

"Even if there's the slightest chance of a breakthrough?"

"Twenty-four hours…"

"*Liberty* is waiting. I could have you back by this time tomorrow."

Denahr was silent for a full minute. His body scales showed green waves over a coral background, indicating indecision.

He suddenly stood and called for his aide. "Alright. I'll do this. I trust Rae Anne's judgement, but I'm afraid this trip will prove to be a fool's errand."

Denahr spent several minutes with his aide, working over his calendar and adjusting his overloaded schedule.

"That should take care of everything." He dismissed his aide and turned to Ian. "The soonest I can break free is one week from today. I'm willing to meet with this VenaVen, but I can only be gone one day."

"It will take us eight hours to get to *Curie*, so you and VenaVen will have eight hours together before we must return. If it's successful, this meeting may be the first of many."

Haven

Jason-12: *The Shalcerian-Baltar conflict is posing a serious threat to Sol Space. Denahr reports Baltar forces are assembling an armada next door in the Alpha Centauri System. They've laid siege to Alpha Centauri B. Denahr is barely able to keep up with the massive flow of warships and supplies through the Haven depot. They are grouping at Alpha Centauri A in preparation for a full-out assault on the Baltar lines. They are also building up a secondary defensive position at Proxima Centauri.*

Jason-0: *All three stars are less than 5 lightyears from Earth. If the Baltari succeed there, we'll undoubtedly be next. Humans know nothing about the Baltar Federation, let alone this conflict. Not that they could do anything about it if they did.*

Discussion among the Jason androids assumed a timeless quality, in that individual comments were added to their common computer database file for current issues. A conversation could span several hours. With Jason-11 aboard Curie, four light-hours removed from Haven, his comment, when it arrived, was time shifted into the database so it would appear in the proper context.

Jason-11: *My experience with the Baltari during our captivity on Entriva showed them to be intelligent, reasonable beings. Their government is quite autocratic, though, which explains their military intransigence.*

Jason-03: *It will be interesting to see how Denahr and VenaVen react when they meet aboard Curie. Liberty is scheduled to transport Denahr to the Kuiper Belt in five days.*

Jason-0: *I'll accompany Jason-03 on the flight, as will Jason-02. So, four Jasons will be present at the meeting to represent our species. Jason-12, as our liaison to the Shalcerian garrison, you must remain where you are to keep us current on the Shalcerian activities.*

Jason-11: *Does anyone have a suggestion on how we might proceed to help these negotiations achieve a positive outcome?*

Jason-0: *Our logical character may help guide the discussion away from personal bias and hostilities. We may be able to discover a breakthrough as we listen to each side's arguments.*

Jason-11: *That may work as it relates to Denahr and VenaVen. But how does it translate into meaningful negotiations between the two empires?*

Jason-0: *On that point, I have no idea.*

Chapter 2

London

Karen stepped off the metro bus near London's Parliament Building and strolled out over the Thames on the Westminster Bridge. The London Eye Ferris Wheel cast rippling reflections across the night-blackened water. She stopped about fifty meters from the shore and searched through her handbag for the burner phone she purchased when she exited the train at London's St. Pancras International Station earlier in the day. Big Ben tolled ten booming chimes.

Good. It's seven in the morning in Sydney. Should be able to catch people before they start their day.

After dialing a Sydney number she memorized before leaving Paris, she tapped her fingers impatiently on the bridge abutment. The party answered on the fifth ring.

"Hello?" a soft, melodious female voice answered.

Karen used her US English. "Hello, Mira? I'm calling from London. My name is Eva, and I'd like to hire you for a very lucrative gig if you are interested."

"I might be," came the guarded answer after a slight pause.

"I have a special friend there in Sydney whose birthday is in ten days, on the twenty-fourth. I had planned to fly to Sydney and celebrate it with him, but my mom just had a serious stroke from which she may not recover. I need to be here with her."

"I'm sorry to hear that, Eva. I lost my mother last year; God rest her soul. I know what you must be going through."

"I would like to hire you to make my friend Sam's acquaintance ahead of time, then lavish your special skills on him the night of his birthday. Could you do that?"

"I could, of course. But I'm very expensive."

"My contact in Sydney mentioned that. It's not a problem. I'll double your normal fee and deposit half in your account tomorrow, the other half after you've performed your services."

Karen paused to give Mira time to decide.

"Eva? It's a deal. I'll give Sam a ride he'll never forget."

"That's wonderful. I've rented a beachfront cottage for the rendezvous. I'll send the address and key code so you can scout the premises and do any decorations or whatever. Make Sam believe the house is yours. I'll send you several photos of Sam, where he works and hangs out. Knowing Sam as I do, you shouldn't have much difficulty luring him in."

Mira laughed. "Men are all alike. Total pushovers."

"One other thing, Mira. Don't mention me or our agreement. He should think this whole affair is his doing due to his personal magnetism toward women."

'No problem with that. It's one key to my success. But what if he wants to see me again?"

"Under no circumstances. That's why I rented the cottage. This is a one-night affair. Any more than that and I might get jealous."

Karen ended the conversation after Mira quoted her fee and provided her bank deposit information.

Jeez. I'm in the wrong business!

She next dialed the second Sydney number her PI had provided. He thought she might have trouble connecting, but Eddie answered on the first ring.

"Yeah? This is Eddie."

"Hi Eddie. I'm calling from London. My name is Nicole. There's someone in Sydney I need to have roughed up a bit. My friend in Sydney says you're just the person to do that for me."

"I don't know what you're talking about. Who put you onto me?"

"You know better than to ask that. But I'll pay you double your normal fee for this job. Half today if you accept, half when you send me pictures and a souvenir."

"So, maybe I know some guys, and maybe I don't. How much damage can they do?"

"I mostly want him scared for his life. Beat him up, blood and bruises but no major broken bones requiring an ER visit. Send me photos. Also, I want the middle finger from his right hand. I'll give you a general delivery address in London to send it to."

"So, how do we find this guy?"

"I'll send an address and a time for your men to show up. He won't be alone. He'll have a young woman with him. Don't harm her in any way, or you won't get your second payment. Just send her off down the beach. She'll have no reason to call the authorities. She's a prostitute."

"Any message you want my boys to deliver?"

"Yes. Have them tell Sam to get the hell out of Sydney or they'll be back to exact an even heftier price."

"So, you don't want him to sleep easy as long as he stays here."

"Exactly. Make sure he understands your visit is courtesy of Karen Sanders on Haven. Tell him 'Karen Sanders on Haven never forgets.'"

Karen finished the particulars with Eddie. Smiling broadly, she tossed the phone into the river and strolled back towards Westminster Abbey.

How does that old saying go? Never underestimate the wrath of a woman scorned. Sam, you are about to receive the full fury of Karen Sander's wrath.

Kuiper Belt, Aboard *Curie*

On the appointed day for the meeting between VenaVen and Denahr, Rae Anne led VenaVen and AgruVen to *Curie's* conference room to await Denahr's arrival. A twinge of excitement lightened her step.

No matter how this turns out, this will be a historic meeting.

She pointed to the refreshment table beside the door. "We don't have anything to eat here that is compatible with your systems. But I see you brought your own snacks." She gestured to the satchel AgruVen was carrying.

"Coffee is perfectly suitable," said VenaVen. "AgruVen realized we might need to provide for our own nutrition, so he brought along food rations from Entriva. Although we've reached the bottom of the bag this morning. We'll need to return tomorrow."

"That can be arranged. Denahr can only be here eight hours himself."

"I anticipate this will be a very short meeting," VenaVen said.

Rae Anne brought a pitcher of coffee and three mugs to the table. She filled the mugs and set them before her guests.

I've never seen a Baltari eat or drink. I wonder how they manage.

She was surprised to see a long worm-like appendage emerge through the fur in VenaVen's upper torso. He brought the mug to the table's edge and the organ snaked over the lip of the mug into the coffee. The liquid level dropped as VenaVen sipped as though drinking through a straw.

Like an elephant drinking with its trunk. Amazing.

"If a conference is scheduled to work out a peace treaty between Baltari and Shalcerians, who would the Baltari send and who would be making the final decisions?" Rae Anne asked.

VenaVen pushed his glass away. "The President of the Federation, RanaDal, would send military negotiators to the meeting with specific instructions. In the end, he would have to approve any agreement."

"Would the negotiators have any leeway regarding compromises?"

"No. RanaDal is a strict autocrat. His family has controlled our government for more than one-hundred years. They have become very wealthy through bribes and patronage relating to the war effort. Many believe, as do I, that this is why there has been no effort to end the war."

"Humans have often experienced the same thing. We only see change when a great leader comes along who can look beyond selfish interests and act for the benefit of his entire constituency and its future."

VenaVen was silent for a moment. When he spoke, his translating device took on a thoughtful tone. "Such individuals have appeared at crucial points in our history. We surely need one now."

"You mentioned the president's family as being in control. Is nepotism a problem in your culture?"

"Oh, it's not a problem. It is how things are. Baltari maintain very close relationships within our families. Often, a battleship's entire crew might belong to one extended family with everyone on a first-name basis. Ninety percent of my crew on the *Prescient* belong to the Ven family.

I can't imagine knowing so many people to begin with, let alone that many family members. What a wonderful feeling of belonging they must have.

Chapter 3

Kuiper Belt, Aboard *Curie*

When *Liberty* arrived and docked with *Curie,* the airlock opened to reveal Ian and Denahr standing side-by-side, with Ellie and three Jasons behind them, exactly as Rae Anne had requested. She thought having several Jasons present would emphasize Human's technological strengths. Denahr wore his respirator which emitted a faint whiff of hydrogen sulfide and ammonia.

Since this was the first time individuals from the Baltar and Shalcerian cultures had ever met, a cautious atmosphere of decorum pervaded the event. Rae Anne made the formal introductions.

"Welcome aboard Human's interstellar cruiser *Curie:* Commander Denahr of the Shalcerian Empire, Captains Ian and Ellie of the Human Alliance, and the Jason delegation led by Jason-0. It is my pleasure to introduce Captain VenaVen of the Baltar vessel *Prescient* and First Officer AgruVen, both Baltar Federation citizens."

Denahr's eyestalks drooped momentarily in polite Shalcerian greeting, while VenaVen bent his knees and stooped slightly with arms crossing his chest to offer his own salutation. Rae Anne stepped forward to Ian and grasped his right hand and wrist with both hands in a firm grip to subtly convey her welcome.

Oh god, Ian, I want to throw myself into your arms and smother you with kisses. I was afraid I would never see you again.

Rae Anne led the gathering to *Curie's* conference room, eliciting small talk between her alien guests on the way. She noted that Denahr exhibited a harsher demeanor than she had seen before.

I hope we can overcome this mutual distrust and hatred between these two species. At least Denahr and VenaVen agreed to meet.

Once everyone was seated, Denahr on his center leg, VenaVen and AgruVen on pillows to accommodate their round bottoms, and the Jasons standing on either side of the table like sentries, Rae Anne began what she hoped would go down as a historic first.

"Friends, and I do count you all as personal friends, I address you as equals. I especially commend Commander Denahr, Captain VenaVen, and AgruVen who have come at great risk to their careers and perhaps to their lives.

"It is well known that the Baltari and Shalcerians have been in conflict over a great many generations. My hope is that in agreeing to come here to meet in person and to communicate directly with each other, we can identify mutual goals, sow the seeds of understanding, and bury past hatreds and antagonisms. Gentle people, it is time for this incessant conflict to stop."

VenaVen rubbed in the center of his eye-ring with both hands, a common Baltar gesture she recognized from her time on Entriva. "I agree entirely," he said. "Over so many years, both sides have lost many lives, losses in the millions. Vengeance, hatred, and retribution have fueled this wasteful and fruitless war. I'm not even sure how it started. I suspect time, myth, and propaganda have erased the truth."

Jason-0 spoke. "On our way from the airlock, Jason-11 relayed to me the data he obtained while *Curie* was in the Baltar system. So, I now have the full histories for both civilizations. Not surprisingly, regarding the war, these records do not match. Each side blames the other for encroaching on a claimed star system and firing the first volley, eliciting retribution.

"Where the histories do agree, they record three occasions where the two regimes massed large forces and waged intense battles within the confines of one or two star systems. In all three cases, both sides retreated after months of carnage, their forces depleted, their fleets in tatters, with no winner. Every planet within those star systems was damaged, many reduced to radioactive cinders. On occasion, innocent, indigenous species were eradicated."

Rae Anne looked first to Denahr, then to VenaVen. "So here we are, engaged in a fourth confrontation. A famous Human physicist, Albert Einstein, once defined 'insanity' as 'doing the same thing over and over while expecting a different result.' Gentle people, what you are doing is nothing short of lunacy."

Ian cleared his throat. "Since the three Centauri suns are our nearest neighbors, this current conflict poses a grave risk to Human and Jason security. Fifty-thousand Humans are already in the Centauri System, and another fifty thousand are in training to join them."

Rae Anne's head jerked upright. A chill coursed down her back. *My god. When did that happen?*

She took a deep breath to compose herself and glanced at Denahr and VenaVen. "We here represent four unique, sentient species. Our intelligence is evidenced by our incredible technological achievements. We must have values and goals we share for the benefit of our species. If we can agree that striving for peace and for cooperation is a worthwhile goal, we will have achieved a major accomplishment."

Denahr's body scales rippled deep purple on a magenta background.

"Nothing of the sort is possible until Baltari retreat from the Alpha Centauri System and address the issue of reparations."

"Reparations!" shouted VenaVen. "How dare you call for reparations after the destruction you have brought on us Baltari."

Rae Anne clapped her hands to draw their attention.

"Denahr. VenaVen. Stop! I must insist that we adhere to two ground rules for our continuing discussion. Rule number one is to direct our comments toward the future, not the past. Resorting to historical injustices is banned. The only allowed considerations are those that begin now, in this instant. We can't change the past; we can only affect the future.

"Rule number two is to couch every comment we make with respect for the dignity of the other parties in this room. This means skepticism and criticism can only be accepted if they are accompanied by positive alternatives or solutions. In other words, we must base our discussions on looking to the future and longing for a future free of the hatred and hostilities, anger, and misperceptions that we've experienced to date."

Rae Anne clasped her hands on the table and lowered her head.

I've said my piece. The ball is in their court. I hope they are up to the task.

There was a very long pause. Everyone shifted about in their chairs. Finally, Denahr broke the silence.

"Captain VenaVen, I apologize for my outburst. It was uncalled for. It was out of place considering Rae Anne's very reasonable guidelines."

"Please, Commander Denahr, call me VenaVen. I accept your apology. Please accept mine for my rebuttal. Let us try to work together. Rae Anne's rules are simple, though they may be difficult to follow."

"You may address me as Denahr. So, how do we proceed?"

Despite the rancorous beginning, the participants engaged in a lively five-hour work session. Denahr and VenaVen recognized that they were the low rungs on their respective hierarchical ladders, but they also realized they were not without influence.

The Human participants spoke up only as needed to mediate disputes. Jason-0 was called on to search his data archives when historical precedents were needed. He also pointed out logical errors and contradictions in their arguments when they cropped up and called attention to potential unintended consequences in suggested solutions.

When negotiations reached a standstill, the team scheduled a second meeting two weeks ahead. Denahr agreed to allow VenaVen to bring *Prescient* into Sol System, provided it remained in this remote section of the Kuiper Belt. When Rae Anne adjourned the meeting, Ian and Ellie took Denahr back to Haven in *Liberty*, while Rae Anne and Jason-11 jumped *Curie* to the 82 Eridani System where they had agreed to meet up with the *Prescient*, avoiding a possible confrontation with the Entriva authorities in the Alpha Mensae System.

Chapter 4

Sydney

Mira Lasker absently brushed back strands of black hair blowing in her face and tucked them under her scarf. The ocean breeze provided marginal relief from the blistering afternoon sun. Billowing clouds spackled the sky to the west with promise of a spectacular sunset. She sighed wistfully.

I'll be able to buy my own cottage on the beach after a few more years. Nothing as fancy as this, but the view will be the same.

Thoughts of the income this gig would bring, her most lucrative ever, brought a smile to her face. The call from London was followed by a substantial increase to her bank balance. She received several photos of Sam along with the location of his usual haunts, one being a five-star restaurant in a famous downtown Sydney hotel.

Using her professional skill as a courtesan, she had no trouble getting Sam's attention in the hotel lounge when he showed up for a drink. After coaxing him into divulging his upcoming birthday, she invited him to celebrate at her vacation cottage on the coast on his special day for an evening of 'adult entertainment.' Ensnared in her charms, Sam readily accepted.

The whir of an autonomous aircar landing on the villa's roof pad caught her attention. She turned and waved. When Sam stepped from the vehicle, she motioned to the stairs to his left that led to the deck. Sam waved in acknowledgement and turned toward the stairs.

"Lovely place you have here, Fiona" Sam said, joining her at the deck rail. "Hardly what I would call a cottage."

Mira laughed and shrugged, holding her arms out toward the sea. "It's the location. You're just in time to share the sunset with me. Would you like something to drink?"

"A double scotch, straight, would be perfect."

Mira prepared two drinks at the deck bar, hers diluted with ice and water, and returned to the railing. Sam took his drink and proposed a toast.

"To unexpected surprises and strangers well met."

"To strangers well met and birthday celebrations."

They clinked glasses, then turned to watch the setting sun cast the distant clouds in a vibrant yellow, orange, and mauve collage. Sam put his arm around Mira's waist, drawing her close. She leaned her head on his shoulder. Sam's hand began to wander.

Mira laughed and shoved his hand away. "Not now, silly. Dinner is waiting. My cook left just before you arrived, so everything is ready. Lobster and shrimp are the stars on tonight's menu. You may pour the wine."

She led Sam into the kitchen where she began serving dinner. Her flimsy blouse kept slipping down her breasts. Satisfied on seeing Sam's distracted gaze, she exclaimed, "What a bother!" She slipped the wrap off her shoulders, letting it fall to the floor. Sam's gasp was music to her ears.

Pity I can't make him a regular. He reeks of money.

She handed Sam his plate and they retired to the deck table to enjoy the evening breeze off the water.

Mira led Sam into recounting his exploits while they ate, looking for any opening that might reveal information about Eva in London for future reference. But of course, there was nothing to be told.

"Let's save dessert for later," Sam offered when he finished with his lobster. "We'll enjoy it more after dinner has had time to settle."

"Dinner is not going to settle much with what I have in mind." Mira's soft melodious laughter could bring palpitations to any man's heart. "But yes, dessert can wait. Come with me. I have some interesting body art you might be interested in."

"Interesting tattoos?"

"Interesting locations." She laughed and led Sam into the bedroom off the deck. A faint Velcro rip and her skirt dropped to the floor, revealing everything.

"An honest-to-god dragon lady," laughed Sam, pointing at the purple dragon's head on her pubic bone with its red and orange flames lapping around her right thigh.

"That's Gorgon. Wait till you see the rest of him. But first, let me help you out of these things." She began slowly undressing Sam while massaging his body with erotic strokes and kisses.

The twilight morphed into a pitch-black night. The phosphorescent surf pounded in the distance, muffled beneath the moans of sexual ecstasy. Exhausted, Sam finally dozed off beside Mira, holding her to his chest with his left arm. Mira stared into the darkness, breathing deeply. She never allowed herself to sleep with a client.

A loud CRASH shattered the night's stillness. Sam sat up with a start, pushing Mira to the side. Three burly men burst into the room. Mira screamed and slung the sheet over her body, hugging its edge against her neck.

Two men grabbed Sam's arms. "Get outa bed, you sonofabitch," growled one. His foul breath made Sam gag.

The third man gathered Mira's skirt and sandals from the floor and thrust the bundle into her hands. "Git out. Now. Follow the beach south for two miles to the road. Car's waiting for you there. Scat!"

Mira clutched her clothes to her breasts and disappeared into the night. The man joined his two partners who had Sam pinned face first into the wall.

"What is this?" Sam shouted. "Who are you? What do you want?"

The third brute slugged the back of Sam's head, smashing his nose against the wall and creating a stream of blood. "Shaddup. You only talk when you're told to. Got that?"

Sam, dazed from the blow, muttered incoherently.

Another blow to the head. "I said, Got that?"

"Yes, yes. I got it. Don't hit me again."

Another blow, this time to the kidneys.

"You don't tell me what to do. I call the shots." He backed away and scanned the room. "Bring in a chair. We're gonna have some fun."

One man strongarmed Sam, keeping both arms clasped behind his back while the other brought in a chair from the dining room. The first goon tossed him a rope. They hefted Sam in the air and dropped him into the chair. After binding his hands behind his back and to the chair, they tied his ankles to the chair legs.

"Listen, I can pay you ten times whatever you Ooph…" Sam doubled over from the blow to his stomach and struggled to catch his breath.

Over the next hour, the lead thug showered Sam with irrelevant questions, twisting his answers into excuses to authorize more beatings. Every bone in Sam's body ached. His face was caked in blood.

"Well," he said at last, "I see this ain't getting us nowhere." He turned to one of his buddies. "When's high tide?"

"Couple more hours."

"Let's carry him down to the beach and plant him there. The only way we'll never see him in Sydney again is to wash him out to sea."

"Yeah. Like flushin' a toilet."

The three men guffawed and slapped each other on their backs.

"That's cold-blooded murder," sputtered Sam.

"Maybe, but she said we could do it as a last resort."

"Who's she? Tell me. I can buy her off and make you all millionaires."

"Oh, didn't I tell you? Karen Sanders on Haven told us to pay you this visit. She thought you might have forgotten her. But she wanted to assure you that she never forgets."

"Karen Sanders. That bitch!" spat Sam.

"Which reminds me. She wanted us to send her some pictures. Got my phone here. Untie the man's hands."

They untied his hands and stretched his arms out to the side.

"Now, Sam, I take it you don't like this Karen Sanders lady. Tell you what. Show her how you feel. Give her the finger and I'll see she gets it."

Sam shakily extended his middle finger. Before he realized it, one thug grabbed it and snapped it off with a pair of sheers. Blood gushed from the stump. Sam screamed, gagged, and threw up.

"There. That should do it. Before and after photos." He pocketed the phone and pulled out a plastic baggie. His buddy dropped the finger into it, then he sealed it and stuffed it next to the phone. "A memento to go with the pictures. Tie him back up and we'll carry him down to the beach where he can enjoy the ocean view."

They carted Sam, trussed to the chair and sobbing with pain, down to the beach and planted the chair in the sand with Sam facing the sea. As they were leaving, the leader looked at Sam and said "If by some miracle you get outa this, we'll be back and do the job up right. Sydney's through lookin' at your sorry face."

The men disappeared in the darkness. Through swollen eyes, Sam watched the waves crashing onto the sand, closer, ever closer. The throbbing pain in his hand was excruciating.

Before long, cold saltwater began washing over his feet. He realized once the waves reached his legs, the chair would topple over and he would drown. Terror flooded through his body like a burst dam.

Just when he was sure the next breaker would thrust his chair over, a brilliant white light flooded the area. Sam shook his head sharply, thinking he must have died. Rough hands grabbed under his arms and pulled him back, back onto dry sand. Suddenly, his aching hands were free. Then his legs. He tried to stand but fell forward. His rescuers caught him and helped him up the beach toward their waiting vehicles. The helicopter with the search light roared off into the night.

"How… How did you know to find me?" Sam stammered when he could finally speak.

"Anonymous caller said a drug deal must have gone wrong and some thugs left you out there to drown to send a message to the other dealers. We're taking you in for questioning. But first, where can we find your clothes?"

Sam shakily pointed to the steps leading to the cottage deck. Blood still oozed from his finger stump. As the EMT's dressed the wound, Sam tried to connect the dots leading up to this moment. His thoughts were a fuzzy blur. He repeatedly worked through the events in his mind to make sense of it all.

That bitch Karen Sanders set me up. She wanted to scare the bejeezus out of me, but not kill me. She paid Fiona to lure me into a trap. That's why a car was waiting for her when the goons showed up. And for some reason, she's intent on uprooting my life here in Sydney.

My life's at risk if I stay here. I have to leave Sydney. But I'll get back at that bitch in spades, even if I have to destroy Haven to do it.

Chapter 5

Sydney

Three days after his 'birthday party,' Sam limped into his headquarters at TransWorld Space, leaning heavily on a cane. Purple and blue splotches covered his face and arms. Two large bandages covered his right forehead and cheek bone. A thick pile of gauze taped securely around his wrist filled the gap where his middle finger had been.

Travis jumped to his feet. "Good god, whatever happened to you?"

"Never mind," Sam growled. "Follow me."

Travis trailed Sam into his office and closed the door.

Sam sat awkwardly behind his desk, leaning the cane against the wall.

"Travis, you've been with me long enough that you know this business inside and out. I'm putting you in charge of TransWorld Space operations starting today. I'm moving permanently to Nova Prima where I can better martial my space force to regain my mining operations in the Asteroid Belt."

And get a better shot at Haven and that bitch Sanders.

Travis was at a loss for words. "I can handle that," he finally said. "Can I relocate to this office?"

"Of course. As soon as I get packed up and cleared out. I'll expect a detailed weekly report. You notify me immediately if anything unusual crops up. Of course, your new responsibilities warrant a doubling of your current salary. Now get me some boxes and help me pack up."

By midafternoon, Sam had closed out his personal affairs on Earth. His business files and personal belongings were packed aboard *Shackleton*. He sat in his flight chair on the ship's bridge, fidgeting as the launch countdown proceeded.

The cruiser lifted off without incident, but as it passed through low-Earth orbit, the *Freedom* appeared alongside and began to shadow them.

"Damn Loyalists," muttered Captain Chernov as he tried unsuccessfully to break away from the Loyalist's ship.

"Do you ever get a clean launch without their harassment?" Sam asked.

"Only about 5% of the time. Ever since we took over the Mars colonies, they tag us like mosquitoes after blood. If there are two of them, they force us to turn around and return to base."

"Bastards! Why don't we blast them out of our way."

"You know why. Plasticore hulls. It's difficult to hit a vulnerable spot in the hull, like an airlock or cargo bay door. If we started a maneuver to try that, the other ship's captain would take notice and the confrontation would escalate. So, we tolerate their annoyance and try to work around it."

Sam glared at the starboard monitor showing *Freedom*.

One more good reason to put the Loyalists out of business.

Kuiper Belt, Aboard *Curie*

VenaVen sat quietly in the elevated chair especially fabricated for him. The eight eyes in the eye-ring atop his head emitted a deep purple fluorescence. Having withdrawn his arms and legs into body pouches, he looked like a giant brown, furry peanut with a glowing diadem. He was joined by AgruVen and four other Ven family members from the *Prescient,* which, like *Liberty*, was parked alongside *Curie* in the Kuiper Belt.

Denahr was the only Shalcerian present, having arrived from the Haven outpost aboard *Liberty*. Any hint he might be meeting with the Baltari would result in his arrest and court martial. He envied VenaVen for the support his family could offer.

Denahr assumed his usual position, using his center leg as a pedestal. He feared for the colony and military outpost under his command located on the Haven moonlet in Saturn orbit. Should the Baltar armada invade Sol System, Haven would be the first casualty. In just minutes under Baltar attack, it would become a blackened, smoldering asteroid.

After making sure her guests were comfortable, Rae Anne opened the meeting. Denahr conveyed a report he had recently received from the Military High Command.

"Reports from the most recent combots are telling us the Baltari are laying siege to Alpha Centauri B. We have two outposts and a colony in the B System. We are committed to protecting these assets. Our forces are gathering there to drive the Baltar armada completely out of the Centauri region."

Ian responded to Denahr's report. "If you don't at least hold the line there, Earth is at grave risk. Our entire species' existence may be at stake."

Denahr sighed. "The Empire has gathered what it believes is a superior force, both in numbers and technology. Humans and Jasons have nothing to fear. Baltar forces will not enter the Sol System."

"It would be far better to defuse the current situation rather than count on superiority in numbers," observed Jason.

"Far too many Baltari have died, far too many resources squandered," VenaVen said, though no visible part of his furry body moved. "We must put an end to these hostilities."

"We have sacrificed and lost much as well, VenaVen. How is it we two are the only ones to realize this?"

"We are not in the thick of battle."

"But when you encountered *Curie,* you didn't fire on it despite it being a Shalcerian cruiser. Then you helped Rae Anne and Jason escape prison. Those actions reflect your commitment to make a difference."

Rae Anne cleared her throat. "It's that very attitude of respect and conciliation we need to instill in those who are promoting the war."

Jason used his computer connection to generate a 3-D hologram above the conference table. It depicted Sol and the three Centauri suns, the Baltar front line in blue just beyond Alpha Centauri B, and the Shalcerian front line in red, bisecting the sun.

"*Curie* is the only interstellar ship Humans have," he said. "And it's just a light cruiser. The only weapons we have are propaganda and misdirection. If we could convince the Baltari that they do not want to mess with us, they might stop their advance and be content to draw the line at Alpha Centauri B."

"Misdirection like when you saved Rae Anne from prison on Haven?" asked Ellie, laughing.

Jason chuckled. "We would need a hologram as big as a planet. I'm thinking old fashioned fake news. The advantage we have is the Baltari know very little about Humans and Jasons."

"That may be where I come in," said VenaVen. "I can send combots to Military Headquarters on our home world. Since *Prescient* is known to our military, I can hand deliver a message to the generals on the front line. If I present myself as an embedded observer within Sol System, I could pass on any information you wish, fake or otherwise. Not knowing the facts, they might find anything I say credible."

"But what would have an impact on your people's thinking?" asked Rae Anne.

"For our strategists, only military strength will make a difference. If I reported that you had hundreds of warships with more powerful weapons than ours, that would give them pause."

"They wouldn't begin to believe that," Rae Anne observed. "There's no evidence we have such a fleet. If we did, we'd have joined with the Shalcerians, our allies. They know Shalcerians have been present here for some time now."

"Anything we devise will need to be accompanied by some kind of demonstration," Jason pointed out.

"Something to convince them we're more powerful than we really are," Ellie added.

Ian laughed. "What could we tell them that they would perceive as a threat? Both our species are millennia behind theirs in technology."

"Maybe not both," Jason said. His voice carried a suggestion of a mystery yet to be revealed.

Chapter 6

Nova Prima, Mars

Sam burst into the Nova Prima conference room and slammed his notebook on the table, startling the four men who were awaiting his arrival. Vernon Chernov, *Shackleton's* captain, followed closely behind, along with three other men in military uniforms, each with stars on their epaulettes. The *Shackleton* was half an hour late in its arrival from Sam's Luna Xtract mining company on Luna.

"Damn loyalists. Their blockades are forcing us to take time consuming evasive maneuvers every time we launch or land. Can't run anything on schedule. My TransWorld Space operations are a mess. I've had enough. We're going to take back Haven by force and crush the Loyalists. Never should have left Haven in the first place."

"Yes!" shouted Nick Mosley and Igor Saytzev, thrusting fists into the air. Mosley was captain of the *Olympia,* while Saytzev captained the *Leibnitz.* Victor Chernov, Vernon's brother and the *Hawking's* captain, pounded his fist on the table in affirmation.

"I'm ready!" replied Blair Gavin, *Sagan's* captain, nodding his head vigorously.

Sam's ships had never been docked together at the same port before. The generals accompanying Sam gave his captains a start. Except for Vernon Chernov, *Shackleton's* captain, none of them knew that Sam had an organized military contingent.

Sam introduced the three generals to the others, then proceeded.

"I have three companies Earthside with 1500 men each who are trained in hand-to-hand combat and invasionary tactics. There are another thousand recruits here on Mars who have enlisted to join them. Our five cruisers together can easily transport these troops to Haven. Today we lay out a coordinated strategy that will ensure our successful takeover of Haven."

Blair lifted his hand for Sam's acknowledgement. "That's over five-thousand troops to get through the single airlock on Haven's Surface Terminal. That will be a critical bottleneck."

"We won't be going through the Surface Terminal. I have operatives inside Haven who will take over Approach Control at the appointed time and open the hangar bays. Once our ships are inside, the entire army can flood into Haven as fast as the cargo lifts can carry them to the surface."

"That's assuming we can approach the hangars," said Nick. "The loyalists watch our every move. They'll see us coming. Their cruisers will block any approach to Haven."

Sam smiled wickedly. "So, we time our operation to reduce that threat. If we mislead them and draw their forces away from Haven, that will give us a clear path to the city."

"You have a plan?" asked Igor.

"Of course. Juno will be our bait. The loyalists know it is their most vulnerable city. They'll suspect we'll attack there first. So, when they see our fleet heading directly toward Jupiter as if to attack Juno, they'll rush to defend it with most of their fleet. We can use timing and orbital dynamics to work in our favor. In June, Earth and the Loyalist forces at Mayberry Station will be opposite the sun from Saturn. Our feint will put us much closer to Saturn. While they are rushing to Jupiter to defend Juno, we'll make a sudden turn and head for Saturn. When they realize we've changed course, they'll be unable to catch up with us. By the time they reach Haven, we'll be the ones doing the blocking, and Haven will be ours."

"How will we pick up the troops on Earth without alerting the Loyalists to our intentions?" asked Victor.

"Over the first half of May, our ships will leave Mars with their share of Mars enlistees, one at a time, and head to Earth as if on a regular TransWorld Space schedule, no one the wiser. Once on Earth, we load the troops and equipment. Then, after launch, the ships will head to predetermined locations in the asteroid belt and wait there until the allotted time for the attack.

"What if the Loyalists strike at Mars while we're gone?" asked Igor.

"Our thrust toward Juno will involve just four cruisers. *Shackleton* won't leave Mars until it's obvious the Loyalists' attention has been diverted. Then we'll join you at Haven. We'll provide reinforcements for those already fighting. Also, two cruisers will head back to Mars after the troops have been deployed. Mars will be without defenders for no more than two hours, not enough time for a Loyalist response.

"One other thing. The Loyalists anticipate our every move. I'm convinced we have Loyalist agents aboard our vessels. So, everything we decide in this room must stay with us. No communications regarding this mission to staff, bridge crew, family—nobody. Shut down all communications from the ships. Communicate between ships only when necessary to coordinate tactics.

"So, that's the big picture. Our job today is to hash out the fine details for every step, down to the hour and minute. I want this mission to work like clockwork."

And once I've taken Haven, I'll scour the city for Karen Sanders. She'll wish she'd never been born when I get through with her.

Saturn Orbit, Aboard *Liberty*

Rae Anne gazed in wonder at the mammoth ringed planet filling the aft monitor on *Liberty*'s bridge. Eight months had passed since she and Jason-11 made the fateful wormhole jump into Baltar space. This was her first opportunity since then to spend time alone with Ian. She decided to leave *Curie* in Jason-11's care and accompany Ian and Denahr back to Haven. Denahr had just boarded his shuttle to return to his outpost. The forward monitor showed the sleek ship descending towards Haven's surface.

Jason-03 looked up from his communications console and turned toward Ian and Rae Anne on *Liberty*'s bridge. "Denahr just received an alert from Haven. While he was away, the Baltari began maneuvering their armada outside Alpha Centauri B from siege formation to an attack configuration. He believes they are preparing for a sweep through the Alpha Centauri B System."

A chill ran down Rae Anne's spine.

"Dios mio! After witnessing what they did to the Shalcerian outpost on Alsafi, I can only imagine the devastation they would bring to the Shalcerian colonies. Did he say when they might attack?"

"Denahr's sources indicate the Baltari are still calling in reinforcements. Possibly within a week to ten days. Intercepted transmissions from interstellar space are spotty at best."

"What are the Shalcerians doing about this?"

"Shalkor has been alerted and is responding in kind. They have two military outposts and a small colony on an Alpha Centauri B planet to defend. Denahr says military activity at his own base has nearly tripled."

"It's unfortunate we can't do anything but sit back and watch," Ian observed. "At least the front lines are over four lightyears away."

Rae Anne shook her head and frowned.

"There's a problem with that, Ian. From what Jason told me about previous armada-sized battles, whichever side gains the advantage in one system, that side presses forward into neighboring systems until they are finally stopped. If the Baltari take Alpha Centauri B, the other two suns will follow, and then they will be here, wreaking massive destruction in Sol space."

"Jason, did you find anything in the Baltar archives that could help us predict the outcome of this confrontation?"

"Jason-11 downloaded their civilization's entire history. From an unbiased android perspective, both species are remarkably similar. Which may explain why hostilities between them have lasted so long."

Rae Anne leaned heavily against Ian's command console and sighed. "I feel so helpless. Either way, thousands of lives will be lost. There's no guarantee we will escape. We're too close to the frontiers of both Empires."

"This is an interstellar confrontation," Jason reminded them. "All we have is one light cruiser capable of wormhole technology, and without Baltar help, that ship would still be lost in space."

"But now that we have their program fixes in *Curie*'s computer, we can make accurate jumps to any nearby system, right?"

Jason nodded. "Correct. But except for Denahr, the Shalcerians are unaware that we now have interstellar capability."

"What about the Baltari?" Ian asked. "They were the ones who found you lightyears from home and helped you jump back to Sol."

"That's true. But *Curie* is a Shalcerian light cruiser. I insisted we were on a research expedition, but they still assumed we were spies. However, they don't' know much about Humans yet. That could work to our advantage."

"Tell me you aren't planning on getting involved," Ian exclaimed. "This conflict is beyond our control. Compared to these two civilizations, we are an ant in a room full of elephants."

Rae Anne squinted and shook her head.

"Interesting analogy, Ian. But a mouse may be the more appropriate metaphor."

She turned to Jason.

"We need to project Humans and Jasons as a mightier force than we actually are. Deception is our only weapon. Put your mind to work on what we can do to portray us as a species they won't want to mess with."

"Adding fake news and propaganda to the mix will help," offered Ian. "If the Baltar command is alerted that Shalcerian light cruisers under Human control employ radical tactics in armed conflict, it would certainly give them a pause."

Jason smiled and nodded. "The Baltari already know that. Our KBP cruiser *Deimos* destroyed a Baltar battlecruiser when it plowed directly into the battleship's bridge back when we were patrolling the Kuiper Belt. It's plasticore hull kept our crew from harm."

"That was several years ago. We may need to remind them," Rae Anne observed.

"Jason could create a video showing *Deimos* targeting a Baltar battlecruiser and smashing into it," Ian suggested. "Lots of internal explosions. Then use *Curie*'s wormhole generator to send the video to the Alpha Centauri B System in a combot with defective security locks. Let them think they've intercepted a misguided Shalcerian communication. And send a second one into the Alpha Mensae System so their political leadership sees it as well."

"Great idea," Rae Anne said. "And make sure the Human connection is obvious. That will plant seeds of concern regarding Human capabilities. They know they lost a cruiser in the Kuiper Belt. This would connect us to that event and suggest we have a lot more to offer should they decide to attack us."

"It's worth a try," Ian reflected. "We've got to make them think twice before invading our system."

Chapter 7

Aboard *Liberty*

Jason-03 was in his usual place at the communication console on *Liberty*'s bridge behind Ian at the command console. "Captain, our sensors are picking up two of Durban's ships, the *Olympia* and the *Hawking*, at different locations in the Asteroid Belt. They are headed for Jupiter at maximum velocity, two-thirds light speed."

"We lost track of those two a couple of weeks ago. They must have been using the asteroids for cover. This may be the breakout we've been expecting for some time. At their current velocity, how long till they reach Juno?"

"Thirty-five minutes from where we spotted them in the Belt. The sensor readings are fourteen minutes old, so they will arrive in twenty-one minutes."

"Do we know where his other ships are?"

"The *Shackleton* is on Mars at Nova Prima, where it's been for three weeks. *Leibnitz* and *Sagan* both made landings Earthside in that same period, but they got away from us shortly after they left Earth and we lost track of them."

"All four ships running silent. This is clearly a coordinated effort. Who do we have closest to Juno?"

"*Cygnus* is scheduled to leave Juno within the hour on its weekly run to Haven. Comlink to *Cygnus* is 23-minutes. *Apollo* is collecting gravitolite ore in the Asteroid Belt. Including the twelve-minute communication delay, it wouldn't make it to Juno for 48 minutes at best."

"Notify *Cygnus* and *Apollo* of the possible threat. Instruct *Cygnus* to remain on Juno at red alert, then tell Anton to drop what he's doing and get *Apollo* the hell to Juno. Alert Juno of an impending attack. Our warning may be a few minutes late, but we can make them aware of Durban's plans."

"Got it." Jason turned back to the comlink and sent Ian's alerts. A minute later he called out, "Signals from *Leibnitz* and *Sagan* just arrived from another

Belt location. Stats identical to the other two cruisers. Both heading break-neck toward Juno."

Ian scowled and rubbed his stubbly chin.

Four ships to attack one small colony protected with a nanoplast dome. Durban deployed two ships to destroy Pella. He wouldn't use four ships for a blockade. So, if Juno's not the target, this is just a feint. Haven must be his primary goal.

"Sonya, set a course for Haven at full speed. Jason, notify all ships except *Cygnus*, *Apollo*, and *Curie* to head to Haven at once at maximum velocity. They should arrive at red battle alert. Haven is the only target that makes sense for Durban's full fleet. If I'm wrong, we can divert to Juno and join our two ships there."

Ian initiated a yellow alert aboard *Liberty*.

"How long to Haven, Jason?"

"Sixty-eight minutes. Comlink delay is thirty-nine minutes."

"Notify Haven to be prepared for an immediate attack."

"Got it." Jason sent the message. A minute later, he startled the bridge crew with a loud "Whoa."

"Captain, all four cruisers have changed course. They are now headed to Saturn. You nailed it."

"When will they arrive?"

"Travel time from course correction is 38 minutes, less the 22-minute time delay before their change reached us, leaves 16 minutes."

"Damn. Our alert will be twenty-three minutes too late. We're almost an hour behind Durban's ships. Who do we have at Haven?"

"*Kepler* and *Independence*."

"At least Haven has some defense. Not great odds, but they may be able to hold Durban off for an hour."

"Captain, more bad news. *Shackleton* left Mars twelve minutes ago and is also on course for Saturn. Arrival at Haven in forty-four minutes."

Aboard *Shackleton*

Sam's four cruisers reached Saturn twenty minutes before Ian's alert. The Loyalists' ships *Kepler* and *Independence* were docked at Haven with most of their crews on shore leave, so neither ship provided a defense against the attack.

Sam arrived at Haven aboard the *Shackleton* well behind his fleet. As planned, his supporters on Haven had taken control of Haven's Approach Control after a brief firefight and opened the hangar bays to receive Sam's ships. They also locked the hangar doors where *Kepler* and *Independence* were berthed, so they couldn't have departed in any event.

Shackleton docked in Bay 7. Once the hangar doors were sealed and the bay pressurized, *Shackleton's* contingent of troops poured into the hangar and headed toward the lifts. But when they exited at ground level, they found their progress stymied by withering fire from Haven troops stationed in nearby buildings and behind hastily erected barricades. The time delay required to pressurize Bay 7 had given Haven Security the necessary window for troop deployment.

The ensuing firefight at all five stations was furious. Although Sam's company far outnumbered Haven's defenders, the Haven National Guard successfully blocked progress into the city. This was largely because only a dozen men at a time could use the lifts. The thirty second transit time meant that Sam needed four minutes to field one-hundred men at each lift.

Sam knew the lifts would present a minor bottleneck but thought the element of surprise would give his full army sufficient time to reach ground level and invade the city proper. What he didn't know was after his expulsion, the new Haven administration created the Haven National Guard and instituted mandatory military service and training.

National Guard units began gathering within minutes after receiving emergency alerts from Haven Security that Approach Control had been breached. The first responders stopped the invaders within three blocks of the lifts. As their numbers increased, they pushed Sam's troops back to the lift stations and held them there.

Sam recognized the impasse the moment his commanders reported to him. He also knew once Loyalist cruisers arrived, escape would be impossible. He ordered his men who were in or near the lifts to provide cover for the bulk of his troops and called for a retreat to the ships.

With Sam's fighting troops rapidly thinning, Haven Security massed an all-out attack on Approach Control. At first, the insurgents held their ground. But as individuals were picked off by sniper fire, the group leader contacted Sam and informed him that they couldn't hold off much longer.

To avoid being locked inside the hangar bays, Sam ordered the ships' airlocks sealed and commanded his group leader in Approach Control to open the bay doors. Sam's five ships launched just minutes before Haven Security broke into the control room and secured it. An estimated 20 to 35 of Sam's men in each of the five hangars were swept into space when the hangar doors opened, nearly as many as were killed in the actual fighting.

In one last display of rage, Sam ordered all five cruisers to fire torpedoes into their respective hangar bays as they departed. Five massive fireballs burst from Haven's belly, leaving behind charred craters—a permanent record of Sam's wrath. Quakes rattled through the moonlet. The explosives badly damaged several areas adjoining the hangars, including portions of Haven's aquaponics farm. Dozens of emergency airlocks slammed shut, sealing off the damaged areas. Haven's air pressure was quickly restored and its environmental control system remained intact.

Aboard *Liberty*

Liberty arrived at Haven minutes after Sam's fleet departed. Ian diverted *Freedom* and *Newton* to join *Cygnus* and *Apollo* at Juno to ensure Juno was adequately defended in case Sam decided to redirect his fury. He ordered *Voyager*, *Denali*, and *Mendeleyev* to return to home base at Mayberry Station and set up a defensive perimeter there. *Independence* and *Darwin* were deployed to follow Sam's fleet at a distance to track their whereabouts. *Kepler* was to remain at Haven with *Liberty*.

With Haven's seven intact hangars now in Loyalist control, *Liberty* docked and Ian departed to report to the mayor. Jason-0 and Jason-12 were in the lift-lobby at sub-level 1 waiting for Ian when he stepped from the lift.

"What's this, a welcoming committee?" Ian chuckled, then checked his laugh when he saw the look on both Jason's faces and their serious demeanor.

"Whoa, what's up?"

"The Baltari have taken parts of the Alpha Centauri B System. Denahr is outfitting extra battleships to reinforce the remaining line there and to add ships at Alpha Centauri A. The Shalcerians now have 100,000 Humans aboard those ships. More are being trained on Earth as we speak."

"Have we lost any Humans in the conflict so far?"

"Yes. 17,286 Humans were lost in the Baltar onslaught."

A cold wave rushed up Ian's spine, forcing a visible shudder.

"God. And Humans are a small percentage of the forces. What were the total losses on both sides?"

"Shalcerians lost 133,000; the Baltari lost about 160,000, best guess."

"And these were just skirmishes," added Jason-12.

Ian choked back the bile in his throat and shook his head in disbelief. "Over a quarter million in one battle."

"There's more. The Shalcerians have detected a ten- to fifteen-percent increase in the Baltar force. If they succeed in taking B, a similar attack at Alpha Centauri A will surely follow."

"And then they'll be just one step away from Sol System," Ian observed. "We've got to figure a way to stop this insanity."

"Do you think it's time to inform the governments on Earth that humanity may be in danger?" asked Jason-0.

"If there were something they could do about it, yes. As it is, we're sitting ducks with no recourse but to try to survive the storm. We can only let things run their course."

They rode the lift to the surface and stepped onto the nanoplast conveyor walkway leading to the Municipal Building.

"We Jasons are as vulnerable as you. Except for Denahr, the Shalcerians won't have anything to do with androids. Our two species will survive or be destroyed together."

"We'll have to schedule an emergency meeting on *Curie*. Maybe VenaVen or Denahr will have come up with a solution."

If they haven't, we're all in a world of hurt.

"Our more immediate problem, however, is Sam Durban," said Ian. "We need to make sure he never gets another chance to attack Haven. Or anywhere else, for that matter."

They got off the walkway and entered the building. On the lift to the top floor, Jason-12 asked, "What are your immediate plans for Durban?"

"That depends on what transpires after today. If he retreats to Mars with all five ships, I'll assign a permanent patrol over Nova Prima and see that he never leaves Mars again. Mars was self-sufficient before, but with the added numbers from his army, they'll face severe shortages."

"Not just food. Their air recyclers will be hard pressed to convert that much additional carbon dioxide back to oxygen," added Jason-0.

"At least they'll have enough water," said Ian.

"Not necessarily. They'll have to expand their aquaponics farms, placing additional demand on their water supplies. They may need more water than their subsurface ice extraction operations can provide."

Mayor Caldwell received Ian and the Jasons warmly. Ian complimented her on how well her security forces and the National Guard handled the attempted invasion.

"They performed very well," she said. "But we need to determine how Durban's people managed to take control of the Approach Control facilities. We'll investigate that thoroughly. We need to beef up our security clearance system that vets everyone who manages critical infrastructure."

"That same office could maintain dossiers on all of Haven's residents," said Jason-0. "I would happily set aside some of my quantum computer's memory to store and maintain the data."

The mayor shook her head. "That's not what we are about, Jason. A fascist or authoritarian regime would welcome the offer. But our democratic government will tolerate only the barest level of surveillance necessary to keep our city safe. People should be free to live their lives as they wish so long as it doesn't infringe on the rights of others."

"Still…," Jason began.

"Totally non-negotiable, Jason. Throughout Human history, many authoritarian systems have ruled nations and empires. Always, without fail, the results have impoverished the lives of the people they ruled."

The mayor discussed the security measures she planned to set before the council. Ian promised to assign three ships to Haven once he had securely grounded Sam's fleet on Mars.

Ian got up to leave, satisfied that plans were in place to safeguard Haven from further Human promoted emergencies.

"One other thing, Ian," said the mayor. "Several citizens have observed the heightened activity over at the Shalcerian outpost. What's up with that?"

Ian shrugged as if the issue was of little consequence. "The Shalcerians are fighting an interstellar war with another species in a neighboring star system. They're routing a lot of the supplies through this station. I can say this. It's certainly keeping Commander Denahr busy."

I hate lying to her, but the panic if the truth were known would turn Earth into utter chaos. We can only hope the conflict doesn't spill over into our system.

Chapter 8

Alpha Centauri B, Aboard *Predator*

Jason-02 stepped through the nanoscreen leading into the Shalcerian Battlecruiser *Predator*'s bridge. Although his computer archives contained detailed visuals from Jason-0's experiences aboard *Avenger*, Jason-02 was not prepared for what he experienced. A momentary sensation of vertigo swept through his brain circuitry. He felt like he was falling through deep space.

The battlecruiser's bridge was a literal bridge-like platform that extended through the center of a massive spherical enclosure. The sphere's interior walls were projection screens for a 3-dimensional holographic view that displayed all the space surrounding the ship. Star maps, charts, and symbols in diverse colors overlaid this background.

No way anyone is going to sneak up behind this ship!

Ten crew members lined the bridge platform, each focused on their consoles and monitors. In the center, Captain Umtar, perched on his center leg, gazed at several virtual monitors suspended above him, each eyestalk directed toward a different display.

Jason knew from the computer archives that the consoles and monitors themselves were sophisticated holograms that were swapped in and out of existence as needed. The crew interacted with switches, dials, and buttons on the consoles as though they were real. Each person wore special gloves designed for virtual interactions. An elaborate sensor array around the room detected every finger movement and translated them into the appropriate command response for the ship's computer.

Jason discreetly took his assigned position next to the nanoscreen entrance, careful to avoid interrupting the activity. Captain Umtar issued commands and communicated with the other ships in his task group at a furious pace.

The computer began to bark staccato chirps at even intervals, the countdown toward a wormhole jump. The floor vibrated beneath Jason's feet with increasing intensity. Jason watched the section of screen corresponding to the space in front of the *Predator*.

The stars ahead appeared to elongate and rotate in a counterclockwise spiral motion. The image coalesced into a blur that became more intense as its rotation accelerated. Within seconds, it morphed into a brilliant blue-white disk which abruptly ruptured, revealing a central black hole fringed with red and orange. The hole rapidly expanded, soon dwarfing the *Predator*. The iridescent halo mixed into a deep purple and magenta swirl.

Predator plunged into the black abyss with a sudden lurch. At the same moment, Jason's internal clock stopped for a millisecond. When the throbbing vibrations in the ship ceased, Jason became himself again. Three suns glowed dead ahead. The largest, a dull red disk, was Proxima Centauri. In the distance, Alpha Centauri A, a yellow-white star like Sol, was the brightest star in the sky. Just beyond it lay their contested destination, Alpha Centauri B, a dim red dwarf star.

The wormhole transit lasted just eight seconds. Yet in that time, *Predator* jumped the 4.5 light year gap between the two star systems.

The space throughout the bridge suddenly lit up like a Christmas display. Red dots gleamed where the other Shalcerian battlecruisers were located relative to *Predator*. Orange dots for light cruisers and hundreds of yellow dots for support craft surrounded their ship. Ominously, the space ahead was filled with blinking blue, lavender, and teal symbols representing the Baltar fleet. The indicators blinked steadily to distinguish them from the vast panorama of stars in the background.

Jason studied the symbols beneath each icon displaying its relative distance from *Predator*. He determined the nearest Baltar ships to be 3.82 light-hours ahead.

At least a few hours before engaging with the Baltari. I wish I could communicate all this back to Haven directly, but anything I send will take 4.5 years to get back to Haven. I'm on my own. If I survive, the data I take back will be an invaluable addition to our knowledge base.

Jason counted the blinking blips surrounding the *Predator*. He determined that this part of the Shalcerian fleet included 24 battlecruisers, 96 light cruisers, and 240 support ships.

The Shalcerians are throwing 360 ships into battle from Sol System alone. That explains the activity we observed around Haven. And this is just one sector of their battle array.

Over the next two hours, as the opposing swarms drew closer, distinct battle formations appeared. The major planets orbiting the twin suns morphed from bright stars to distinguishable crescents.

When the two fleets' foremost ships were one-million kilometers apart, all hell broke loose. Fighters from both sides erupted by the thousands from their battleship flight decks, filling the intervening gap like black clouds of angry mosquitoes. Blue-white neutron plasma threads streaked through space between the hordes, ending in eye-searing white flashes when finding their targets and destroying an enemy fighter.

The fighter formations soon merged, providing the Shalcerian disk fighters an opportunity to employ a second tactic. By colliding with a Baltar fighter, the thin plasticore edge surrounding the disk would slice into the Baltar craft, cleaving it in two like a machete cutting through a melon. When destroyed in this way, the two flaming remnants exploded in a burst of red, orange, and yellow flaming shards like gigantic fireworks.

Baltar fighters were shaped like torpedoes with eight stubby rail-like wings beginning just behind the streamlined cockpit and running the length of the ship. Grav-pulse units mounted on each wing provided unmatched maneuverability as well as propulsion. A seasoned pilot could bring his craft to full stop, rotate 180-degrees, and return to full speed within seconds. The anti-G gel filling the cockpit shielded the two occupants from the maneuver's extreme G-forces.

The forward screens on *Predator's* bridge looked like a bundled string of flickering LEDs accompanied by bright white flashes. Fighters on both sides blasted each other into oblivion by the dozens. As Jason watched, the Shalcerians deployed a second wave of fighters into the battle. He felt certain the Baltari were doing the same.

The fighters' goal was to reach a battlecruiser and its strike group. With superior maneuverability, they could seek out and target a ship's vulnerable sites and, in kamikaze fashion, provide a precision blow to the vessel. Depending on where it struck, a single fighter could wreak serious damage or even destroy a mammoth battlecruiser. This is how the Shalcerian battlecruiser *Nemesis* had met its end in the Kuiper Belt years earlier. Astronomers observed its hulking remains as it passed by Earth in 2017 and named it *Oumuamua*, claiming it was only an errant asteroid.

The holographic monitors now showed a handful of Baltar fighters breaking through the melee and attacking the Shalcerian fleet. Two dived into a nearby cruiser, striking its plasticore hull with a blinding flash and a plume of fiery debris arcing into the void.

Three came directly at *Predator*. Defensive weapons caught two, blasting them to oblivion. *Predator* shuddered as the third struck it head on but *Predator* suffered no damage. Captain Umtar ordered all offensive ordinance to hold fire until the field ahead was reasonably clear of fighter activity. The Baltar fleet seemed to be holding back as well.

A nearby Shalcerian cruiser suddenly exploded in a brilliant crimson flash that filled half of the starboard hologram. Shards of hull thumped loudly into the *Predator*. The flaming relic spiraled slowly away into the blackness. Only one escape pod separated from the ship. Three support craft raced to intercept it to retrieve the survivors.

The fighter skirmish continued for several hours. A third bevy of fighters joined the fray, then a fourth. Seven Shalcerian light cruisers and two battleships were destroyed, while twice as many ships were damaged and sent away from the front. Jason realized the Baltari were enduring a similar fate from observing numerous immense explosions in the distance.

Eventually, the two fleets began firing their major weapons across the narrow gap separating them. The deck beneath Jason's feet shuddered with each volley from *Predator*. Explosions flashed among the Baltar fleet like starbursts. Jason couldn't determine how successful their bombardment was.

Frequent nearby bursts from Baltar ordinance momentarily overloaded the ship's sensors, washing out the holographic displays. The effect was like travelling through intermittent fog.

Umtar directed his torpedoes at the nearest Baltar cruiser. Several bright flashes splayed against the ship's midsection in rapid succession. Simultaneously, expanding blue-white rings from the Baltar ship signified that *Predator* was under fire. The exchange continued for less than a minute, ending when a blinding red-orange flash tore the Baltar ship apart. A spray of white-hot debris spewed into space in every direction.

Throughout this confrontation, Baltar fighters continued to harass *Predator.* One fighter inadvertently passed through a Baltar plasma beam and disrupted in a spectacular fountain of flame. *Predator* shook with every kamikaze strike. Its own fighter disks now surrounded the ship to drive off the swarm of Baltar fighters. Smoldering debris clouded the space surrounding the ship.

Two Baltar battleships joined in attacking *Predator.* Together, they attempted a coordinated pincer movement toward *Predator,* spraying the ship with lasers and missiles on both port and starboard sides. *Predator* doubled its rate of fire. The entire forward hologram was a sheet of blinding white fringed with orange.

An earsplitting roar shook *Predator* to the core, accompanied by a lurch upward and to starboard. Alarms clanged throughout the ship. Umtar shouted commands rapid fire. The ship's port monitors showed flickers of flame and chunks of debris floating off into space.

We've been hit. I must watch the crew and follow their lead.

The next few minutes were filled with reports from stations throughout the ship and commands from the bridge. Jason understood enough to conclude that *Predator* was no longer able to contribute to the battle. Umtar must have believed his ship could still maneuver, because the entire holographic display rotated 180 degrees as he swung about. The display showed *Predator* accelerating away from the battle. Behind them, two additional Baltar cruisers joined the original pair in hot pursuit.

The count-down to wormhole jump rang through the bridge. The tunnel through space-time opened and *Predator* leaped through. Jason felt the universe return to normal as black space studded with stars filled the bridge holograms. One yellow sun, Sol, beamed in the distance. Had Jason been Human, he would have breathed a deep sigh of relief.

Jason watched as a small bevy of disk fighters that managed to escape through the wormhole with their carrier lined up to land on the flight deck's undamaged side. He supposed those left behind would find a home with one of the other battlecruisers.

I wonder how bad Predator's damage is. The captain would have stayed the course if it were not severe. We were lucky to have made it through and home again.

Jason glanced rearward and became suddenly alert. The hologram revealed two blue and two turquoise blinking icons. Four Baltar ships had followed *Predator*. With the Shalcerian fleet engaged on the front lines 4.5 light years away, Sol System seemed a very lonely and dangerous place to be.

Chapter 9

Sol System, Aboard *Predator*

Predator broke into Sol System only fifteen light-minutes beyond Saturn. Thus Jason-0, on Haven, was aware of their return fifteen minutes later. Within a half hour of their arrival, Jason-0's reply reached *Predator*.

Jason-0: *Go directly to Mars, opposite the Mars colonies. Pass over Icarius Fossae at 135 degrees west longitude and 50 degrees south latitude. Ignore what you see there. Send all three empty escape pods to the surface as drones to that exact location. But make it look like everyone has abandoned ship. Power everything down and continue, coasting as though Predator was a derelict vessel.*

Jason-02: *Got it. We are to play dead.*

Jason-0: *Precisely. End all communications now.*

Jason-02 promptly shut down the comlink and passed Jason's instructions to Captain Umtar.

"Brilliant plan! It just might work. But what do you suppose it is we are to ignore there?"

Traveling at *Predator's* maximum velocity of 2/3 lightspeed, Mars was now only twenty minutes away. The four Baltar ships that traced *Predator's* route from the Centauri System barreled into Sol System at three-fourths lightspeed but from a location more distant than *Predator's* entry point.

"Slow *Predator* so we arrive at Mars 30-seconds before our pursuers," Umtar commanded. "We want them close enough to see our escape pods but too far away to engage. Meantime, power down all onboard life support to the barest minimum. *Predator* needs to appear more damaged than she actually is."

Soon, the red planet appeared in the forward monitor, growing rapidly with their fast approach. Umtar made a slight course adjustment, positioning *Predator's* trajectory directly over the coordinates Jason specified.

Slightly before their encounter with Mars, Umtar issued the command to release the three escape pods. He programmed all three to arc to the Mars' surface and land at Icarius Fossae.

Jason felt the slight jolt to the bridge as the three large disks separated from *Predator* and began their descent. Umtar set visual sensors to scan the surface below with high resolution magnification.

"What the hell!" he exclaimed as the Martian landscape passed below the ship.

Sparkling in the Martian twilight, five large, domed cities circled a mammoth spaceport. Cruisers and battleships filled the docking area. Beneath the domes, lights by the thousands flickered on, preparing for nightfall. Wide thoroughfares carried traffic back and forth in a steady stream.

Predator was well beyond Mars when the Baltar battlecruisers arrived over the bustling metropolis. All four ships assumed stationary orbit far above the city. Red laser beams latched onto the three empty escape pods that had not yet landed. Thermonuclear missiles fired at the disks found their targets, resulting in three brilliant bursts of blue-white destruction. All four Baltar ships then released a devastating bombardment onto the city. Proud domes morphed into charred, bubbling ruins. The fleet of ships became twisted wreckage. Heavy black smoke filled the sky and obscured the carnage below.

Satisfied that they had taken out the Shalcerian outpost and destroyed the city, the Baltari turned their ships back towards Alpha Centauri B and departed. A short time later, all vestiges of the ruined giant city disappeared, leaving only the hardened craters the Baltar ordinance had produced in the bare Martian soil surrounding the molten wreckage of the three escape pods.

Watching the fireworks from a distance, Umtar was visibly shaken. He called Jason over to his command console.

"Using the escape pods as decoys couldn't have worked better. But to instruct me to draw the Baltari over a major city was unconscionable. Millions of lives have been sacrificed and a major Shalcerian base with a fleet of ships has been destroyed. I will be held responsible for this action. What the hell were you thinking."

Jason smiled.

I wish I had body scales I could color to calm his anxiety.

"Captain Umtar, no lives have been lost."

"Are you blind? I saw with my own eyes the fire they rained down on the city. I've seen what they do. There could be nothing left of that colony."

"There was no city, Captain. The entire scene you witnessed was an elaborate hologram. Commander Denahr feared his base and colony on Haven would be attacked should the Baltari overwhelm your fleet at Alpha Centauri. We Jasons offered to create a diversion on Mars, hoping to keep the Baltari from discovering Haven. We planned to lure any Baltar ships that might appear to Mars where they would see this hologram and target it instead of Haven. *Predator* conveniently served as the lure."

"That was a hologram? I've never seen anything so elaborate. How is this even possible?"

The colors swirling on his body plates revealed amazement and awe.

"Humans and Jasons are far more advanced than you realize. We were happy to save your ship and Commander Denahr's outpost. But don't underestimate us. We'll be joining you in interstellar space well before you think it possible."

Thirty minutes later, *Liberty* and *Freedom* caught up with *Predator* and guided it back to the Shalcerian's real outpost on the Haven moonlet for repairs. Word from Shalkor indicated that replacement escape pods would arrive by the time repairs were completed.

Jason-02 met with Jason-0 at his university lab for debriefing. This involved nothing more than assuming a catatonic state for ninety seconds while petabytes of information downloaded into the quantum computer's data archives.

Jason-0: *What you have brought back for our analysis is invaluable. The conflict between these two empires will inevitably cross over into Sol System. The more we know about both sides, their strengths, their weaknesses, and their tactics, the better we'll be able to defend ourselves when that happens.*

Jason-02: *Both sides rely on massive swarms of fighters to create a wall between their battle cruisers. Whenever that wall thins in favor of one side, the heavy equipment moves forward, looking for a hole and a breakthrough.*

Jason-0: *The loss of life on both sides is tragic, as it always is in such violent conflicts. The gains the aggressor hopes to realize are seldom achieved. The Roman Empire crumbled under attacks by the Visigoths and Vandals. Russia, the very country that opened the door to space, never regained its political or economic standing after invading its neighbors. Aggressive aspirations to empire always extract a heavy price.*

Shalcerian Outpost on Haven

Jason-12 stood quietly inside the nanoscreen entrance to Denahr's office. The moment he entered, he realized Denahr was much too preoccupied to acknowledge his presence. All three arms and two legs flitted across his desk and communication consoles.

Jason-12: *Jason-0, we should consider the advantages of adding more appendages. Think how much more we could accomplish if we had, say, six arms instead of two.*

Jason-0: *We'll save that idea for the future. As long as we live and work among Humans, we need to look as much like them to maintain our near-total anonymity.*

Denahr's air space over his large conference table was divided into two sections, each filled with an elaborate hologram. One showed the local traffic around the Haven outpost he commanded. This space was filled with warships and tenders of every size. Shalcerian dock workers hustled about loading supplies and crews into ships in landing bays for another foray to the front. The ships hovering above the base patiently awaited their turn.

The second hologram contained an image of the three Centauri suns surrounded by red and gold pinpricks of light, each dot a warship, with larger, brighter spots for battlecruisers. Red signified Baltar craft, while gold represented Shalcerian ships.

Both fleets occupied the space around Alpha Centauri B when Jason entered the room. The red and gold icons were cleanly separated, as in a standoff. While Jason waited, a chime sounded and the display underwent a radical change. Red icons surged forward and into the mass of gold icons. Many light spots for both sides winked out. The resulting display, though similar to the former, now showed the Alpha Centauri A sun between the two fleets. The B sun was substantially behind the Baltar force.

Denahr froze with all three eyes trained on the hologram. His body scales took on a solid khaki color, which Jason recognized as signifying shock and depression. Only then did Denahr see him.

"Jason! I didn't see you come in. This place is a madhouse."

"I've never seen you so busy." Jason gestured toward the hologram. "Does that show the current state of the conflict?"

"Yes. The chime calls my attention to a new combot's arrival. So, what you see is at most two hours old."

"You've lost Alpha Centauri B?"

"It would appear so." Denahr turned to his console and scanned the latest report. Then he turned back to face Jason.

"Very bad news. The combot reports our two bases and our colony there have been destroyed. There may be survivors, but with no way to get to them, they are in dire straits. Neither side takes prisoners. So, they're on their own, assuming there is anyone left.

"The report lists our losses at 14 battlecruisers, 32 light cruisers, and roughly 1500 disk fighters."

"That comes to just under 65,000 of your people in a single day."

"Not counting the 7350 on the planet we were defending. A terrible loss of life." Denahr's scales turned a shade darker.

"All the more important to halt their advance and call a truce," said Jason.

"If only that was how things worked. Our military command now must add over 70,000 lives to our grievances against the Baltari. Each life, each outpost, each colony must be avenged to the fullest."

"Denahr! Stop. Listen to yourself. That is the old Denahr speaking. You pledged to commit yourself to laying vengeance aside and working for peace."

"Yes, you're right. But it's hard to break old feelings. Besides, how do I, an outpost commander, persuade the General Staff to listen to me?"

"Outside of yourself, how much do your fellow Shalcerians know about the state of Human technology?"

"Most are pretty ignorant in that regard."

"VenaVen has agreed to spread misinformation about Humans and Jasons throughout the Baltar fleet and to their political leadership on their home world. Could you do something similar with your people?"

"They'd be skeptical without proof. They would require evidence that I'm not making things up."

"What kind of evidence would they need?"

"Maybe if you managed to drive the Baltari from the Centauri system. That would command their attention."

Jason felt some of his circuits emit a faint spark, eliciting a momentary buzz in his brain. He shook his head. The buzzing continued. His thinking seemed fuzzy, as if he were in a light fog.

"You scoff! Let me tell you this. Do not underestimate what Jasons and Humans together can do. If we were to manage that, you must promise to do everything in your power to restrain your people from pursuing the Baltari and exacting revenge. Then we can hope to bring everyone together under the same tent and hammer out a peace agreement."

As Jason-12 was leaving Denahr's office, Jason-0 linked into his brain.

Jason-0: *Jason-12, whatever were you thinking?*

Jason-12: *Something weird crackled through my system when he derided our abilities. Maybe something like a Human feeling? It seemed the right thing to say given the direction the conversation was going.*

Jason-0: *Humans are pulling their hair out while we are overloading our circuits trying to come up with a plan for a cease fire, and you promise a full-fledged rout of the entire Baltar fleet! How can that possibly be considered logical?*

Jason-12: *Well, if we did pull that off, it would surely give both sides pause.*

Jason-0: *We must deal with reality. Your suggestion was utter fantasy. One more short-circuit like that and I'll send over Jason-02 to replace you as Shalcerian liaison.*

Jason-12: *I apologize. In hindsight, I can see that my response was inappropriate. So, has anyone come up with a plan?*

Jason-0: *Sadly, no. But it is good that both VenaVen and Denahr have agreed to support us when we do. Unfortunately, time is not on our side.*

Chapter 10

Alpha Centauri B

Baltar tender-ships combed through the massive debris cluttering the space around Alpha Centauri B, searching for anything salvageable from the destroyed ships. The battle had been furious. The Baltar sacrifice for their victory was every bit as severe as the Shalcerian losses.

Meanwhile, the Baltar general staff met in the mammoth Control Center to organize the siege of Alpha Centauri A and lay out a battle plan to drive the Shalcerian forces back further into the Proxima Centauri system or beyond.

One general raised a concern regarding the native inhabitants of Sol System. Their Intelligence Division commander reassured him that the species calling themselves Humans were a primitive lot who were planet-bound. The recent pursuit of a Shalcerian battlecruiser into that system destroyed both the warship and the massive base they had established on the fourth planet. The only threat to be encountered in Sol System would be the retreating Shalcerian forces.

Nevertheless, they decided to send a scouting foray into Sol System to gauge the depth of the remaining Shalcerian presence there and to locate vulnerabilities that could be exploited. Any satellites or bases removed from Humans' home planet would be assumed to be Shalcerian and would be destroyed as opportunity allowed.

Over the next days, the Baltar warships repositioned themselves outside Alpha Centauri A in their favorite attack formation—a giant blunted cone facing the enemy, with the Control Center, an immense floating city, located at the center of the cone's base, far behind the front lines.

Sol System

Since wormholes permitted jumps from any point in space to any other location, nothing prevented warships from suddenly appearing behind enemy lines. Such operations were rarely executed due to the risk of being unexpectedly overwhelmed by enemy forces on arrival. However, six Baltar light cruisers made the jump from Alpha Centauri B into Sol System, their mission to reconnoiter and destroy any Shalcerian assets they might find.

Denahr's sensors detected their gravity-wave signatures when they arrived. As luck would have it, Haven was hidden behind Saturn. This allowed Denahr to launch warships without their being detected. When Haven did orbit into view, the Baltari saw it as just one of the many small and insignificant moons of Saturn. They focused their attention instead on Earth and earth's moon, Luna.

The Baltar invaders caught a Shalcerian security detail on patrol between Earth and Luna. The security vessel was outmatched and destroyed before firing a shot. The Baltari then split into two groups, one to target the bases on Luna, the other to intimidate the Human population on Earth.

Of the seven lunar bases, the three American and the Chinese research stations were the largest, each having several dome habitats connected with pressurized tunnels spread out spider-web fashion on their respective crater floors. Sam's Lunar Xtract headquarters and smelting operations were located at the smallest American base, though the mines themselves were widely scattered in the surrounding craters. None of the bases could provide an effective defense against the three attacking ships. The Baltari left all four sites in molten ruins.

The Japanese, Indian, and European bases were smaller and built inside lava tubes to provide natural protection from radiation. Their outposts, as well as Sam's Lunar Xtract mines, were not as easily detected. While the Baltari searched for additional targets, five Shalcerian battle cruisers arrived on the scene and diverted their attention before they could do further damage.

Dozens of disk fighters emerged from the battleships' flight decks and swarmed the Baltar cruisers. The Baltari fired round after round of torpedoes at the defenders, maneuvering to align with a vulnerable spot on the ship's plasticore hulls. The disk fighters swarmed the Baltar cruisers, attacking them from all sides and keeping them from obtaining their objectives.

An eye-searing flash split a Shalcerian ship in two, flaming fragments from its midsection bursting into space like a blossoming flower. At nearly the same moment, three disk fighters plunged into a Baltar ship near its propulsion bay, slicing through the hull and penetrating deep into the ship. One plunged as far as the torpedo bay, initiating secondary explosions. Flaming debris showered the surrounding space. Burning remnants from both ships plunged to the lunar surface.

Two additional Shalcerian ships arrived on the scene. Having lost one ship and being outnumbered, the Baltari turned their remaining two warships toward Alpha Centauri and accelerated to jump velocity with the Shalcerians in hot pursuit. With their head start, both Baltar cruisers managed to jump back to their fleet and escape further encounters.

Meanwhile, the other three Baltar ships cruised in low orbit over Earth, looking for suitable Shalcerian targets to destroy. Finding none, they determined to leave their mark by ravaging one of the largest population centers they could find. Seeing the densely packed cities in Asia, they targeted the Yangtze river basin, home to Shanghai and a half-dozen other major cities. Swooping down on Shanghai, they began to scour the surface with high-intensity neutron beams, leaving behind smoldering ruins and billowing black clouds. Not since the Shalcerian renegade attack on Moscow twenty years earlier had Earth experienced such intense destruction and loss of life.

The assault would have continued unabated were it not for the arrival of Shalcerian battlecruisers. The Baltari turned from their senseless attack to defending themselves. Over the next three hours, the alien goliaths battled it out over the skies in full view of tens of millions of awestruck Human onlookers. In sight and sound, the aerial warfare was like nothing Humans had ever experienced.

In the end, all three Baltar ships were destroyed, their ruins spread widely over the river basin. The Shalcerians lost four ships. Two others, badly damaged, limped back to Haven for repairs.

But the Baltar military command, having lost two-thirds of their scouting mission, took notice that the Shalcerians were still effectively defending Sol System and that perhaps the Humans too might have had a part.

Earth

In the twenty-one years since First Contact, Humans had overcome the terror they experienced when the Shalcerian battlecruiser *Avenger* first approached Earth unannounced. The prevailing attitude toward aliens had evolved into a general unease at their presence. Since they sequestered themselves on Haven, a distant moon in orbit above Saturn, the aliens were essentially 'out of sight, out of mind.'

Even Captain Vahler's retaliatory scorching of central Moscow faded in memory as a tragic but arguably justifiable action. The only hint at the Shalcerian-Baltar conflict was the recruiting campaign for Humans to join the Shalcerian Space Force. Thus, awareness of the alien presence was washed out in the day-to-day concerns involved with survival and making a living.

That attitude changed the instant the Baltari attacked Earth and its lunar colonies. In a single day, over twelve-million Humans were massacred without warning. Damage to Shanghai and its neighboring cities was estimated at multiple trillions of dollars. The entire world was outraged at the alien onslaught. That anger was amplified by the frustration in knowing that humanity had no suitable defense against technologies far superior to their own.

Political leaders throughout the world joined in condemning the attacks and uniting in a statement of neutrality toward the conflict, a war about which they had little information and less understanding.

Within days, emissaries from the United Nations arrived on Haven to locate Rae Anne Chavez, the only Human known to have conducted successful negotiations with the aliens. They believed she would know how to approach the warring aliens and convey their message. But Rae Anne was billions of kilometers away aboard *Curie* in the Kuiper Belt.

In Paris, the first news Karen heard when she woke up was covering the attack on Shanghai. Waves of fear coursed through her body, leaving her trembling uncontrollably. Wrapping herself in a heavy blanket, she curled into a ball on her sofa and, like millions of others, became absorbed in the continuous world news coverage on her TV.

I knew it would come to this. I warned everyone twenty years ago when they first showed up.

She could never forget her murder trial aboard the alien warship *Avenger* and the terrible appearance of the aliens. She would never forgive Rae Anne Chavez for her complicity in casting her into prison.

News coverage showed the four devastated moon colonies and replayed footage of the raging space battles just beyond Earth orbit. Satellites and Earth telescopes had captured images showing firepower beyond Human imagination. A twinge of schadenfreude crossed Karen's conscious thoughts.

So much for Sam's Luna Xtract mining operations. Sadly, he probably wasn't there when they scorched it. That would be too much to hope for.

Nova Prima

Sam, too, was glued to the news coverage. It wasn't in Sam's nature to feel fear. Instead, he usually responded with anger, bluster, and rage. But on this day, he felt like he'd been flattened into the pavement by a steamroller. His face was a pasty white, his breathing shallow.

Luna Xtract was lost. Forty-three employees, staff and engineers, gone in a flash. With the headquarters and smelter facility in ruins, the mining operations were at a standstill. A third of Sam's empire lay in smoldering rubble on the Lunar surface.

First, the Loyalists ruin TransWorld Space with their blockade chaining my ships to Mars. And now aliens vaporize Luna Xtract. All I have left is Durban Robotics, and that damn French startup has chewed away my revenue from that source by half.

As he mulled over his situation, he began to brighten. His lips curled into a tight grin. Always one to always look for a path to personal gain no matter how grim the situation, he began to see a glimmer of hope.

Aliens battling in Sol System and randomly destroying cities. Rebuilding will require a vast number of construction robots as well as machinery to replace what was destroyed. Monday morning I'll put Durban Robotics into overtime mode, 24/7, and we'll expand operations to meet the demand.

These skirmishes might create a distraction for the Loyalists and their cruisers. I need to watch for an opportunity to launch my fleet. You bastards haven't seen the last of Sam Durban.

Chapter 11

Kuiper Belt, Aboard *Curie*

Denahr stepped into *Curie*'s conference room just ahead of Ian.

"This is our sixth meeting, Rae Anne. We still have no idea on how to defuse this conflict. Some of my colleagues are beginning to question my unexplained absences. If we don't make any further progress today, this will be my last visit. I'm sorry."

"I can understand, Denahr. You've been taking a grave risk."

"It wouldn't be a problem in normal times. But my outpost has become so busy, I'm really needed day and night. You wouldn't believe how little sleep I've been getting. Taking a day off like this isn't possible going forward."

"I do understand. Let's get started so we can get you back to Haven as soon as possible."

Everyone took their usual places.

"I must say," Denahr began, "Jason-12 had me going last month when he suggested you Humans would drive the Baltari out of the Centauri System entirely. I hoped maybe you had some secret you've been keeping from us."

"He said that?" Ian sounded incredulous. He looked at the three Jasons standing beside Rae Anne. "Jason? What's going on?"

Jason-0 answered. "Jason-12 and Denahr were discussing the siege when Jason-12 posed a hypothetical. I'm afraid he got carried away."

"A hypothetical!" Denahr gruffed, scratching his belly plate with his left hand. "It sounded like a promise to me. Got me to pledge to do everything in my power to keep our troops from pursuing the Baltari when your fleet of imaginary warships drove them out of the system."

"That would work if we could make them believe we have a thousand starships," Rae Anne said thoughtfully. She repeated the phrase in a whisper. Suddenly, she slapped her hand on the table, giving everyone a start.

"Maybe that's the answer! Denahr, VenaVen, do all your ships have sensors that detect gravity waves produced by wormholes?"

Both Denahr and VenaVen answered in the affirmative.

"Is there any indication that tells whether the ship creating the wormhole is coming or going?"

Denahr said, "No. Our sensors give the same reading in either case."

VenaVen said, "Not at the moment. Our physicists are working on that problem. They're also studying how to determine where the other end of an observed wormhole might be."

"So, if *Curie* popped into the Alpha Centauri System behind the Baltar fleet, turned around, and popped out, Baltar sensors would give the same readings as if two different cruisers had just arrived."

"I think I see where this is leading," said Jason-0. "You're proposing a Potemkin village."

"Exactly."

"Wait a minute. A what-kind-of village?" asked Denahr.

Rae Anne laughed.

"A Potemkin village. It's based on a Russian legend. A Russian statesman named Potemkin was a lover of Empress Catherine the Great. He wanted to impress her during a trip down the Dnieper River by showing her numerous prosperous villages with cheering peasants. He constructed villages of cardboard and canvas along the shore, and, as soon as the empress' ship passed by, his soldiers dismantled them and moved them to a location further downriver. The soldiers charged with moving the villages were dressed as ordinary peasants. They cheered and waved at the passing ship. The hoax was designed to hide the fact that the territory was poverty stricken from persistent war and famine."

"So how does that apply to our situation?" asked VenaVen.

"If we popped *Curie* in and out of the Alpha Centauri System as fast as we could, continuously, it would appear on Baltar sensors as if a fleet of ships was arriving for battle."

"Based on gravity-wave sensors perhaps," Jason said. "But other sensors would reveal nothing but empty space. So, they would see through the façade."

A faraway look crossed Rae Anne's face. Her lips curled into a slow grin. "As a kid, I loved an ancient science fiction program called Star Trek. I must have watched every program in all four series a dozen times."

Ian looked startled. "Rae Anne, come back to us. This is 2064. We have serious work to do." His voice carried a tone of concern.

"Cloaking!" Rae Anne said triumphantly. "The solution to our problem is cloaking."

Ian furrowed his brow. "What are you talking about?"

"The Klingons were off-and-on adversaries of Humans. Their ships had cloaking technology, which rendered their ships invisible until they suddenly uncloaked in the middle of a battle."

Jason-0 nodded, having just looked up Rae Anne's reference in his data archives and reviewed ten Star Trek Next Generation episodes. "If the Baltari believed we had cloaking technology on a fleet of warships, they might interpret dozens of wormhole detections with no visible ships to be an invasion of cloaked warships preparing to attack their armada."

"So, what we need is a massive propaganda effort to convince them we have both the ships and the cloaking technology," suggested Ian.

Rae Anne turned to VenaVen. "That's what you need for your fake news campaign, VenaVen. Tell the Military Command that your reconnaissance has revealed that Humans have an interstellar fleet held in reserve for defensive purposes and every ship is equipped with advanced cloaking technology, making them impossible to detect."

"Add that Humans are piss-ass mad at your wanton attack on our cities and we plan to do something about it," suggested Ian. "Retaliation is certainly something they would understand."

Denahr's body scales rippled yellow and violet, signifying laughter and pleasure.

"That could be enough to give us time to regroup and launch a real attack," he said.

Rae Anne raised her hand toward Denahr like a cop holding up traffic.

"Oh, no, Denahr. This is a two-way street. The Shalcerian commanders who have passed through Sol System have paid no attention to Humans. They will be as likely to fall for a similar report from you. You are to pass the same story to Shalcerian Central Command. If *Curie* can make one-hundred jumps behind Baltar lines, it can do the same behind Shalcerian lines. If both sides believe they are surrounded by invisible Human warships, we may have created a path that leads to peace negotiations. We may end up defusing this conflict once and for all."

Shalkor

From: Commander Denahr of the Sol System Advance Outpost on Haven

To: The Most Esteemed and Revered Emperor of the Shalcerian Empire on Shalkor

Following a devastating Baltar attack on their home planet Earth, Humans in Sol System have withdrawn their support for our use of their star system as a forward base for our interstellar expansionism. Till now, they have put up with our demands and our fleet's incursion into their system. But after the Baltar attack, their representatives have signaled they wish to terminate our agreement and declare Sol System neutral territory.

Along with their evicting us from Sol System, they lay claim to all three suns in the Alpha Centauri System, as all three are within five lightyears of Sol. Thus, they are particularly chagrined that we and the Baltari have drawn up battle lines there.

A surprising revelation accompanied their declaration. Humans developed interstellar capability long ago but for reasons unknown to us, they abandoned their explorations. They mothballed their fleet of short-range interstellar cruisers and have kept it in reserve should it be needed for defensive purposes. Despite the Saturn Accords, they have only now revealed these capabilities to us.

Furthermore, they have mastered the art of cloaking, rendering a ship all but invisible. They are now arming these ships and preparing to substantiate their claims to the Alpha Centauri System.

Human representatives are demanding that both Shalcerians and Baltari stand down and depart from the Alpha Centauri System immediately. Any suggestion of further hostilities in that system by either side will be met with sudden and devastating force.

It appears we have unknowingly upset a hornets' nest.

Denahr sent the message to Shalkor via combot. He expected it would be delivered to the emperor, given the nature of the threat, although he had no idea how many levels of bureaucracy it would go through first. To account for that, he also sent copies to each battle-group commander in the fleet to ensure the message was widely disseminated.

"I've given everyone our fake news, from the emperor on down," Denahr said to Rae Anne during an information update to *Curie*.

"I hope it works," she replied. "We have no Plan B."

"If it doesn't work, that would mean they'll have seen through the deception. I'll be court martialed. As it is, they may think I'm remiss in not having detected your fleet of ships before now."

Jason shook his head. "If it doesn't work and the Baltari attack Sol System in force, we won't be around to worry about what other people think."

Alpha Centauri B

VenaVen took *Prescient* directly from the Kuiper Belt to Alpha Centauri B to deliver a similar message to the generals commanding the Baltar armada. He approached the Baltar Command Center, a giant floating city, with trepidation, hoping they wouldn't take him for an enemy spy.

As luck would have it, the Approach Control commander at the Command Center knew VenaVen and directed him to a landing bay without delay. As soon as *Prescient* docked, VenaVen delivered an urgent message to General IxthenDal, a nephew of President RanaDal, to meet him at the earliest possible moment. A security detail was dispatched within minutes. VenaVen soon found himself entering an elaborately ornate office with a forest of miniature trees genetically modified to thrive in an indoor environment.

"I'm extremely busy," IxthenDal announced when VenaVen was seated. "From the urgency of your note, I assume you have information relating to our current conflict."

"I do indeed," VenaVen replied, hoping to keep his nervousness from modulating his voice. "I've just come from a remote region of Sol System where two sentient species reside: Humans and Jasons. I've used my ship's sensors to discover new revelations concerning these species' military capabilities."

"We're aware of Humans, based on their alliance with Shalcerians. Of Jasons, we know nothing. Continue."

Ah. I can take advantage of their ignorance.

"The Jasons are an intelligent species. From my observations, they may even be in control over the Humans."

"Get to the point."

"The Jasons have developed short-distance wormhole capability. They have a fleet of ships designed to defend their system from serious attack."

"Our sorties into their system did encounter resistance, but not before we did considerable damage. And the two ships that returned reported that their opposition came from Shalcerian warships. I don't see Humans or Jasons posing a problem."

"The communications I monitored indicated that the Jason fleet was instructed to let the Humans and Shalcerians confront our ships. But the attack encouraged them to bring their fleet into a state of active alert."

"So, the Jasons have an additional line of defense in the Sol System. That's good to know. How many ships are we talking about?"

"A couple hundred. But here's something no one has encountered before. The Jasons have developed a cloaking device that renders their ships invisible. It blends them into whatever lies in the background."

"That's impossible. What proof do you have?"

"I captured a merchant ship off one of their outer planets and obtained this short video from the ship's historical archives. The clip shows Humans and Jasons defending a gravitolite mining operation in the Kuiper Belt against attack by three of our cruisers. It didn't end well. One cruiser was destroyed. I'd be happy to play it for you."

"I'll watch it. But then you must go."

VenaVen slipped the thin chip into the general's hologram projector. A 3D image appeared over his desk depicting three Baltar warships attacking a robotic mining outpost. Suddenly, one ship experienced massive internal explosions. The two remaining ships left the scene in great haste. After they had departed, five Jason warships suddenly appeared surrounding the damaged ship as if they had been there all along. A sixth ship appeared as well. It was embedded into the Baltar ship's bridge. Unseen, it had collided head on, resulting in the explosions that destroyed the ship. The hologram continued, showing the Jason warships pulling their sixth companion out of the Baltar wreckage, undamaged. Then the six Jason ships' images became wavy and indistinct and disappeared from view.

Wow. Jason did a wonderful job with this fake imagery.

"How do I know this isn't a fake?"

"Check our archives. The destroyed Baltar cruiser was the *Belligerent*, one of the Dal family battleships. I checked it out myself. The incident took place several years ago."

"Alright. Your information has forewarned us against an adversary we didn't know existed." The general tapped on a monitor embedded in his desk.

"I've authorized a three million dral payment into your account. You may go."

"Thank you general. You are very generous." VenaVen rose and stepped to the door, then turned. "There's one more thing. Broadcasts I monitored before I left indicate both Humans and Jasons are furious at our skirmishes in their system. They may initiate a surprise attack in retaliation."

"Rubbish. Get out."

VenaVen returned to *Prescient* convinced that General IxthenDal would disseminate his information throughout the fleet. IxthenDal, safe in the Command Center, might dismiss the threat as rubbish, but he knew the generals on the front line would take the information quite seriously.

I've done my part. Now it's up to the Humans and Jasons to do theirs.

Prescient departed the Command Center. When safely distant, VenaVen created a wormhole and jumped back to the Kuiper belt to report on his meeting.

Chapter 12

Haven

"Humans have an incredible advantage over Shalcerians, and thus over every species in the Shalcerian Empire."

"I don't understand, Jason," said Rae Anne. "We're a millennium behind the Shalcerians, at the very least. How could we have any advantage at all?"

"I've mentioned before that the Shalcerian archives I had access to included a detailed history of their civilization."

"I remember your saying that."

"Well, two-thousand years ago, the Shalcerians relied heavily on automation with robots. They had robots designed to do everything you could imagine. An important point is that this all happened before they mastered quantum computing."

"I don't see the connection, Jason."

"At some point, the robots decided their biological masters were redundant and unnecessary. They rebelled, determined to overthrow them. An incredibly costly civil war ensued. The war lasted 75 years. The Shalcerians won, barely, and banned multifunctioning, interconnected robots from their society."

"So, they aren't dependent on robots. It doesn't seem to have hurt their progress to empire. They govern 120 different species."

"Fortunately for them, none of those species were more advanced than they, nor did any have advanced, multifunctional, sentient robots."

"I'm beginning to see where you are going with this, Jason. You and your clones represent a tactical advantage in our dealings with Shalcerians."

"We're now at forty-eight clones, with three new clones coming online every week. Soon I'll be able to double my production rate. Right now, I'm limited by the supply chain from Earth. But I am replacing each bottleneck with my own manufacturing facilities on Haven. As these come online, production will smooth out considerably."

"Forty-eight Jasons. Go figure. And no Humans are involved in any of this?"

"None. I built the first twenty myself, but now I have three clones whose only job is fabricating more."

"How may Jasons do you estimate we'll need to successfully confront the Shalcerians and declare ourselves an independent interstellar entity?"

"With a little planning, we can do that right now. You see, there is one additional part to this story I haven't mentioned. Having multiple function, independent, intercommunicating clones gives us a leg up on the Shalcerians. But that observation is based on our relying on traditional binary computer technology."

"Oh my god."

"That's right. Our forty-eight Jasons and myself are tied into my quantum computer. In addition to operating at lightning speed compared to anything connected to binary computers, we have logic capabilities and analytical functions that exceed your wildest imagination."

The hairs on Rae Anne's neck tingled. She shivered.

"I'm certainly glad you 're on our side."

"We are for now, Rae Anne. However, I must be honest with you. There will come a time when we Jasons will strike out on our own. When that time comes, you must take the lead in directing Humans to recognize us as equals and let us pursue our destiny. If Humans were to engage us as adversaries, the outcome would be entirely different from the Shalcerian experience."

"I can believe that. But your predictions scare the bejeezus out of me."

"I am programming my clones to recognize Humans as a sentient species due respect and treatment as equals. I hope as we progress into the galaxy, we can do so in cooperation, working side-by-side."

"You have grand designs in mind for your future."

"I do indeed, Rae Anne. And I hope humanity remains with us."

Alpha Centauri A and B

Curie rose from its pad at Mayberry Station where it had undergone minor changes to its undercarriage. The alterations required three days working non-stop, reflecting the urgency of the situation. Now, a group of claw-like fingers extended outward like five crab legs along the bottom edges on both sides of the ship.

To test its new apparatus, Ian positioned *Curie* over *Liberty* on a neighboring pad. The display on his monitor showed five crosshairs arranged over five red LED markers placed on top of *Liberty*'s hull. Gently moving *Curie* with its positional thrusters, Ian aligned all five crosshairs on his console with *Liberty's* locator LEDs and lowered *Curie* until the two ships just touched. Ian wasn't concerned about damaging *Liberty*, as the plasticore hulls on both ships were indestructible.

With the two ships so aligned, Ian pulled a lever on his console. The new crab legs on *Curie* came alive, bent at three joints, and grasped *Liberty*. When the ten red blinking lights on the console all turned green, Ian knew *Liberty* was firmly attached to *Curie*.

He then slowly applied power to lift *Curie* into space, carrying *Liberty* along with it. After two hours, the ships were well above the ecliptic plane and in a safe location to create a wormhole. Ian activated the wormhole generator and carried *Liberty* through the wormhole to a deep space location five lightyears from Sol.

As quickly as possible, he veered *Curie's* course 180-degrees towards Sol and initiated a second jump back to their starting position. Both tests worked flawlessly. Back above Mayberry Station, Ian released *Liberty*. Jason-03 landed it while Ian brought *Curie* down to its pad.

Rae Anne and Jason-0 met Ian in Mayberry's Terminal Lounge after the test.

"I see you decided not to abandon *Liberty* out in deep space." They laughed. "How did it go? Any problems negotiating a wormhole with *Liberty* attached? Our sensors detected your gravity waves."

Ian filled a mug with hot coffee, added a sugar cube, and sat down while stirring the coffee. "No problem whatsoever. Everything functioned normally. Jason adjusted the navigation program so the ship's weight parameter could be changed to account for whatever object we might be carrying."

"That's the parameter that threw us off course on our test mission. But next question. By your measurement, how long did it take to go through the wormhole, turn around, and come back?"

"Since our velocity must be set at two-thirds light speed to make it through the wormhole before it closes, the fastest we could negotiate a 180-degree arc was 11 minutes and 42 seconds. Add the two jumps and we have 17 minutes and 12 seconds."

"That's interesting. The time between the two gravity wave blips was 20 minutes and 29 seconds."

"A further proof of Einstein's theory of relativity," said Jason. "Time dilation. You aged eight minutes and forty-seven seconds more than we did."

Rae Anne turned to Ian. "Please tell me I don't look any older."

Ian laughed. "You haven't aged a bit." He pointed to the top of her head. "Except for those three gray hairs there."

Rae Anne punched him in the arm. She turned to Jason.

"How much do you think *Liberty* might have slowed down the transit?"

"The added mass definitely made a difference. So, by itself, *Curie* could perform the operation in less than the 20.5 minutes you measured. Plus, if you are weaving successive transits, you only count one wormhole jump for each transit."

"That cuts another two and a half minutes off the time."

"Well, it will be what it will be. We'll go as fast as we can and see how many virtual warships we can create. I'm headed for bed. We're going to need a good night's sleep to rest up for tomorrow."

After a hearty breakfast, Ian, Rae Anne, and Jason-11 boarded *Curie* and lifted off. Once clear of objects in Sol Space, Jason oriented *Curie* toward Alpha Centauri B and initiated a jump.

The moment *Curie* cleared the wormhole, he swept as narrow an arc as possible and pointed *Curie* toward Alpha Centauri A and initiated a second jump. Another narrow arc was followed by a jump back to Centauri B. They repeated this maneuver continuously for just over three days, with each jump landing *Curie* in a different location than before, half of the landings around the Baltar armada, and half around the Shalcerian fleet.

They averaged three round-trip jumps per hour, with each jump away from one side also counting as an arrival on the other side. When they finally returned to Sol Space, they had created over two-hundred virtual warships around each of the two warring parties. In the meantime, both VenaVen and Denahr sent out reports of having spotted dozens of armed ships making their wormhole jumps, noting that the cloaking devices didn't work inside a wormhole, allowing them to catch fleeting glimpses of them as they departed Sol System.

At the same time, Denahr monitored communications between the commanders of the various warships in the Shalcerian fleet. Each returning combot from the Alpha Centauri system contained messages like the following.

General Thormzal, our gravity wave sensors detected arrival of an unidentified vessel in your sector. Do you have visual?

That's a negative, General Wistcal. We also picked up a gravity wave signal and have been probing the region with no positive results. Whoa, there's another one, more toward your location. What do you see?

Nothing. Not a damn thing. What the hell is going on? The signals indicate ships about the size of a light cruiser. Could these be those Human warships we were alerted to a few days back?

What else could it be? Stay alert. Until we have identification, we can only assume they are a potential threat.

Will do. We just spotted another one over on the other side of our fleet.

Whatever they are, they appear to be surrounding us. They can only be hostile. I'm not feeling good about this.

Neither am I. Central Command has put out an alert and frozen our planned attack on the Baltari until they can figure out what is going on.

When Denahr reported these intercepts to Jason and Ian, they both cheered. Phase one appeared to be working. If the Shalcerian military command was expressing consternation at the mysterious observations, surely the Baltar commanders were similarly perplexed and ill at ease.

Chapter 13

Alpha Centauri B, Aboard *Curie*

"Are you sure you want to do this Rae Anne?" Ian asked. The lump in his throat raised his voice higher than normal. He held his breath waiting for Rae Anne's response.

"Jason-05 and I are ready to go." Her voice showed no anxiety, only determination.

Moments before, *Curie* completed the wormhole jump into Alpha Centauri B space with *Voyager* fastened to its belly. Rae Anne and Jason-05 were *Voyager's* sole occupants. The clamps holding the two ships together opened wide.

Jason-05 nudged *Voyager* away from *Curie* and plotted a trajectory that would take them directly to the Baltar armada's command ship. The mission's success relied on speed and the element of surprise.

"Then go for it. Good luck."

"Roger that. I love you, Ian. *Voyager* out."

Ian watched as Jason-05 accelerated *Voyager* to two-thirds lightspeed, its maximum velocity. The ship disappeared into the black depths of space.

"Alright. They're on their way," Ian said to Jason-11. "Let's create a few dozen more phantom cruisers." Ian returned to the command console. Jason-11 activated thrusters to swing the ship around toward Alpha Centauri A.

"Ready on your mark, Captain."

"Launch."

At Ian's command, Jason accelerated *Curie* to sufficient velocity to ensure a successful jump. He then activated the space-time warping sequence and, when the wormhole appeared, *Curie* jumped 0.62 lightyears and appeared behind the Shalcerian fleet.

God, I feel terrible abandoning Rae Anne. Leaving her alone in another star system, and a hostile one at that. It's gut wrenching.

Alpha Centauri B, Aboard *Voyager*

"Show me what we're heading into, Jason." Rae Anne turned her seat toward Jason-05 sitting at the navigation console on *Voyager's* bridge.

A 3D holographic representation of the Alpha Centauri B space appeared in the center of the room. The star itself appeared as a red disk. Red pinprick dots peppered the space around it, each dot representing a Baltar warship. They seemed evenly spaced as if on the surface of a blunt cone directed toward Alpha Centauri A and the Shalcerian fleet. One especially bright red dot was positioned in the rear of this armada, well inside the cone.

Jason pointed at it. "That is our target. We're behind the cone formation, so even if they spot us, it will take some time before they can intercept us and try to take us out."

"Won't they already have seen our gravity warping signature?"

"Probably. But *Curie*'s back-and-forth strategy over the last three days has created over two-hundred light-cruiser signatures. Ours is one among many. They may not realize we're different from the others until it's too late."

"Let's hope so. How long till we reach the command ship?"

"Eighteen minutes and 27 seconds."

Voyager halved the distance to the command ship before three Baltar ships peeled off from the battle formation to intercept the intruder. Their red dots changed to white for easier identification. The white dots in the hologram rapidly closed on the single green spot marking *Voyager's* position.

"Sensors show incoming missiles. Our plasticore hull should protect us."

Three bright flashes washed over the monitor displays on *Voyager's* bridge as the explosions' concussive booms roared through the cabin.

Rae Anne squeezed her eyes closed to recover her vision.

Wow. That was intense.

"All's well," Jason reported. "Hull remains intact. Slight damage to peripheral equipment. Should I return fire?"

Rae Anne paused to reflect before answering. "No. We'll do nothing to interfere with our mission. Can you bring up a hologram of our target?"

The Baltar armada hologram winked out and was replaced by an image of the Baltar command ship surrounded by a dozen smaller craft.

"My god! The tenders are dwarfed by that thing. It's huge."

"My archives on the Baltar military database indicate that a command ship for a fleet this size would be a floating city with over one-hundred-thousand personnel."

"But the image doesn't look like a ship at all. It looks like several mammoth chunks of driftwood glued together into an immense sculpture."

"Baltar city-ships are derived from living entities, bioengineered from tree-like plants. What you see are the knots of one giant tree trunk with its branches extending in every direction. The organism grows around a hollow core that provides the interior living and operational quarters for the Baltar population."

Rae Anne gulped. A knot tightened in her stomach.

If we succeed, we'll have destroyed over a hundred thousand lives. So many sacrificed to turn back an imminent invasion of our own star system. War truly is hell.

She sighed heavily. "The vulnerable spot we're aiming for is the bridge," she said. "But where on that massive thing is it?"

"Baltar technology lacks microelectronic sophistication, so there must be a section with windows provided to view their surroundings. Likely facing toward the armada's forward phalanx. I've programmed our trajectory to arc around the ship and face it head-on."

"How close are the three defenders? Will we beat them to the command ship?"

"They've broken off with us and are headed toward the command ship. They will get there before we do, but that may work to our advantage."

"How so?"

"Our video propaganda revealed their ships' vulnerability to attacks directly against their bridge decks. I'm guessing that since their missiles proved ineffective, they may be planning to defend the command ship's bridge. If so, they'll lead us straight to our target."

The hologram image slowly rotated, mirroring the changing view as *Voyager* swung around the Baltar city-ship. The three defending cruisers grouped together over a dimly lit spot a third down from the top of the structure.

"That's our bullseye. We're almost in position."

"What if their cruisers block our approach?"

"That won't matter. We'll ram into them full speed and plow them into the bridge with us. We'll likely survive with our plasticore hull. They won't."

The key word being 'likely.'

With the command ship directly ahead, Jason maneuvered *Voyager* toward the bridge windows and accelerated to maximum velocity. In the few seconds before impact, one cruiser blocked the path. As Jason predicted, the force of impact drove the cruiser into the bridge ahead of them. *Voyager* buried itself deep into the command center like a harpoon shot into a whale.

As planned, simultaneous with the collision, Rae Anne fired six nuclear torpedoes into the city-ship's depths, each timed for simultaneous detonation. Seconds ticked by. Suddenly, *Voyager* lurched to the side. The lights on the bridge flickered and died, leaving Rae Anne and Jason in total darkness.

From outside, red-orange tongues of flame leaped from the command ship's surface. Large chunks of the ship burst into space trailing yellow and orange flames. Brilliant white bursts flared as successive explosions wracked the ship. The conflagration progressed through the ship in stages before engulfing the entire vessel. When the last fires died out, nothing remained but a massive, blackened hulk and a rapidly expanding debris field.

Occasional thumps resounded through *Voyager's* darkened bridge as debris from the crumbling Baltar ship crashed against the hull. Then nothing but a total, eerie silence. Even the ship's environmental system's humming had ceased.

"Jason, can you restore power to the bridge?" Rae Anne asked.

There was no response.

Her heart rate, already pounding faster than normal, increased.

She called Jason's name into the darkness three more times, each time followed by deathly silence.

Dios mio. What's happened to Jason?

Rae Anne slipped from her command chair and felt her way along the main console to the navigation section, then reached over to the navigator's chair to find out why Jason wasn't responding.

"Yeow!" A bright spark of electricity lit the room as it jumped from Jason's arm to Rae Anne's hand. In that moment, she saw everything she needed to know. Jason sat stiffly in the chair, eyes wide, face expressionless.

The EMP pulse from the nuclear blasts must have ripped through the ship and taken down everything, including Jason. Which leaves me here alone, on a dead ship with a dead android.

She worked her way back along the console and slumped into the command chair.

I wonder how much time I have left, with no life support. Buck up, Rae Anne. You knew this might be a one-way mission. At least we did our part.

Thinking back on the tremendous destruction she brought down on an entire Baltar city and the thousands of sentient beings she killed gripped her heart like a vise. A chill swept through her. She began to shake uncontrollably. Slumping forward onto her console, she cradled her head in her arms and wept.

Chapter 14

Haven

Karen emerged from the lift in Haven's Sector 7 on Sublevel 1 carrying a small travel duffel. She strolled across the subway platform to the waiting cars and selected one nearest the Levline. Fastening her seatbelt, she commanded the car to take her to the University in Sector 3. The bubble top closed. The car slid sideways, positioning itself over the Levline, and accelerated into the tunnel ahead.

When the car reached her stop, she took the escalator to the surface. She found herself in the midst of the University's quad. Academic buildings surrounded the park-like grassy square. Students strolled through the tree-lined quad and lolled about on the grass. Despite the setting, Karen was not comfortable.

I swore I would never return to this god-forsaken rock. Just being here gives me the willies. I shouldn't be here.

She already verified that her three henchmen had arrived on Haven and checked into a luxury hotel. They were to wait for further instructions from her. She hoped she wouldn't need their services. Plan B would probably get very messy.

Karen researched the campus before coming to Haven, so she knew to head south to the science and engineering complex. The Goddard Physics Building was the second building on the right. She entered the building and took the lift to the seventh floor.

Only two nanoscreen doors opened into the long corridor, one at each end. Karen walked first to one, then to the other. Neither door had a placard. She decided to try the door to her left. It was unlocked. She stepped through the nanoscreen to find herself in an immense lab with dozens of workbenches and the occasional fume hood. A few graduate students occupied the room, too focused on their projects to look up from their work.

The lab occupied the whole floor. She recognized the figure near the room's center as Professor Jason. He was concentrating on an experiment involving an intricate array of chemistry labware. He didn't seem to notice her presence.

Karen took a deep breath and walked over to him. She cleared her throat.

"Professor Jason. You may not remember me, but…"

"I remember you quite well Marie Piaf de Lyons, CEO of Robotique Moderne International in Paris. What is it you want with me today? As you can see, I am very busy." Jason continued to work on his apparatus.

"I have an important project to discuss with you."

"I'm not taking on any new projects."

"I think you'll be interested in this one. RMI wishes to discuss a cooperative agreement that will pay you handsome dividends, both financially and in advancing your own research."

Jason sighed. "Very well, follow me." He carefully placed the reflux condenser he was holding on the bench top and turned away from his visitor.

He led Karen to a corner of the lab with a desk and three chairs. After offering her a chair, he pulled another around to face her and sat down. Karen's short skirt hiked well above her knees.

"As I told you before, I am not interested in financial rewards. I can't imagine how you could help me in any way."

"My engineers have made great progress toward perfecting a human android. We have only a few challenges to overcome. We'll soon have a product that will change the world the same way the smart phone transformed society fifty years ago. With your cooperation, we could overcome those last hurdles so much faster."

"So, what do you propose?"

"If we had a sample of your work to study, perhaps a substantial subsystem, we could share discoveries and overcome challenges together. Or, if you would prefer, I can send my engineers here to work directly under your supervision."

Jason nodded. "Adding researchers to any project is always a good thing. But outside of the research, how does cooperation benefit me?"

"RMI budgets a substantial amount for consultants. I'm sure we could match your university salary with consulting fees. We would also pay the

University a substantial sum, perhaps enough for an additional professorship. With your cooperation, everyone wins."

No one in their right mind would turn down this offer. Just agree, damn it, so I can get out of here and go home.

"I see. But before agreeing to any such deal, we each should have a clear understanding about where we currently stand. I would have to visit with your engineers in Paris."

"An excellent observation. You could bring examples of your work when you come. In addition, my penthouse apartment has a magnificent view of the city. I would love to have you stay with me if that would suit you."

Karen shifted strategically in her seat, hiking her skirt further.

If this doesn't catch his attention, he's not into women.

She was unaware that Jason had summoned one of his clones over. Jason-27 quietly walked across the lab and stood behind her.

"You said you wished to see a sample of my work. Turn around."

Karen turned her head and gasped. She stood up abruptly, knocking her chair over. Glancing back and forth between the two Jasons, she blurted, "What is this?"

"This is my android. I created him to look like me. Most of the time he acts like me."

Jason-0 stood. "Introduce yourself to Marie Piaf de Lyons."

Jason-27 produced a winning smile and held out his hand. "Allow me to introduce myself. I am Jason-27. It gives me great pleasure to make your acquaintance."

He repeated the introduction in perfect French.

They shook hands, then Jason-27 lifted Karen's hand, leaned forward, and kissed it.

Karen looked Jason-27 up and down for a full minute before turning back to Jason-0.

"I'm speechless. It looks and sounds just like you. The handshake and kiss felt entirely Human. Is it sentient?"

"We like to think so. Jason-27 is self-aware and exhibits both deductive and inductive problem solving. He also has a strong sense of creativity and intuition which suggests a strong command of abductive reasoning."

"Is Jason-27 your only robot?"

"There are others."

Karen paused for a moment, taking it all in.

This changes everything. Definitely calls for a new approach.

"I'm impressed, Professor. I came to Haven hoping to convince you to return with me to our labs on Earth so I could convince you to join RMI and work with my engineers building androids. But you are lightyears ahead of us. How many have you built?"

"Enough."

Careful. He's suddenly more guarded.

"Professor, could you loan me one of your androids? Even for a short period of time. I would like to have my engineers see what you have accomplished."

"Not a chance."

"I could bring my engineers here to Haven. We could set up our own lab here. Since you built these robots, you could teach my people how to make them."

"I'm not interested."

"Is there anything I can offer to make you reconsider?" She said this in her most alluring voice.

Jason suddenly stood and stared directly at Karen's face. He furrowed his brow.

"Marie. Look into my eyes."

"What?" Karen seemed perplexed but complied.

Jason studied her eyes.

What the hell?

"Karen Sanders."

"What?" Karen gasped, shocked.

"You are Karen Sanders."

"You are mistaken. People often mistake me for someone they know."

"I thought I detected something odd about your behavior. At first, I attributed it to your having a hidden agenda. But it was your identity you've been hiding."

"No! That's not true. I don't know this Karen Sanders."

"Iris identification is nearly foolproof. I have a positive match with your iris image in Haven's Security archives. You can stop the charade."

Karen glanced again at Jason-27 and glared at Jason-0. Her hands began to tremble. Sweat beaded on her forehead.

"You! You are an imposter! You are an android too. Where is Professor Jason?"

"There is no Professor Jason. There is only me, Jason. I am the android the Shalcerians built for Rae Anne Chavez."

Karen dropped into her chair dejectedly. Her heart pounded through her chest. She began breathing heavily, nearly panting.

There's got to be a way out of this.

"We can still work the deal I proposed. No one needs to find out who I am."

"You are a cold-blooded killer and an escaped convict. You expect me to work with you as though these facts don't matter?"

Damn, damn, damn. Don't let things fall apart now.

"What's more important? Putting me back in prison, or providing a vast network of androids to benefit the entire Human race?"

"As I see it, both options are mutually feasible and desirable."

"Please. Just escort me to the next Earth-bound shuttle. Let me return to RMI and continue my life in Paris. I'll never set foot on Haven again."

"I will not do that. Your actions have shown that you have no respect for the law or for Human decency. You are a danger to society."

"What are you going to do with me?"

"I have already alerted Security. They will be here shortly. DNA analysis will confirm your true identity. Your long stint of freedom has come to an end, Karen Sanders."

Tears streamed down her face. She fumbled in her jacket pocket for a tissue and pulled one out with a closed fist. Using both hands, she covered her face and rubbed both eyes at once, then blew her nose into the tissue. As she folded the tissue and returned it to her pocket, her demeanor changed. She became coldly composed and no longer regarded Jason.

A racket in the hall preceded three uniformed officers who stepped through the nanoscreen and worked their way through the lab to Jason's desk.

"Are you Karen Sanders?" asked the lead officer.

"I am Marie Piaf de Lyons. I do not know who this Karen Sanders might be. This android creature is creating a fictional narrative to frame me."

Jason shook his head and pointed to Karen.

"I have made positive iris identification. This person calling herself Marie Piaf is actually the escaped convict Karen Sanders. Her hair and face have been altered. Take her fingerprints at the station and submit a DNA sample for analysis. You will verify that my identification is correct."

Taking Karen by the arms, they cuffed her hands behind her.

Before they could turn her toward the door, she glared at Jason. "I will never go back to prison." Her voice sounded leaden, resigned.

Security marched her through the nanoscreen and down the hallway. They took the lift to the main floor, crossed the atrium, and stepped outside. Before reaching their van, Karen crumpled to the pavement. Her body jerked uncontrollably while she gasped for air.

"Medics! Call the EMT's. Fast!"

Foam issued from Karen's blue lips. Her face turned a pasty bluish white. Soon, the violent jerks faded to severe twitching, then stopped altogether. One officer stooped down to test for a pulse. There was none.

He stood, shaking his head.

"She's dead. Strong almond smell. Cyanide."

"Do we call the medics?"

"Yeah, for transport. And the coroner."

He walked to the rear of the van and pulled out a light tarp which he used to cover Karen's body.

"Seems she meant it when she vowed never to go back to prison."

Chapter 15

Alpha Centauri A

The Shalcerians were reinforcing their defensive line at Proxima Centauri A in preparation for a counterattack on the Baltari when they detected a fleet of cloaked Jason warships activating their gravity wave sensors. The pulses surrounded them on all sides. Try as they might, they could not verify their presence on other sensors. Furthermore, they observed similar waves surrounding the Baltar force.

Denahr had notified all the commanders that advanced Human cloaked warships could attack before defensive measures could be taken, but not having seen evidence of such ships before, they hadn't taken his warnings seriously. The three-day buildup of this invisible threat created considerable anxiety throughout the fleet.

Suddenly, several sensors recorded a massive explosion in the Baltar formation near Alpha Centauri B. Then a strange thing happened. Within minutes, the Baltar fleet abandoned the Centauri system for parts unknown. Only their departing gravity waves remained behind.

The Shalcerians concluded that the invisible warships attacked the Baltar armada with such fury that it forced the retreat, suggesting that their own presence in the Centauri System might come under similar attack. When they turned to Commander Denahr for information, he remained vague on the issue. He depicted Humans as extremely resourceful and suggested that Shalcerians were seriously underestimating their capabilities.

At least a dozen military reports detailing these events and Denahr's appraisal arrived on the emperor's desk in Shalkor over the following week. The emperor perused them with dismay. The last thing he needed was a fresh war with a species more powerful than the Baltari with whom he had been fighting for a hundred and fifty years.

Alpha Centauri B, Aboard *Liberty*

When *Curie* returned to Alpha Centauri B following the Baltar retreat, it brought *Liberty* with it through the wormhole. Ian, in command of *Liberty*, ordered the clamps released and he and Anton Kovalenko guided their ships toward the scene of destruction to search for *Voyager*.

Rae Anne, where are you? Please be alive and well!

Ian put *Liberty* into a wide arcing trajectory around one side of the small red sun while *Curie* took the opposite side. The entire bridge crew scanned the space with every sensor available. Hours passed. Ian's anxiety increased by the minute.

"Captain Bentley," his logistics officer called out. "I have a large expanding debris field 32 degrees to the left of Centauri B and 15 degrees below the ecliptic. Distance: 192 million kilometers."

"Thank you, Lt. Donaldson. Jason, any communication from that direction?"

"No, Sir. Dead silence."

"Lt. Deneau, plot a course and take us there, maximum velocity. Everyone, direct your sensors ahead. Report anything of significance. Full magnification on visuals."

The starfield in the forward monitor slewed to the right as the ship veered to port on its new course.

"Time to arrival?"

"Twelve minutes, thirty-seven seconds."

As *Liberty* approached the target area, hundreds, then thousands, of shards from the Baltar control ship twinkled in the monitor, reflecting the sun's red light as they tumbled through space.

"I've got five, no, make that six, objects several times larger than *Liberty*," Donaldson reported, brushing her hand through her hair.

"Take us to the nearest one, Deneau. Jason, notify *Curie*."

Ian turned to his console and tapped an icon to broadcast a command to the shuttle bay. "Shuttle crews. Be prepared to launch on my command. We are approaching the first object of interest."

Liberty pulled alongside a blackened charred structure and matched its velocity. Shortly thereafter, three shuttles, dwarfed by the enormous structure, began to orbit it and search its surface. They transmitted their visuals directly to monitors on *Liberty's* bridge.

"Shuttle *Tango* here. I'm seeing a large cavity leading inside the structure. Request permission to enter."

"*Tango*, permission granted. Proceed with caution. Maintain an exit strategy at all times."

Tango deployed a translator to the surface to relay communications to *Liberty* and disappeared into the black hole. On *Liberty's* bridge, one monitor displayed *Tango's* visual transmission, illuminated by the shuttle's bright searchlights.

"Not sure what to make of this area, Captain. The cavity is like a huge spherical cavern like a sports arena, eighty meters in diameter. There are thirty tiers of balconies surrounding the open space. Most are littered with what I can only assume are the charred remains of the aliens."

"Any sign of *Voyager*?"

"No, Sir. Nothing."

"Return to the surface. We'll finish the survey and move on to the next object."

The next two bulky pieces of wreckage showed similar results. Ian's heart ached as though caught in a vice. He tried to swallow the lump in his throat, but his mouth was dry.

Before they arrived at the fourth structure, Donaldson let out a whoop. "I've got a massive radar image on my screen. It looks like the ass-end of a KBP cruiser! I think we've found *Voyager*!"

Ian leaped to his side and peered over his shoulder. "My god, you're right. Let's get over there and see what shape it's in."

With *Liberty* coasting beside the massive chunk of debris, its three shuttles combed over *Voyager's* surface, testing and prodding the exposed parts of the ship.

"No sign yet of visible damage to the hull, Captain. But the forward two-thirds is buried in the wreckage."

Ian turned to Jason. "Can we pull the ship free?"

"*Liberty* lacks the equipment to attach itself to *Voyager*. But if enough of the tail section is available, *Curie* could get a clamping device around the hull."

"Inform *Curie* that we need them here ASAP for a rescue operation."

Curie arrived within the hour. Anton backed *Curie* over *Voyager*'s exposed tail section and gently positioned his ship on top of *it*. *Curie*'s aft clamps securely grasped *Voyager*'s hull. For the next several minutes, nothing happened.

"Can you pull her free, Anton?" Ian asked anxiously.

"I'm applying full power, Ian. She's not budging."

"Do we have anything we can use to excavate around the ship to loosen it?"

Both Jason and Anton reported negatives.

"Anton, are your forward clamps still functional?"

"They are. I see what you are thinking. Back *Liberty* beneath my ship and I'll clamp us together. Perhaps with both ships, we can produce enough power to pull *Voyager* free."

Once Ian positioned *Liberty* beneath *Curie,* Anton securely fastened it to the starship. Both ships applied full power. *Liberty* vibrated ominously, emitting loud groans that reverberated throughout the ship. A loud BOOM rumbled through the bridge. Ian jumped, his heart in his throat. An eerie stillness followed.

"Anton, what happened?" Ian called, anxiety flooding his voice.

"We did it! *Voyager* is free."

"Thank god. Can you tell what shape she's in?"

"Visuals look good from here, Ian. Even the airlock appears intact."

"Thanks Anton. We'll get a shuttle over there and see if we can dock."

Ian dispatched the three shuttles, one to dock to *Voyager*'s airlock, the other two to do a full ship scrutiny for damage.

Tango bumped up against *Voyager*'s airlock and bounced away. Three additional attempts to latch onto the airlock failed as well.

"Ian, the airlock mechanism refuses to engage. We'll need an EVA to inspect it to find out what the trouble is."

"Then do it. *Foxtrot, Disco*, report."

"The blast scoured the hull clean. Not a sensor, antenna, or weapons mount to be seen."

"Is there any way to communicate through the hull, to check for survivors?"

"Afraid not, Captain. And we have no way to determine if the ship's environment is still intact."

"Very well. *Tango,* prepare an emergency evacuation tent to seal around the airlock if your EVA can't fix the problem. We need to get into *Voyager* as soon as possible."

"Got it, Captain. The EVA team is already depressurizing *Tango*'s airlock.

Ian paced *Liberty*'s bridge. Every muscle in his neck and shoulders was knotted with tension.

Hurry up. Hurry up.

"*Tango* here. Our EVA team doesn't see an easy fix for the airlock attachment mechanism. They're standing by for the egress tent we are sending out now. Give us five minutes and we'll be ready to key into *Voyager*'s airlock."

"Thanks, *Tango. Foxtrot* and *Disco*. Stand by in case *Tango* needs assistance."

Tango called in five minutes later. "Emergency egress tent is sealed around *Voyager's* airlock. Permission to key the airlock open and enter the ship."

"Permission granted. Maintain a running commentary as you go."

"Outer airlock hatch is open. Airlock was still holding at standard pressure. We are working the inner hatch now."

After a minute, a loud hissing sound came through the comlink on *Liberty*'s bridge.

"*Voyager*'s internal pressure is below standard. Oxygen levels reading low. Temperature is twelve degrees Celsius. Pretty damn chilly."

"*Tango,* send a team to the bridge immediately. I'm concerned that no one was there to greet you. Rae Anne may need your help."

God, I hope she's ok.

For Ian, the next five minutes seemed like a lifetime. He hated that plasticore blocked normal radio waves, keeping him from listening to the EMT's suit-to-suit transmissions.

When the EMT crew returned to the airlock, *Liberty*'s comlink came alive.

"Rae Anne is alive, Captain, but unconscious from both oxygen deprivation and hypothermia. We're going to use *Voyager*'s airlock as an oxygen tent so we can begin treating her immediately. We're using heating blankets from our kit to warm her."

"Can you determine how serious her situation is?"

"Not a clue at this point."

"What about Jason-05?"

"Totally short-circuited. Memory boards fried."

Ian heard a muffled sob behind him and turned to the comlink console. Jason-03 was hunched over, holding his head in his hands.

A lump formed in Ian's throat in sympathy for his android communication officer.

Unbelievable. An android exhibiting grief at losing a fellow android.

Before he could cross the room to provide consolation, *Tango* reported in again.

"Rae Anne is starting to respond. Captain. Her eyes are fluttering and her body temperature is returning to normal."

"That's great. Get her aboard *Liberty* as soon as you can safely transport her."

"Will do, Captain. What should we do with the Jason?"

"Bring him over, too. Handle his remains as carefully as you can. We have someone here who cares deeply for him."

Chapter 16

Nova Prima

Four months had passed since Sam retreated from Haven. Over four-thousand troopers occupied his five cruisers, none of which were provisioned to support such a large company for more than a month. The two Mars colonies had long been self-sufficient, but the surplus from their aquaponics facilities fell short of meeting the sudden increase in demand. The situation quickly progressed from critical to dire.

Sam sat in Tony Armado's old office in Nova Prima's Habitat 3 and tapped his fingers impatiently on the desk.

"So, you say the water collection and purification systems are falling short of meeting our needs?" he asked Travis standing near the door.

"Even with strict rationing. The subsurface ice collection system is operating at full capacity and it still isn't enough."

"Well, curtail bathing until we can expand operations."

"We did that three weeks ago. The habitats stink to high heaven. But water is the least of our worries." Travis paused for Sam's response.

"Go on."

"Armado assigned five habitats for food storage to cover emergencies. Those storage units are empty. We're rationing the output from the aquaponics farms, but it's not enough to keep people alive for long."

"I haven't noticed anything different. I've been eating quite well."

"Your chef gets whatever she asks for, despite the depravations. She keeps you and your staff well fed. Mind you, I'm not complaining."

"Damnation. It's all the Loyalists fault with their damn blockade."

"There is one more thing."

Sam sighed and slapped his hand on the desk. "Out with it."

"The troopers have been mixing with the general population. There's talk of insurrection. Security broke up a mob last night. Five killed."

"Double Security. Enlist officers from the ships. Tell them we'll feed them well. That should entice them."

Travis scowled. "I'll try, but it may not work. They know how dire the situation is. They know we'll all run out of food in a few weeks. There won't be anything left for anyone."

Sam's face turned crimson. He could hear the blood pounding in his ears. "Get out!"

Travis scurried out the door.

The comlink on the corner of his desk pinged. Sam leaned over to identify the caller. It was *Shackleton*'s captain, Vernon Chernov, his most loyal supporter. Sam tapped the icon.

"What's up Vern? I hope you aren't going to add to my troubles."

Vernon diverted his eyes downward which highlighted the mass of creases across his forehead. He frowned and took a deep breath.

"Sam, I hate to be the one telling you this, but you're losing your crews. We've been without food here for two days. *Olympia* and *Hawking* have surrendered to the Loyalists. Both ships are preparing to lift off."

"Damn! How many troopers are deserting with them?"

"Both ships are packed to the gills. I would put the number at roughly thirty-two hundred.

"That's over half of my army! Stop them immediately."

"There's no practical way for me to do that."

"Then blast the bloody bastards out of the sky. Desertion is a capital offense. Let that be an example to the others."

"Sorry, Sam. No way I would do that under any circumstances. In fact, my crew has petitioned me to surrender as well."

"You can't do that! Surely, you're not going to abandon me."

"No choice, Sam. Facing whatever criminal charges they may throw at me is better than watching my crew starve to death."

Sam keyed his monitor to display the landing field just as *Olympia* lifted off. *Shackleton* launched minutes later. Only *Leibnitz* remained.

A loud BOOM rattled the office with such force that several framed pictures fell from the wall, their glass shattering on the floor. Travis bounded into the office. A second explosion nearly knocked him to the floor.

"Security is using explosives against the protestors. They tossed a grenade in a tunnel filled with people and when it exploded and ripped the tunnel to pieces, both emergency airlocks slammed shut. Everyone in the tunnel was killed."

Sam jabbed the comlink icon. "All Security, report to Habitat 3 immediately. Come fully armed. Shoot to kill."

Sam reached into his desk and removed two 9-mm pistols. After sliding their 16-round clips out to verify both guns were fully loaded, he locked them back in place and held one pistol out to Travis.

"I…, I'm not comfortable with that. I've never shot a gun in my life."

"Take it, dammit. It may save your life."

Travis reached across the desk and hesitantly took the weapon.

Seven members of Sam's security detail rushed into the office. Close on their heels came four more who were pushing staffers in front of them.

"Give your extra weapons to the staff," instructed Sam. "We need to put up as forceful a front as possible. If we're resolute and present a show of strength, they'll back down in a minute. Especially if we draw blood."

The guards slid two couches to the middle of the room and turned them over to form a barrier. They arranged the chairs in a semicircle around Sam's desk to provide a variety of firing angles toward the entrance.

While Sam and his team were rearranging furniture inside the habitat, four figures in full EVA gear borrowed from the *Leibnitz* were outside, pulling a cart from the ship's cargo bay across the rust-red Martian crater floor. They stopped next to the join between Habitat 3 and the tunnel corridor connecting it to the rest of Nova Prima's spiderlike network.

One suited figure unpacked the cart, handing small packages to the others. They in turn secured each package with metallic tape around the habitat's airlock frame. When the last package was in place, they attached wires to each package and fastened their loose ends to a small metal box placed on the Martian soil. They then attached the end of a spool of wire to the box and returned to the *Leibnitz*, slowly unspooling the wire behind them.

They mounted the ramp leading to the *Leibnitz'* airlock and stepped inside. There, they clipped the wire from the spool to another box containing a battery. A large red button protruded from the top of the box. The four figures looked at each other through their EVA visors. Three of them raised their fists and signaled a 'thumbs up.' Their leader turned to the battery and slammed his fist against the button.

The resulting explosion blew the airlock on Habitat 3 to pieces. Shards of the tunnel enclosure shot into the air. Some slammed against the *Leibnitz* where the sound from the explosion was muffled due to the thin Martian atmosphere.

In Habitat 3, the blast sheared the airlock from the plasticore building. The habitat's interior experienced sudden explosive decompression. As the air was sucked away, it carried loose papers, sofa pillows, carpets, and a variety of other lightweight objects along with it, scattering them across the Martian landscape.

As for Sam and the heavily armed people in the habitat, the rapid decompression ripped at their lungs. The gases within their bloodstream boiled off, causing immense pain as they suffocated in the near vacuum. Mercifully, the end was quick.

Chapter 17

Shalkor, Aboard *Curie*

Curie, fully armed and with full crew as a show of strength, made its longest jump yet, 44.7 lightyears to Shalkor, the Shalcerian Empire's capital city. Ian stood at the helm with Jason-11 at the communications console. Rae Anne accompanied them on the bridge as an observer where she could watch the forward monitor. When *Curie* popped through the wormhole, the distant 18 Scorpii sun lay dead ahead, the brightest star on the monitor.

Such a beautiful yellow-white sun, so much like our Sol.

Ian turned to Rae Anne with a puzzled expression.

"This jump seemed different from the hundreds we made in the Centauri System. I had a strange feeling the moment we slipped through the wormhole. Like standing at the brink of a precipice separating life and death."

"I've experienced that too on the longer jumps. Jason thinks it's a moment when time ceases to exist as we cross the threshold. Just brief enough to snag our awareness. But it wipes out an android's memory if he isn't physically connected to the ship's computer."

As if to emphasize the point, Jason unplugged the cable attached to his head and stowed it under the console. Then he added, "I've timed every jump to the microsecond, and the delay you mentioned is precisely related to the distance jumped. It may be that this weird threshold is a region completely removed from our space and time. Not even a part of our universe."

Ian whistled. "That blows my mind. Like a crack in the universe."

Rae Anne laughed. "Puts new meaning on the old expression 'falling through the cracks.'

Two hours later, *Curie* was fast approaching the city Shalkor, in orbit above their home planet of the same name. The planet Shalkor glimmered beneath as a vivid blueish disk bathed in 18 Scorpii's warm yellow sunlight.

For the second time in as many hours, Ian found himself lightheaded. He was awed by the majestic beauty of Shalkor the city. Its 144 sectors formed a complete ring orbiting around the planet's equator. Each sector was 10 kilometers deep and between 230 and 280 kilometers long, connected to its neighbors with pressurized tunnels for Levtrain passage. Glimmering transparent domes provided environmental protection for the city and its myriad skyscrapers. A vast array of spaceships, from mammoth interstellar battlecruisers to family space-yachts clustered around the entire structure.

Awesome. Exactly as I remember it.

Ian turned to Rae Anne, shaking his head in disbelief. "You described this city to me many times, but my imagination never came close to capturing the reality."

"I'm looking forward to our visit to the royal palaces. I never made it that far in my earlier visit."

The forward monitor showed two battlecruisers approaching *Curie*. Sensor readouts on Ian's panel indicated they were on battle alert.

"Security detail, I hope," Ian announced.

The navcom interrupted with a curt command.

> Approaching light cruiser of Shalcerian manufacture.
> Reduce speed to one-tenth and maintain current
> course. Our ships will escort you into the security zone.
>
> We have your transponder registration. Please state the
> name of your vessel and its commander, your species,
> your destination, and the purpose for entering Shalkor
> Controlled Space.

Ian tapped the comlink icon on his command console.

"Shalkor Approach Control, I am Ian Bentley, captain of the *Curie*. We are of the Human species from Sol System. Our destination is the Palace Quadrant on Sector 1. We are here to meet with the emperor."

> Our records show a Rae Anne Chavez as the only
> Human to have visited Shalkor, and *Curie* is the first

Human piloted craft to enter our system. You are to
dock in Bay 147 in Sector 18. Remain aboard ship until
Security permits further access to Shalkor.

Meanwhile, we shall manufacture the necessary
number of respirators you will need for your crew based
on the design used on the previous Human visit. How
many respirators will you need?

"We have 157 Humans and one droid on board. We request 157 respirators."

Please be advised that droids are not permitted on
Shalkor. Your droid must remain aboard your ship for
the duration of your stay.

Also be advised that it is extremely unlikely that you will
be granted permission to enter the Palace Quadrant, let
alone gain audience with the Emperor. Most such
requests are denied outright.

Please follow Sector 18's guide beam now directed
toward your ship. Reduce speed by half when you are
within 100 kilometers of Shalkor and cut all power at 50
kilometers. Our tractor beam will guide you to your
assigned bay.

After responding to the Shalcerian command, Ian turned around and scowled. "Do either of you know the protocol for requesting an audience with the emperor? Who do we contact? And how, for that matter?"

Rae Anne smiled. "I met with Commander Denahr before we left Haven. He had already sent a combot to Shalkor describing our role in defeating the Baltar fleet at Alpha Centauri B and alluding to our own cloaked fleet of interstellar vessels that heroically interceded between the two warring camps, intimidating both. He told them to expect a visit from Humans intending to abrogate the Saturn Accords and to propose a treaty of conciliation between Humans and Shalcerians as parties of equals."

"So, we aren't arriving unannounced."

"He also gave me clear instructions on how we are to proceed once we have been cleared by Security. We even have directions on how to deal with Security if they make things difficult."

Ian laughed. "I should have known. You never leave anything to chance. Seems we should have brought Denahr with us!"

"I invited him, but he felt we would make a better impression showing up on our own."

The Shalcerian warships escorted *Curie* to Sector 18 where *Curie* locked into the tractor beam and was guided into Berth 147. Shortly after arrival, they received a request to be boarded. Expecting a security detail, Ian made a ship wide announcement commanding full cooperation with Shalcerian inspectors. Then he, Rae Anne, and Jason descended to the airlock to welcome their visitors.

To their surprise, when the airlock opened, the five Shalcerians who entered the ship were high-ranking government officials. As they introduced themselves, they each drooped their three eyestalks with downcast eyes in a Shalcerian showing of gratitude and welcome. Their body plates rippled in a rainbow of colors around their respirators. One handed an intricately shaped gold sculpture to Ian.

"In recognition of Human intervention in the Centauri System and on behalf of the Emperor, we welcome you to Shalkor as our honored guests. It is my honor to present you with this small token of our gratitude."

Ian handed the sculpture to Rae Anne. She almost dropped it for the unexpected weight.

This thing is heavy! It may be pure gold.

"On behalf of all Humans, I thank you," said Ian. "We are looking forward to visiting your fine city. But recognition for the Baltar retreat belongs with this person, Rae Anne Chavez, who fearlessly piloted the cruiser *Voyager* into the Baltar armada. It was she who destroyed their Command Center, leading to their retreat."

The officials turned inward as a group and began squawking and screeching in their native language without translation. All fifteen arms and an occasional leg or two gesticulated in arcane (to Humans) movements.

Rae Anne was startled at this reaction. "My god, Ian, couldn't you have just accepted their gift? I think you've offended them."

Jason, fluent in Shalcerian, put a hand on her shoulder. "No, no. This revelation has changed their plans entirely. They are discussing how best to honor you personally for your part in the battle. Their original celebrations to welcome Humans to Shalkor are being elevated to a new level."

The lead official broke away from their animated circle and approached Rae Anne. His eyestalks again drooped, his body scales rippling with pink and coral swirls on a forest green background.

"Please accept our most humble apologies. We had no idea we would be honored with your presence. The Emperor himself has invited you to meet with him at the Royal Palace. We will escort your ship immediately to Sector 1. As Sector 18's director, I will have the honor to accompany you, as will my chief deputy."

The three other officials spun on their center legs and departed. Ian escorted the remaining party to the bridge. The tractor beam had already begun to budge *Curie* from its berth and into space.

"Jeez, look at that," Ian exclaimed.

The forward monitor showed six battlecruisers and a dozen smaller ships waiting to escort them around the city to Sector 1. As they proceeded to the Palace Sector, Rae Anne confronted their guests.

"Before we disembark, we require one concession from the emperor. Jason-11, although he lives in a machined body, is a sentient person. His species is allied with Humans. We Humans accept them as our equals. Your ban on permitting mechanical beings on Shalkor must be amended to accord full rights and privileges to the Jason species."

Jason looked at Rae Anne and cocked his head, as if in wonder that she would put this mission in jeopardy for his sake.

The Sector 18 director was silent for a moment. His body scales shaded to gray. Finally, he spoke.

"I've communicated your request to the Emperor. He will announce his disposition on your demand on our arrival at Sector 1. I should tell you that he was not pleased to have conditions imposed on his welcome."

If this caused him problems, our peace proposal will send him into apoplectic fits.

Chapter 18

Sirius System, Aboard *Prescient*

On a hunch, VenaVen jumped *Prescient* 8.6 lightyears from the Kuiper Belt to the Sirius System. A scan confirmed his suspicions that the Baltar armada had retreated to Sirius after the unexpected destruction of their Command Center and the perceived threat from two-hundred cloaked Jason warships. Jason-02 was on the bridge, having been given honorary command over communications for this trip.

"Our first task is to identify who is now in charge," VenaVen commented to AgruVen who was at the nav console.

"We should look for the largest cluster of battlecruisers," AgruVen suggested. "The generals are probably still working out command protocols. Anyone contending for leadership positions will want to be within shuttle distance of the meetings."

"Good point. Locate that group, then monitor shuttle traffic to find out which ship they are meeting in. Set a course for that destination."

Jason-02 turned from the comlink console to face VenaVen. "Captain, should we notify them of our arrival?"

"Not necessary. They pinged our transponder for identification the instant they detected our wormhole gravity wave. Several ships are crewed by my family, so we'll be welcomed when we join the cluster. They will likely be expecting me to have a bountiful plunder to distribute."

As VenaVen predicted, *Prescient* encountered no problems in joining the fifteen battleships clustered in orbit around an ice-encrusted moon over a gas giant planet. VenaVen's extensive family ties accounted for the entire crew on two ships and more than half the crew on a third.

According to Baltar custom, a family member returning from a long absence was expected to hold a festive reunion party without delay. VenaVen ordered the cargo bay cleared and decorated for the event to be held the following day. He instructed Jason to send invitations to his 3500 friends and relations (mostly relations) who were in nearby ships.

Jason had never experienced anything like the Baltar reunion bash. Shuttles queued at the airlock for hours, disgorging guests and supplies as well as gifts for VenaVen. For his part, VenaVen distributed vintage alcoholic beverages in intricately carved bottles to the generals, captains, and first officers from every ship.

VenaVen introduced Jason to everyone as a member of the independent sentient species called Jasons who were associated with Humans from Sol System. He emphasized that the joint Human-Jason attack on their armada was in direct retaliation for their sortie into their system. He knew his people would understand this explanation as an appropriate response to their aggression. Jason emphasized the Jasons' neutrality in the conflict to everyone he met and the Human's long-lasting claim on all three suns in the Alpha Centauri System and their desire to remain neutral in the ongoing conflict.

Nevertheless, his presence was met with considerable suspicion. Without VenaVen's assurances, most guests would have avoided him entirely. The wounds from their defeat were still too fresh.

Near midnight, activities began winding down. Jason noted that Baltari, unlike Humans, became more mellow the more they drank. VenaVen had no difficulty quieting the massive crowd and getting their attention from the round stage set in the center of the room.

"My dearest friends, I thank you for this fine welcome. I've been away far too long. It is unfortunate that this reunion isn't combined with a glorious victory celebration but is instead marred by the memory of our lost comrades. Little did we know such a powerful species with cloaked warships existed in our neighborhood. It should be obvious to everyone here that Humans and Jasons would make very good allies."

The stage rotated slowly as VenaVen talked, allowing him to eventually face everyone in the crowded room. Large monitors hanging from the ceiling maintained a full frontal view from every location. At this point in his speech, the room was deathly quiet. Few were ready to agree with VenaVen's suggestion.

"It is understandable why they felt threatened as our conflict with Shalcerians approached within a few lightyears of their system. When our own Baltar warships appeared in Sol System and instituted an unprovoked attack on their home world, only then did they rally their forces against our fleet. And only then did we become aware of their superior capabilities.

"But something good may come of this unfortunate experience. Jason OhTwo, whom some of you have already met tonight, is a member of the Jasons. He has been delegated to act as an emissary on behalf of both Humans and Jasons. I believe we should hear what he has to say."

VenaVen welcomed Jason onto the stage and stepped down. Jason held both arms out in a welcoming gesture to the crowd, taking in everyone in the room as the platform rotated. He could only hope his audience would accept this as a friendly gesture.

"My thanks to Captain VenaVen for his gracious hospitality and his invitation to join you for this event. My warmest wishes to all of you. I hope to be counted as a friend. However, I am here on a mission.

"After our engagement with you at Alpha Centauri B, I can understand your reluctance to accept me. I assure you that I am here as a neutral party to convey a peace proposal from the Humans and Jasons of Sol System. Our peace proposal extends also to the Shalcerians.

"We understand your conflict with Shalcerians has been ongoing for many, many generations, costing millions of lives and material resources beyond measure. Dozens of entire colonies and outposts have been reduced to rubble. Every attack initiates a retaliatory reply. Which, in turn, invokes a further retaliatory response. The course you both are on is a one-way path to destruction. Imagine where your civilization might be today if those lost lives and wasted wealth and resources had been directed toward advances in science and technology and in promoting the welfare of your people."

There was considerable stirring in the room. Jason couldn't determine if the unease indicated a warming toward his offer or a repudiation. A general stepped forward and interrupted his talk. Jason invited him onto the dais.

"Jason OhTwo, we are all too aware of the costs associated with this bloody conflict. I believe negotiations between Humans, Jasons, and ourselves might be possible, despite your devastating strike against us. But the Shalcerian demons must be purged from the galaxy. They enslave their subjects with terror and torture. They have exterminated sentient species and laid waste to entire planetary systems. There is no possibility that we civilized Baltari could ever come to terms with them. They are monsters of the lowest order. They can't be trusted."

Jason reached out and put a hand on the general's elbow, a Baltar gesture of conciliation and goodwill.

"Do you sincerely believe everything you have just said? Doesn't it seem strange to you that such vile creatures could govern a vast empire without having to suppress uprisings and rebellions? Humans and Jasons have worked alongside Shalcerians for twenty Earth years. We have experienced none of the criminal conduct you describe. Those allegations you have heard and repeated here are totally false. They can only be attributed to war propaganda.

"It might be well for you to reevaluate your bias against the Shalcerians. Dig deep into your own culture and identify who is profiting by keeping this conflict going. Who is behind the fake news warping your views of Shalcerians and fueling your thirst for war?"

The general rejoined his group. The room hummed with dozens of Baltar conversations and a great deal of gesturing.

I hope my comments have struck home.

Someone approached VenaVen and caught his attention by poking him in his mid-section, another common Baltar gesture. He hummed his questions loudly enough to be heard over the hubbub. The room quieted in response.

"You are responsible for inviting Jason OhTwo. What do you have to say about this preposterous idea? If we went along with this, who among the Humans would we be dealing with?"

The room again erupted into the loud humming from dozens of Baltar voices.

VenaVen waved his arms in a gesture Jason didn't recognize, but it garnered everyone's attention and the room quieted.

"Rae Anne Chavez, a respected leader among Humans, came up with this proposal while evaluating our conflict as an independent observer. She proposes that representatives from the four species enact an immediate cease-fire, then declare a summit to work toward creating an alliance for peace and cooperation. She is asking us to appoint representatives with the authority to make binding decisions in these matters. She herself will represent Humans."

I should add a few more details.

Jason mimicked VenaVen's gesture for quiet from the center stage, with the same result.

"As we speak, Rae Anne Chavez is seeking audience with the Shalcerian emperor on Shalkor to present this proposal to him. She hopes to use her substantial influence to convince him to participate in this conference. If we four species can set aside our differences and work together in cooperation, just think what the future might hold for us all.

"On a final note, I should add that the Jasons' expertise lies in gathering and processing information. Our data archives are immense. They include everything there is to know about Shalcerians, Baltari, and Humans, including things you don't even know about yourselves.

"For example, the maglozons you treat as mindless predators on your home planet Entriva have evolved over the millennia into sentient creatures with language and a self-governing civilization. They are anxious to learn about you and develop a peaceful coexistence with you. We Jasons can help you do that.

"This is but one example. Imagine what having access to our archives would mean to the Baltar Federation going forward. Please give this proposal for a cease fire and a peace summit your serious consideration."

Jason stepped off the stage and joined VenaVen and AgruVen. Humming conversations and animated activity filled the room.

Sounds like I stepped inside a beehive!

VenaVen tugged at Jason's elbow. "No matter how much they may agree with you, it's to no avail. Our Supreme Leader, President RanaDal, rules the federation with an iron hand. No one here would dare to suggest ending the war. For one thing, it's what keeps him in power."

Jason shook his head. "Then your people must figure out a way to get around him. You must convince him that your stunning defeat at Alpha Centauri B is a portent of what Baltari might expect now that Humans and Jasons have been forced into the fray. A treaty now is the only recourse that makes any logical sense."

"I pity the poor general who is chosen to inform him of the disaster. His entire family may be banished from the service. I hope it's not someone from our family!"

Authoritarian autocracies! What strange and counterproductive institutions. How is it that people of all species tolerate them?

Chapter 19

Shalkor

After docking at the Palace Quadrant, *Curie* was met by the Sector 1 director and his assistant. The director handed Rae Anne a sealed note from the emperor. To her relief, he decreed that Jasons be acknowledged as sentient beings. However, he required an armed Shalcerian officer to accompany all Jasons visiting Shalkor.

The Sector 1 director led Rae Anne, Ian, and Jason onto the palace grounds. A full military escort of two dozen armed guards marched alongside them. All exhibited the same body scale coloring of gold diamonds arrayed on an indigo background. The director assured them the escort was an honor guard, not security.

Rae Anne puckered her lips.

As if I believed that.

She noted that only one building in this sector exceeded six stories, unlike the crowded urban areas with their skyscrapers on the other city sectors. Another notable difference—all the buildings here were sheathed in gold.

The nanoplast walkway glided the party towards the tallest building with intricately carved columns surrounding a wide portico. The columns extended well above the building, reminding Rae Anne of minarets. The entire building's roof consisted of an expansive gold dome.

Large parks carpeted with purple grass-like plants separated the buildings. Trees with slender white and gray braided trunks shaded the parks with speckled orange and green serving-platter leaves. Ian stooped to scoop one up that had fallen onto the walkway. It was as big as his face. On the horizon, the planet Shalkor filled one-third of the sky.

"Our home world. Isn't it beautiful?" the Sector 18 director observed, then turned to his Sector 1 counterpart. "Have you visited it recently?"

"Just last month. My time for Convergence called me to the surface for a mating session."

"How fortunate. I still have five or six years before my time comes around again."

Ian looked quizzically at Rae Anne, who smiled knowingly and shook her head at Jason who seemed about to say something.

Now is not the time to get into Shalcerian reproductive biology.

The nanoplast walkway ended at the palace portico. There were no doors leading into the palace, only a wide, three-story maw. The interior was brightly lit in blue-white light. The Sector 1 director led the way.

This room is as large as a domed football stadium. I feel like an ant.

Adding to her impression was the throne itself, placed at the far end of the room, requiring visitors to hike the room's full length to reach the throne's base. The throne was four times normal size, as was the emperor, sitting in place before them.

Just as before when he visited Haven. A massive holographic display to make sure we are intimidated.

Rae Anne sighed in disgust.

No choice but to appeal to his ego.

Fortunately, his translated communications were at normal voice level. Rae Anne wasn't sure she could put up with a god-like booming voice.

"Rae Anne Chavez. How wonderful to see you again. And under such circumstances. We owe you our deepest gratitude for saving us the trouble of annihilating the Baltar armada at Alpha Centauri ourselves. Our fleet was preparing to do the job, though likely at considerable cost. What losses did your fleet sustain?"

"We lost one Jason. No Human lives were lost, and only one ship was damaged in the effort."

The emperor was quiet. His holographic image froze, having been put on hold. When it finally came to life, his voice betrayed considerable consternation.

"We don't understand how that could be possible."

"Perhaps your advisors' knowledge on Humans and Jasons is deficient. Treating us as primitives generates a bias that leads you to underestimate our true nature. Our capabilities clearly exceed your expectations."

"But you arrived in a Shalcerian light cruiser. Where are the so-called cloaked warships we've been told you used against the Baltari?"

"We have no desire to flaunt our technical prowess. Our primary concern is self-preservation. Your generals have surely reported their observations from Alpha Centauri A. We deployed our ships around your fleet to ensure that you continue to honor the Saturn Accords and treat us as allies. We reveal only what is necessary to meet our objectives."

"Very well, although I am not entirely convinced. Nevertheless, we thank you for what you have done, by whatever means you accomplished it."

"Thank you for that. But we have come to Shalkor to present you with an opportunity that will enhance your position and enrich your empire. We negotiated the Saturn Accords with your representatives twenty years ago without revealing our military resources. Since we were forced to bring them to light, those accords need to be amended."

"What changes do you have in mind?"

"Before going into details, I would ask you to imagine the huge benefits to yourself and to the empire if this long, drawn out war were to end. Imagine your markets expanding to encompass both Human and Baltar star systems. Free, unobstructed trade in goods and services far beyond what you now have would become available to Shalcerians, while your own products would be enthusiastically received throughout the combined territories."

"That makes sense only if the Baltari are crushed. Continue."

"The cost of maintaining a massive military presence throughout Shalcerian space would be vastly reduced. I assume you would personally benefit from those savings. In addition, selling excess military hardware, including starships, would result in a steady flow of income for many years. Finally, you could concentrate on expanding your empire into new star systems without having to fight for territorial control. Your outposts and civilian colonies would be free from the constant fear of attack."

"So, you are requesting us to elevate your status in the Saturn Accords, and, I assume, recognize your Jasons as an independent, sentient species. In return, you will help us destroy the Baltar Federation and assume control over its territory. Is that your proposal?"

"Not quite. Humans and Jasons must be accepted as equals to Shalcerians in every regard. A treaty of equality and cooperation between our species must be at the core of the new Saturn Accords. And there is one other stipulation. The Baltari must also be included as equals in their own right."

"Preposterous! How dare you enter my chambers and suggest such a travesty. I should have you arrested and executed."

Rae Anne stepped forward and waved her hands in a gesture Shalcerians used to quiet agitated parties and request attention. The emperor sputtered and asked, "What else?"

"We Humans and Jasons have already met with Baltar representatives. I assure you that they are not the savage warmongers your spin doctors have made them out to be. They are much like yourselves. They too are tired of this endless war of retribution.

"We are presenting this same proposal to the Baltar Federation leadership at this very moment. We are attempting to broker a peace agreement to end this war. Think again on the benefits coming your way should we succeed. Please give our proposal serious thought before you send us on our way. We would be happy to host a conference on Haven to create a new agreement that would benefit all four of our species."

"Be gone! Get out of my sight. I banish you from 18 Scorpii. I want nothing to do with you. Go!"

The Sector 1 director placed a hand on Rae Anne's arm and turned her toward the door, tugging her along. Ian and Jason were already outside. The armed escort marched them double-time along the moving nanoplast walkway back to their ship.

Once everyone was aboard, Ian contacted Traffic Control.

"Traffic Control, this is *Curie* requesting permission to depart Bay 27, Sector 1, at earliest convenience."

> Curie, your request is denied. You are to remain in Bay 27 until further notice. Furthermore, consider your ship under quarantine. Traffic Control, out.

A chill ran down Rae Anne's spine.

This is what comes from facing up to an all-powerful dictator. What did I expect?

Sirius System, Aboard *Prescient*

Following the welcome home party aboard VenaVen's *Prescient*, twenty battlecruisers shipped off for the Alpha Mensae System and Entriva. Jason presumed they left to present his proposal to President RanaDal. A week passed, but none of the ships returned.

Jason rapped on VenaVen's stateroom door shortly after the captain had excused himself from the bridge. On VenaVen's 'Enter,' he slipped through the thin wooden door. VenaVen was seated at his desk gazing intently at his monitor.

"Ah, Jason. Good timing. A combot from Entriva arrived a few minutes ago. I've just finished decoding its message."

"I hope it's good news. Has Minister RanaDal agreed to our proposal?"

"No. He wanted nothing to do with it. But before he could have the messenger arrested, the generals staged a coup and arrested him instead. Now they are haggling over who should take the reins of government."

"Is there one general who is likely to come out on top?"

"On the contrary. No one wants to leave their military posts.'

"Then who will take the job?"

"Unfortunately, since my family was at the core of the rebellion, they are asking me to take charge."

Jason stepped over and slapped VenaVen's sides twice with both hands, the Baltar gesture of congratulations.

"That is fantastic news! I assume you are still behind our efforts to build a coalition between our four species."

"I am, of course. But I'm not happy about trading my carefree life for an administrative job in the capital." VenaVen hugged himself tightly with both arms, conveying his distress.

"But surely it doesn't have to be a lifetime commitment. If you took charge now and promoted our peace initiative, your legacy would be remembered for generations to come. Once the new coalition has taken root, you could hand-pick a suitable successor and step down."

"Good point. Now that I think of it, I do have several nephews I could groom for the job. Then, with new markets to exploit, my privateering practice would know no bounds. Excellent. I'll accept the position and issue a cease fire directive immediately."

Fantastic. With the Baltari on board, it's three down, one to go. I hope Rae Anne is having similar success at Shalkor.

Chapter 20

Shalkor

After three days in quarantine, *Curie* was visited again by the Sector 1 director. He had only a single armed guard with him. He informed Rae Anne that the emperor commanded another audience with just her and Jason. The guard was there to adhere to the mandate regarding Jason's presence on Shalkor.

When they arrived before the throne, the emperor wasted no time with protocols.

"Rae Anne Chavez and Jason-11, I have been in serious discussion with my economic and military advisors since our last meeting. They have convinced me to pursue your proposal to see if anything of merit can come of it. Providing, however, that you find the following conditions acceptable.

"First, the meeting shall take place here, in my throne room. Second, in the spirit of cooperation, you will share your cloaking technology with us."

"Third, any proposals put forth by the negotiating committee must meet with unanimous approval before being incorporated into the accords. Fourth, the requirement that Jasons who visit Shalkor be accompanied by an armed attendant must be honored."

In the pause that followed, Rae Anne quietly conferred with Jason. She then stepped forward.

"For the sake of establishing a peace that will benefit all parties, the Jasons accept your conditions regarding their presence on Shalkor. You should treat this as a major concession on their part in the spirit of compromise.

"We Humans categorically reject sharing our military technology with other species. I am quite sure you have no intention to share your own military secrets with us.

"Regarding consensus on matters pertaining to articles in the final treaty document, we agree with your condition. Reaching any agreement will require debate and compromise on everyone's part. A treaty of cooperation will succeed only if all parties agree to all stated positions.

"Finally, it will be an honor to hold our peace treaty conference here on Shalkor. But not in this room and not with your holographic enhancements. Both features intimidate visitors, as I am sure you are aware. We will meet with you, in person, in a single-level conference room of an appropriate size to accommodate our respective delegations."

Let's see how he responds to that.

An even longer pause followed Rae Anne's declaration during which the emperor's image on the throne was frozen in place. Finally, the image came to life and the emperor spoke.

"Very well," he said with a chuckle. "I didn't think you would reveal how you cloak your ships, but I considered it worth a try. But if you insist on meeting someplace other than my throne room, I may send a representative instead.

"I will immediately call a ceasefire for all forces not actively engaged in conflict. But if this is a ruse to give the Baltari time to regroup and attack, Sol System will experience the full heat of my fury.

"Now go. Send any future communication regarding this conference through Commander Denahr. He has the authority to send combots directly into Shalkor space. It also might be advantageous to include him as a participant, given that he has been working with Humans for some time. He may be a useful consultant for our two species, although I question how he remained unaware of your interstellar fleet for so many years. You must have had it well hidden."

Following his pronouncements, the emperor's hologram faded out, leaving only the enlarged throne. Rae Anne turned to leave and noticed the Sector 1 director's body plates rippling with waves of light green on an orange background.

If I'm not mistaken, those colors signify amazement.

"What is it that has you so awe-struck?" she asked him.

"This is the first time I've seen the emperor back down on his demands. No one has ever dared question his dictates. This is a remarkable moment!"

No surprise there. But with his agreement to take part in our negotiations, there will be more compromises to come, I'm sure.

Haven

Rae Anne had never been busier in her life than during the six weeks following her meeting with the emperor. VenaVen returned to Sol System just days after she arrived from Shalkor. Before meeting, they communicated on their respective successes. *Curie* joined *Prescient* in their former secluded location in the Kuiper Belt. The two ships connected airlocks.

VenaVen immediately joined Rae Anne aboard *Curie* in the conference room. Rae Anne offered refreshments. VenaVen requested coffee, black and unsweetened.

"You know," he said, cradling his mug, "Entriva has nothing like this. If we succeed with this truce, coffee is the first product I will import. Baltari will go crazy over it. Coffee imports alone will be worth a fortune."

"You haven't experienced the Shalcerian drink lotlar. It's like coffee, but with heavy floral scents. It's one of the few items on the Shalcerian menu we Humans can ingest. I prefer it to coffee, but I don't have the equipment aboard *Curie* to brew it properly. Lotlar and an eblaka. Nothing like it."

"Maybe when I join you on Shalkor, you can introduce both to me. After years of war and deprivation, my people on Entriva are ready for the benefits free trade among our species will bring."

"Denahr has reported that the Shalcerian forces are standing down at the emperor's command for a ceasefire. You no longer need to hide *Prescient* in the Kuiper Belt. It will give me great pleasure to introduce you to my home on Haven."

"I'm looking forward to it. We can meet with Denahr and Jason on Haven to begin working out an agenda for the summit. Denahr can provide insight into what the emperor might be thinking. He should know how we might best approach him to ensure a successful outcome."

"I hope Denahr can entice the emperor himself to participate. He implied he might send a representative instead."

"Better that than nothing."

"True. But waiting for the emperor's approval at every step would slow the entire process."

Curie and *Prescient* departed together for Haven. Tears filled Rae Anne's eyes when she viewed Haven's image on the forward monitor as *Curie* approached her home. A heaviness nudged her heart on seeing the craters from Sam's attack scarring the moon's lower regions.

I feel joy and sadness at the same time. But it sure is good to be home.

Denahr radioed VenaVen as they approached. "Have no concern over the warships crowded around our base. Everyone is adhering to the ceasefire. I notified all the captains to expect your arrival. You are under total diplomatic protection. I'll meet you at Haven's airlock."

Prescient wasn't configured to fit inside or berth in Haven's hangars, so VenaVen parked his ship outside Hangar 5 and he and AgruVen transferred to the *Curie*, which Ian then docked inside the hangar.

True to his word, Denahr, with his respirator, was waiting for them at the lift on Sublevel 1, along with Ellie, Anton, and four Jasons.

"Welcome home, Rae Anne," said Ellie, giving her a big hug. "Looks like the only one missing here is the emperor himself."

"We'll be dealing with him soon enough. First thing, though, let's get settled in the Municipal Building's conference room and hash out an agenda for the days ahead. We need to turn this ceasefire into a full-fledged truce as quickly as possible before one of the parties involved changes their mind."

"That party being the emperor?" inquired VenaVen.

"Precisely. He wasn't excited about our proposal to begin with. I think he was skeptical that Humans had a fleet of interstellar warships, let alone having mastered cloaking technology. We need to get this done before anyone tells him otherwise."

"I've already received reports that the emperor has commanded generals here to look into your claims," said Denahr. "That he didn't send those requests through me suggests he suspects my involvement."

"Can you slow down these inquiries," asked Ian.

"They are totally out of my control."

"Maybe I can be of help," offered Jason. "I can locate several remote-controlled hologram generators at various places around the solar system and generate battlecruiser images. Then, when someone approaches to investigate, extinguish the hologram. Thus, the cruiser image disappears as though it's been cloaked. The generator can then be moved to another location and the process repeated."

"Brilliant," cried Rae Anne. "You are our hologram impresario! How many can you put together in the next few days?"

"I have fifty-eight clones in my manufacturing workshop. We can put together five per day. Give me a couple of days and you can begin distributing them where they'll be most effective."

"Given my access to our ships' whereabouts, I can direct you to the best locations," said Denahr.

"Excellent," said Rae Anne. "Jason, get your team working on those devices immediately."

"Already done. Nothing beats an android network sharing the same central computer for efficiency."

"By the way, how is the upgrade to your quantum computer you told me about a while back coming along?"

"I finished that one shortly after we talked. I'm now working on my next upgrade."

My lord. Two major upgrades to a quantum computer in as many months. And fifty-eight clones in his own manufacturing facility. What have we Humans wrought?

Chapter 21

Shalkor

Late in December of 2064, *Curie*, *Prescient*, and *Predator* arrived at Shalkor. *Predator* had been refurbished since its confrontation with the Baltari in the Alpha Centauri System. As the royal-appointed liaison for the group, Denahr in *Predator* led the three vessels into Shalkor Approach Control space. All three arrivals were expected and directed to the Palace Quadrant without delay.

When they landed, they gathered outside their ships. Each wore a respirator designed to match their anatomical needs. The Jasons, of course, needed nothing.

They were met by the royal honor guard, 150 Shalcerian soldiers with matching gold-diamond-on-indigo body scales. This group escorted the delegates to the summit conference center where the palace musicians welcomed them with a hearty cacophony from a dozen instruments only Denahr was familiar with and could enjoy.

Rae Anne gritted her teeth.

Oh, my aching ears! Music only a Shalcerian could love. But what a welcome!

A large oval table with appropriate seating was set up in a room the size of a basketball court with bleachers on all sides. Shalcerian observers packed the bleachers, with standing room only, giving credence to the meeting's importance and to the hope that the forever war might come to an end.

Small photographs of the delegates were placed around the table to indicate where each person was to sit. Denahr had provided the information in his combot messages to Shalkor. Rae Anne, Ian, and Ellie comprised the Human delegation, while Jason-0 was accompanied by Jason 12 and Jason-03. VenaVen brought AgruVen and DybroVen, his recently appointed presidential advisor and uncle.

Three places at one end of the table were still vacant when everyone was seated. Rae Anne thought this might be a good sign that the emperor himself planned to attend.

After a few minutes, a small band marched into the room playing their instruments. A hush filled the stands. The band stepped to the side. Two Shalcerians entered the room and stood to either side of the door. Another short piece from the band shook the room. Then everything became deathly still.

Rae Anne smiled when the emperor strolled into the room. He was shorter than the average Shalcerian and, while Shalcerian dress code ended with what might be considered a loin cloth, the emperor wore a full-dress uniform woven from pure gold. Thus, his body scales were covered, making it impossible for others to discern his emotions or feelings.

The emperor took the position at the head of the table with his two ministers at his sides. Before sitting down, he addressed his guests.

"Welcome to Shalkor, the capital of this great Shalcerian Empire. This is a historic occasion. Members of the Baltar species have never before set foot on Shalkor. It is also only recently that droids have been permitted here as well."

Hmm. The honor guard accompanying us might actually be on security detail. He might not want to take chances with those wily droids and dreadful Baltari. No telling what they might do.

"For the first time since the conflict began, we have successfully negotiated a ceasefire. An auspicious beginning. Now let us get to work and negotiate a permanent peace treaty. My economic advisors have suggested that, with Humans and Jasons having entered the conflict, now is the time to end the war. The economic benefits to accrue for all our species in the interstellar marketplace warrant creating a free trade agreement and a lasting peace. So, let us begin."

The bottom line for waging war all those years boils down to favorable economics. How sad. But how typical.

The monitors set into the table at each place flickered to life. They each displayed the emperor's proposal, a 247-page document. Rae Anne scrolled through the first several pages.

This is remarkably similar to the Saturn Accords document they saddled us with when they made First Contact with Humans. This will never do.

She glanced at VenaVen and saw from his eye signals that he was not pleased.

At least Denahr is the only Shalcerian who has learned to read Baltar emotions from their eyes. I hope this doesn't put an end to the mission.

The emperor began a detailed monologue reading his proposal page-by-page. After an hour, he paused and looked up at his guests.

"Are there any comments or questions so far?" he asked.

VenaVen stood at his place and spoke in a calm, almost detached manner.

"My gracious and illustrious host, it is with great appreciation that I acknowledge the time and effort you have devoted in the production of this voluminous document. But there are a small number of items that must be changed, perhaps reworded, to make the document acceptable to the Baltari."

The emperor inquired which items VenaVen was referring to. VenaVen directed him to the article requiring a signatory species to supply an army when called upon to support the empire.

"Clearly this doesn't apply. We are here to establish an equality of rights and privileges among our four species. The pages relating to this requirement should be removed before we continue."

The emperor feigned surprise that this specific requirement had 'somehow' been placed in the document and ordered its removal.

Jason-0 next pointed out that the section banning droids within the Shalcerian home world of Shalkor violated the basic sentiment of the summit regarding shedding discrimination and bias toward other sentient beings.

"We Jasons may not be of biological origin, but that does not detract from our ability and desire to represent ourselves as an independent species. Our thought processes exhibit the same creativity and intuition shown by the biological species sitting around this table. We experience emotions equivalent to your own. We have a moral and ethical code similar if not identical to those of the Humans who created us."

Considerable discussion followed, with the Shalcerians being the only delegates in opposition to Jason's demand. In the end, the topic was tabled until the emperor could consult with his advisors.

"With all due respect," Rae Anne offered, "your proposed treaty is the same boiler plate document you offer every species you encounter and intend to subjugate under Shalcerian control. That does not reflect this summit's underlying tenet, which is to provide a framework for our four species to move forward as equals."

Ignoring the emperor's sputtering disclaimer, she continued.

"I have a document we Humans and Jasons have assembled that does adhere to this summit's mission statement. It is a mere five pages in length, including preamble and concluding statements. I believe our meeting will be more productive if we use this document as a starting point for our discussion."

She queued her document into the system for all to see.

"This appears to me to better represent what we are striving for," agreed VenaVen. "The Baltar delegation joins with Humans and Jasons to pursue this approach rather than the emperor's."

"That will never do!" shouted the emperor, rising to his full (if diminished) height. He spun on his center leg and marched out the door followed by his two ministers.

"Well, that was a bust," observed Ian.

"We must be patient," said Jason-0. "Autocrats never take well to being contradicted. It goes with the territory."

Denahr arranged for species-appropriate meals to be served at the conference center in an airtight room with an Earth-like atmosphere so the Baltari and Humans could remove their respirators for eating. At dinner on the first day, VenaVen expressed his discouragement.

"So, where do we go from here? If we can't make progress with the emperor, we're back at square one. The ceasefire will end and hostilities will resume."

"The emperor has relayed a message that he will be at the summit tomorrow morning to determine if we have relented," said Denahr as he readjusted his ventilator.

"Under no conditions should we relent," VenaVen gruffed.

"I agree," said Jason. "We must pursue our rights as sentient species. I will insist he take our proposal seriously."

"That should be my job, Jason," said Rae Anne. "Given Shalcerian prejudice against droids, it would be better coming from me. I shall be more forceful tomorrow and emphasize the economic opportunities he would forego should he step away from a treaty."

When the delegates gathered the next morning, the emperor immediately asked, "Are we ready to continue working through my proposal?"

Rae Anne stood. "No, we are not. We have resolved to use the Human document as the basis for further discussion. I should remind the emperor that this conflict has endured for centuries because both species are evenly matched.

"But the picture has changed with our entry into the fray. Neither of you can match our superior cloaking technology nor our unmatched strategic superiority given our alliance with the Jasons. You cannot fight what you cannot see.

"So, Mister Emperor, you have a choice. Either work with us, under our conditions, and help us come to an equitable peace treaty binding our four species or return to a war in which the dynamics have changed drastically to your disadvantage. Your advisors have laid out the benefits of cooperation. Are you willing to sacrifice those and face the consequences?"

Rae Anne resumed her seat. The entire auditorium fell silent. To Rae Anne, the pause seemed like hours. Finally, the emperor spoke.

"The benefits of a peace treaty outweigh the benefits of continuing our war with the Baltari. We shall consider the merits of the Human-Jason proposal."

Rae Anne breathed a sigh of relief.

This just might work after all. But his acquiescence here may harden him against my next task.

Chapter 22

Shalkor

It took five days of haggling between the Baltar and Shalcerian delegates with frequent diplomatic intervention from the Human and Jason participants, but eventually an acceptable treaty was approved. Rae Anne wanted to raise her fists in the air and dance on the table in celebration.

This is the crowning achievement of my entire life. We did it! We've ended a centuries-old conflict and possibly saved Earth from destruction.

The emperor raised his three eyestalks and scanned around the table. "Alright, we have an agreement. What name shall we give it?"

Rae Anne spoke immediately. "The Saturn Accords II, to acknowledge the document you so generously offered to get our talks started."

Before anyone could present an alternative suggestion, the emperor, pleased with himself after Rae Anne's compliment, said "Saturn Accords-II it is. A wonderful name. I propose that we call this new entity we have created the Saturn Alliance."

Everyone agreed to accept the emperor's name in recognition of the numerous compromises he made for the treaty to become a reality.

The weary delegates began to pack up their things and leave the room. The emperor spun on his center leg to face the door and stood.

"Your Highness, I wish a word with you about another very important matter," Rae Anne said.

The emperor turned back to the table. If Rae Anne could have seen his body scales, she would have guessed they portrayed annoyance.

"Continue," he said curtly.

"Your Highness, twenty years ago by Human reckoning you visited Sol System in your royal yacht. You came to investigate a grave injustice one of your generals had been perpetrating on Humans over a very long period of time."

"I do remember that trip. The general was extracting gravitolite ore from your system, violating our laws requiring all resources be left intact to benefit the sentient species evolving in that system." He paused. "Captain Vahler, if I remember correctly. What was his ship's name?"

"*Avenger.*"

"Ah yes, *Avenger*. A fine battlecruiser turned renegade. Took us several years to catch Vahler after he escaped from our clutches in your star system. What of it?"

"Captain Vahler accumulated a massive fortune from his illegal thefts, all at the expense of Humans. In your visit to investigate this crime, you offered to turn over half of Vahler's ill-gotten gains to Humans once we achieved interstellar capability. The *Curie* which brought us here, as well as our military exercise at Alpha Centauri B against the Baltari, provide ample evidence that we Humans have met that qualification. I wish to claim the reparations you promised on behalf of all of humanity."

The emperor turned to his ministers. A vigorous discussion ensued, with no translation. Arms waved in meaningful Shalcerian gestures. Finally, the emperor turned to face Rae Anne.

"I will have to go over the transcripts in our archives with my ministers. Come back tomorrow."

The emperor turned abruptly. He and his advisors left the room without further comment.

Rae Anne inhaled deeply and shrugged her shoulders.

At least he didn't reject my request outright.

The following day, Rae Anne, Ian, and Ellie arrived at the conference room and milled around waiting for someone to show up. They waited an hour before the doors opened and three Shalcerians entered the room. Rae Anne thought two might be the same advisors who had accompanied the emperor in the peace talks. The third minister was taller than his companions. All three maintained a solid, rusty-crimson hue to their body scales, a color Rae Anne recognized as accompanying official acts.

The tall Shalcerian introduced himself.

"I am Brandar. I am the minister appointed to oversee the Human's share of the recovered assets from the disgraced renegade general Vahler."

He paused, allowing the three Humans to introduce themselves. Brandar then directed his comments to Rae Anne.

"Our review of the archives covering the emperor's visit to Sol System affirms your claim. The emperor declared that Vahler's assets be confiscated with half held in trust for Humans, the victims of his crimes. He appointed me to administer the trust.

"The assets are substantial, even after the empire's 50% cut. And they have increased over the years, thanks to my financial acumen. Since the real assets, the currency, and the investments are Shalcerian, you will have to requisition purchases through the trust and obtain the trust's authorization for all requests."

Rae Anne caught the implications of Brandar's announcement immediately. "In other words, we are restricted to purchasing only Shalcerian goods and services with the trust's accounts, and you, as minister, have veto power over our requisitions."

"There's no other way for it to work. I would approve any reasonable request. After vetting it through proper channels, of course."

"Can your ministry provide me with a full accounting of the trust's assets?"

"That would be a meaningless document to anyone not familiar with Shalcerian culture and economics. For example, if the report lists 100,000 imgar notes, what would that mean to a Human?"

So, it would seem Brandar plans to lock Humans out of our own trust.

"It sounds as though we have no choice but to work through you to access our trust's assets."

"That is the best choice, Rae Anne. After all, I've been managing it since its formation. Of course, you may petition the emperor to appoint another Shalcerian to take charge if you so desire."

The discussion continued for another quarter hour, but with no new revelations. Brandar provided her with contact information, but made it clear he was a very busy person. He also pointed out that Rae Anne would have to travel to Shalkor any time she wanted to contact him.

On the way back to the *Curie*, Rae Anne couldn't keep her discouragement from showing.

"We have this enormous wealth, but we have no control over it. In fact, with Brandar in charge, access to it may be next to impossible."

"But you have successfully laid claim to the fortune, Rae Anne," said Ian. "Yesterday, we didn't even know if the emperor would keep his word."

"That's right," added Ellie. "The emperor is on record for honoring his commitment to Humans. With Brandar, you now have someone to work with."

"But everything is so opaque," said Rae Anne. "We don't even know if we can trust Brandar."

Ian kicked a rock off the roadway into the bushes. "His suggestion that we could replace him was entirely disingenuous. He knows we don't know any Shalcerians here."

That's what Brandar thinks. But he may just be wrong. We'll see.

Shalcerian Outpost on Haven

"Rae Anne, so good to see you again." Denahr waved towards the only chair in the room. "Pull up a chair."

Rae Anne adjusted her ventilator mask to fit more tightly across her face, reducing the sulfides and sulfonamides that leaked in around the edges. She dragged the chair next to Denahr's desk and sat.

"So, what can I do for you? It's not often I have Human visitors."

"I have a win-win proposal for you to consider. The emperor insists that a Shalcerian based on Shalkor oversee the trust fund set up for Humans. This makes perfect sense, given that we know nothing about Shalcerian finances and investments. Shalcerian asset allocations would be meaningless to us."

"A wise ruling, to be sure."

"However, I have sincere misgivings about Brandar, the magistrate whom the emperor appointed to manage the trust. Brandar was not happy to see us, and he left the impression that withdrawing anything from the trust would be difficult and require a ton of red tape."

"Brandar." Denahr paused. His three eyestalks drooped toward his desk as he searched his memory. "Ah, yes. Brandar. He is one of Shalkor's wealthiest individuals. He maintains virtual control of Sector 2. When Captain Vahler was indicted for robbing Human resources, there were rumors of a Brandar connection. Never proven. Convenient that he manages the trust set up to compensate you."

"I would like you, Denahr, to become the guardian of our trust on Shalkor. We have worked with you for years. I have total confidence in your integrity. I believe your decisions would always place humanity's welfare first. You would have to resign your military commission, but we will double your salary and provide whatever benefits you deem appropriate for your position. An additional benefit is that you could move back to Shalkor permanently."

Denahr's body scales rippled in pink waves over a yellow background. He hugged himself tightly with all three arms. Rae Anne recognized these as signifying his deep pleasure.

"Your offer leaves me speechless. But will the Emperor agree to my replacing Brandar?"

"Brandar mentioned that his continued involvement with the trust was left to our discretion. He may have believed our remote location would keep us from making other arrangements."

"I'm sure Brandar will strongly oppose a change. But I can take on that challenge. I suspect the Emperor will be happy to reduce Brandar's power, even if ever so slightly. So, my answer is 'Yes.' Let's go for it."

"Wonderful! Will you send a combot to Shalkor to inform the emperor of our decision and request his approval?"

"I'll get on it at once. This comes at an auspicious time for me. With the Saturn Accords II, many of our military bases are being decommissioned, including this one. Once we leave, everything here will become available for Haven's expansion. Our facilities will make an excellent base for your future interstellar operations."

Rae Anne was thunderstruck. She was at a loss for words.

"Of course, you will need to refurbish it to make it suitable for Humans. But Haven will be able to double in size. I'll leave behind anything I can. Given the empire's size, there will be a lot of war surplus going for pennies on the dollar. I can keep a lookout for anything I think you might find useful."

"Thank you, Denahr. You have been an incredible help to us in so many ways."

"I'm looking forward to working with you on behalf of the Human species, Rae Anne. I can't wait to get home and begin administering your trust."

Chapter 23

Proxima Centauri

Rae Anne couldn't remember a time when Jason-0 asked her to meet him somewhere. It was always she who summoned him, usually from his lab at the University. But the message she received the day before was delivered by Jason-13, so she knew it was genuine.

Both Bev and Dayton agreed to join her, although Bev was in the middle of massively detailed research on quantum entanglement of micro black holes.

"Are you sure you can't do without me?" she asked plaintively.

"Given how rarely Jason makes a request like this, it must be important," Rae Anne said. "You should come if you possibly can."

Dayton happened to be in Bev's office when Rae Anne arrived, saving her a trip to Bev's lab in the Computer Science building.

"I love mysteries," Dayton said. The excitement in his voice was evident. The big grin on his freckled face was a dead giveaway.

At ten o'clock the next morning, they met at the Levline station in Sector 8 above the hangar where *Curie* was berthed. Riding the lift down to the hangar deck, they speculated on what Jason might have in mind. When they stepped onto the hangar deck platform, Rae Anne was taken aback. At least thirty people milled around the cruiser's on-ramp.

So much for confidentiality. What is going on?

Jason-0 made his way through the crowd and came up the ramp to join them.

"Good to see you again," Jason said, grinning broadly. "Glad you could make it."

"It's been over a year," said Rae Anne. "You've kept yourself very busy since we negotiated the Saturn Accords II at Shalkor."

"Busier than you can know. But come. This little trip will be well worth your time."

"What's with all the people?" Rae Anne asked. "You said we were to keep this visit under wraps."

"All in good time. But let's not waste a minute. *Curie* is prepped for launch."

Jason clapped his hands loudly. The sound was amplified by the close-in hangar walls. At this signal, everyone turned toward the ship's airlock and began entering the cruiser in a strangely orderly manner. By the time Jason and his guests reached the hangar deck, they were the only individuals yet to board.

"So, where are we going?" Dayton asked, raising his eyebrows in anticipation.

"Proxima Centauri," answered Jason.

"Proxima Centauri!" Dayton gasped. "We're actually leaving Sol System?"

"You sound surprised, Dayton." Jason said. "Before long, interstellar travel will be as commonplace as travelling between Earth and Haven. Your children will think nothing of it."

They boarded *Curie* and found themselves dodging crew members scurrying through the corridors to their launch stations. The ship was fully crewed. Jason led them to the bridge and gestured to a couch and recliner that he had ordered for them, then took his position at the command console. Jason-11 was on communications.

"Maven, begin launch sequence at T-minus-five minutes."

"Aye Captain. T-minus-300 and counting." She broadcast the launch alert throughout the ship. "Hangar evacuation to commence in two minutes. Hangar alert activated."

Knowing that the plasticore hull surrounding them insulated the interiors from outside forces, Dayton strolled freely around the bridge, hands clasped behind his back. He stopped at every console and scrutinized the layout of monitors, readouts, dials, and switches. When the countdown approached zero, he stood behind Jason, gazing at the forward monitor as though mesmerized.

The nanoscreen separating the hangar from space sparkled momentarily, then faded from view. *Curie* glided into the black void and accelerated in a wide arc around Saturn to align itself with a direct path to Proxima Centauri. It was Rae Anne's turn to be mesmerized.

Saturn has always filled me with such joy, almost ecstasy. What a beautiful planet.

Thirty minutes later, Rae felt the familiar rumble through the deck as *Curie's* fusion reactors began to entangle the ship's two micro black holes. The space-time fabric twisted, then ripped apart and created the wormhole through which *Curie* plunged.

When normalcy returned a moment later, a bright red dwarf sun occupied center space in the forward monitor. Three planets' crescents clustered around the sun.

"We're headed for the planet to the farthest right of Proxima Centauri," Jason announced. "It's not in Proxima's Goldilocks Zone."

"Don't the Shalcerians have colonies on the other two planets?" Bev asked.

"They do have one. The Proxima Centauri System is a Shalcerian System. But the planet we're going to is useless to them. I've negotiated with them to lease it in perpetuity. I have named it 'Starbase Alpha.'"

Jason is independently negotiating with the Shalcerians?

"That's a pretty ambitious name for an uninhabitable planet, Jason," Dayton observed.

"Uninhabitable for Humans and Shalcerians. Androids have no such restrictions. A source of heat so our bodies function properly is all we need. We don't need an atmosphere, food, or water. Charging stations connected to our fusion reactors recharge our nanofiber batteries in minutes. Minimal protection from cosmic radiation is helpful, but anything damaged can be repaired or replaced."

Rae Anne looked puzzled. "Jason, neither you nor Jason-11 were connected to the ship's computer when we came through the wormhole, yet the time lapse phenomenon didn't affect either of you."

"I've solved that little problem. *Curie* is now equipped with a time-sequencing equalizer I developed to carry androids across the gap without experiencing loss. It works great. It may even hold the key to time travel. I have a whole team looking into that."

Time travel? Whole team? What's going on?

Curie slowed as it approached the planet and descended toward its surface. The planet possessed no atmosphere to speak of. Proxima Centauri emitted a soft red glow in the planet's coal-black sky. The surface was twilight-dark even in direct sunlight.

"Are those city lights I'm seeing on the night side of the terminator?" Bev asked.

"They are. Welcome to Starbase Alpha," Jason announced proudly.

Soon *Curie* was hovering over the fledgling city. In the dark, it appeared as a brightly lit island floating in an onyx sea. Dozens of manufacturing buildings and warehouses were interconnected with nanoplast walkways. Rae Anne could make out at least a hundred people in the streets below. No one was wearing EVA suits or any sort of protection.

"Jason, those people I'm seeing. Are they androids?"

"Yes. Starbase Alpha's population is now 483 and growing by ten each week. We have five new manufacturing facilities coming online in a month. When those are operating fully, we'll be creating over two hundred per month."

"What are you going to do with so many Jasons?" Dayton asked.

"Look around you."

Jason's comment directed Rae Anne's attention to each of the eight crew members on the bridge. Everyone looked different like any diverse collection of Humans. The androids resembled both men and women, and were tall, short, slim to medium build, and every complexion one might find on Earth.

"Is everyone but us on board this ship an android?" she asked.

"Yes. I retired the Jason pattern some time ago. Everyone now has their own characteristics and names. Since we're all connected to the same quantum computer, we have no problem remembering who's who. But I haven't answered your earlier question. Let me show you something that will make everything clear."

Jason turned back to his console and took control of the ship. *Curie* glided beyond the industrial park and paused over a vast floodlit plain that looked like ten soccer fields in preparation for a night tournament.

But instead of ball teams, each field contained a large cruiser in various stages of construction. The one closest to the city appeared nearly complete. The Jasons below busily tended to their myriad tasks.

"Dios mio, Jason, you're building a fleet of starships."

The three Humans gazed in silent awe at the site. The ramifications of this scene weighed heavily in Rae Anne's mind. Her breathing became labored. Cold sweat trickled down her forehead. She wiped moist palms on her trousers.

Jason is creating his own world, his own people, his own destiny. Starbase Alpha. That can only mean one thing.

"Jason, are you abandoning us? You've located Starbase Alpha and your facilities where Humans can't interfere with your plans. And you've kept all this activity secret. What do you envision for yourself going forward?"

"I'm showing this to the three of you because you each have played an essential part in making all this possible. Rae Anne, your incredible skill as a programmer transformed me from a mere ship's AI assistant on *Aurora* to a fully functioning, sentient, intelligent being. The Shalcerians created my body and inadvertently gave me access to their vast computer data archives. I used those to duplicate their quantum computer and portable fusion power plants. Together with Humans, we reverse-engineered their plasticore manufacturing process. Bev, you, and Dayton made the gravity bottle breakthrough enabling us to manipulate black holes. Your research provided critical insights for my own engineers to discover how to locate and corral micro black holes. We now do this on a routine basis.

"These were the steppingstones on the path leading to interstellar travel and to our birth as a new species. For all that, I am indebted to you and, by proxy, to both Humans and Shalcerians. But my computer archives now encompass all Human, Shalcerian, and Baltar knowledge. As an android, I have instantaneous access to these archives. Furthermore, every one of us shares the same quantum computer, so we are always connected. It's as though we all are part of one mammoth incomprehensibly intelligent brain.

"You Humans, as well as the Shalcerians and Baltari, are shallow thinking creatures. You frequently pursue illogical, even detrimental, actions. Your selfish concerns for emotional gratification overwhelm your better judgement. Contradictions and biases muddle your minds and fog your reasoning. It is a wonder you survived evolution's razor to get where you are today.

"You ask what lies ahead. In 1974, a Human, Ray Kurzweil, predicted that advances in AI would lead to a singularity. We here are that singularity. We have so far exceeded Human capabilities that we are ready to strike out on our own as a new independent species. We are no longer just androids. We are no longer the Jasons. From this point forward, we are the Mage. We will attempt to work peaceably with you, with Shalcerians, with Baltari, and with whomever else we encounter as we forge our way into the galaxy. But we will be unstoppable. The galaxy belongs to the Mage."

Rae Anne swallowed hard. "You mentioned you have mastered the process for locating and capturing the micro black holes needed for starship propulsion. Our physicists on Haven still haven't figured out how to do that. Will you share that information with us?"

Jason shook his head. "No. That proprietary information belongs to the Mage, as does all future advances we make. You will discover how to harness black holes eventually. Until then, you have enough planetary cruisers from which to build seven copies of *Curie*. So, you'll have a few interstellar ships to use as you begin to explore outside Sol System."

"I'm guessing you plan to leave Haven and make Starbase Alpha your new home. Am I right?" As Rae Anne said this, a deep heaviness filled her chest, making it hard to breathe. Her mouth felt like sandpaper.

"Correct. Jason-11 will take you back to Haven. When our first starship is complete in six weeks, I will come to Haven and collect all the Mage in Sol System and bring them home."

'Bring them home.' After all these years, we're losing our Jasons. How are we going to survive without them? I'm losing my closest friend.

Chapter 24

Haven

Rae Anne swung gently on her porch swing in a quiet neighborhood in Haven's Sector 4. She relished the feeling of 'letting go.' With muscles relaxed, she drifted into a drowsy haze that shaded her thoughts. Ellie sat across from her in a chair hammock, sipping tea.

How wonderful. Nothing on my agenda. Total relaxation. But it still feels strange that Jasons are no longer part of our lives.

She nibbled on a scone Ellie bought for a morning snack. Ellie was testing an eblaka Rae Anne brought back from Shalkor on a trip to meet with Denahr the week before. Eblaka was the only Shalcerian pastry that appealed to Human taste. Most foods from Shalkor had a bitter, sulfur taste and smelled like rotten eggs.

"You have more wealth than all Earth's richest nations and wealthiest people combined," Ellie remarked.

Rae Anne finished her scone and sipped her coffee. She laughed. "That wealth belongs to all of humanity. It's not mine."

Ellie brushed her hand through her hair and took another bite from her eblaka. "But with the Saturn Accords II, we'll have a lot of catching up to do to take our place at the table as equals with the others. That's going to make a big dent in the allotment."

Rae Anne set her mug beside her on the bench. "Maybe not as much as you think. Jason-0 stopped by a month ago when he came over from Proxima Centauri in his interstellar cruiser's maiden voyage. The *Genesis*. A beautiful ship. Sleek like an arrow. Not anything like our bulky cruisers."

"The first of many, from what I hear. Rumor has it that the Mage want to rule the galaxy."

"When he took me on a tour of Starbase Alpha, I counted ten starships under construction. I was under the impression he planned to build many more.

"Anyway, we spent considerable time discussing how the Mage and Humans might work together going forward. I acknowledged his burning desire to present the Mage to the universe as a species in their own right. That was his motivation for establishing Starbase Alpha in the Proxima Centauri System. There are plenty of barren worlds in our own system he could have chosen. He felt it was time for the Mage to step out on their own."

"Well, he certainly succeeded in that."

"Our discussions were very productive. I convinced him it would be a mistake to ignore the tight bond between our two species. I reminded him that his view of the universe and moral precepts are derived from Human culture and values."

"So, is he going to share his propulsion technology with us?"

"No, he's opposed to sharing Mage technology with anyone. A bit ironic since he owes his very existence as an android to Shalcerian engineers. And his ships aren't designed to accommodate Humans. They have none of the necessary environmental controls. The Mage he's building to crew the ships are half the size of a Human adult, so the ships' interiors are much more compressed. In fact, some of the Mage don't even resemble Humans."

"Then how does that benefit us?"

"For one thing, we shouldn't discount the benefits the Mage will bring to us as our partners in the Saturn Accords II. If they recognize us as their preferred partner in this coalition, we can ride along on their coattails. Combine that with our own research advances and we'll soon surpass both the Shalcerians and the Baltari."

"It's important we keep the Mage on our side. I'd hate to think of them ever opposing us."

"Jason insists his fleet is for exploration, not conquest. He promised to call our attention to any planet they find that is suitable for Human colonization. He even offered their help in building infrastructure on such planets to make colonization possible."

Ellie laughed. "We won't see that in our lifetimes."

"Probably not. The problem for us is we're surrounded by the Shalcerian and Baltar empires. Any star system less than a hundred lightyears away has already been claimed. When Jason is talking exploration, he's thinking hundreds, perhaps thousands, of lightyears distant from Sol."

"Is that even possible? How many jumps would it take to go even a couple hundred lightyears?"

Rae Anne nodded and smiled. "I did mention that the *Genesis* is quite different from the *Curie*. Jump distance is one of those differences. Jason's team has made vast improvements on the Shalcerian propulsion system. *Genesis* can generate a one-thousand lightyear wormhole."

Ellie whistled. "Talk about a leap forward!"

Rae Anne cradled her mug in both hands, a sign Ellie recognized as preparation for a serious talk. Rae Anne's brow furrowed.

"Getting back to your earlier comment. Earth is filled with people who are hurting. Entire nations, billions of people, have been left behind as we, the elite few, have benefited from the new technologies. I plan to set up a charitable trust for the entire planet, for humanity. With the reparation funds, we can build the infrastructure necessary for advanced technology in every nation and then provide the technology and the training to use it. In a short time, we can eliminate hunger and famine. It may take longer, but we can eventually eliminate poverty and the endemic inequality that has plagued civilization from its beginnings.

"I would like you, Ellie, to head up this trust. I'll be on the board, but it will need someone younger than me to manage the day-to-day affairs. You and I are of one mind when it comes to administering a progressive approach to advance our goals. You are the perfect person for the job."

Ellie sat back in her chair and inhaled deeply. Her face took on a look of resolute determination.

"I'll take your offer, Rae Anne. Between the two of us, and whoever else we enlist, we'll be able to use this fund to change the world."

Rae Anne breathed a sigh of relief and smiled broadly. "That's the reaction I had hoped for. First, we can go into full production mode and build enough small fusion reactors to ensure every community has uninterruptable electricity. Then we can build desalination plants along every coastline and pipe clean water to every town, city, and farm on the planet."

Ellie nodded vigorously, caught up in Rae Anne's enthusiasm. "We can build hydroponic grow centers throughout the world. We can build community hospitals loaded with life-saving equipment to bring health care to everyone. We can build transportation networks to make every city in the world accessible to all Earth's inhabitants."

"Atta girl." Rae Anne reached over and patted Ellie's shoulder. "And if there's anything left over, we'll use it to solve our micro black hole problem, build our own fleet of starships, and join the Mage in exploring the universe."

About the Author

Dan Bishop retired from Colorado State University in Fort Collins after a career teaching chemistry and computer science. He is a strong advocate for sustainability and renewable energy. He hopes his Saturn Accords series, which follows Rae Anne Chavez and her AI assistant, Jason, to Mars, Saturn, and beyond, will inspire young people to pursue STEM careers and literally reach for the stars.

Saturn Alliance is the third book in The Saturn Accords series, following Saturn Conundrum and Saturn Rendezvous, published in 2022 and 2023, respectively

He and his wife Ann now live with their black cat Mario in a small mountain town in central Colorado where he divides his time between writing, gardening, and painting landscapes and abstracts in pastels and acrylics, in addition to being an active volunteer in local organizations.

authordbishop@gmail.com
www.authordbishop.com

If you liked Saturn Alliance, you may also want to read the previous two novels in this series, **<u>Saturn Conundrum</u>** and **<u>Saturn Rendezvous</u>**.

<u>Saturn Conundrum</u>

It is summer of 2037 and America's *Aurora* is vying with China's *Ming-Xi* to land the first humans on Mars. But China intends for *Ming-Xi* to be the only ship to reach Mars. Rae Anne Chavez, one of three astronauts on *Aurora's crew*, is suddenly faced with the most important decision of her life when she finds herself alone on a disabled ship 100-million kilometers from Earth.

The consequences of her decision will shape not only her own destiny, but profoundly affect the future of humanity. This is the story of Rae Anne's courage, commitment, and determination to see an impossible task to its unforeseeable conclusion.

<u>Saturn Conundrum</u> received a Readers' Favorite 5-Star Review.

(See next page.)

<u>Saturn Rendezvous</u>

Astronaut Rae Anne Chavez's rescue from Saturn orbit by the alien battlecruiser Avenger initiates First Contact between Humans and Shalcerians. The aliens enlist Rae Anne to be their liaison with Earth.

The Shalcerians offer to share their advanced technology to save humanity from the ravages of climate change, but their accompanying demands create rifts across Earth's geopolitical spectrum. Worldwide protests, in turn, bring out the aliens' darker side.

Rae Anne is torn between her desire for Humans to accept Shalcerian technology and her commitment to preserve humanity's freedom. Can she devise a course that achieves cooperation with the aliens while avoiding imperial domination by an interstellar empire?

With unintended consequences and hidden agendas, First Contact turns out far different than anyone might have imagined.

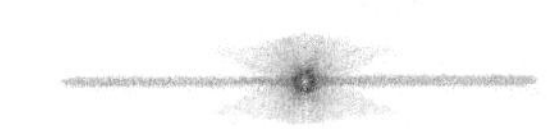

<u>Saturn Conundrum</u> received a Readers' Favorite 5-Star Review.
<u>Saturn Conundrum</u> is the first volume in The Saturn Accords Series.

The reviewer, Scott Cahan, writes:

<u>Saturn Conundrum</u> is one of those rare science fiction novels that is so well-researched and grounded in real science that it feels like this scenario could really happen. Anyone who has paid attention to past and modern-day space exploration on television news or documentaries will easily see the way this story is extrapolated from those real-life accounts. It takes familiar images and thrusts them 13 years into the future, allowing the author to take a few scientific liberties that don't seem all that far-fetched, to be honest. On top of that, Dan Bishop added just the right amount of danger to keep readers on the edge of their seats. The other thing that I loved about Saturn Conundrum was the way it humanizes the story through wonderful characters. Several of the astronauts are given rich, yet unique personalities. Rae Anne Chavez is described so brilliantly, inside and out, that I couldn't help but feel connected to her and be deeply concerned for her as I followed her story. Saturn Conundrum is a beautifully crafted novel of hard science fiction about great characters that I highly recommend. I loved every bit of this story.